BOOK ONE OF THE REFORGED TRILOGY

CRUCIBLE OF STARS

ERICA LINDQUIST &
ARON CHRISTENSEN

LOOSE LEAF
STORIES

This is a work of fiction.
All characters, organizations, places and events portrayed in this book
are either the product of the authors' imagination or are used fictitiously.

Find more of our books at LLStories.com

For my mother, Doré Lindquist,
who taught me how to fly.

"One need not be asleep to dream."

- ARCADIAN PROVERB

When life first contemplated leaving the sea, they believed that distance was the greatest of all barriers. The line of the shore, etched in gold by sunlight cutting through the thin, toxic atmosphere, seemed so very far away. Certainly not worth the effort required to crawl toward it on limbs so poorly evolved for land.

So life remained in the sea for another million years, never straying too far from its spawning ground and fearing what lay beyond. Only when food became too scarce and mates too hard to find did the young creatures of the worlds finally venture out of the water. As eons passed, fins and flagella gave way to limbs of all sizes, numbers and uses. But as life spread across the land, food and resources grew scarce once more.

And so billions of eyes turned up toward the stars. When life first contemplated the skies, they believed that distance was the greatest of all barriers.

They were wrong.

[1]
HAWKS AND DOVES

"You shall know the last days by the coming of the three: the hungering father, the mad mother and the undying child. Beware these signs of the end times and open your heart to the One God, for He alone offers you His love and His salvation."

- THE BOOK OF LIGHT (23 PA)

Maeve Cavainna stared out at the elongated rainbows of stars as the Blue Phoenix raced between them. Superluminal flight scattered their spectra into a thousand subtle hues, transforming starlight into something strange and unfamiliar. At these speeds, even the brightest sun was only a colorful smear against the perfect black of space. A heartbeat of light, and then each one vanished again.

How many billions of lives did the Blue Phoenix fly past, unnoticed by people living on the worlds circling those hazy little rainbow stars? But those planets were invisible to Maeve, too small and gone too fast to see. The universe was a cold and empty place.

Maeve pressed her fingertips to the glassteel of the viewport, searching through the darkness. It was like no one else was out there, as though she were utterly alone. But Maeve knew better.

Where are you?

He was out there somewhere: Logan Coldhand, the bounty hunter. Tiberius was sure they had shaken him from their trail, but that seemed unlikely. No matter how many worlds Maeve fled to, Coldhand always found her. Whatever stinking alleyway she hid inside, he would be there, the silencing hand of the Nameless closing around her at last.

There, that spark of light... Was that Coldhand's ship? But no, it couldn't be. Maeve frowned as the ember glow faded once more into nothingness and she struggled to remember what Gripper had told her about SL flight. At superluminal speeds, there was no way Maeve could see a pursuing vessel, right? The Blue Phoenix was flying faster than light, outrunning sight of anything that might be behind them.

Everyone expected time dilation and lapses at superluminal speeds. All of the math predicted it, Gripper said. They called it relativistic travel, but it never happened. No one stepped off a starship to find themselves years younger than their own children. Time wasn't the mutable, changeable thing that physicists and chronologists expected, not stretched and twisted by superluminal speeds like cloud-candy. Time didn't behave according to the mathematical models, but as a strange, steady galactic constant, a mysterious and unwavering interstellar heartbeat that no one seemed to understand.

Least of all Maeve. If there were a way to change the flow of time, she wouldn't be here at all. But Maeve leaned against the window and her breath clouded the glassteel pane. She squinted through the fog, willing herself to see the impossible.

Where are you, Coldhand?

Here in the back of the ship, Maeve could feel more than hear the deep thrum of the Blue Phoenix's superluminal drive. There was a clang and a shout from Gripper as he tried to wring more speed from the old machines. Maybe she could...

Maeve's com chirped insistently, interrupting her thoughts. Where had she put that thing? She patted at her threadbare spacer's pants until she found the small device. Maeve turned on the audio with a flick of her finger, but left the tiny video screen dark.

"I am here," she answered. "What is it?"

"We're almost ready to drop out of SL," came the muted, tinny response. "You might want to strap in."

The voice was masculine, but muddied by a buzzing sound on the com channel. Probably the engines interfering with the signal, even at this short range.

"If you are the one landing us, Duaal, then I had best say my final prayers," Maeve answered. "How close are we?"

"Sink you. We'll be coming in about ten minutes from Axis. Just sit down and strap in, Maeve. It's going to get choppy. Axis' gravity well is an absolute Nnyth."

"I will tell Gripper."

Maeve keyed off her com and half turned away from the viewport, but she caught her dim reflection in the glassteel and hesitated. At a glance, she might have passed for human, if a very small one. She had two arms and two legs, and a head of tangled hair the black of a starless midnight.

But Maeve wasn't human and any human would have been insulted by the comparison. She was Arcadian. Under that mess of dark hair, Maeve's ears tapered to imperfectly hidden points and her stained shirt did even less to conceal the pair of wings that arced up from between her shoulders. Each of them was as long as the fairy was tall and covered in feathers that would have been white if they were ever clean.

Maeve turned away from the depressing view, ducking down through the hatchway and into the engine room. The ceiling here was so low that she had to fold her wings tightly against her back to avoid tangling them. According to the ship's original design, this ceiling should have been considerably higher. But the Blue Phoenix was old, several times reclaimed from the scrap heap and repaired just enough to get it back into the sky. Any room that would have let Maeve stretch out her wings was now taken up by jumbles of retro-fitted pipes and cables that connected the ship's outdated systems. The cargo hold was the only place left that Maeve could spread her wings without knocking into something and causing a problem – for her or for the rest of the crew.

There was another loud thud and some more shouting up ahead. Maeve brushed dangling wires out of her face with the crest of one wing and wondered how Gripper managed to keep the Blue Phoenix flying at all. She caught sight of the grumbling's source and stopped in the narrow passage.

Anandrou – or *Gripper* as he very much preferred to be called – was squeezed into the cramped corridor, plucking at the exposed circuitry behind an open panel. He cradled a length of frayed wiring in his massive hands and eyed it mournfully. One long, brown-mottled ear twitched at Maeve's approach.

"The FMS relay is shot," Gripper said. He craned his thick neck awkwardly in the tight confines to shake his head morosely. "We need a new one. Are we there yet?"

Maeve had no idea what the FMS relay did, or why the chewed-looking bit wiring in Gripper's hands meant the machine's death. But the Blue Phoenix was a coreworld construct and made little sense to her. Arcadians didn't need starships to travel between worlds... At least, they didn't used to. Now the fairies traveled how-ever they could manage. When they could travel at all.

But Gripper loved the Blue Phoenix like a living creature and Maeve couldn't help being momentarily charmed. The inevitable failures of the old ship always seemed like personal wounds to Gripper, while the numerous cuts and scrapes in his brown hide went utterly unnoticed.

"Duaal is almost ready to take us out of superluminal flight," Maeve said.

"Shimmer's landing?" Gripper asked, even as he began an urgent wriggle out of the hatchway and into the engine room. "We better go tape ourselves to something!"

Watching him leave, Maeve's heart clenched. Gripper was so very much like her little brother, though the thought surely would have offended them both. Boys treasured their pride like favorite toys and hated to be reminded of their youth.

"Hey, Smoke," Gripper shouted to Maeve over one lumpily muscled shoulder. "Come on! You have to strap in, too!"

Maeve followed Gripper as he picked his way through the cluttered engine room. The fibersteel floor was dark and patchy from countless coolant and oil spills, so many times cleaned up and re-spilled that they had seeped into the very metal. The hatchway on the far side of the engine room was larger, tall enough that Gripper could pass through without hunching his bulky brown shoulders. He didn't bother with the stairs, but jumped instead and grabbed the joint of the heavy ceiling plates. He swung on his long arms to the top and by the time Maeve caught up, Gripper was already inside the crew mess, tugging impatiently at the too-short safety belts on one of the acceleration couches.

Xia had arrived before them and the Ixthian's expression was one of carefully composed serenity. Only the tightness of Xia's harness and a faint red sheen to her gem-like compound eyes betrayed any concern about their copilot's skill. Her slender, long-limbed build and six-fingered hands hearkened back to her race's insect origins. Xia's skin was a polished pewter color and a pair of slim antennae rose up from her short white hair, waving toward Maeve and Gripper as they hurried through the door.

The deck of the Blue Phoenix pitched beneath them and Maeve tried to spread her wings for balance, stumbling the final distance to throw herself down into a seat beside Xia. It was uncomfortable to cinch her wings so tightly against her back, but it was better than taking the beating of Duaal's amateur flying. Strapping himself into the opposite couch, Gripper grimaced and clapped his hands over his stomach.

"Hasn't Shimmer been flying for like four years now?" he asked with a groan. "And the guy is still wasp-crap at piloting. Do you think Claws could teach him the SL drop some other time? Like some time I'm not here?"

"How could he when you never leave? You're married to this ship," Xia said with a short, clicking laugh.

Gripper flushed. "Hey, that's not my fault. She's old and needs a lot of care."

Maeve let her head fall back across the patched cushions of the couch. The harness straps dug into her narrow chest as the sudden deceleration to sublight speeds made the Blue Phoenix buck and shudder. What if the ship *did* crash? What if Tiberius or Duaal had miscalculated their drop time? What if they smashed into the planet, crushing flesh and steel and stone? At least it would be an end...

No. Maeve had a better way to finish this story.

Outside the viewports, the colorful streaks shortened, blurred and then burst into hundreds of thousands of stars that filled the blackness with blinding white points of light. The thrum of the superluminal engines and clanging of metal finally stopped.

The ship intercom buzzed. Maeve could just make out the loud sound of Duaal cheering his successful SL shift from the cockpit.

"Welcome back to Axis," Tiberius announced over the noise of his copilot. "Our home away from scattered homes."

Axis was a silver-blue planet positioned only a few hundred light-years from the precise center of the galaxy, but it was not that location for which it was named. By agreement of the member planets of the Central World Alliance, Axis was the capital of the largest government in the galaxy and a vital checkpoint for travel and trade throughout the stars.

On a lesser planet, the colossal Central World Alliance capitol complex alone would have covered an entire nation. From its heart rose the vast Lyceum, the galactic parliament in which every world of the CWA had a voice. Four species and thirty-six planets argued in the Lyceum daily for – or sometimes against, when certain debts were called in – the interests of their homeworlds.

Axis' megatropolis had swallowed the world's land and seas long ago, burying them under a planet-spanning city of concrete and fiber-woven steel. Axis was divided into ten distinct levels, each a world unto itself. Level One was the outermost shell, the glittering crown jewel and the only part of Axis with true sunlight and open air. Aglow in the radiance of the system's bright yellow sun, Level One was the shining face that the Alliance presented to the galaxy and the great glass and metal heart of the CWA that moved a lifeblood of trade and bureaucracy.

The deep lower levels of Axis, however, were a different story altogether.

When Duaal finished another bumpy landing onto the planet's surface, Maeve followed the others down into the cargo hold of the Blue Phoenix. They gathered around the airlock, waiting to venture out into the city.

Xia stood to one side of the bay, smiling and joking with Duaal. Like many Ixthians, Xia was a doctor and served as the ship's medic when trouble inevitably caught up with them.

The planet of Ixth had been one of the eight responsible for founding the Central World Alliance. Under Ixthian care, all life flourished. They were masters of genetics and medicine, their colleges producing the best doctors and biologists in the galaxy.

Before the Ixthians, most species had to replace lost limbs or organs with unwieldy and unresponsive metal cybernetics. Now Ixthian cloning tanks had all but eradicated such barbaric practices.

"So I gave him the redprints and that was the end of it," Xia said. "I never saw the man again."

Duaal laughed. The Blue Phoenix copilot was one of the several human species found throughout the core worlds, this particular example born on the watery planet of Hyzaar. Duaal's skin was dark and his bleached-blond hair was cut in a short, ragged style that was popular all across the Alliance.

Like Ixth, Hyzaar was a founding member of the CWA. The sapphire-blue planet boasted a surface area that was ninety-five percent ocean and the humans of Hyzaar considered themselves experts of every aquatic sport. Since no other race in the galaxy could best a Hyzaari ship in the annual Beven competition, no one disputed their claim. Of course, those were bragging rights that only the Hyzaari seemed to care about.

But Duaal didn't dress like other Hyzaari. Instead of the loose, comfortable clothes favored by most of his subspecies even off world, Duaal's choices were... exotic. Today, the Blue Phoenix copilot wore a long coat of black and purple leather, closed down the front with bright gold clasps. Beads and charms dangled from every hem and chimed with each step. Duaal covered himself in such expensive, ridiculous extravagance that Maeve wondered sometimes if it was the boy's face she recognized or just his clothes.

Duaal's wardrobe wasn't half as strange as his studies, however. Maeve had lived for a century in the galactic core – since the fall of the White Kingdom – and in all that time, Duaal Sinnay was the only human she had ever met who knew any sort of magic.

But his understanding of her people's craft was deeply flawed. Did Duaal think his magic required the arcane symbols embroidered all over his clothes? Perhaps. Maeve wasn't sure where Duaal might have learned that, but she had no intention of wasting her time correcting him. Besides, the young human seemed to take great pride in his strange appearance.

Boys and their pride...

Gripper hung from the ceiling supports by his long arms, impatiently digging his huge fingers into the metal hard enough to make it creak. He wore basic spacers' pants and shirt, like Maeve and Xia, though his were all cut much, much larger. They were sized for a Hadrian, but even those seams had to be let out in places.

Gripper towered over every other member of the Blue Phoenix crew, almost nine feet tall and powerfully built. The Arboran's body was protected by leathery, mottled brown skin. His ears were pointed, like Maeve's, but considerably longer. Gripper's arms, too, were elongated, and hung nearly to his knees. No hair grew on his head, but his thick forearms were covered with green fur. Maeve wasn't sure what evolutionary advantage that fur might offer, but Gripper was clearly made for climbing and swinging through the trees of his homeworld, not for cramming himself into an engine room.

Gripper dropped to the floor with a loud clang. He eyed the damaged ceiling support, coughed and sidled quickly away.

He had told his crewmates that he looked just like other Arborans, if a little on the short side. Of course, they all had to take his word for it. No one in the Alliance or in the rim kingdoms had ever seen another Arboran. Gripper's sudden appearance in the core was a mystery, even to him.

People stared at Gripper wherever he went, but not many challenged him. It was much easier to harass the less intimidating and far more numerous Arcadians. Which was lucky for Gripper – for all his great size and strength, he was a shy young man, awkward and more or less a coward. His world was a peaceful one, Gripper said. The Arborans lived high in the huge trees of their homeworld, far from the predators below. They were all herbivores and knew nothing of hunting or bloodshed.

The captain of the Blue Phoenix, Tiberius Myles, stood at the airlock controls. He cleared his throat loudly, silencing Duaal and Xia. Though hardly as massive as Gripper, Tiberius was large for a human, with broad shoulders and a wide barrel chest. His hair was short and steel-gray with age. Tiberius' stubbled face was worn by years of heavy burdens – burdens of which this unruly crew was only the most recent. When he spoke, it was in a rough, deep voice with the rolling accent of his homeworld, Prianus.

"Listen up," Tiberius said. "We've got about eight hours on Axis. We haven't seen any sign of Coldhand yet, but that doesn't mean he's not out there. We're ahead of him, but not by much. Not with that leak in our core."

Gripper held up his huge hands at Tiberius' accusatory glance.

"Hey, I'm going to buy a new venno plate today," said the Arboran. "Even the FMS relay is broken. The recycling system is old, Claws. What do you expect?"

Tiberius sighed. "Fine. But if we can get off Axis before Coldhand touches down, he'll have a hard time following us out. Don't make a fuss and don't give anyone something to remember. Let's not invite trouble. That means you, princess."

Tiberius leveled a hard, blue-eyed glare at Maeve and the fairy shrugged. Her battles with Coldhand were her own business. And even if the bounty hunter caught up with them now, all he wanted was Maeve. The rest of the Blue Phoenix crew was unimportant – unless they tried to interfere.

Gripper watched Maeve and shifted his considerable bulk uncomfortably. He obviously worried about her, but knew better than to say so.

"Gripper, you get that shielding taken care of," Tiberius said. He waved his hand toward Xia and Duaal. "You two, we need supplies. Especially water. With the recycling system working at half, we're losing a lot of it. Duaal, let Xia handle it. We don't have much colour to throw around. Just help her get it back here."

Duaal pouted less than subtly at his uninspiring planetside duties. Tiberius ignored him.

"Maeve, take care of the datawork and landing fees," Tiberius ordered. "I'll get the ship refueled. That should leave each of you more than enough time to do anything personal on Axis. Remember, be back on the Blue Phoenix in eight hours or you'll need to find another bird off this rock."

Everyone in the cargo bay nodded, except Maeve.

"We had to take off from Hadra before we could finish restocking or pick up new work," Tiberius said. "So keep your eyes open. Salvage has been pretty thin lately, so we need cargo and we can't afford to be picky."

With that, Tiberius pressed the glowing green airlock button. The cargo ramp hissed as the seal broke and then lowered with a mechanical whir that grated and ground more than it should have. Gripper wasn't exaggerating the Blue Phoenix's age or disrepair.

Outside, the blastphalt abutted expansive metal walls studded with fluorescents and striped by colorful map tracks. The landing that Tiberius told Maeve to pay for wasn't enough to buy an expensive Level One open-air pads. The ceiling overhead was ribbed with arcing beams as wide as Maeve was tall and covered by a network of yellow-white daylights, all dimmed to simulate nighttime for the late evening traffic.

A massive mechanical claw still held the Blue Phoenix where it had set the cargo ship down between a huge Hadrian bulk transport and a shorter Dailon carrier. The Blue Phoenix wasn't a large vessel, which made it well suited to handling jobs too small for the major shipping companies or whose owners wanted to avoid official attention.

Most of the Blue Phoenix's length was dedicated to the cargo hold and engines, without much space left over. That made the corridors inside narrow and quarters cramped, resulting in a lot of scraped knuckles for Gripper and tangled wings for Maeve.

The Blue Phoenix was shaped like half a cone, bisected from base to tip and set on its flat side. The cargo ramp and three stout landing legs extended from the bottom of the ship. But the rest of the shape was almost lost under a multitude of sensor spars – invaluable in scanning for salvage – that thrust out in every direction like the spines of a drunken porcupine. A pair of wings with stabilizing jets and a matching rotational thruster in a fin on top seemed nearly an afterthought.

The only other break in the forest of sensors was the cockpit. The windows there were not strictly necessary, since pilots flew almost entirely by instruments and computer readings, but shipbuilders had learned centuries ago that pilots liked to see where they were flying.

Xia wrapped her long silver fingers around Duaal's embroidered sleeve, leading him away from the Blue Phoenix, and Gripper knuckle-walked behind them with a small computer folded under his chin. Maeve moved to follow. She was eager to finish her task and attend to her own business, but Tiberius caught her by the shoulder.

Maeve rustled her wings and the captain glanced at them. The humans of Prianus adored birds over all other animals and Maeve was sure that her wings had a great deal to do with Tiberius' patience with her. Of all the coreworld species, Prians alone treated the Arcadians with anything like respect. It was a shallow sort of respect, based only on the fairies' superficial resemblance to their beloved birds, but it was something.

Maeve rarely hesitated to use that advantage. But not this time, it seemed. Tiberius held her fast.

"I'm serious," he said. "Stay out of the lower levels. I don't want you coming back to the ship low on some chem or beat up from a fight that *you* picked."

Maeve narrowed her eyes. "What I do with my own time is my business and none of yours."

"It's every bit my business! I didn't make you my first mate for your looks, dove. If I'm going to keep the Phoenix in the sky, I need you to put the crew in order for me and you can't do that when you're out of your skull on some chem."

"I will... consider your request," Maeve said.

Tiberius grunted and released her. It was the best he would get for now.

"You've got eight hours, princess," the captain reminded Maeve before stumping down the cargo ramp.

Tiberius vanished into the throng of travelers pouring from the other ships and out onto the busy streets of Axis. Maeve closed the ramp behind her and then punched a code Gripper had given her into a keypad. The airlock hummed and cycled, then the light ticked from green to red. Secure.

When the Blue Phoenix was locked, Maeve turned away and hurried into the city.

[2]
AXIS

"One hundred years ago today, our predecessors brought together hungry, desperate worlds into a new constellation. This constellation wasn't a symbol or a picture, but a promise. The promise of a better future."

- NANSHI CRESTONE, 32ND LYCEUM PRESIDER (202 PA)

For most of their history, each species of the galaxy believed themselves alone. Planetary governments had work enough for generations just managing their own ever-dwindling supplies of food and fuel, air and other natural resources. No matter how carefully tended, these assets vanished alarmingly quickly until every world had no choice but to turn their attention out to the stars.

All races were equally astonished to discover intelligent life beyond their own stellar systems. Humanity particularly so as they discovered more or less their own species exploring with the same desperate need. The native humans had named their own worlds Hadra, Hyzaar, Mir, Prianus and Vanora.

Bitter decades of war ensued before the humans found the commonalities that bound them together. Vanora's military and then diplomatic victories secured its place as the center of the growing galactic alliance, and a new name: Axis.

Though the human subspecies appeared quite different, they were pronounced by the Ixthians to be nearly identical at the genetic level – a verdict borne out by years of breeding between the five races of humanity. But each planet had left its mark. Hadrians were large and muscular from generations of high gravity living, with dark skin and eggshell white membranes to protect their eyes from their blinding binary suns. The people of watery Hyzaar were long-limbed and bronze-skinned, with powerful lungs and strong stomachs. On Mir, striped skin and hair colors ranging from brown to bright green camouflaged humans from their fast grassland predators. The humans of Axis and Prianus bore few obvious adaptations to their homeworlds, but no one would ever mistake the urbane Axials for backwater Prians.

Along with the Lyrans, Ixthians and Dailons, the human races founded an interstellar government to regulate their shared needs for scarce and precious resources. They named their coalition the Central World Alliance and the newly-minted CWA struck out into the unexplored sectors of the galaxy with renewed hope.

It took an hour for Maeve to track down and pay the harried-looking Dailon dockmaster. She thought it might have been a male, but discerning Dailon genders was notoriously difficult for outsiders. They told one another apart easily by scent, but of the other species in the galaxy, only the canine Lyrans could smell the difference. Like the rest of their race, the Dailon's skin was dark blue over a muscular, long-limbed body.

The dockmaster regarded Maeve with large black eyes for a moment, then unceremoniously thrust a datadex out at her. Maeve thumb-printed the screen and then paid the landing fee with a few colored plastic chips. The dockmaster hurried off, rubbing blue hands off on their pants after even momentary contact with an Arcadian.

The Blue Phoenix was berthed on the second of Axis' ten levels, in one of fifty thousand or so docking circles. Landing pads and fueling stations dominated this part of the megatropolis and the streets were filled with sky cars suspended on cloudy null-fields, as well as older wheeled and bearing-mounted vehicles. Crowds pushed along the sidewalks, genders of all species absently shouldering past each other as they went about their business on this level or making their way to one of the many lifts that would take them up or down into the rest of Axis.

The air was alive with voices. In the early days of the Alliance, the founders had agreed upon a common language that they named Aver. Because humans were by far the most numerous and widespread race in the galaxy, Aver was primarily made up of human dialects. But hoping to forge a lasting understanding between the members of the Central World Alliance, each of the four core species took a hand in perfecting Aver. The black-haired Dailons contributed their rolling, sibilant hisses and from the Ixthians came clicking names for all manner of medicines and chemicals. The canine Lyra voiced their deep love of machines, as well as the *chagri* – an open-backed chair that let them freely swing their furry tails.

As Maeve made her way past the docking circles and fueling stations, ship airlocks were replaced by tastefully holographed storefronts with windows displaying fashionable flight suits and polished starship parts. Sidewalks and roads were kept painstakingly clean and in excellent repair despite the traffic of millions of feet and vehicles. Most visitors to Axis came by way of Level Two and so, in the interest of ongoing trade and good public relations, the city-world went to great lengths to keep the upper levels pleasant, relaxing and beautiful.

The streets had glassteel skylights arcing overhead, vast windows that opened out on the starry Level One sky. Maeve stopped to look up. The sky of Axis never ceased to amaze her. It was alive with stars, as close and numerous as the people of the great city. The stars blazed even at midday, too bright and too many for the sun to eclipse. By night, their light was glorious.

The White Kingdom of Arcadia had been far, far away from here – out on the edge of the galaxy. Maeve never saw a sky like this when she was a girl. Axis was the breath-taking, glittering heart of all the stars. Maeve felt as though she could reach up and touch one of those countless brilliant points of silver light. But not even an Arcadian could fly that high.

Somewhere out there, among all those stars, was the shattered remains of her home. Maeve turned away, but the view on the street was no better, just as full of life and untouchable joys. A smiling human couple brushed past, ignoring the dirty Arcadian and laughing together at some private joke.

Maeve very nearly fell off the sidewalk when a tall Hadrian man ran into her. She stumbled and only barely managed to catch herself on the man's sleeve. A stylish silver com was hooked around his ear, flashing in the starlight. He stopped speaking into it to look down at Maeve and tugged his arm out of her grasp.

"What are you doing up here, bird-back?" the man hissed under his breath. He pointed down the street with a finger almost as thick as Maeve's wrist. "The lifts are that way. You better get off this level before someone else sees you!"

He glanced about with white membrane-covered eyes and then hurried away, grumbling into his com. Maeve turned and pushed a path through the crowd in the direction the Hadrian had indicated. Nothing she wanted would be found this high up on Axis anyway, only more undesired attention.

Maeve stalked down the walkway – marked out with a red mapline – until she reached a mirror-polished elevator. Several other passengers got out when she entered, muttering about crowds and that they would just catch the next one. Maeve went inside and the doors slid shut.

A controlled ten-minute drop finally deposited the lift down on Level Seven and a computerized chime roused Maeve from a half-doze. She shook out her wings and stepped out of the lift canister. By now, this low in the city, the canister was nearly empty.

And it was easy to see why. The Level Seven streets were dark with grime and deep, secretive gray shadows. Close-leaning apartment blocks and dim-lit shops were foreboding with broken, taped windows caked in layers of lumapaint graffiti. The paint's glow had long since faded, whatever opinion or territorial claim it had once advertised now gone. Overflowing trash bins and even less ordered filth choked narrow alleys between the buildings. Perfect.

Maeve thrust her hands into her pockets and pulled her wings close. She hurried furtively along the road, scanning the shadows. A few cracked streets away, Maeve found a run-down med clinic, surrounded by trash that was only half-heartedly cleared back from the doors. The place was still open despite the hour, which must have been well past midnight local time.

Through a small window crisscrossed in steel mesh, Maeve could see a pair of tired-looking Ixthian doctors working diligently over a human man stretched out on the metal table between them. Their short antennae waved in shallow, weary arcs as they labored. The preservation and purification of life was very nearly a sacred Ixthian obligation and they sold their services at a fair cost even on the lower levels of Axis.

Maeve circled around behind the clinic, where there were no windows. Back here, she knew, would be operating rooms and a streamlined cloning facility. Cybernetics so galled the Ixthians that they charged bare minimum prices to run their cloning tanks – only the truly destitute or unlucky resorted to primitive machine replacements.

But Maeve didn't need cloned organs or even cybernetic ones. Axis was the center of the galaxy and capital of the Central World Alliance, but beneath the gleaming skin of the city above, darkness thrived. On Level Seven, everyone needed drugs – patients and doctors alike.

Maeve found a chem dealer slouched beside the clinic. It was a Lyran woman with matted fur, no taller than Maeve. Lyrans were built much like bipedal dogs or wolves and were among the shortest of the CWA citizens. This one had a pelt dyed in brilliant purple and her black nose ran wetly, but her predatory golden eyes were alert and watchful. The Lyran sniffed the air as Maeve approached.

"You're a long way from home, fairy," she growled.

"The White Kingdom fell before you were even born. I have no home," Maeve snapped back. "And I have no time or inclination to argue with an ill-tempered wolf. You know what I want and I will pay you better than I should for it."

Closer now, Maeve could see the Lyran was quite young. Just out of puppyhood, really. An oversized plastihide jacket poorly hid her starvation-thin frame. She bared her yellowing fangs.

"You're wanting for a rip with a mouth like that, bird-back," the Lyran snarled.

"What are you selling?" Maeve asked.

"Vanora White."

"Give it to me!"

The Lyran reached into her pocket and pulled out a plastic-wrapped bundle about the size and shape of a human's finger. Maeve grabbed for the package, but the other woman snatched it away. She extended her empty paw, leathery pads turned up.

"Color first, bird-back," she said. "Two hundred cen."

Cen was short for *cenmarks*, nicknamed *color* for the brightly hued chip denominations. Maeve's jaw clenched. A hundred cenmarks would have been outlandish, but she needed the White and had admitted as much. Maeve dug two squares of red plastic from her pocket and thrust them into the Lyran's paw. The dealer examined them for a moment, then nodded and gave up her goods. Maeve took the bundle with shaking hands.

"Hardly a pleasure, but you have my thanks," she said by way of farewell.

The wolfin girl spat onto the sancrete as Maeve left and turned one of the plastic coins over in her paws. Did she wonder how a fairy had come by that much money? Maeve doubted the dealer really cared. She was probably already thinking about catching a pounceball game up on Level Five or perhaps scoring some chems of her own.

Maeve hurried away and managed to restrain herself – barely – long enough to find a darkened alcove a few dirty blocks from the Ixthian clinic. She turned down the narrow alley and crouched behind a rusted trash bin. Dusty windows stared blankly at her; flat glass eyes blind to her indiscretion.

Biting her lip, Maeve unwound the needle and tossed the wrapping away, off into the rest of the trash, then held up her purchase for inspection. The substance inside – barely visible through the plastic cylinder – was the color of tar. This drug was named *Vanora White* for the blank, pure white stupor that it induced, not its actual appearance.

There were better delivery devices than this, high-tech coreworlder medical equipment that could pump the Vanora White right into Maeve's bloodstream without even breaking the skin. But this was just a cheap hypodermic needle. No Ixthian would ever have touched the thing and Maeve knew that sticking it into her arm was a terrible idea.

Maeve pulled a fraying piece of twilight purple silk from her pocket and knotted it awkwardly around her upper arm with one hand. The scarf had come with her all the way from the White

Kingdom, one of the colorful windings she used to wear under her glass armor. Long ago, when Maeve was still a knight...

She gripped the cloth tight in her teeth and flexed her fingers rhythmically, watching for the telltale dark bulge of a vein beneath her pale skin. There. Maeve's hands trembled with anticipation and she fumbled the syringe.

"You've got it tied too far up."

His voice came from above, punctuated by the sharp click of a gun safety being turned off. It was a sound Maeve had come to know very well. She looked up, heart racing.

Logan Coldhand was already too close, just outside the reach of Maeve's wings, his gun drawn and leveled at her. She recognized the weapon: his Talon-9 laser pistol, with its long refraction barrel, deadly in both power and accuracy even at great distance. And at this range, Maeve would never survive a hit if Coldhand pulled the trigger.

The gun and its owner were both Prian, forged on the same world as Tiberius. Coldhand had the same blue eyes and strong accent as Maeve's captain, but the similarities ended there. Tiberius Myles was built as thick and wide as an auroch, but Coldhand was smaller, more like a mountain cat. The bounty hunter couldn't have been long into his twenties – less than half Tiberius' age – but his eyes had an icy hardness that even the old man's stern gaze somehow lacked.

Coldhand's dark blond hair was damp against the back of his neck. He smelled of sweat and his chest was heaving. The bounty hunter was fit and well-muscled; he must have run hard to catch Maeve here. He was dressed in plain, utilitarian clothes that would neither stand out in a crowd nor impede him on a chase. But Maeve had known Logan Coldhand even from their first meeting by his namesake.

The right hand gripping his Talon-9 was unremarkable enough, if steadier than most. But Coldhand's left gleamed unnaturally in the dim light of Level Seven. From the elbow down, his arm and hand had been replaced by metal – silvery nanostructured titanium and scarred gray illonium plating. The cybernetics looked as much like a hand as a mask did like a face. Coldhand could have worn longer sleeves or a pair gloves to conceal it, Maeve supposed, but he never did.

"You should not be here," Maeve hissed. "Gripper said that you were light-years behind us."

Coldhand's finger tightened on the trigger of his gun. Maeve wasn't frightened. She was ready for whatever verse came next in her song... but she had no intention of making it easy for the hunter. Maeve flipped the needle in her hand and closed her fingers in a tight fist around it. It wasn't much of a weapon, but Maeve had nothing else. Not here, at least.

"You flew away from an old pod programmed with my Raptor's transponder signal," Coldhand said. "I've been on Axis for three days, Cavainna. Your ship always comes back here, sooner or later."

"Why chase me across the Alliance when you can simply wait here?" Maeve asked. "Well planned."

"Yes," Logan agreed.

His accented voice remained flat. Coldhand never gloated.

Maeve let herself go deceptively limp, sagging into the side of the alleyway in apparent defeat. Let Coldhand think that he had won, that she had finally given up the chase. Maeve curled her wings against the nearest building and waited.

Coldhand took the bait. Or maybe he saw the trap and just didn't care. He stepped in closer and Maeve lunged at the bounty hunter, using her long wings to push off the wall. Maeve slammed her small body into Coldhand as hard as she could. When he staggered, she raised the needle and stabbed it at his eyes. Coldhand brought up his cybernetic arm to protect his face and Maeve's needle struck harmlessly against the metal. The impact jarred her fingers and she gasped in pain.

But by protecting his face, Coldhand had exposed his stomach. Maeve jabbed her elbow into his abdomen and then punched him in the jaw. Coldhand fell back again, red blood blooming at the corner of his mouth. The Arcadian leapt, trying to catch enough air under her wings to fly up and away. But Coldhand recovered his balance and bounded toward Maeve, lashing out with a hard kick. It landed against one of her wings and Maeve crumpled to the alley floor once more. Her remaining wing barely turned aside a punch from the hunter's cybernetic hand, but Maeve was too slow to avoid the second. She took the blow on her ribs and sucked in a wounded hiss of breath.

"Use that Aes-be-stilled gun and end this," Maeve groaned.

"You're worth twice as much alive," said Coldhand.

The Talon-9 was on his hip, reholstered at some unnoticed moment and never fired. Maeve launched herself at the bounty hunter once more. Coldhand's glacial blue eyes were impassive as he kicked low, sweeping Maeve's legs out from under her. She rolled away and jumped to her feet again just before he could bring a crushing boot down on her wing. Coldhand drove her back with a pair of high kicks, landing another metal-plated punch as she stumbled into the graffitied wall.

Maeve caught herself against the trash bin and pulled her wings protectively around her body. When Coldhand battered aside the meager shield, Maeve was ready. While he was half-blinded by feathers, she ripped the syringe along his stomach and pushed down the plunger. The needle tore through Coldhand's shirt and left a narrow gash in the flesh beneath. Red blood and black Vanora White oozed across his skin. Had any of the White found its way into his blood? Probably not much, but the drug was a strong one. Coldhand would still be asleep in this alley long after Maeve had returned to the Blue Phoenix.

She leapt up, beating her wings hard, and managed to push herself into the air. But Maeve's injured wings buckled under the strain and she fell, landing awkwardly on top of the trash bin. Coldhand pressed one palm against his bleeding stomach and looked down at the streaks of black and red with clinical detachment. Without changing expression, he bounded toward Maeve, caught the toe of his boot on a corroded groove and vaulted up onto the trash bin.

Maeve staggered back until she felt only air under her probing feet. Cornered, she dove off the bin into a wing-tucked roll that carried her out of the alley and onto the sidewalk. Coldhand gave chase, following Maeve into the street. Sweat streamed down his face and blood ran across his stomach, but he showed no signs of stopping.

"That White should have put you to sleep," Maeve gasped. "Its effects rival a night after delberry wine!"

"Vanora White slows the heart," Coldhand said, touching his metal fingers against his chest. "It doesn't work on me."

What did that mean? Maeve didn't understand. But then something smashed into her from the side, bowling her over. Maeve realized almost too late that it wasn't Coldhand. The bounty hunter had stopped in the mouth of the alleyway, blue eyes narrowed in suspicion as Maeve hit the ground.

Someone else had collided with Maeve, pulling her down into a tangle of clumsy arms and legs. The fairy threw her wings around the stranger and they tumbled together along the road. Her wings took the worst of the fall, but they were fragile and already injured. Maeve winced and drew a breath to scream at whoever was stupid enough to run right into the middle of an earnest battle.

"By Anslin!" Maeve swore instead.

It was a girl. She kicked in instinctive fear at Maeve's wings, forcing the fairy to release her thrashing burden as gently as she could. The girl was a Dailon, with bruised blue skin smeared in dirt, and wide black eyes. But unlike the dockmaster, there was no question as to this Dailon's sex. Despite her thin limbs, her body was curved and full-breasted. Only the hormones of childbearing could change a Dailon like that. She clasped her hands protectively over her round belly.

The Dailon stared up at Maeve and Coldhand with stark terror, but didn't recoil. The girl was afraid of them, yes, but she was more afraid of something else. She pushed herself to her knees and held her hands out to Maeve.

"Help me!" she cried. "Please, they'll take my baby!"

Coldhand had moved no closer, still standing some distance away and slowly drawing his laser pistol. He watched the girl and Maeve could read nothing of the hunter's thoughts on his hard face. She stood gingerly – her bruised ribs protesting loudly – and pulled the Dailon to her feet.

"What?" Maeve asked. "Who would take your child?"

"My Sisters," the girl answered, still clutching at Maeve's hand. "Please, they're coming! Don't let them find me!"

Maeve glanced at Coldhand. The bounty hunter stared at her for a moment and then nodded curtly toward the alleyway they had just tumbled out of.

"Back here," he said.

Cradling her unborn baby, the girl followed Coldhand's instruction. He beckoned her behind the trash bin where he found Maeve only minutes ago.

"Now stay low and stay quiet," Coldhand told her. "Don't move until I tell you to. You'll be safe."

Coldhand's tone was unexpectedly soft and soothing. The girl nodded and huddled behind the trash, obedient as a gentled colt. She bit her lip and her huge black eyes shone with frightened tears.

Maeve heard voices and looked up. There were people shouting in the street and they were approaching quickly.

"Kessa, come here! Come on home, girl!"

The owners of the voices came into view – a dozen women, all dressed in rough, bright outfits. Each of them wore a red band of cloth around their right arm, painted with an upward-pointing black triangle, and brandished nanoknives in their hands or on their belts. The surface of the blades swam with colors like oil on water as programmed nanites busily maintained the weapons' molecule-fine edge. The women swaggered down the sidewalk, calling and laughing to one another. Sky and ground cars raced past the armed gang, not slowing down until they vanished safely into the distance.

Maeve almost fell again as Coldhand leaned against the graffiti-caked wall and pulled her on top of him. The bounty hunter thrust his Talon pistol into her hand.

"Rape me," he whispered, urgent but not panicked.

"What?" Maeve gasped. "Are you mad?"

"Do it. Quickly."

The women were strutting down the road and would be close enough to see down the alleyway in seconds. Maeve took the Talon-9 and jammed the barrel up under Coldhand's chin. With a sharp jerk, she finished the work of her first needle slash and tore off the Prian's already ripped shirt.

Maeve stared. A stark white scar ran down the center of Cold-hand's chest, as wide as two of Maeve's fingers and as long as her hand. There was no way he could have survived such an injury. Whatever had struck Coldhand there must have gone right through his heart.

Cold hand, cold heart... That was what he meant about the Vanora White, when he said that the drug didn't work on him. That arm wasn't the only part of Logan Coldhand that had been re-placed. His heart was cybernetic, too, a machine. The hunter caught Maeve staring and narrowed his ice-colored eyes.

"Cavainna," he said.

Maeve shook herself and stood up on her toes to grab Coldhand by the throat. The alleyway was suddenly full of raucous laughter and jeering cheers as the women saw them and stopped in the road.

The gang held their nanoknives aloft and howled at Maeve in vicious approval. A tall Ixthian missing three fingers on her knife hand whistled.

"Don't bleed him just yet," she said, smirking at Coldhand. The Prian turned his face away and made an impressive show of looking ashamed. "Lose too much and he won't do you any good, eh?"

"Damn, you like 'em ugly, don't you?" a human woman asked. She thrust her hips suggestively. "How much of that boy is metal?"

Maeve forced herself to smile. "Nothing will remain when I am done, metal or not."

"Just be sure to clean up when you're finished," the Ixthian said. Her eyes glittered red. "Don't make me come find you later, little bird-back."

Maeve nodded. She ran the barrel of Coldhand's gun down along his chest and prayed that no one actually wanted to see a show today. But the women laughed and hooted, making obscene gestures at Maeve. Coldhand watched her from the corners of eyes slit nearly shut as she reached for the waist of his pants.

"Let's go," the Ixthian said at last. She raised her voice. "Kessa! Where are you, girl?"

Taking up their leader's call, the gang of women continued off down the road. Maeve held her breath until their voices faded into the rush and growl of traffic. Finally, she stepped back from Coldhand. But Maeve kept the gun pressed against his stomach.

"Ja'hiraa ilvae," she said. *It would be so simple.*

The Sisters would say nothing if Maeve left a dead body here. There would be no witnesses. For a year, Coldhand had hunted her. Thousands of cenmarks poured into nanite surgery, days guarded in a hospital bed for the injuries that this man had lavished on her... But he had never captured Maeve, never killed her.

There was another scar on Coldhand's chest, smaller than the one over his heart – a slender white line across his ribs. That was hers, a bloody slash Maeve had cut into the hunter's side early in their chase. Coldhand had nearly as many scars from their battles as Maeve did.

It could all be over right now. Maeve tightened her trembling finger on the laser's trigger. All she had to do was adjust her aim a little and then...

Maeve flipped the gun in her hand and offered the grip out to Coldhand. He took the Talon and quickly thrust it back into the holster on his belt, then turned to the alleyway.

"They're gone," he said.

The girl, Kessa, tumbled from her hiding place. She lurched forward and threw her arms around them both, sobbing in barely coherent thanks.

"Those women are still canvassing the area," Coldhand said.

Maeve nodded in curt agreement. "We cannot leave the girl here. She is still in danger."

"I'm not letting you out of my sight, Cavainna."

Hunter and prey stared at each other, eyes narrowed – his ice blue and hers steel gray, both hard and unforgiving. Their fight might have been interrupted, but it was not forgotten.

[3]

THE BLUE PHOENIX

"Life is one journey in which we hope never to reach the inevitable destination."

— HADRIAN PROVERB

"Stop, damn it! Put that away," Tiberius shouted. "Gripper, get down from there!"

Xia lowered a silver laser pistol fractionally and Duaal dropped gloved hands back down to his sides. Gripper was still clinging to the ceiling, eyes squeezed closed and shaking with terror. Tiberius growled under his breath. The Arboran had dug his huge claws almost knuckle-deep into the Blue Phoenix's fibersteel bulkheads. It was going to take days to hammer those marks out.

"What's he doing here? What's going on?" Gripper asked, eyes still screwed tightly shut. "Is it over yet?"

The source of the crew's alarm waited silently in the airlock. Logan Coldhand seemed utterly unfazed by the frightened, violent greeting. He stood close beside Maeve and a young Dailon woman sobbed between them.

"Princess, get that girl away from him," Tiberius said, stabbing a calloused finger toward Coldhand.

The bounty hunter narrowed his eyes, but Maeve took the blue-skinned girl by the arm and pulled her back.

One problem at a time. And Tiberius' first mate had brought back several of them, as usual. There was a heavy thump as Gripper dropped to the cargo bay floor and sidled nervously over to Maeve, hunkering near her for protection. In any other situation, Tiberius would have laughed to see the massive Arboran trying to hide behind a fairy a quarter his size. Gripper awkwardly patted the weeping Dailon on the shoulder.

"It's okay. You're safe now," Gripper assured her, then looked at Tiberius. "Uh... she is, right? We're not going to let him get her, are we?"

"I'm not after the girl," said Coldhand.

"Then why–?" Gripper started to ask.

Tiberius waved him into silence. He didn't care about the answer. Prians weren't exactly known for their tact or grace, but Coldhand was worse than most. Prianus was the furthest planet of the Alliance, thousands of light-years from the nearest major out-post. Not much trade and no military presence made Prianus a poor, unimportant and unprotected planet. As a result, few Prians managed the journey off world and those that did were generally considered uncultured bumpkins, little better than fairies.

Coldhand wasn't doing very much to improve that perception. Tiberius took in the younger Prian's appearance: no shirt and blood drying on his bare chest, streaked with something black and sticky. Tiberius detected the over-sweet scent of Vanora White. He had been a cop on Prianus too long to mistake that smell.

"What the hells are you doing here?" Tiberius asked.

Coldhand arched a blond eyebrow. "You know the answer to that. I'm chasing Cavainna."

"That's not what I'm asking," said Tiberius. "What are you even doing on Axis? We were a day ahead of you, at least!"

Coldhand shrugged. He watched Xia and Duaal, attentive but not at all afraid. Tiberius' crew stood to either side of the airlock, tensed to move if the bounty hunter twitched toward his Talon-9.

Tiberius drummed his fingers on the stock of his own weapon, a stubby old-fashioned null-inertia gun. It worked more or less like an ancient gunpowder weapon, but helped along by a null-field to minimize the recoil. Guns like this used to be the height of modern efficiency, but then manufacturers like Starwind had perfected the laser. The new guns were smaller, lighter, and could fire hundreds of shots before they had to be recharged. Overnight, lasers transformed NI guns into antiques.

Old and outdated, Tiberius thought. Just like him.

What was he supposed to do now? It was Maeve's job to keep the Blue Phoenix crew flying smoothly. Tiberius knew only bits and pieces of the fairy's life, but Maeve had said that she held a command position before the fall of the White Kingdom. She wasn't the smart choice for first mate that Tiberius had hoped for, however. Maeve brought Tiberius little luck and a lot of trouble.

And today was no exception. Maeve had returned with not only the bounty hunter who had been chasing her for the last year – for reasons that Tiberius still didn't understand – but a pregnant and hysterical Dailon girl, too. So much for a quick stop on Axis and an easy getaway. Tiberius turned to Maeve.

"Damn it, dove!" he snapped. "Is someone still looking for this girl, whoever she is?"

"Kessa," Maeve said. "And yes."

"What happens when they find her?"

"They'll kill you," Coldhand said in a flat voice. "The men first."

"Why did you bring her here?" Tiberius asked.

"I could not leave Kessa where her enemies would catch her," Maeve answered.

Tiberius balled his hands into fists and braced them against his hips. "There are police on Axis, princess. Why didn't you just go to them?"

"I... I told them not to," Kessa said in a voice so shaky and quiet that Tiberius almost missed it. "The Axis police can't help me."

"Why the hells not?" Tiberius asked.

"The Sisterhood operates openly on Level Seven," Coldhand said. "They've bought off at least some of the cops there."

"Bribed? The police?" Tiberius repeated, eyes narrowed.

"They're not like the ones on Prianus," Coldhand told him. "And while a single precinct might be the only one compromised, all of their computer systems are connected. As soon as someone reports picking Kessa up, it's just a matter of time before that information and some cenmarks trade hands."

Tiberius shot a glare at the bounty hunter and then scowled at Maeve. He thrust his chin at the pregnant blue girl still huddled in her arms.

"Fine! Then we better get this bird up into the black," Tiberius growled. "You brought the girl, princess, so you go strap her down. And when we're safely off Axis, you're going to tell me what you were thinking."

"What about Coldhand?" Duaal asked.

"I don't want him on my ship, but I want him chasing us even less," Tiberius said. "He stays until I figure out what's going on. Xia, search and disarm him."

The Ixthian's eyes flashed a darker red. "You want me to disarm him?"

"My Raptor—" Coldhand began, then fell silent. He clenched his jaw shut, unwilling to say more.

Tiberius regarded the other Prian without pity – bloody, shirtless and stinking of drugs. Bounty hunters were no better than the criminals they chased. Worse, sometimes.

"Duaal!" Tiberius said, turning away. "Get this bird ready to fly!"

"Already on it, captain!"

Duaal dashed up the stairs with a grin and vanished into the ship. A moment later, the Blue Phoenix rumbled, the deck vibrating as the engines charged. The cargo bay airlock hissed, cycled and slid shut. The intercom clicked on.

"She's all warmed up and ready for you, captain," Duaal said through the speakers. "I've put in for liftoff."

Xia had stepped in behind Coldhand and was gingerly patting the human down. She took his Talon, holding it at arm's length like a snake. When she had set it aside, Xia unbuckled and removed the entire holster, including a battle-scarred com and a pair of hand-cuffs.

"He's clear," Xia said. "I think. But this isn't a prison ship. What are we supposed to do with him now?"

"Take him to one of the extra rooms and lock him in," Tiberius ordered. "We're taking off in five minutes."

"Even disarmed, Logan Coldhand is a dangerous man," Maeve said. She was still standing in the cargo bay with a wing held pro-tectively around Kessa. "I doubt our ability to contain him."

Maeve seemed almost pleased by that prospect.

"Get out of here! I said to get that girl belted down," Tiberius told her.

He jabbed a thick finger toward the metal stairs that led into the rest of the ship. Maeve's storm-gray eyes narrowed and she held the Dailon girl close, not moving. Xia gestured at Coldhand with her laser pistol and directed him up the steps. Maeve watched with a frown until the bounty hunter had disappeared into the Blue Phoenix before finally escorting Kessa away.

Shaking his head, Tiberius climbed the stairs and hurried up to the front of his ship. Duaal was waiting for him in the cockpit. The boy was strapped into the copilot's chair and his hands hovered ready over the glowing control panels. Tiberius dropped himself into the pilot's seat.

"Get us disengaged," he said.

Duaal nodded and punched three buttons in rapid succession. A deep boom rang through the Blue Phoenix as the mooring clamps unlocked. The black- and orange-striped mechanical arm grasped Tiberius' ship, carried it along a massive rail to a huge hatchway and set it onto a platform beneath. The doors grated open and flooded the cockpit in bright silver starlight, but the automated lift plate didn't move them up toward the surface.

"I thought you already put in for takeoff," Tiberius said.

"I did," Duaal answered. "But the wait time is three hours."

Tiberius flicked a switch and opened a channel to the control tower.

"Axis Flight Control," he said. "This is the Blue Phoenix. We're requesting immediate departure."

There was a loud burst of static, and then a clipped female voice answered. "Midnight push is on, Blue Phoenix. It's going to be a few hours yet before we can get you out of here."

The channel hissed again and then went silent. Tiberius looked up through the massive hatch above. True to the controller's words, the starlit sky was full of ships taking off and landing, swarming like a hive of great fibersteel bees. A sleek chromite Hyzaari skimmer flew low overhead, down under a lumbering Starwind Enterprises freighter.

Tiberius sucked a long breath between his teeth. Was whoever chased Kessa really that dangerous? Tiberius wasn't sure, but he had no intention of sticking around to find out. He activated the channel again.

"Control, this is the Blue Phoenix," Tiberius said. "We need *immediate* flight clearance."

"Blue Phoenix, this is Axis Flight Control," the same crisp voice replied. "*Everyone* needs to lift off immediately. I'm afraid that you'll just have to wait your turn."

"Axis Control..." Tiberius said, but the frequency went dead once more.

He pounded his fist down onto the radio panel. The lights flickered, dimmed then resumed their defiant red glow. The Phoenix was accustomed to her captain's less-than-gentle attention. Tiberius glanced at Duaal, who was toying with the beaded hem of his coat.

"So... we're waiting?" he asked.

"No," said Tiberius. "We're getting out of here."

He punched the ignition switch and the ship's engines ceased their sleepy rumble, roaring to life. Duaal grinned and grabbed at the arms of his chair. Tiberius slammed the throttle pedal to the floor, throwing pilot and copilot against their seats and kicking up a storm of loose blastphalt. The Blue Phoenix hurled itself off the ground, into the air and toward the waiting stars.

The runstrip lights below flickered from steady blue to angrily flashing red as the plates registered an unapproved takeoff. In the cockpit, the communications panel lit up with a riot of flickering indicators.

"*Now* they want to talk to us," Tiberius said.

Hydraulics grated through the Blue Phoenix's wings as they rotated in their sockets, turning the blasting engines away from the ground and toward the tail of the ship. The sudden transition from upward to forward thrust lurched the starship into a stomach-churning dip. Tiberius swore and yanked on the control yoke to pull the Phoenix's nose back up. Outside, the landing field was a raucous symphony of blaring alarms and proximity warnings as they flew overhead. Klaxons screamed from the runstrip and sensor spires, all ablaze with strobing red lights.

"I sure hope everyone's secure," Duaal said over the intercom. "Tiberius is taking us up!"

"What? I thought that had to be you flying, Shimmer!" Gripper's small, plaintive voice came through the speaker. "Can we go back for my guts?"

The ventilation system gave a strained groan as it struggled with the pressure change. Tiberius winced. Their hasty departure from Axis hadn't given Gripper time to fix the air scrubbers.

"We've got contacts, captain," Duaal said. "Four of them and they're close!"

A display showed Tiberius a storm of blue and green indicators scattering in their wake, ships milling in confusion as their crews tried to recover altitude and adjust their courses. But four dots broke from the pack and raced after the Phoenix. Duaal flipped over to a different screen and it lit up with a hazy video feed from the rear of the ship. The horizon was full of swirling pewter pre-dawn clouds as the freighter shot through Axis' atmosphere toward the rising sun.

"Where are they?" Tiberius asked.

Before Duaal could answer, another ship punched through the clouds, followed closely by the other three and all flying together in a tight diamond formation. Each one was a sleek silver blade under Axis' brilliant starscape, like soaring nanoswords. The ships were narrow and angular, with cockpits pressed forward into the nose to keep their pilots far away from the powerful engines.

Not just any ships, Tiberius noted with dismay. Those were police-issue fighters. He saw the guns affixed beneath their shiny, backswept wings. Pulse cannons, by the look of them. The electro-magnetic bursts would do minimal damage to Tiberius' ship, but were designed to burn out all of the electronics inside. The Axis cops had to be equipped with clamps and cables to keep the dead starships from simply tumbling back down to their planet's silver surface. Standard police equipment and procedure, Tiberius knew. Clip and capture. He never thought he would be on the receiving end of those magclamps.

The four fighters split off into pairs and gunned their engines to swoop in alongside Tiberius. Every screen in the cockpit crackled and went black, then lit up with the same image as the lead fighter overrode the Blue Phoenix's com frequency to display a Lyran pilot, age and gender obscured by the hose-covered mask.

"Civilian transport Blue Phoenix, power down and prepare to be escorted back to the planet's surface," the Lyran growled. "If you comply immediately, you will only be charged with traffic disruption. Your ship will be impounded and you will be fined."

Tiberius lifted one hand from his control yoke long enough to clench it into a fist. He raised his thumb and last finger at the Lyran. *Fly off.*

Even if the other pilot wasn't familiar with Prian obscenities, they understood enough to snarl and end the transmission.

"Impound? No one takes my bird," Tiberius growled.

"So… what now?" Duaal asked. "We're a bit outnumbered and we don't have any weapons."

Tiberius grinned tightly in his beard and toggled up the superluminal controls. Duaal laughed and switched on the ship-wide intercom again.

"Everyone hold on to something," he said. "We're about to go flying in fire!"

The Blue Phoenix hurtled across the Axis terminator line, from darkness into the dazzling dawn. Tiberius raced up through the swiftly thinning atmosphere, pointing the nose of his ship toward the stellar system's brilliant yellow-white sun. The polarized viewport saved them from the worst of the sudden glare, but it was still enough to make Duaal throw an arm across his face. Sweat beaded on Tiberius' brow and ran into his eyes, but he squinted and moved his thick old fingers over the controls. The entire ship thrummed and shook as the superluminal engines cycled up. Monitors flickered throughout the cockpit again and the Lyran growled at them over the connection.

"Blue Phoenix, disengage your engine! What are you doing? You can't use SL in-system. Do you want to tear your ship apart? Disengage!"

"Just a short hop from the nest," Tiberius said. "Don't you worry about us."

"What the hells are you doing? You're nosed right at the sun!" shouted the Lyran pilot. "Are you trying to kill everyone on that ship, old man?"

"You'll never take my wings," Tiberius said. "Never."

"Blue Phoenix–!"

Tiberius flipped up the ignition cover and punched the button. In a flash and then a shuddering lurch, the Blue Phoenix jumped. The engines hurled the starship at faster-than-light speeds for less than a second before the navigational computer errored out and pulled them back into subluminal propulsion.

The searing, burning light of Axis' sun filled the viewports, eclipsing everything in blinding white radiance. Control panels all through the cockpit lit up with warnings – the Blue Phoenix was too close to the star. Great looping streams of plasmic hydrogen and helium coiled through the corona, so vast that entire planets could have fit inside their arcs, and burning like the flame of a celestial dragon. Tiberius brought shields slamming down over every viewport on the ship as radiation readouts leapt into the red.

But the Blue Phoenix lived up to its name. The hull glowed an angry scarlet as the sun's heat enveloped it in a deadly tide of primal fire. Sparks raced across the metal like their own miniature stars, and then the whole ship burst into sapphire-blue flame. The shielding burned but held, even under the brutal onslaught of the stellar inferno. Tiberius smiled and patted the consoles.

"Good girl," he said.

[4]

SIBLING RIVALRY

"The Lyceum is like a choir of children... beautiful, if you can ever get them to stop squabbling and actually sing together."

- ANNU MARTH, HYZAAR REPRESENTATIVE (125 PA)

With a population of over a trillion citizens on thirty-six planets, the Alliance was spread thin. Necessity sent the CWA flying from star to star, forever searching out the means to support its growing population. But space was vast, and even the fastest starships took years or more to reach neighboring stellar systems.

For the Alliance to survive, they needed a way to cover much more distance in much less time. The scientists and engineers of the CWA were tasked with creating this solution. Faster-than-light engines were a simple enough prospect, in theory. But at superluminal speeds, mass was a major problem. As a ship approached the speed of light, its mass increased exponentially. When the inertia of the ship became too great, even the most powerful engines lacked the ability to propel them.

The answer to the prayers of physicists and shipbuilders alike came in the form of the newly-founded Starwind Enterprises and their revolutionary null-inertia technology. Through a clever trick of quantum gravitational thresholds, null-fields reduced the effective mass of everything contained within them to zero. Suddenly, superluminal travel became a real possibility.

But there was one complication. Interactions between shielded mass and normal matter proved to be... problematic. Theoretically, anything enfolded within the null-inertia field had no effective mass and should have been able to slide right through unshielded matter. But in practice, these interactions with normal mass tended to rip test ships back down into subluminal speeds – usually in pieces. Perhaps the same unknown physics that kept time mysteriously pinned into place had some other effects...

So engaging superluminal drives near planets or deep inside a stellar system – where planets and moons held captive by a star's gravity were most numerous – was risky. Faster-than-light speeds made reacting to such barriers a dangerous roll of the dice.

Despite their imperfections, however, null-inertia fields were an overnight sensation throughout the CWA. Starwind stockholders became the richest beings in the galaxy.

Since matter contained inside null-inertia fields had no mass, it was immune to the effects of gravity. The fields were incorporated into all manner of technology, from replacing wheels on vehicles to reducing the gunpowder required by projectile weapons. Expensive hair accessories even utilized tiny null-fields to create ever more wild and imaginative styles. Of course, only those who had first invested in Starwind could afford the most extravagant uses of their technology.

The Blue Phoenix burned at the edge of the sun's corona for the better part of an hour before Tiberius would consider venturing out of the sheltering plasma for a quick scan around. Radiation from

Axis' star made it impossible to perform even the most basic sensor sweep, but it hid them from the patrolling Axis orbital enforcement fighters, too. The Blue Phoenix's hull still rippled with azure fire and inside, the passengers waited.

With Duaal in tow, Tiberius stumped down to the crew lounge. It was a round room located in the middle of the ship with a large viewport set into the ceiling, covered by thick illonium radiation shielding for the moment. Duaal followed his grumpy Prian captain to the battered dinner table.

Duaal had been flying with Tiberius the longest, but he was the youngest member of the Blue Phoenix crew – somewhere around eighteen central standard years old. He wasn't exactly sure. But it didn't matter if he was young, Duaal often reminded himself. He was special.

The air moving sluggishly through the broken recycling system was hot and wet and smelled like burning oil. Maeve perched up on one of the acceleration couches, watching the door. The white feathers of her wings stuck against the fairy's pale, sweaty skin. They looked... itchy.

Gripper sat beside Maeve, alternately clenching and relaxing his hands. His huge claws were black with engine grease. But the mechanic grinned at Tiberius.

"Right into the sun!" Gripper said. "The phenno did great, huh? We just about ruined the SL engines jumping them like that, though."

Tiberius shrugged and grunted. "They did the job. We're safe... For the moment, at least."

Kessa wandered a slow circuit of the room, her mouth hanging open. The pregnant Dailon woman had been terrified down in the cargo bay, but now she stared at everything in frank wonder. Duaal surreptitiously combed his fingers through his hair. Her pregnancy certainly suggested there was already someone in the picture, but it never hurt to make a good impression.

"We need a new coat of phenno," Tiberius said. "We don't have a replacement for the one we're burning."

"Phenno...?" Kessa asked.

"Phennomethylln," Gripper told her. "That's the stuff keeping the heat and radiation out right now, or we'd get cooked inside the ship!"

Kessa flinched a little. "Oh."

"Phennomethylln is useful for all sorts of protection," Xia said. She gave Kessa a reassuring silver-lipped smile. "The Lyceum hasn't *quite* approved its production, though."

"Why not?" Kessa asked.

"It's a protein secreted by the Nnyth," Xia explained. "Phenno shields them from heat and radiation when they fly in space. But it can be dangerous to collect samples and the Alliance doesn't want to encourage ships broaching Nnyth territory."

"The wasps fly in space? Without ships?" Kessa asked. "But... no one can do that!"

Maeve leaned forward and shook her wings like an angry bird. "Coreworld arrogance. Whatever you do not understand, you call impossible."

"I didn't–" Kessa said in a tiny voice.

"Don't bother," Duaal whispered.

"For generations, your kind told stories of fairies and angels and enchanted trees," Maeve hissed. "But when you found us, you recoiled! You treat us like refugees!"

"But... Arcadians are refugees," Kessa protested.

Duaal snorted and Maeve's eyes narrowed. She half rose to her feet and spread her wings, making Gripper scramble away with a shout. Kessa shrank back behind Xia.

"Easy there, princess," Tiberius said.

Maeve snapped her glare up to Tiberius. She held his gaze, every muscle in her small body tensed. Duaal touched his fingertips to one of the embroidered stars on his coat. If the fairy decided to actually attack Tiberius, he would make her regret it. But Maeve just pushed a tangle of dark hair out of her face and nodded.

Xia cleared her throat. "At any rate, the phenno on our hull isn't designed to withstand the kind of stress we're putting it through. Nnyth occasionally skim stars but they never stay close for this long. That's why the phenno is burning."

"Burning?" Kessa's black eyes widened. "Will it burn off?"

"No," Xia answered. "At least, not for a while. The heat from the sun has crystallized the phenno and it should hold for another five hours at this range."

"But as soon as we fly out of the corona, the temperature differential outside will crack the finish," Gripper said. He flicked one of his fingers as though chipping imaginary phenno off the hull. "We need a whole new batch."

A sun blazed just outside the Blue Phoenix, on the other side of a few layers of metal and phenno. Sweat ran down Duaal's back. Maybe Maeve didn't really have it so bad with those wings, he decided. She only had feathers to deal with, but the leather of Duaal's coat was as heavy as lead in this heat. He shifted uncomfortably, but he couldn't take it off. Duaal *needed* the stars and sigils that he had stitched there. Without them – without his magic – Duaal was only a useless kid.

"Where is Coldhand?" he asked, more to distract himself from the sticky feeling of sweat streaming down his spine than actual curiosity.

"I locked him up in one of the spare rooms," Xia answered. "Number six."

"What are we going to do with him?" Duaal asked.

Tiberius rubbed his rough cheek, considering. "I'm not sure. We have some other things to figure out first. Like who exactly our new passenger is and why we just spent three thousand cen getting her off Axis."

"We never pay for the phenno," Duaal said. "Xyn owes us."

"But we *did* run away from Axis police," Xia pointed out. "If they ever discover that we survived jumping into the sun, we just earned ourselves some criminal records."

"Those who did not have them already," Maeve said.

"Damn it," Tiberius sighed. "How the hells did this happen? Start talking, princess."

Maeve turned one of the chairs at the table backwards and sat, crossing her arms over the back. She couldn't sit normally with those wings behind her, Duaal supposed. The fairies didn't fit anywhere in the core. The war that had driven them from the White Kingdom was over now, wasn't it? Why didn't the Arcadians just go home?

"Logan Coldhand found me on Level Seven," Maeve said. "We fought, but we were interrupted by Kessa's arrival. She was being chased by her Sisters and needed our help."

"Sisters...?" Gripper asked. "Why would she be running away from her family?"

Kessa shook her head and gulped. "They were my family once, but not like that. They're called the Sisterhood."

"The Sisters are a gang of sorts," Maeve said. "Their outlook on other genders is... unkind. I have encountered them before."

Of *course* she had, Duaal thought. If a bounty hunter was after Maeve, that meant she was a criminal, didn't it? She would fit right in with a gang of violent women.

"The Sisterhood's membership is entirely female," Maeve said. "And deadly when provoked. More than that, I do not know. But Coldhand seemed to. He was the one who suggested how to deal with them."

Duaal took a chair across from Maeve, who was now describing tearing off Coldhand's shirt as a part of their ruse. That, at least, sounded interesting. But then Maeve's story moved on to the arrival of the Sisterhood and trying to distract them from Kessa hiding nearby. Duaal's attention swiftly wandered.

Why did Tiberius put up with Maeve? The fairy woman was pretty enough, Duaal supposed, with her delicate features and long midnight hair. Maeve attracted Duaal's attention when she first joined the Blue Phoenix crew, but that died off quickly. He doubted that Tiberius had designs on Maeve, either. Orphia was the only woman in the old Prian's life.

Duaal kicked his silver-buckled boots up onto the table and glanced around the room, past Maeve to Gripper and then Xia. Why had Tiberius hired *any* of the others? Things were so much better when it was just the two of them, Duaal and Tiberius. Before Maeve and her chems and her bounty hunters. Before Xia and her mothering. Before Gripper and his questions.

Of course, keeping the ship running had been harder back then, too. Duaal had to admit that having a mechanic and a medic was helpful, at least: someone to fix broken machines and someone to fix broken bodies. But Maeve? Maeve was useless.

Tiberius was frowning and rubbing his jaw again. It was already dark with a day's gray stubble. Maeve seemed to have finished her story and fell silent. Tiberius looked at Kessa.

"What the hells, girl?" he asked. "You don't seem like the kind to join a gang. Too fragile. What's going on? And why did they turn on you?"

Fresh tears ran down Kessa's blue cheeks and she covered her face with her hands. Xia gave her shoulder a comforting squeeze and Maeve scowled at Tiberius. Duaal badly wanted to kick her under the table. Wasn't it just a few minutes ago that Maeve was the one yelling at Kessa?

"You're right," said the Dailon. The words were muffled through her blue fingers. "You're right about me. I know I'm not strong or fierce like them…"

Kessa hiccupped and Gripper held out a wad of paper towels from a dispenser next to the sink. She blew her nose into them and wiped her cheeks.

"That was the whole point," Kessa said when she could speak again. "My dad left us alone, Herra and me. Herra was my sister – my actual sister – and she took us both to the Sisterhood. Herra said we needed them. She always told me to just stay quiet and wait when things got bad.

"So I did. I stayed quiet and waited one day while some of the Sisters went out for men. They hit up against some other gang. It... didn't go well. Herra didn't come back. But they brought another Dailon. They chained him up in a room so... so the girls could use him. He cried at night sometimes. His name was Vyron. I think his line name was Fethru.

"I felt sorry for Vyron. I brought him food if no one was watching, and we talked. Vyron was nice, and smart. I liked him and he seemed to like me, too. After a while we... uh... got up to the same sorts of things that the other girls did with him. But... better."

Here, Kessa blushed deep violet and touched her fingers to her rounded stomach. So this prisoner, Vyron, was the baby's father. Where was he now? At least Kessa was calming down a bit as she told her story.

"I wanted to let Vyron go," she said. "But I was scared of what the others would do if they thought I actually cared about a male. They would kill him and hurt me. Vyron said he understood, that he loved me and didn't want me to take any chances for him. I didn't like it, but I had no idea what else to do.

"Vyron was around for about three months, I think, when the other men came for him. His gang, the ones the Sisters attacked when they caught Vyron. They killed four of my Sisters during the fighting and we got five of them. But they took Vyron back."

"Were you there when it happened?" Xia asked.

Kessa shook her head. "No, I was off buying food. They told me about it later. I missed Vyron, but I was glad he was out of there. I guess I wasn't very good at pretending to be angry about the whole thing, though. My Sisters got suspicious."

"Did you know you were pregnant at the time?" Maeve asked. "How did that occur? Surely birth control is a simple matter, even on Level Seven."

"It would be, but it's kind of frowned upon," Kessa said. "We're not supposed to get the shots. Mothering is really important to the Sisterhood. I didn't know I was pregnant until after Vyron was gone, but then it was pretty obvious."

The Dailon gestured to herself and Duaal nodded. It would be hard to overlook that body.

"They were all excited about a new Sister, but I was frightened," said Kessa. "What if it's a boy? They only keep female babies. And even if I have a girl, she would grow up hating her father..."

Kessa let out a shuddering sigh and wiped her face again. She took a deep breath before continuing her story.

"So I ran away. It didn't take my Sisters long to figure out that I hadn't just gone shopping. They chased me across Level Seven, where I ran into her–" Here, Kessa pointed to Maeve. "–and the human male with the old metal hand. You know the rest."

Duaal looked at Tiberius.

"I see," the captain grunted and scratched his rough cheek. "You ran to keep your baby safe."

Everyone waited.

Duaal tugged at his collar. God, it was hot. Sweat streamed into Duaal's eyes and blurred his vision. He blinked it away and hoped no one noticed how much he was fidgeting. Tiberius folded his arms on the scuffed plastic table and peered at Kessa. The pregnant girl squirmed in her seat, too, clearly aware that her fate hung in the balance.

"I never had any children myself," Tiberius said at last. "Always too much work to do. But if I had, seems I would want the best for them. Can't exactly blame you for the same."

The old Prian slapped his hand down on the tabletop, making Kessa jump.

"Besides, we've already flown right out from under the Axis police and burnt off thousands of cen in their sun," Tiberius said. "Might as well finish what we started."

Gripper grinned and Kessa's face lit up with confused hope. She reached out to take Maeve's hand, but the fairy pulled away. Kessa deflated a little, then brightened again as Xia enfolded her blue fingers and her own silver ones.

"Once things have settled down a bit, I'd like to examine you and the baby," said the Ixthian doctor. "Just to make sure you're both healthy."

Kessa nodded and Duaal caught Maeve's eye. This wasn't a paying job and having Coldhand onboard was dangerous. Duaal couldn't quite hate the fairy for bringing Kessa to the Blue Phoenix, but he wasn't happy about it, either.

"Now, what are we going to do with you?" Tiberius asked Kessa. "Don't suppose we could just put you back down on the other side of Axis?"

"My Sisters will find me there," Kessa said. "Sooner or later. Probably sooner."

"Fine," Tiberius grumbled. "Forget that. We'll take you somewhere else. Any ideas, dove?"

Kessa shook her head. "I've never been off Axis before."

"Maeve, you and Coldhand seem to know about that Sisterhood bunch," Tiberius said, shaking one rough finger at his first mate. "I want the two of you to help me figure out where Kessa can get some damned peace from them."

"Be careful with him," Xia said, looking up from Kessa with a deep frown. "That man is dangerous."

"I will speak to Coldhand," Maeve said.

She stood and headed for the door. Tiberius heaved himself to his feet and grabbed her arm.

"Not alone," he told Maeve. "I'm coming with you."

"Wait," Kessa asked suddenly. "What about Vyron?"

Tiberius turned his attention back to the Dailon, though he didn't release Maeve. The captain sighed.

"Wouldn't be right to make you do this on your own. We'll find your hawk, if we can. But let's start by figuring out where to take you two," Tiberius said and then corrected himself. "Three."

He and Maeve moved toward the door again. Duaal tried to think of some good reason to go along or at least an intelligent suggestion. But by the time Tiberius and Maeve left, Duaal still hadn't come up with anything. Gripper grinned at Kessa and gently took one of her blue hands in his huge claws.

"Come on," he said. "I want to show you the garden. It's the nicest place on the Blue Phoenix."

"A garden? On a ship?" Kessa asked.

"Yeah! It's wired up high," Gripper told her. "So we can keep the cargo floor open for crates and stuff. But you can see it pretty well from the catwalks."

Kessa stood and let herself be led away until their voices faded into echoes. Xia sat down in the recently vacated chair and laced her six-fingered hands together. The Ixthian doctor rested her pointed chin on her knuckles and looked at Duaal.

"What is it?" Xia asked.

Her eyes shimmered alternately blue and green. Duaal wondered how a species who displayed their mood so obviously could ever hide anything from each other.

"Shouldn't you be off examining Kessa?" Duaal asked.

"I will when Gripper's done showing her the garden. But I know something's bothering you. What is it?"

Xia could be such a mother sometimes. But Duaal didn't remember his own parents... Maybe it wouldn't be so bad to have a mother. Just for a little while.

"I don't know," Duaal admitted. He leaned back in his chair, balancing it up on two legs. "I'm not saying we shouldn't help her, but did Maeve have to bring Kessa to the Phoenix? Don't we have enough to deal with?"

Xia's short antennae curled. "Where else could she have taken Kessa? Maeve has no home except this ship. You know that."

Duaal pulled his feet off the table. His chair thumped back down to the floor.

"But that meant bringing Coldhand, too," Duaal said. "That was dangerous. Maeve should have gotten rid of him first."

"And risk fighting him off with a pregnant girl on her arm?" Xia asked. "Besides, all he managed to do was get himself caught. Coldhand is locked up now, away from his ship and his weapons."

The Ixthian's voice faltered a little, perhaps trying to convince herself that the Blue Phoenix was actually safe from Logan Coldhand.

"I guess so, but I don't trust her. Or him," Duaal said.

"You think this might be some kind of trick?" Xia asked. "How? Coldhand couldn't have known that Kessa would run into Maeve."

"You want to know what I think?" Duaal snapped. He kicked his chair back from the table. "I think that a good first mate wouldn't do things like this! Maeve has never been anything but trouble. Why the hells does Tiberius let her stay?"

Xia blinked and sat back, her eyes darkening to a deep blue and pursed her lips.

"I... I don't know why Tiberius had to hire her," Duaal said. He didn't look up. "It used to be just him and me. I was here before this was even the Blue Phoenix, when it was only the Phoenix."

"I didn't join up until after that," said Xia. "How did a Hyzaari boy end up on a Prian ship?"

Duaal closed his eyes.

It was cold. It was dark.

Duaal pulled his knees up to his chest, wrapping thin arms around them and shivering. Sparks of color danced in his vision. Was it really dark?

Or was he blind now? The child rocked back and forth on the hard floor, crooning to himself. It didn't matter. Blind or just condemned to live in darkness, at least Duaal had escaped. Anything was better than... than before.

"Two hundred eighty-eight days of light..."

"I was hiding on the ship when Tiberius bought it," Duaal said.

There was more – much more – to that particular story. Even Tiberius didn't know the whole thing. Duaal closed his hands into fists and felt sweat on his palms. It had nothing to do with the heat this time.

"I had run away," Duaal told Xia. "A bit like Kessa, I guess. We were on Prianus when I escaped and I found my way to an old shipyard. There was an unsecured hold and I hid inside."

Duaal knew he should be quiet, as silent as a stone, but it felt so good to hear his own voice, his own words. His own words, when he wanted to sing! But Duaal only knew his master's songs... His teeth chattered in the cold, surrounded by the empty crates he had pulled together into a sort of cave.

"...Will be desired by a Night..." Duaal sang.

He didn't hear the footsteps over the sound of his own voice. It was his master's song, the one he sang so often. Not a spell like the others, but it seemed to hold another kind of power. Or a promise, at least.

And then a huge, rough-calloused hand caught Duaal by the scruff of the neck and hauled him into the light. The boy screamed and writhed, but the hand held him fast.

"When Tiberius found me down there, he threatened to toss me out an airlock," Duaal said. "Then he threatened to leave me on the nearest planet. But he never did. He gave me a room and said that if I was going to fly with him, I was damned well going to pay my way. So he found me some work around the ship and he even started teaching me how to pilot the Phoenix."

Duaal opened his eyes and saw Xia smirking at him. She didn't comment on his flying, though. Duaal felt heat in his cheeks.

"For a few years, it was just the two of us," he said quickly. "Until Tiberius hired Maeve."

"Did you ever question that?" Xia asked. "A first mate manages a crew. But if there were only two of you, then what did Tiberius need Maeve for?"

"I have no idea." Duaal shook his head and stood up. His shirt stuck uncomfortably against his ribs and he pushed sweaty hair back from his face. "I should get up to the cockpit and check on the readings. If the captain missed a bit of hull when he put the phenno on, some radiation might be getting through. I don't feel like baking inside my own skin today."

Xia reached out and placed her hand on his arm. The Ixthian looked as though she wanted to say something else, but Duaal pulled his sleeve from her grasp and made his way up toward the front of the ship. He really didn't want a mother, Duaal decided. Tiberius was all the family he needed.

[5]

COLD HEART

"I think the stars shine so bright in the sky to remind us to look up from the mud."

- MICHAEL CYRUS, PRIAN POLICE PILOT (102 MA)

Not all civilizations prospered equally under the Central World Alliance. One of these unlucky planets was Prianus, which had the misfortune of being located on the edge of the core and outside regularly traveled galactic trade routes.

Prianus was a tectonically volatile world covered in deep forests and high, rocky mountains. But there weren't many useful metals or minerals in those mountains, and the frequent quakes made large-scale mining operations infeasible. Being of such little interest to the Alliance, Prianus didn't benefit very much from the cooperative efforts of the CWA.

Like other founding worlds of the Alliance, Prianus was vastly overpopulated. Only the terrible cold and thin air of the high Prian mountains preserved any of the planet's wilderness. In these places, birds held the evolutionary advantages of mobility, range and larger hunting territories than animals on the ground. Recognizing the uses of these traits, the humans of Prianus domesticated dozens of bird species and brought them down from the mountains.

Far below, the cities of Prianus were bursting with people. Too many people. Prian life expectancy was ten years less than on any other human planet. Long before joining the CWA, death had become an accepted part of Prian existence, codified into a culture of ritualized dueling. Predatory birds became prized weapons, trained to fight to the death with humans and animals alike. Such duels were considered barbaric by the rest of the Alliance, but remained a cornerstone of tradition in Prian society.

Being so remote also meant that Prianus received little military support from the Central World Alliance Armed Forces. CWAAF was a vast galactic army made up of soldiers from every member world and charged with the protection of the entire core. In theory, this included Prianus, but the logistical details of mobilizing troops across such distances usually resulted in years-long response times. When the CWAAF could respond to a Prian call for aid at all.

To prevent any one planet from being able to subjugate another, individual Alliance worlds were forbidden to maintain their own armies. Prian delegates strenuously objected to this decision, but were overruled and the already wild fringe world lost all control of its own population. Competition for Prianus' sparse resources was vicious and the planet became an open, festering wound of crime and corruption.

Denied the ability to raise an army as the populace tore each other apart, the Prian government turned to their domestic police precincts to restore order. The cops of Prianus accepted this duty with grave pride, even as they were warned that no additional resources could be spared to assist them.

The Prian police had been charged with the task no other force in the galaxy was willing or able to undertake, so they went to work. The cops were underpaid and overburdened, with the highest mortality rate of any profession on their planet. The badge of a police officer became a mark of integrity and bravery on Prianus, a modern knighthood of the strictest moral code. New recruits willingly endured rigorous and often painful physical and psychological tests to prove their worth. Necessity and devotion bred strong ties between the officers, and an even stronger sense of honor and civic duty.

The crime rate on Prianus remained the worst in the CWA. But for more than two hundred years, the Prian police held back the bloody tide of total chaos and brought some measure of peace to their planet.

Xia left Coldhand alone in darkness. The lack of light bound him more efficiently than any restraints. The bounty hunter had only one brief glimpse of the bunkroom as Xia had locked him inside, leaving his improvised prison largely a mystery.

Coldhand felt his way slowly across the room and sat down on the corner of the single small bunk. The sheets were rough and stiff under the fingers of his right hand. By the feel of them, the bedding was cheap and infrequently used. The Blue Phoenix didn't take on many passengers.

The hunter ran his cybernetic left hand along the frame beneath the bunk, but the scrape of his illonium fingertips was a dull and distant sensation. The supports were metal, probably more fibersteel – most starships were predominantly built of the stuff – but Coldhand couldn't get much more information than that from his artificial nerves.

Twenty percent.

Coldhand stood and reached out through the darkness again with his right hand. There was a jarring impact as his fingers encountered the wall sooner than he expected, but then Coldhand felt the smooth plastic of the door controls. They were all deactivated, of course. If he was going to open the locked door, he had to get to the wires behind this panel.

Coldhand felt along the edge of the control pane until he found a small indent in the wall – the repair access point. There were specific tools designed to fit into that notch, but the hunter figured he could probably muscle the latch open. He worked the fingers of his right hand into the divot and pulled. The panel didn't move. Coldhand tugged until his fingers throbbed and stung, but the plastic held.

Twenty percent.

The fingers of his new hand were numb and slow. Like they were too cold.

Or dead.

His guitar hit the floor with a discordant shriek. The broken strings curled up like the legs of a dying spider. Jess buried her face in her hands and started crying again. Logan only watched in clinical disinterest.

The seal on that control panel would be no match for Coldhand's cybernetic servos. He clenched his left hand in the darkness, listening to the metal-on-metal clack of his fingers. But he remembered what the surgeons had told him, too – the artificial hand had only twenty percent feeling. That was the best their technology could manage. Twenty percent sensation was far too clumsy to pry off the control facing without snapping or shattering it. Once it was broken, there was no hiding what he had done.

How had Coldhand gotten himself captured by a band of barely armed civilians? It would have been illegal to simply shoot Kessa for interfering with his hunt... but Coldhand didn't have to help the girl and certainly didn't have to go with Maeve to get her to safety. The advantage of staying close to his mark had vanished as soon as Coldhand stepped onto the Blue Phoenix.

It had been a gamble. Trying to take Maeve down with Kessa nearby wasn't impossible, but it put the pregnant girl in danger. Maeve might even have been willing to turn Kessa into a hostage to ensure her getaway, if the fairy's bounty posting was any indication. But she hadn't done anything like that.

In fact, Maeve's entire demeanor was... confusing. She taunted Coldhand and didn't seem particularly interested in preserving her own life. Yet when cornered, Maeve fought more like a demon than like an angel. But even that had fallen away when Kessa appeared and begged for their help.

It would have been smarter to press his attack back on Axis. Injuring or killing Kessa in the crossfire might have generated some extra datawork, but Coldhand promised himself that he would *not* hesitate again.

What was done was done, and now Coldhand needed to regain control of the situation. Here, Maeve had all the advantages – she was on her own ship, with her own crew. She had weapons and Coldhand did not. He had to get out of this room, off of the Blue Phoenix and back to his ship. And then he could resume the hunt and finally capture Maeve Cavainna.

Coldhand sat back on the bunk. The fibersteel bulkhead was cold against his bare skin, but he didn't shiver.

The bounty hunter was still considering how to proceed when he heard the sound of footsteps outside. Coldhand couldn't pick out any voices, but the door gave a warning chirp as it unlocked and then hissed noisily open on old compressors. Green-tinged light from the hall flooded into the room, silhouetting the unmistakable bulk of Tiberius Myles in the doorway. Coldhand stood up and squinted into the sudden brightness.

Whatever access code had unlocked the door also reactivated voice control over the lights. The bunkroom lit up at Tiberius' curt command and Coldhand was finally able to inspect his prison. He took it in at a glance, though, and then returned his attention to his visitor.

Visitors. Maeve Cavainna stepped into the bunkroom behind her captain and the door slid shut once more.

"Sit down," Tiberius instructed, gesturing to a desk now visible on the other side of the bunkroom and the chair bolted in front of it.

"I'll stand," Coldhand said.

Tiberius looked annoyed, but only sighed and then shrugged. "Fine. It's your spine."

"Your copilot shouted something about fire over the com," Coldhand said. "Since you're still flying, I doubt that he meant weapons fire."

"No," Tiberius agreed with a nod. "We're in orbit around Axis' sun right now."

Coldhand felt the sweat running down his skin. The air was hot, but not as hot as it should have been. Maeve watched the bounty hunter, her gray eyes lingering on the scar over his heart. Or what used to be his heart before the surgeons replaced it with metal and plastic.

"Phenno," Coldhand concluded. "Lots of it. Enough to cover the entire hull?"

"That's right," said Tiberius. With a grunt, he dropped into the chair that Coldhand had declined. "The Axis police birds chased us halfway across the system. You're right, though. That *is* a lot of phenno and we'll have to fly all the way out to Stray to replace it."

"But you're still in orbit of the sun," Coldhand said. He hadn't felt the superluminal engines engage again after that first short jump. "Why?"

"We do not yet know where to go," Maeve answered. She remained standing in front of the door. "You are more familiar with the Sisterhood than I am. We require your assistance."

Her words had the formal, musical cadence that was distinctly Arcadian. Most of the refugee fairies had learned Aver only late in life and spoke it with a thick accent that often made them difficult to understand. Of course, the rest of the Alliance considered the Prian accent nearly indecipherable, too.

"The princess here thinks you can tell us where to take Kessa," Tiberius said. "Somewhere she'll be safely out of the Sisterhood's reach."

"I don't have to tell you anything," Coldhand answered. "Except that you wasted a great deal of money."

Tiberius opened his mouth to say something, but Maeve was faster. She lunged toward the bed and seized Coldhand by the shoulder. Her high cheeks were flushed scarlet.

"You *will* help us, Logan," she hissed.

The fairy's grip tightened under Coldhand's collarbone, digging her fingernails into his skin, but he felt the pain only distantly – just a dull pressure against his chest. Tiberius was standing again, his brow folded into deep, furious lines.

"Maeve!" he barked. "What the hells are you doing?"

Coldhand grabbed Maeve's hand and pried it off of him. She struggled in his mechanical grip and beat her long wings once, but couldn't keep her balance. With a yank and twist, Coldhand locked her wrist and drove the fairy down to her knees. Her wings slapped against the steel floor, shaking loose a few white feathers.

Coldhand looked down at her. Beneath the dirt, Maeve was a beautiful woman. Her body was slim and well muscled, but she dressed herself in stained spacer's pants and a torn, dirty shirt. Her long black hair hung in tangles around her shoulders. Maeve's face was recently washed, still damp and beaded with water at the hairline, but the skin around her eyes was purple and bruised-looking. The veins of her contorted arm were dark, scabbed along the inner elbow with a dozen needle punctures. Why did Maeve do this to herself?

The Arcadian hissed in pain, spitting her rage at Coldhand. She was little more than an animal, and a sick one at that. Why did she even fight for her own miserable life, much less that of the Dailon girl? He didn't understand.

"Why do you care about any of this?" Coldhand asked.

Maeve stared up defiantly from the floor, her hand still twisted unnaturally in his cybernetic fingers. She bit her lip so hard against the pain that blood ran from one corner of her mouth. The fairy was just another fragile thing protesting Coldhand's touch.

The hunter tightened his grip and Maeve's gray storm-cloud eyes burned with furious agony, but she refused to cry out. Coldhand should have felt her hand in his, the warm softness of her skin and the heat of her blood rushing to her reddening fingers as he crushed them. But he felt nothing in his cybernetic hand, nothing in his cybernetic heart.

Something clicked. Coldhand looked up to see Tiberius pulling a bulky null-inertia gun from the rig under his arm and thumbing off the safety. NI weapons were dangerous on ships in the vacuum of space – their massive lead slugs could all too easily punch through the hull of the Blue Phoenix and vent precious oxygen to freeze uselessly in the darkness beyond. And there was a sun out there to consider, as well.

The old captain must have been very certain of his aim to draw such a weapon on his ship, or else very stupid. Tiberius leveled his gun at Coldhand.

"Let go of her!" he ordered.

Wresting the gun away from Tiberius would mean losing his grip on Maeve and giving her the chance to resume her attack. Trying to fight them both at once might force Coldhand to kill the fairy, just to reduce his opponents.

He released Maeve. Another opportunity would present itself. Coldhand simply had to be patient.

Maeve jumped quickly back out of reach. The white skin of her hand was already darkening with bruises to match the ones around her lips. She flexed her injured fingers experimentally. Apparently content that no permanent damage was done, Maeve shoved her hands into her pockets. Tiberius frowned at her.

"You're not helping anything, princess," he said. "Get out."

Maeve glared and then nodded curtly to her captain, angry color bright in her pale cheeks. Stiffly, she spun on her heels and stalked out of the room.

"Princess?" Coldhand asked.

Tiberius was still frowning at the door. He turned back to the bounty hunter. "What?"

"Why do you call her princess?"

"Oh. That." Tiberius sat down again and scratched at his gray beard. He didn't reholster his weapon. "Maeve says she's the last survivor of the Arcadian royal family."

"And you believe her?" Coldhand asked.

"Why not?" said Tiberius. "As I understand it, that black hair of hers is a dead giveaway. Mark of the royal line. Have you ever seen another Arcadian with anything but blond hair?"

Coldhand shrugged in answer. Hair could be dyed and Maeve was still his target, royalty or not. But it could be true, he supposed. She might have come from the actual White Kingdom. If so, that made Maeve Cavainna at least a hundred years old. And unless she was a baby at the time of the Arcadian kingdom's fall, probably more like two hundred. Old by human standards, but a fairy could live for several centuries.

None of the coreworld species had such long lifespans, even with the best Ixthian medical care. The canine Lyra survived only seventy-five central standard years. A human – one with a safer occupation than bounty hunting, at least – might expect to see a hundred and forty CSYs before cloned organs couldn't compensate for the deterioration of age.

But Arcadians and the other rimworld races lived much, much longer. A rooted Jinn might survive for millennia before finally withering. No one had any idea how long the Nnyth lived, but if the Jinn and Arcadians were any indication, it was centuries or more.

Maeve Cavainna had surprisingly little self-control for a woman who had lived for more than a hundred years, Coldhand thought.

Tiberius rested the gun against his knee, still aimed at the captive bounty hunter.

"Alright, let's get on with it," said the captain. "Do you know anything useful about the Sisterhood?"

"Yes," Coldhand answered.

He had encountered the fanatical women too many times since leaving Prianus to avoid learning something about them. Coldhand had even taken a few bounties on particularly dangerous members of the Sisterhood.

"Well, don't keep it to yourself," Tiberius said. "Tell me what you know and I'll drop you back on Axis."

"Or I can kill you and your crew, then take this ship," Coldhand countered. "I could pick up my Raptor and be one bird richer."

Tiberius glowered at him. "What the hells is wrong with you, hawk? Maeve told me you helped Kessa. So why won't you help the girl now?"

"My business isn't with her. I'm only interested in Cavainna."

"There's no profit in Kessa's death or her baby's," Tiberius said. "What would it cost you to give me a little information?"

Coldhand was silent. Tiberius growled in frustration and stood. He began to pace, gesturing with his null-inertia gun.

"God, I hate this," said Tiberius. "I'm just a beat cop, damn it, not a detective!"

Coldhand narrowed his eyes at the other Prian. "You were a police officer? Back home?"

"Police! Stop where you are!"

The command echoed down the rain-soaked alleyway, but the sound of it was thin and fragile. The deep night was misty and dark, lit only in the staccato red and green of the squad car's lights. Most of the dealers were already running, vanishing into the mist, but no one chased them. It wasn't a few petty street sellers that the police wanted tonight. This was a much bigger bust.

Logan stood in the fog, gun raised and finger tight on the trigger.

"Yeah, sure was," Tiberius said. He thumped the heel of his free hand against his chest. "Flew a wing team when I was young. The Blacktails."

"Where?" Coldhand asked.

"Oak District." Tiberius sighed and combed his fingers through his short steely hair. "But I got old and somehow not dead. When I couldn't do the job anymore, I was out on my ass and there was just never money for a pension. I'd saved a bit. Not enough to retire on, but enough to hit the shipyards."

"This ship is a Starwind TT-40 mark 3," Coldhand said. "They scrapped this model sixty years ago."

"She was all I could afford." Tiberius stopped pacing and patted a dented fibersteel bulkhead affectionately. "I bought her for seventeen thousand cen, cargo and all."

A shadow passed over Tiberius' face, but it vanished swiftly. The old captain was proud of his ship and eager to talk about it. He gave away information like Docinia presents, more than Coldhand could ever have uncovered on the Axis mainstream.

"How could you afford a crew?" the hunter asked.

Tiberius didn't seem able to pay them much. Maybe one of them could be easily bribed. Or was there something else that bound the crew together? But Coldhand's tone must have given him away. Tiberius scowled and resumed his pacing.

"I think I've talked enough," he said. "If you won't be helpful, I'll go spend some time with Orphia before this whole thing makes me crazy."

Orphia? Coldhand knew the Blue Phoenix's crew complement, even if he didn't know a great deal about them. But he had never seen that name on any datawork.

"I'll come back later," Tiberius grumbled. He keyed open the door. "Maybe you'll feel like sharing then. But we'll be flying out of here soon. The longer you wait to talk, the further we'll be from Axis. I can have Gripper bring you a shirt."

"And a datadex."

Tiberius turned in the doorway. "What?"

"I'm going to be here a while," Coldhand said. "Give me something to read. I don't care what it is."

"Fine. Clothes and a datadex," Tiberius agreed.

He left the bunkroom, leaving the lights on when he locked the door behind him. Coldhand spent the next half hour inspecting his prison until there was another tone from outside.

"I... I'm coming in," said a voice.

The door slid open and a massive alien ducked through, with thick brown skin and green fur on his long, muscular arms – Gripper, the ship's mechanic.

Gripper held out a faded gray shirt in one huge, shaking hand. Coldhand took it, which made the mechanic flinch violently. The shirt was printed with the white starfield logo of Starwind Enterprises and several sizes too large. Too large for Coldhand, at least – it would have been a comically tight fit on Gripper. The shirt must have belonged to Tiberius.

Coldhand pulled it on over his head and then looked up.

"The datadex?" he prompted.

Gripper dutifully removed a datadex from one of his pockets. The screen was tiny in the big alien's hand and he flinched again when Coldhand took it. *The Still Wind* was on the datadex display, an old Prian book scrolled about halfway through. The screen was scuffed and scratched almost beyond legibility, but Coldhand didn't care. He turned it over, illonium fingers clicking on the plastic. The datadex was an older, heavier model, nearly too thick for his needs. But it would do.

"Need... anything else?" Gripper asked in an unsteady voice.

"How many people are on this ship?"

"Um, five of us," Gripper answered, taking a step away from Coldhand. "There's me, Claws, Smoke, Silver and Shimmer. Uh, that's me, the captain, Maeve, Xia and Duaal."

Orphia wasn't on his list. So who was she and would she be a problem? Coldhand didn't know, but one problem at a time.

"Why the nicknames?" he asked.

"It's a uh... a thing from back home. We don't use birth names much on Arborus," Gripper explained. "They're useful for yelling at babies not to fall out of their tree, but that's about it. I mean, Anandrou doesn't tell you anything about me, does it? But *Gripper*..."

The young alien brandished his massive hands. His fingernails were long and nearly as thick as the datadex Coldhand held.

"I never let go of something once I grab on," Gripper said. "Not a branch or a job. I never give up, right? Like this one time–"

"Cavainna," Coldhand interrupted. "Maeve. Why do you call her *Smoke*?"

"I uh... I don't really know if I should say. I've never even told her that."

Coldhand fixed his gaze on Gripper. The mechanic hunched until his long arms brushed the floor, then pressed his balled-up hands against the deckplates. He shifted his weight back and forth on his knuckles.

"Smoke is just so tiny and light, and not just compared to an Arboran girl," Gripper answered at last. "But she's... poison. I mean, I like her – I think – but Smoke's got a temper even worse than the captain. She's destructive. To herself and everyone around her. Like fire."

"Then why not call her that?" Coldhand asked.

"Because fire still burns," Gripper said. He shook his huge head. His voice had gotten small and quiet. "I don't think Smoke does anymore. I think she's given up. I don't know if there's anything left inside her. Oh... and smoke flies. So does she."

Gripper made a ridiculous fluttering motion that looked very little like Arcadian wings, but Coldhand got the idea. The Arboran fell silent and took another shuffling half-step back toward the bunkroom door.

"And what do you call me?" Coldhand asked.

"Um... Coldhand," Gripper answered. "You've already chosen your own name."

Coldhand said nothing. Gripper stood awkwardly in the door for a moment, then turned on his knuckles and squeezed back out into the hallway. It locked behind him with a beep and a muffled clunk.

When Gripper was gone, Coldhand crouched next to the door and slipped the corner of the datadex into the dimpled wall beneath the access panel. He worked it painstakingly up and down, and was rewarded with a loud click as the hatch swung open. The space between the bulkheads was filled with circuit boards and bundles of coiled wires. Coldhand considered the controls.

He wasn't an engineer. Rewiring the bunkroom door would take time and a great deal of trial and error, but the unbroken access panel would let Coldhand conceal his work from his captors for as long as necessary.

Carefully, he pulled a red wire out of the wall and got started.

[6]
SMOKE AND FLAME

"You can lift a gun, but I can lift a heart. So I ask you: which of us
has the greater gift?"

- YINAAL DEVRA, HYZAARI SINGER (780 MA)

Even with the invention of superluminal engines and their
ancillary null-inertia fields, it took months for a starship to reach
the rim worlds, stellar systems that lay on the outermost edge of the
galaxy. When the CWA arrived on the rim, they were shaken by
what they found there. Most planets on the galactic fringe were
barren, but not all. Before the Alliance decided that rimworld
exploration was financially unsustainable, their pioneers discovered three kingdoms in the outer reaches.

First were the Jinn, a strange tree-like species with long lifespans and not much interest in contact with the Alliance. Next, the
CWA encountered the great star-hive of the Nnyth, called The
Tower by its inhabitants as best Alliance linguists could guess. But
the vacuum wasps quickly chased off all exploration vessels.

After two such expensive and unproductive encounters, the
Central World Alliance approached the third rimworld civilization

with caution and distrust – the White Kingdom of Arcadia. The fairies were more human in appearance than the Jinn or Nnyth, but their worlds were still so... alien. While the CWA built massive starscrapers of fibersteel and tough ceramic, the fairies made their cities out of glass. Not the thick tempered stuff that gave Axis its mirror shine, but delicate crystal in brilliant colors. Alliance scientists discovered a high and well-organized carbon content in Arcadian glass, similar in structure to carbon fiber or diamond.

But far more shocking than the fairies' glass cities was their knowledge of both the Jinn and Nnyth worlds. The Arcadians were natural fliers and had never developed any kind of aerial transportation, which included a total ignorance of space travel. Instead, they journeyed to other planets through the use of constructs they called Waygates, which allowed the White Kingdom to span every world of their stellar system and trade with the other rimworld kingdoms. Exactly how these gates functioned could only be understood as 'magical' by the Alliance explorers, like so many facets of rimworld existence.

A deep and mutual distrust quickly developed between the Alliance and the White Kingdom. Each was utterly alien and suspect to the other. The fairies were not invited to join the CWA or to trade with their outposts. A handful of Union of Light missionaries ventured out in an attempt to win the polytheistic aliens over to worship of the One God, but found no converts.

Twenty years later, the already unfriendly relationship between the Central World Alliance and the fairies fell apart entirely when the White Kingdom suddenly and mysteriously collapsed. Two million refugees – many wounded or dying – appeared without warning across the five human homeworlds of the Alliance. The fairies were greeted with almost universal hostility. There was no room in the CWA for two million Arcadian refugees.

And in the century that followed, sentiments changed very little.

Orthain Fyre stood in front of Maeve's tent. He wore his golden hair unbound to frame his beautiful face. The fine plates of his glass armor shone in the bright sun with the edges picked out in delicate scrollwork of red and violet, the colors of his house. Light silk wrappings were visible through the glass of his armor, wound close around his long, lean body. Orthain was tall for an Arcadian – nearly the height of a coreworld human – and could boast an impressive wingspan twice as long as he was tall.

Not that Orthain would ever boast. Not Sir Orthain Fyre, the perfect knight, humble and handsome. Maeve's heart beat fast at the sight of her teacher. How long had she been his squire? Forever, it seemed sometimes.

"Your time has come, Highness," Orthain said. He gestured up toward the sun. "Aes has reached the pinnacle of her dance and Anslin waits to hear your vows."

Maeve rose from her kneel and almost fell down again as her legs shook. Orthain laughed and offered his hand. He wrapped strong fingers around Maeve's and led her out from the red and gold striped tent. The audience stands bloomed with snapping pennons of every hue, dancing banners of color in a bed of thousands of white Arcadian wings. In the lower working-class rows, Maeve caught sight of nyad blues and dryad browns and green. The assembled crowd sang out their approval, thundering voices shaking the very air as Maeve appeared.

Orthain grinned at her and hummed softly. "Courage, Highness."

One of Maeve's handmaidens, a pretty young nyad girl with pearls braided into her long blue hair for the occasion, scattered rose petals and flakes of beaten gold on the grass before the princess' feet. Orthain guided Maeve across the field to a dais covered in flowers.

The king and queen of the White Kingdom sat in their birchwood thrones on top, worn smooth and polished by millennia of hands. They wore flowing silks of House Cavainna red and gold and smiled down at Maeve. Her mother, Princess Beltain, stood beside her brother's throne *and pushed back the black curls of her hair. Even baby Caith squealed in Beltain's arms and waved his tiny fists at Maeve.*

On King Illain's other side, Crown Princess Titania – Maeve's cousin – lifted her wings and silence fell across the field.

"Who stands for Maeve Cavainna, child of Princess Beltain and Sir Arlinn?" the king asked.

Orthain bowed until his white wingtips brushed the grass. "I am Sir Orthain Fyre and I stand for my squire. By the stone of Erris All-Singer, Maeve has proved herself to be of strong spirit. By the fire of Aes Cloud-Dancer, she has proved herself a fierce warrior. By the wind of Anslin Sky-Knight, she has proved herself to be fair and just."

Maeve drew herself up proudly. For fifty years, she had dreamed of this moment, toiling and training as Orthain's squire and student. Her father, Sir Arlinn, stepped forward on the dais, carrying a long spear with a glittering glass blade. His eyes shone with tears and he beamed down at his daughter.

King Illain rose and took his own spear from where it stood beside his throne. He thrust the blade out toward Maeve, who knelt to receive his blessing. She waited, but didn't feel the cool glass against her shoulder. Something was wrong.

No. It did not happen like this…

Maeve looked up from the grass and stared at her uncle, her king. His eyes rolled back, leaving white crescents, and blood ran from the corners of his mouth. The spear in his hand had turned a sickly gray and twisted this way and that like an angry snake.

Please, no! Leave me this. Do not take this memory from me.

Dark clouds filled the sky, turning the sun into a flat iron-colored coin. Muttering from the assembled fairies rose to a terrible wail, and then terrified screams. The grass was red with blood. The birchwood thrones were in flames and their black smoke was a spreading, choking cloud.

Maeve lurched and beat her wings, trying to fly away from the carnage, but Orthain was suddenly holding her hand again and didn't let go.

"Courage, Highness," he said.

Smoke swirled around Orthain and he closed his eyes, waiting to die.

The chirp of the ship's com woke Maeve. She jerked upright in her bed, kicking. The sheets were a sweaty tangle around her ankles, leaving the rest of her bare body uncovered and shivering.

The Blue Phoenix was two days out from Axis' bright sun. With the ship presumed destroyed by their star, the Axis control officers had quickly stopped searching for the missing ship. Cautiously, Tiberius flew the Blue Phoenix to the edge of the system, waiting until their next move was decided well outside the deadly heat and radiation of the sun.

Maeve shoved messy black hair back out of her eyes and stood. She groaned as her wings cramped, stiffened by the narrow confines of the bed. Crumpled paper wrappers and plastic narcohol bottles littered the floor and rolled under her feet as Maeve made her way to the beeping communications console. Still naked, she opened the channel.

The screen lit up, displaying Xia's smiling silver face. Behind her, the rest of the crew was gathering around a table in the mess and chattering over breakfast. Xia took in Maeve's state of undress and tactfully placed herself between the table and the video feed.

"Good morning, Maeve," Xia said. She gestured back with a six-fingered hand to the pile of pancakes on the table. "I made breakfast, if you'd like to join us. Hurry, before the others eat it all."

Xia closed the channel with a conspiratorial wink, her jeweled eyes whirling a mischievous sky blue. Maeve grimaced at the darkened screen. Xia was a kind woman who treated everyone like a treasured friend. Even those who didn't deserve it.

A used needle rolled under Maeve's foot as she dug through the filth for something to wear. It spun away and came to rest against the spear propped up in one corner of the room. The spear Maeve had seen in her dream, with a haft of smooth-polished birch and a glass blade colored by delicate swirls of red and gold. There were dozens of ribbons tied along the spear's handle, each of them a prize from some tourney or competition and boasting rights for the knight that carried it.

The ribbons were frayed now and there was no one left to recognize them. The knights of the White Kingdom had all died defending it. All except Maeve.

She found a pair of denims with only one torn knee and put them on. Maeve fished around for a shirt and untangled a red scarf from an empty narcohol bottle. She pulled it free and ran the fabric between her fingers. The ends were embroidered with graceful golden loops and circles. It had been a gift from her father so many years ago, when a younger Maeve flew away to serve her first post as a full-fledged knight of Arcadia.

But Sir Arlinn was dead now, along with the rest of her family. Caith had been too gentle and clumsy to follow Maeve into the knighthood, but he was one of the first to die when the White Kingdom fell. Orthain survived a little longer, but Maeve wasn't there beside him when he died. She was already gone when they killed Orthain, flying as fast as her wings would carry her.

Maeve seethed with the familiar molten heat of hatred. She screamed in fury and smashed her fist into the nearest bulkhead as hard as she could. Everything beautiful in the universe was dead, leaving Maeve behind and alone.

But she lived. So, for the moment, did Kessa and Coldhand. How could the bounty hunter let himself be captured so easily? For days now, Coldhand merely sat in the room that served as his cell while the Blue Phoenix waited outside the Axis system. When Maeve brought him aboard, she assumed that Coldhand had only accompanied her as part of some clever ploy to finally take down his mark. When would he *do* something?

Maeve looked down at the scarf still in her hands. Her knuckles were bleeding and left smears of darker red on the fabric. Maeve wound the scarf around her chest and tied it off just beneath her wings. Good enough.

When she was dressed, Maeve made her way down the narrow corridors of the Blue Phoenix to the mess. It doubled as a kitchen, with a stove, oven and counter along one wall. The rest of the crew was gathered around the table. They laughed as Gripper – who took up an entire side of the table – folded three pancakes in his claws and devoured them in a single bite. Xia pulled a few from the pile in the center, covered them in sweet amber mantle syrup and then handed the plate to Kessa, who was eating almost as ravenously as the Arboran. Maeve ignored Gripper's invitation to sit.

"What about Logan?" she asked. "Has anyone fed him?"

"I'm not walking into a room with that man unless I have to," Xia answered with a shudder. "Did you see that hand?"

"Coldhand isn't going to starve to death," Tiberius said. "But no, he hasn't been fed yet today. You can take care of that, princess. After we talk."

Duaal nodded. "We need to figure out where to go next. The Sisterhood is widespread, but we didn't get much else out of Coldhand. So where can we take Kessa that she'll be safe?"

"And how do we find Vyron?" Xia asked. "Kessa doesn't know where he went. Is he still on Axis? We're not exactly popular with the Axis police right now, so going back to look for him isn't really an option."

"They believe us dead," Maeve said.

"True," Xia agreed. "But I don't know that we want to rely on that so soon after our disappearance. Our registry is still flagged in the Axis system, I'm certain."

Kessa sighed and wiped syrup from her mouth. Gripper patted her shoulder, almost knocking the young woman face-down into her breakfast.

"We'll find him somehow," he promised. "I'd love to leave some kind of message, but we're way out of range of the Axis mainstream now."

"One problem at a time," Tiberius said. "We didn't have the chance to finish refueling and restocking on Axis before we took off. This bird can't fly forever. We've wasted several days waiting for Coldhand to talk, but that man's lips are sealed tighter than an Axial's wallet. We'll have to get Vyron later. Somehow."

Kessa looked as if she were about to object, unwilling to leave the world where her mate might still be hiding. But the Dailon laid her hands against her belly and nodded. There were new burdens in her life now, but burdens coupled with blessings.

The sun was brilliant in the sky, as though Aes Cloud-Dancer herself was celebrating. Orthain grinned at the news, too. He leaned on his spear, silk wrapped around the blade so that he could practice safely with his young squire.

"And now you have a little brother," he said. "I suppose I should release you from today's lessons."

"The gods have been kind," Maeve answered. "But I... I will remain if that is your wish, my teacher."

Orthain laughed and there was a bright twinkle in the older knight's eyes that made Maeve's wings go weak.

"The All-Singer must have gifted your father with a mighty spear indeed," he said, "to have granted your mother so many children."

The young princess blushed furiously. "You should not say such things! My father is your ranking officer, Sir Fyre."

"Of course, Highness," said Orthain. He covered his broad, handsome grin with a deep bow. "Now is no time for crude jokes. Go, Maeve. Go meet your new brother. We will resume your training later."

Maeve stammered out her thanks and launched herself into the air. Orthain watched the princess soar up into the cloud-dappled blue sky with a smile. She looked down and thought she saw his lips moving. Maeve knew that song.

"Two hundred eighty-eight days of light..."

"What about Stray? It's only about a week away," Xia suggested. "We have to go there for some new phenno, anyway."

"That's not a bad idea," Gripper said. "Stray is on the edge of Alliance space and pretty close to the rim. Even if Blue's Sisterhood sent word that she's run off, that message isn't getting all the way out to Stray for a while."

"But Stray is a cesspool," Maeve protested. "That is no place for Kessa to raise a family."

"Anything's better than going back to Axis," Kessa said. "I can go to Stray."

Tiberius nodded. "Fine then. Stray it is."

With their next step decided, the crew of the Blue Phoenix went back to their breakfast and conversation turned to the current CWA fashion; tight-fitted Ixthian styles in stately monochromatic color schemes. Kessa listened in awe as Xia and Duaal argued the merit of human versus Ixthian models.

Maeve paid little attention. Instead, she fumed silently. Stray? Stray was a *terrible* choice. It was a dangerous planet, perhaps even more crime-ridden than the lower levels of Axis. What were the chances that the Sisterhood hadn't taken up residence there? Bad, Maeve thought. Very bad.

Maeve collected some of Xia's pancakes onto a plate, not bothering with the butter or mantle syrup. Coldhand was their prisoner, after all. No one noticed Maeve leaving the mess.

When she arrived at his door, Maeve keyed it open and stepped inside without announcing herself. She found Coldhand sitting on the corner of his bed. Wordlessly, the bounty hunter took the plate with his right hand when Maeve held it out. He set the food on his knees and balanced it there as he ate, leaving his metal hand curled motionless over the edge of the bed. There was no hate in the man's pale blue eyes, no anger or even fear.

"Are you not worried that I might have put something in your food?" Maeve asked.

"Poison me, you mean?" Coldhand said between bites. "No. I've studied your record, Cavainna. You have sixteen attempted murder charges, but nothing so premeditated – mostly self-defense against other hunters. Or are you talking about the charge on the main bounty posting, the private one...?"

Maeve ground her teeth and couldn't bring herself to answer. Coldhand needed to be more careful if he was to live long enough to complete his hunt. He finished off his breakfast and held out his plate.

"I am not your servant," Maeve snapped.

"I can take the dishes myself," Coldhand said evenly. "Just un-lock the door. I'm sure I can find the way."

Maeve snatched the plate and cocked it back over one shoulder. Fury turned her blood into acid and it burned through her body. Coldhand watched her with clinical detachment, gauging her reac-tion, but didn't move. Was he that sure Maeve wouldn't hit him? Or simply didn't think she could harm him if she did? If so, he was wrong on both counts... But Maeve dropped the plate onto the bed. It bounced across the covers and landed half on top of a worn datadex.

Maeve recognized the device – it belonged to Tiberius. She picked up the datadex and found *The Still Wind* displayed on its scuffed screen.

"*Elonna's shining black eyes had become pale and dull,*" she read out. "*Blind. Elonna trembled in my hands and I promised my falcon ven-geance for what they had done to her. The wind grew still and silent, as though God had bent close and held His breath to hear my vow.*"

Maeve rolled her eyes and dropped the datadex back on top of Coldhand's empty breakfast plate. Only Prians could write about birds with that kind of overwrought passion. *Other* Prians, at least... Coldhand didn't wear any of the leather gloves or sleeves that

Prians used in order to safely handle their predatory birds. There were many deep scratches in the metal of his cybernetic arm, but none of them looked like those left by a hawk.

Leaving backwater Prianus wasn't cheap. How could Coldhand afford the journey but not a hawk or falcon? Hunting and dueling birds were precious on his homeworld and no respectable Prian would be without one.

"Where is your bird?" Maeve asked.

"Back on Axis," Coldhand answered. "Tiberius flew away without letting me retrieve it."

"Not your ship. Your actual bird – a hawk or a falcon, as favored by your people."

"I don't fly hawks anymore," Coldhand said in an icy voice that didn't invite further conversation.

Maeve ignored his tone. "Prians are well known for their love of birds. Even your ship is called a Raptor. But if you had the money to buy it, why not a hawk?"

"I didn't buy my Raptor," Coldhand said. "When I left Prianus, I took it with me."

"You stole it?" Maeve asked. She shook her head and laughed. "How... appropriate. The bounty hunter is himself a criminal. The Nameless has a truly wicked sense of humor."

Now it was finally Coldhand's turn to look curious. "Nameless?"

"A god of my people," Maeve said. "The goddess of death who waits to take all of creation back."

"No one sent me," Coldhand answered. "Unless you count the bounty boards."

Arcadian religion was considered a fringe cult by the Alliance and studied by only a handful of exopologist. The refugee fairies' private worship wasn't expressly forbidden, as long as it didn't bring them into conflict with the Union of Light, the CWA's official and almost aggressively inclusive church. But few non-Arcadians were familiar with their mythology.

"Erris All-Singer was the first god of my people," Maeve said. "But he was alone, with no one to hear his songs. So Erris created three other gods to be his companions."

"I didn't ask, Cavainna," said Coldhand. But he leaned forward on the bed, listening.

"From the soft down feathers of his wings, Erris created Aes Cloud-Dancer," Maeve told him. "She was the most beautiful of his creations. Erris fell instantly in love with Aes and claimed her for his wife."

"Romantic," Coldhand said.

Maeve glared at the bounty hunter, but he quieted again. She cleared her throat and continued.

"From the strong pinions of his wings, Erris created Anslin Sky-Knight to watch over the All-Singer and his bride. Anslin was the first knight and the father of spearcraft.

"But Erris All-Singer was wearied by his creation and made the last god from the sweat of his brow and only half his heart. The Singer gave this final goddess no name and no purpose. The nameless god was furious with her creator for his inattention and fled the heavens, swearing revenge on the other gods. She hid in darkness so long that her wings turned as black as midnight."

It felt good to tell the old stories. For a little while, at least, it was like Maeve was back home. Like the White Kingdom still stood and she wasn't the last survivor of her house. Maeve could almost hear her father's voice and feel his strong wings around her.

"Erris sang in the heavens and Aes danced to his every song until her heart and her wings ached. The gods grew to know every note and every step until their delight faded. Aes and Anslin came to Erris and begged him to make others, creators of new songs and new dances. But Erris was too proud and refused, saying that his creations were already perfect.

"So Aes and Anslin conspired. When the All-Singer called upon them, Aes would not dance and Anslin covered his face with his wings, refusing to watch or listen. They told Erris that they would not serve their purpose until Erris promised to do as they asked.

"Enraged, the All-Singer turned his back on Aes and Anslin. But in time, he grew lonely for his bride and his friend. That was when the Nameless returned to him.

"She wore Aes Cloud-Dancer's form, with wings as soft as whispers and hair as golden as the dawn. The Nameless embraced him in lover's arms and Erris was overcome with joy. He agreed to all Aes had asked, but the Nameless demanded one more thing."

"Death," Coldhand guessed. "Every culture has a death myth."

"Yes," Maeve said with a nod. "The Nameless told Erris that his new creations must be mortal or else their songs, too, would grow ancient and stale. Erris was consumed by passion and agreed.

"The Nameless cast off her disguise and laughed at Erris. Death was promised, the Nameless gloated, and every life that the All-Singer created would fall ultimately into the endless same dark to which he had condemned her.

"Erris was furious at the Nameless for her trick. He tore the wings from her shoulders and left the goddess naked and shivering, bound forever to the ground. But Erris could not take back the promise he had given. As the All-Singer wept, the Nameless fled on bare feet like a low beast."

One of Coldhand's eyebrows rose a bit at that, but the bounty hunter didn't interrupt again.

"Erris confessed his terrible mistake to Aes and Anslin. He could not bear to forge new life only to let their Nameless sister take it away. But he had made promises , so he would give his new creations a gift he had not even granted Aes and Anslin.

"'You have given us power, beauty and strength,' Aes told her husband. 'What else can you give them?'

"'I will give them the one gift I always kept for myself,' Erris said. 'The ability to create life. New life, born of love. Perhaps with the gift of life, they will forgive death...'"

Maeve looked up at Coldhand again. The warm feeling of home was gone and she was back in cold black space, the domain of the Nameless. Coldhand was watching her closely, but he hadn't taken advantage of her distraction to attack.

"That must be the Arcadian creation myth, too," Coldhand said. "You were the new singers Erris made, correct?"

"Yes."

"What about the other fairies?"

"The gods created them later, to serve the Arcadians," Maeve answered. "...Or so it is said in our oldest songs. During our brief contact with Alliance scientists, though, they found our genetics to be very similar. Like the human species, we were told. The dryads and nyads might even have been able to interbreed with us, had our culture permitted it."

"What happened to the dryads and nyads when Arcadia fell?" Coldhand asked.

"They died," Maeve said. "All of them. Only a small percentage of the fairies escaped the destruction."

"Only Arcadians?"

Maeve nodded. Coldhand had another question, but her com chirped and Tiberius' voice crackled over the line when she turned it on.

"Maeve, I need to talk to you," he said. "Get up to the cockpit."

Coldhand leaned back on his bed, gesturing for her to go. Maeve bent to take the plate from beside him. She could drop it in the sink on her way to the cockpit...

The borrowed datadex slid as Maeve pulled the plate out from beneath it. Coldhand reached out with his cybernetic hand. It was an unthinking, reflexive motion and the datadex slipped through his metal fingers. He tightened his grip, clamping down on the thin screen until it cracked with a sharp snap.

Coldhand stiffened and his illonium hand opened as though burned. The datadex fell to the floor and the hunter stared down at it, his glacial eyes blankly unreadable. Maeve sighed and reached for the broken device. It was trash now and as long as Maeve was serving as Coldhand's maid, she may as well throw it away.

Maeve paused when her fingers closed on the datadex's casing. The corner was rough against her skin, covered in fresh, jagged scratches. Maeve picked up the datadex to inspect the roughened metal. Even Coldhand's cybernetic hand couldn't have damaged it this way. The datadex had been used to scrape or pry at something. Used as a tool. So he wasn't just sitting idle in this room.

Maeve held the datadex out to Coldhand. He narrowed pale blue eyes at her, but took it.

"It is said that the Nameless, too, learned the secret to creating life," Maeve told him. "There are stories of her children on other worlds, creatures of death with short lives and no wings. When they could bring no more death to their own planets, they learned how to create great metal wings to carry them further out into the darkness."

Coldhand tucked the broken datadex under his mattress. Maeve turned away and opened the door with her handprint.

"You're flying on those metal wings, too, Cavainna," Coldhand reminded her.

"Our kingdom and our home is gone," Maeve said. "The dryads and nyads are dead. We are homeless and despised. I doubt my species will survive very much longer. We are all sons and daughters of death now."

Maeve stepped out of the door and locked it behind her. She made her way through the Blue Phoenix, pausing to deposit Coldhand's plate in the mess, then headed up to the front of the ship.

The cockpit was small, not much more than a pair of pivoting chairs bolted down in the middle of a busy crescent of displays and controls. Duaal was somewhere else in the ship, but Maeve's wings made sitting comfortably in his seat impossible, so she stood in the open hatchway.

Tiberius wasn't alone in the cockpit, though. Orphia watched Maeve coldly. The hawk perched on the back of her master's chair, carving another deep set of gouges with her talons to match a hundred others in the hard plastic. Orphia's once-vivid black and brown markings had faded with age, but the old police hawk was still as deadly and grumpy as her master.

Orphia clicked her wickedly hooked beak at Maeve, cocked her head to one side and then decided that the other bird was no threat. With that, Orphia flipped her wings and ignored Maeve.

"Princess, I need to know something before I take us to Stray," Tiberius said. The captain rubbed his bearded chin. "Well, two somethings."

"What are they?" Maeve asked.

"Why the hells did you bring Kessa *here*? I can barely rely on you to come back to the Phoenix yourself. You don't care about much. Not even your pay, as far as I can tell."

Tiberius glanced up at Maeve, perhaps to see if he had insulted the fairy. But she just shrugged and gestured for him to go on. Orphia preened her feathers, ignoring the conversation entirely.

"You're a wild one, dove," Tiberius told her. "Always have been. Coldhand was in the right to wonder why you give two cen about Kessa, and you were right not to answer him. But now I'm the one asking."

"My kind gives birth only infrequently," Maeve admitted. "It is a sacred gift granted by our first god."

Tiberius' brow furrowed. "That's it? You're helping Kessa because your god says so?"

Maeve made herself meet her captain's gaze, but it wasn't easy. "No. But you would not understand."

"Try me, princess."

"Kessa was just a girl when she followed her sister into that gang. Young and stupid and afraid to be parted from her sibling," Maeve said. She heard the raw red wound in her voice and hated it.

"I have seen the pain that results from such a decision all too near and would spare Kessa that loss."

"You're saying that what Kessa's going through hits a little close to the nest?" Tiberius asked. "That's why you got us all into this?"

Maeve didn't answer. It was more complicated than that but... yes. Eventually, Tiberius grunted and spoke again.

"Fine, then. Look, I've given up on Coldhand being any help to us, but I need a warning if the man will be a problem. Of everyone on this bird, you're the only one who knows much about him."

"As well as any prey knows her hunter," Maeve said.

"Coldhand must have realized we weren't going to release him once he was on the Phoenix. Why did he come at all? Not to let you out of his sight, he said, but now he's in a bind. Coldhand should have known – or at least suspected – that this would happen. So why did he stay with you?"

The princess shrugged. She didn't know, but Coldhand never did anything without a reason, usually one involving money or his job or... something else. Tiberius sighed when Maeve did not respond. He turned on the ship's com.

"Duaal, get up here," Tiberius said. "It's time to fly ourselves out of here."

[7]
STRAY

"Experiences are like feathers. Some may get ruffled, but all of them are important if you want to fly."

Stray was eight days from Axis and the galactic core at superluminal speeds. Gripper spent most of the journey working down in the cramped engine room. Without ground time on Axis to make repairs, the atmospheric recycling system and FMS relays were still broken. Gripper watched the SL drive jolt and shudder with almost paternal worry, clenching and unclenching his huge hands at every grating sputter.

In her usual caring – end meddling – fashion, Xia made sure that the fretting mechanic ate and slept on something like a regular schedule. She brought Gripper plates of vegetables from his garden in the cargo bay and remained with the Arboran even after he had eaten them all. When the Phoenix's lights dimmed in the evening, she lured Gripper away from the engine room with questions about his homeworld until the words became a tired mumble and he finally fell into much-needed sleep.

On the fourth such night, Xia sat up with Gripper in the cargo bay. He perched on the edge of one suspended planter, mournfully inspecting his garden. New seeds and fertilizer had been ordered back on Axis, but they left before receiving the shipment and now Gripper's garden was looking more than a little empty.

"Claws let me install these," Gripper told Xia. "When he found out I couldn't eat that protein goo. He said a sick engineer wouldn't do him any good and to set up whatever I needed."

That sounded like something Tiberius would say, Xia thought. Cranky but caring. Tiberius obviously liked the eager young alien, but it would never occur to him to say so.

A catwalk ran along the top of the cargo bay, connecting the fore and aft of the Blue Phoenix. Steel mesh stairs led down from the walkway to the floor of the bay. Xia sat at the bottom of the steps, balancing her elbows on her knees and her chin in her hands.

"Tell me about Arborus," she said.

Xia hoped that Gripper would tire himself out talking. It was already late and she was too sleepy to think of a less obvious ploy. It was the same one she had used last night – and the night before – but Gripper was always delighted to talk to anyone who would listen about his homeworld. If he knew what Xia was doing, he didn't say anything.

"I downloaded the latest planetary surveys from the Axis mainstream," Gripper said. "Before everything went crazy with Smoke and Coldhand."

"Have you been able to look them over?" Xia asked.

Gripper nodded, making his long ears bob. "Yeah, a little. No sign of Arborus yet, but all of the updates are to stellar systems in the core. Do you think the Alliance will ever send more ships out to the rim?"

"I don't know," Xia said. "It's expensive to fly out there and the Nnyth make it dangerous. Not to mention whatever wiped out the Arcadian White Kingdom."

"I suppose," Gripper agreed. "And I'm not sure Arborus is in this galaxy at all. It's the most beautiful world I've ever seen. Still, even after all the places we've gone."

Xia leaned against the railing of the stairs. Her antennae felt heavy and she fought back a yawn.

"Arborus is all forest. Huge, gorgeous green trees everywhere," Gripper said. "I never saw the edge of the forest. Maybe there wasn't one. You know the starscrapers on Axis? There are trees on Arborus just as big."

Xia knew the story of how Gripper left Arborus. Everyone on the Blue Phoenix did, but that didn't mean Gripper was tired of telling them. Xia's eyes fell shut and she smiled. She could see the whole thing as he spoke.

The world was a green one. The very air seemed alive. Leaves the size of CWAAF starcruisers overlapped and wove together to create a landscape of jade, complete with lakes and streams of clear, sweet rainwater.

Arboran villages dotted the smooth emerald hillocks. They built their homes out of deadfall and strips of leaf tied with vines. Simple but sturdy. Stone and metal were almost unknown to these tree-dwellers. The dangerous places where they could be found were far below the canopy where the Arborans made their homes. Here amongst the treetops, the threats of the world on the ground seemed so very distant.

"There aren't any computers or ships on Arborus," Gripper said. "Not that I ever saw, and I visited four different villages. There's just the trees and the sky. We all stay up in the leaves with the rain and sun. Unless one of the trees falls."

Xia cracked an eye open as Gripper climbed down from his suspended planter garden and wove his way carefully around the slender illonium cables that attached it to the ceiling struts. He grabbed onto a support, sinking his clawed fingers easily into the tempered fibersteel. Arborans often slept hanging from the limbs of their trees with no fear of falling, he had told Xia. Gripper dangled above her.

"My mother warned me not to climb the old sycona tree, but I didn't listen. I liked the big purple flowers. They were sweet and a little crunchy. I was hungry, so I climbed out there. But the tree was sick and it fell."

The air was filled with a terrible tearing, wailing sound as the sycona fell. Huge branches, grown entangled with its neighbors for hundreds – perhaps thousands – of years finally ripped free. Young Anandrou must have screamed as he fell with the old tree, but his voice was lost in the thunder. He leapt, scrambling to find a hold, searching for anything that wasn't plunging toward the ground. But the tree was dying. Leaves weakened by sickness wouldn't support his weight and Anandrou couldn't climb fast enough to get away. The ancient sycona pulled him down to the forest floor far below.

"I was holding onto the tree and the fall was pretty slow – compared to a ship crashing, I mean – but I think the sudden change in altitude knocked me out. When I woke up, I was down below the canopy. It was so dark and I was so scared."

Gripper swung slowly back and forth on the cargo bay support. Xia leaned against the stairs to look up at him. The young alien was massive, his huge hand strong enough to crush metal... but there was true terror in his eyes just at the memory of his fall into what must have amounted to the Arboran underworld.

"I was on the ground," Gripper said. "Not the real ground, you know, but the dirt one all the way down in the roots. I could barely see anything – all of the leaves on the trees are up high, near the sunlight, and they grow really thick. So I ran for the nearest tree and started climbing.

"But then I saw something, some kind of light. Not sunlight, even the weak stuff that comes through the canopy. This was bright blue, like phenno when it burns. There wasn't supposed to be anyone down there. I had to find out where it was coming from."

Anandrou moved carefully on bruised knuckles, picking his way between the vast tree trunks, each one tower-wide and gnarled with age.

The ground was a tangle of thick roots and slimy soil. He squinted after the blue glow when it vanished behind the trees as he wound through them. Mud squished between Anandrou's fingers. The Arboran boy fought down a sharp surge of panic each time he lost sight of the azure light, the only beacon he had here in the darkness.

But his curiosity was stronger than his fear. What could be down here, in the forbidden, dangerous depths of his world?

"I didn't really think there was anything in the dark except that blue glow... until everything started changing. I didn't realize that I could see the trees, but I knew when they were gone.

"I was in a city. I think... I couldn't see much, but there were definitely buildings. They kind of reminded me of Axis, down on the lower levels. There were these huge towers, but it was all falling apart. I wanted to look inside them, but I was still trying to find the blue light."

"And you did," said Xia.

"Yeah. It was in the middle of all the buildings, and there was a sort of clearing with a smooth white floor. All around were these... rings. They were different sizes and made of different stuff. Some of them were just barely big enough for me to squeeze into, but there were rings that the Blue Phoenix could fly right through. But one of the little ones was glowing bright blue."

Anandrou's pain and fear were forgotten in a second. What was that glowing ring? The surface was segmented and densely packed with writing that he couldn't read. And inside the ring, through the sapphire light, was... something. Another place that wasn't Arborus.

"It was a gateway of some kind, but there was someone inside it. They were a lot smaller than me and wearing a cape or something, I think. It was hard to tell – they were already stepping through the blue light and it was all blurry. I shouted, but whoever it was didn't seem to hear me. So I tried to grab them."

Hanging overhead by one hand, Gripper mimicked reaching into the light to seize the stranger. Almost anyone else would have run away from the strange, rotting city and certainly wouldn't have stuck their hand through an unknown portal trying to save a mysterious shadow inside.

Xia shook her head and then looked up at Gripper as he told his story. She could at least stay awake for it.

"As soon as I touched the light, there was... blue," Gripper said. "I couldn't see the city or the ring or anything else. Just blinding light. When it finally faded, everything was different, even the sun. I was in the middle of a big grassy field."

The blue glow was gone and a pair of small, bright suns lit the sky. Whoever he had been reaching for was gone, too, and Anandrou was alone in the field. He whirled, searching, but there was no blue light, no caped shadow, no glowing ring. And no way to get home. Anandrou was stranded.

"I found some humans and Lyrans, eventually," Gripper said. "Once I learned a little Aver, they told me the planet was named Kahl and it was part of the Central World Alliance. No one seemed to know what to do with me, but some of the Lyrans taught me about engines and computers. I guess that's not telling you about my home, though."

"No," Xia agreed. "But I'm still listening."

"Smoke says the thing I went through sounds like a Waygate."

Xia blinked and looked up. "Those only exist on the rimworlds, as far as we know. That's why you think Arborus might be out there, isn't it?"

"Yeah. But Smoke also said the Waygates just go one way. They can send you almost anywhere, but there doesn't have to be a Waygate on the other end. Kind of like a slingshot, I guess. You can shoot a rock off in any direction and be pretty accurate, but unless whoever finds that rock has a slingshot, too, they can't send it back."

"Did Maeve say anything else about the Waygates?" Xia asked.

"Not much. Just that the thing I went through doesn't look quite like the Waygates in Arcadia," Gripper answered. "But they're all unique and no two are exactly alike. Apparently. Smoke wouldn't say a whole lot, you know?"

Xia nodded. "Yes, I do. Arcadians don't often discuss the Waygates. But I've been told that it's not because they're trying to keep secrets. A gate was involved in the fall of the White Kingdom, somehow, and most of their Waygate specialists died during the resulting violence."

"Do you know what happened?" Gripper asked.

"No," Xia said. "There are a few accounts from the survivors, but they are... unreliable. I have a friend who specializes in archaeogenetics that might have access to those records, but I'm a doctor. I've never read them."

"We could ask Smoke about it," Gripper suggested.

"I don't think that's a good idea." Xia stood and stretched, her multitude of knuckles cracking as she flexed her long fingers. "Can you sleep yet?"

"Nah. I'll go check on the engines and make sure they haven't thrown a rod," Gripper said, shaking his head. "Thanks for staying up with me again, Silver. It was really nice."

Xia waved and retreated up the stairs. Gripper would just have to get himself to sleep tonight. The Arboran dropped with a loud thump to the floor of the cargo bay and headed into the aft of the Blue Phoenix.

When she reached her quarters, Xia quickly stripped and slid into bed. She told the lights to turn off and pulled the sheets up around her shoulders. But she didn't fall asleep.

Gripper had joined the Blue Phoenix crew a year ago, hoping that Tiberius' travels might lead him back to Arborus. But as far as Xia knew, Gripper was no closer to home now than he was the day he appeared on Kahl.

What if Gripper's homeworld *wasn't* in this galaxy? There was no way to cross the great black emptiness that separated galaxies. No one in the Alliance built a ship self-sufficient enough to make such a long journey. Even the three-month flight out to the rim was so taxing that the CWA had given up on exploring it. In the century since the Arcadians had appeared in the core, they hadn't returned to the White Kingdom. If an entire species couldn't make the trip home, how could one lonely Arboran?

Under Gripper's watchful eye, the Blue Phoenix limped to Stray. On the eighth afternoon, the ship dropped out of superluminal flight and the sandy beige planet leapt into focus outside. A computer-generated signal gave Tiberius clearance to land in Gharib, one of only four large cities on Stray.

Duaal watched Tiberius take the Blue Phoenix down through Stray's thin, dusty atmosphere. A few shiny blue flecks of phenno flaked away in the heated air. Duaal leaned forward, scowling at the controls. They just seemed to operate more smoothly for Tiberius...

Orphia gave a warning sound somewhere between a hiss and a screech. Duaal glared at the hawk.

"Hey, watch it," he said. "I can light your tail on fire with a word, remember? Well, a couple of words..."

The Blue Phoenix bumped lightly down onto Stray's surface and Duaal turned his glare back to the controls.

"I swear I did it just like that on Axis," he protested.

"You need more practice," Tiberius said. "A lot more practice."

Duaal sagged back into his seat and sighed, rolling his eyes. The old Prian captain shrugged and switched on the intercom.

"I want to see everyone in the cargo bay before we all fly off into the city. We're here to do a job," Tiberius said. As an afterthought, he added: "Coldhand, this doesn't apply to you."

Duaal stopped frowning and laughed. "You really like to rub it in, don't you?"

"What?"

"Never mind."

Duaal glanced up through the cockpit's solar shield at the fat, swollen red sun hanging low in Stray's sky. Another hot day on another hot planet. His outfit was going to be a sauna out there. But Duaal pulled on his gloves and stood. Tiberius coaxed Orphia up onto a leather sleeve and they headed out of the cockpit, down to the cargo bay.

Kessa waited with the others assembled in the hold, standing behind Xia and eying Maeve warily. The Arcadian princess was about as welcoming as a block of ice. No, not a block of ice – the cold sounded damned welcome right now, Duaal thought. Maeve looked as friendly as a drawn gun, then.

Despite the fairy's prominent role in saving Kessa from the Sisterhood, the Dailon still treated Maeve cautiously, spending her time instead with Xia or Gripper. Tiberius shook his head at the pregnant woman and jerked his thumb over his shoulder.

"No, you stay on the ship," he said. "We don't know if this place is safe for you yet."

Kessa looked disappointed, but nodded and rubbed her hands over her round belly. A week confined on the Blue Phoenix must have had her itching to go outside and stretch her legs, but not enough to risk the life of her baby.

Tiberius gestured to Maeve. "Take Xia and go find out if the Sisterhood is around. Gripper, get working on those repairs. If we're wrong and this place is trouble, I want to be ready to fly."

"Will do, Claws," Gripper said. "I bought most of the parts back on Axis. All I need is enough ground time to install them."

"Get on it," Tiberius told him. "I'll go talk to Xyn about getting some more phenno. Duaal, we've had an extra mouth for the last week. We need food."

The captain pulled a red cenmark chip from a pocket of his black vest and tossed it across the cargo bay. Duaal caught Kessa's eye and winked. If she couldn't leave the ship, he would at least give her something to watch... But by the time he managed to murmur the levitation spell, the scarlet chip had fallen onto the floor and Duaal hastily scooped it up.

"What's he doing?" Kessa whispered.

"Magic, I think," Xia answered.

"Is that how it's supposed to work?"

"No," Maeve said.

Flushing, Duaal shoved the money into his pocket. Tiberius grunted and stroked one of Orphia's faded wings. The old hawk didn't hiss at *him*, Duaal noticed.

"Stray gets shipments from all over the galaxy," Tiberius said. "Take your time and look around. You can use whatever's left on that chip to get something for yourself."

Duaal perked up a little and shot a sidelong glance at Maeve. *She* didn't get extra spending money.

"But stay sharp," Tiberius warned. "Stray can be dangerous."

"Hey, can I go shopping, too?" Gripper asked, raising his hand. "Stray is one of the best places in the Alliance to buy used parts."

"No," Tiberius answered. "Repairs. Xyn's shop isn't far from the landing crescent and I'll be back with the phenno in less than an hour. I expect you to have some progress to report, Gripper."

"Aw," the Arboran grumbled. "Alright, Claws."

Kessa waved farewell to everyone and wandered back toward the stairs and her quarters, humming tunelessly to herself. Gripper turned on his knuckles in the direction of the engine room to begin his work. Tiberius opened the airlock and Duaal followed him out onto Stray's dusty surface.

[8]

WAYWARD WINDS

"Proximity denotes association. Why else would the mouth be located so close to the brain, if not designed to speak one's mind?"

Bannon 3 was an arid planet, only barely habitable and far from welcoming. A weary, ancient red star served as its sun and cast just enough visible light on the sandy little planet to illuminate it, but enough infrared to turn Bannon 3 into a furnace. Located inconveniently on an otherwise uninhabited edge of Alliance space and a source of almost no valuable natural resources, the Bannon system was ignored for decades.

In 132 MA, an ambitious young Lyran by the name of Channik Grale purchased all land, mineral and mining rights to the entire planet for only four and a half million cenmarks. Channik was mocked all across the galaxy for spending his inheritance on Bannon 3. The only thing worth mining on the remote dust ball seemed to be hafnium, but all substantial deposits were located deep underground. Hafnium wasn't particularly precious or rare, found on thousands of other planets, several of which had been successfully colonized years before. It certainly didn't seem worth the effort to mine Bannon 3 for such an inexpensive and relatively common element.

The mockery continued for the next seven years as Channik purchased cheap equipment and set up a mining camp in Bannon 3's northern hemisphere. As expected, the machinery broke down so frequently in the dusty, sandy climate that Channik had to fly a non-stop supply of parts and engineers out to his planet.

But the jokes turned into curious whispers as miners and engineers flocked to Bannon 3 by the thousands. There were plenty of jobs and Channik paid. He didn't pay well, but it was work for those who couldn't find it elsewhere in Alliance space. Instead of waiting for the frequent replacement part orders, Starwind Fabrications set up a small factory on Channik's planet to cut down their shipping costs. The new factory brought in more jobs and all manner of beings that needed work. Workers brought families that required food and clothes.

More jobs, more money.

Before two decades had passed, the single mining camp on Bannon 3 had grown into a full-fledged city. Satellite towns grew up almost overnight as the city expanded. By the time Channik's fur was turning gray, the entire northern hemisphere of his planet was settled and thriving. His people were poor and often desperate, but the same could be said of Prianus and the lower levels of Axis, both founding worlds of the CWA.

Opponents of Channik's success nicknamed his planet *Stray* – taunting that it attracted every stray dog of the galaxy – and the name stuck. Channik Grale died a rich man at a venerable Lyran age of eighty-two, never having successfully mined a single ounce of hafnium.

Everything was covered in dust. The people, the streets... Even the buildings seemed shrouded in dirty veils. They were all constructed of simple, unadorned siltstone blocks laid with little attention. Joints were rough and crooked, as though the builders were in too much of a hurry to spend more time on their work than they absolutely had to. The cities of Stray were quickly and hastily built with minimal investment. Gharib was no exception.

Xia sneezed and rubbed at her eyes. The static charge on the window coatings wasn't strong enough to repel the dust. It lay thick and yellow over everything, making the entire city look as though it were built of sand. Xia sneezed again.

By necessity as much as any desire to blend in, she and Maeve had adopted the local dress. Both women had donned scarves and veils covering their hair and faces, long sleeves and pants to keep out the dust. The scarf that Xia wore tied across her mouth was borrowed from Maeve's wardrobe and smelled sharply of spilled narcohol.

Xia cast a sidelong look at Maeve. The fairy hadn't covered her wings. There wasn't a scarf or cape or coat large enough to conceal them and her feathers were soon yellow with dust. Maeve shook them out a few times, but swiftly gave up as the grit just settled right back into place.

But the Arcadian wasn't attracting the stares that Xia expected. No one in the core liked the fairy interlopers. Wherever they went, Arcadians tended to be sneered and spat at. Here in Gharib, though, few seemed to take much notice of Maeve at all. There were a handful of distasteful looks – at least, as best Xia could judge them through protective scarves and veils – but nothing compared to the sort of anger she had come to expect from traveling with a fairy.

Maybe Maeve was prepared for more trouble, too. She walked with her glass-bladed spear tapping on the sidewalk at her side. The multicolored ribbons tied along the haft rippled and snapped in the hot breeze like tattered pennons. Xia didn't see Maeve carry her weapon often. But not even the spear attracted much notice on Stray. Xia guessed that no one cared. Probably because the robes and scarves all around them concealed weapons of their own. Xia could see the weight and outlines of knives and guns through cloth all along the street.

Perhaps no one else cared about Maeve's spear, but Xia found herself drumming her fingers against the chromite grip of her own laser. The Arcadian princess usually carried her weapon when she was expecting an encounter with Logan Coldhand. Xia knew how deadly that archaic weapon could be in Maeve's hands. The glass blade wasn't nearly as fragile as it appeared – and neither was the woman who wielded it.

Xia averted her eyes to stare out through Gharib's dusty street, then grabbed Maeve's arm. She pointed across the road.

"Look," Xia said.

There was a barren dirt lot on the other side of the busy street – recently emptied to judge by the sancrete and rebar jutting up through the dust like skeletal remains. Three Arcadian men sat perched on the remaining half-height wall. Each of the fairy men was short and slender, with long golden hair and fine, delicate features. Maeve glared across the road at the other Arcadians, but her gray eyes didn't change color, so Xia had no idea how to read the look there.

"Let's go talk to them," Xia suggested. "Maybe they know something about the Sisterhood."

Maeve pulled her arm out of the Ixthian's long-fingered grasp. Her lips pressed into a thin line.

"There are many Arcadians here on Stray," Maeve said. "The Alliance would not help my people when our kingdom fell and

Stray was one of few places that would take us... or at least did not turn us away."

"Aren't you excited to see some of your own species?" Xia asked.

"No. I have been on Stray before and this is a world of outcasts and criminals. My people deserved better."

Xia glanced out at the trio of Arcadian men again. They were watching the street and one of them arched his back, stretching his long wings out behind him. Maeve began walking briskly away. Like she didn't want the fairies to see her. Xia grabbed Maeve's arm again and pulled her to a stop. Other pedestrians pushed past them with low grumbles.

"Wait, we still need to learn about the Sisterhood," Xia said.

"And you think those men might have that information?" Maeve asked.

"Yes. Look, I know how other species tend to treat Arcadians," Xia explained quickly. "So you have to stick together and help each other out."

"Do we?" Maeve asked, arching one black eyebrow.

"*Other* Arcadians, then," Xia said with a sigh. "Look, Kessa says the Sisterhood likes to hunt and capture men for sport."

Maeve nodded. Xia rushed on with her theory.

"If they are here on Stray, they've surely preyed on some of the Arcadian men. They're sick and weak and no one would pay much attention if a few of them went missing. Except other Arcadians. They would know, right?"

"They... may," Maeve admitted reluctantly.

Xia tried to guide her toward the road, to cross and question the men, but Maeve pulled back with shocking strength. Xia jerked to a stop and released the smaller woman.

"You don't think it's a good idea?" Xia asked. "Do you?"

"No," Maeve answered in an even icier tone than usual. "Mine are a desperate and unhappy people."

Xia blinked at the other woman.

"You mean they might try to pick a fight?" she asked. "Maeve, I know what kind of people you deal with to get your chems! And Coldhand... I can't believe you're worried about some fairies. And you have that spear! You brought it along to keep us safe, right?"

Maeve stepped back, out of the crowd of people. She folded her wings and leaned against a wall, the name and window display obscured by dust. Maeve crossed her arms over her chest.

"That is not what I meant," she said.

"What *did* you mean, then?"

But Maeve only shook her head and would not answer. Xia remained on the sidewalk and stared at the tiny fairy woman.

"I know you're not afraid of a fight," Xia said. "I've never seen you back down from one. So come with me? Please?"

Maeve shook her head again. "Go. I will be nearby."

"What if they don't speak Aver?"

"You will manage," Maeve said shortly.

Xia couldn't think of any more arguments, so she turned on her heels and squinted through the dust. The Arcadian men hadn't moved, so Xia adjusted the scarf across her mouth and waited for a break in traffic. Maeve watched without comment.

Maeve Cavainna was... difficult to understand. Maybe impossible. One moment, the fairy seemed utterly cold, composed and uncaring. The next, she flew into uncontrollable rages or long, sullen silences. Tiberius said that she used to be a knight back on her homeworld, before the fall. It was difficult to see anything like that in the temperamental, narcoholic wreck of a woman. There was nothing knightly or honorable about Maeve anymore. The princess was unpredictable, wild and very dangerous.

Xia paced with her medical bag clutched in shaking silver hands. She didn't want to be there, but the pirates had hijacked her ship weeks ago and left her no choice but to become their medic. The captain of the Caitiff was a vile little rat of a man with a long nose and even longer ambitions.

His dreams of easy wealth and total lack of ethics or sense drove his crew into one hopeless fight after another, each with promises of greater riches than the last. The latest target was a small freighter carrying a hold full of expensive gallium-errol transistors.

There was a heavy thump from the airlock. Xia whirled, ready to treat whatever injured pirate stumbled through. The men of the Caitiff lacked nothing in brutality, but their skill never managed to match their bloodlust. Xia froze, her heart pounding loud in her ears. It wasn't one of the pirates at the airlock.

A winged woman stood in the door, with black hair and a bloody glass-bladed spear in her fists. For all her tiny size, she looked like some kind of pagan war goddess. She wore no clothes, but her white skin and wings were spattered with blood. The Arcadian's bare feet were red, as though she walked through wet paint. And her eyes were bloodshot and deeply shadowed, like she had just been woken from an unsettled sleep.

She leveled her spear at Xia, who dropped her supplies and reached for the gun she carried in case of situations like this. The fairy spun her spear in an arc, cracking the haft against Xia's knuckles and her laser spun away across the dented airlock. The doctor cried out in pain and fell to her knees before Maeve, waiting for the killing blow that never came.

A truck rumbled past Xia on an orange-tinged null-field. The blue and white Starwind logo was only half visible through sand and graffiti. Xia didn't see any sign of the triangle that Maeve had described as the Sisterhood's mark, so she stepped out into the road. A Lyran on a streetcycle swerve and snarled something Xia couldn't quite hear as she jogged across the street.

Duaal wandered aimlessly through the huge bazaar that squatted in the center of Gharib. There were hundreds of counters and tent-stalls set up in concentric rings, though dust and sun had bleached all color from the vast display of wares. Walkways carved through the circled stalls like the spokes of a wheel and converged on a towering siltstone statue of Channik Grale. The larger-than-life monument to Stray's lupine founder had an expression of nobility and visionary magnificence on his face that Duaal doubted the real Channik had ever worn.

The mage shoved his sweaty way through the market crowd. He had made none of the concessions to local dress that Maeve and Xia had. Shoppers whispered and stared curiously at his strange, ornate costume and Duaal grinned to himself. The thick dust and heat were oppressive, but the attention felt almost good enough to make up for it.

He passed a young Lyran pup with braided fur, who pointed a clawed finger at the intricate interlocking star across Duaal's back. The little girl was fascinated by the pretty design, embroidered in shiny golden thread that flashed even in the dim light of Stray's red sun. But her mother grabbed the puppy by the scruff of the neck and hauled her away, growling a low warning. Duaal waved and winked.

His work was done and there were crates of dehydrated protein and drums of water already on their way to the Blue Phoenix, along with the other necessities Tiberius had asked for. But nothing else in Gharib's dusty market caught Duaal's attention. Most of it was basic and functional, ship parts or mining supplies or boring clothes in the same colors as the sandy city.

Duaal rolled a plastic chip between his fingers – change from the color Tiberius had given him – and began making his way toward the edge of the market. The sunlight was faint and hazy. It cast thin, indistinct brown shadows, but the heat cut as sharp as a nano-blade.

In the outer ring of the bazaar, Duaal bought a tube of sweet ice for the long walk out to the landing crescent. It was flavored with some kind of Hadrian fruit juice and Duaal sucked gratefully on the coldness, but it vanished swiftly in the midday heat and left him with an empty plastic wrapper. The mage was considering going back to buy a couple more when he heard a soft, hissing voice.

"*Ksst!* Over here, boy."

Boy? Duaal bristled and whirled to find the speaker, but saw only a black-eyed Dailon who walked quickly away, casting worried glances back between steps. There were too many desperate souls and fugitives on Stray to risk making even casual enemies.

"Boy!" came the voice again. It had a strange, crackling intonation. Whoever it was, they had an awkward handle of Aver.

"Stop that," Duaal said sharply. "I'm not a child!"

Why did everyone fixate on his age? Duaal wasn't *that* young and he knew things that no one else in the core did.

Well, *almost* no one else...

But that was the point. Duaal was a mage! He knew *magic*. Some Alliance citizens didn't even believe in it and who could blame them? Other than Duaal, practitioners of magic were found exclusively on the outer worlds of the galaxy. The Jinn and the Arcadians studied magic, and so did the fearsome soldier-drones of the Nnyth Tower. But not humans.

Duaal was tempted to cast some kind of spell just to make his point, but who was talking to him? He narrowed his eyes and stared about for the speaker, but all Duaal saw was a withered tree hunkered between a pair of closed stalls wrapped in static sheets.

"Ah, my apologies, young man," whispered the tree. "But come closer. I have things to show you."

"A Jinn!" Duaal said.

A very old one, he noticed. Its branches were twisted with age and covered in dry, papery brown leaves. What looked like shiny blue-black berries peeked out from under the leaves, but Duaal knew those were the alien's many eyes. The fronds around the Jinn's eyes lifted out of the way so it could see properly, appearing for all the worlds like an old man raising his bushy eyebrows in surprise.

"Ah, an *educated* young man," rasped the Jinn. It rubbed and rustled its leaves together to produce the odd, windy speech. "I thought that I recognized some of the symbols you wear, though I haven't seen them since the last time I gated to lost Arcadia..."

"What do you want?" Duaal asked. Despite the thick heat of the Gharib day, he shivered.

"Be cautious when dealing with the Jinn," his master read out from a folded sheet of paper. There was a broken seal of red wax on the front. "Though you may have to before this is done."

Duaal cringed in the corner of the room, fearful but attentive. The old man wasn't speaking to him, but that wouldn't stop him from kicking or cuffing the boy if he got in the way.

"They are slow to anger and as patient as trees. The Jinn value wit and wisdom over wealth or beauty. If you cannot hold your own in debate against the Jinn, they will think nothing of abusing your hospitality. Learn what you can from the Jinn, should you meet one, but move on quickly before a dull moment turns them against you."

Duaal's master swept past the boy. His black robes – like something from a show, or that a college professor would wear – whispered over the floor. The old man sat down at his dusty computer to type out a letter of his own.

"I want only what any merchant in Gharib does," rustled the Jinn. "To do business."

"What?" Duaal asked. "Jinn never want to trade with the core."

"With the fall of the Arcadian kingdom, many of us must look somewhat further afield to make a living."

"That was a hundred years ago," Duaal said.

The Jinn swayed in what seemed to be a shrug.

"There are plenty of other vendors all over the market that don't have to hide or beg," Duaal pointed out. "So what do you have that they don't?"

"A very good question," the Jinn said, rubbing its leafy branches together. "Which I will answer shortly. My name is Ssassi. And who is the strangely dressed young human before me?"

"You don't need my name to sell me something."

"Ah, quite true," Ssassi hissed with a laugh. "And to answer your question, my nameless new young friend, you are correct. There are many other vendors here, all selling the same things: coreworld goods available all across the Alliance. But what *I* carry comes from the edge of the galaxy, worlds that – as you say – do not often trade with yours."

Duaal was still nervous, but now he was curious, too. Ssassi was right: the CWA and the rimworlds had no trade agreements and Duaal couldn't bring himself to walk away from such a rare and exotic opportunity.

"Alright, what have you got?" he asked.

Ssassi's wrinkled gray bark folded into something like a smile. The effect was disarming, but Duaal reminded himself that the Jinn wasn't a kindly old grandmother. He was a trader trying to get a good price.

"Now, where did I put them?" the Jinn asked himself.

Punctuated by sharp creaks and groans like the settling of an ancient house, the alien reached with branches into his browned upper foliage. From his leaves, Ssassi began producing small items, laying them out in a neat row on the dusty ground for Duaal's inspection.

"A runic from the Tower itself," said the Jinn, holding up a geometric piece of glistening stone.

It was marked with a crossed spiral a lot like those on the back of Duaal's gloves. Ssassi withdrew a few midnight black fragments that looked almost as much like stone as the runic.

"Also taken at great personal risk from the Tower, shards from a Nnyth egg."

A stout ceramic jug joined the pile.

"Delberry wine from Usarral, my world. A hundred fifty-seven years old and quite delicious. It has potent properties, of course. One drink will keep you awake and alert for a month."

Duaal weighed the bottle in his hand. About half full. He was familiar with delberry wine – they made him drink it many times when he was a boy – and knew Ssassi had neglected to mention the weeks-long coma that came after that drink. Duaal picked up a slender shape wrapped in layers of silky cloth. He squeezed it gently, trying to feel out the shape of whatever was inside.

"What's this?" Duaal asked.

"Assssh ks ree!" Ssassi shrilled, lapsing momentarily back into his own native tongue, the sound of the wind in leaves and creaking branches. "Put that down!"

Startled, Duaal dropped the bundle, then inspected his gloves. There was a neat slice across the leather of one finger and into the skin beneath. Duaal pulled off his glove and sucked at the wound. The cut wasn't deep, but he hadn't even felt it happen. Carefully, Ssassi retrieved the fallen item and unwrapped it.

"A dagger of Arcadian glass," said the Jinn. "Brought from the fairy kingdom before its fall."

The weapon the Jinn held out was shorter than a nanoknife, with a blade only about the length of Duaal's finger and a hilt not much bigger. Maeve was a tiny woman and her entire species was considerably smaller than humans. She would have no difficulty wielding such a small weapon to great effect. The dagger was made entirely of glass and the blade glistened like ice melted impossibly thin. Only the hilt had any color, wrapped in alternating blue and silver cord. Duaal took the dagger and held it up to catch the dim sunlight. The glass threw back rainbows that filled the shadowed alcove with multicolored light.

"Not as good as a *k'saar* staff, I say," Ssassi told Duaal. "But we Jinn have never cared for blades. Still, this Arcadian stuff is stronger than heartwood and sharper than jealousy."

"Do you have a sword?" Duaal asked.

Ssassi shook his withered branches. "No. I'm afraid Arcadians never made such long blades. Spears, certainly, but no swords. It has to do with their anatomy, I'm told. Most of the muscles in their backs are bound up in operating those lovely wings. Their shoulders aren't terribly strong and without the power for a mighty swing, the fairies prefer short blades and stabbing weapons."

"How much do you want for the knife?" Duaal asked. It was small, but beautiful and obviously still sharp.

"One hundred cenmarks," Ssassi told him. "Arcadian glass is no longer made anywhere in the galaxy, after all. And you see those ribbons on the hilt? Those are the colors of the royal family."

"You're lying," Duaal said. He didn't know who the glass dagger had belonged to, but it wasn't a Cavainna. "Their colors were red and gold, you old cheat."

The Jinn made a sound that might have been a laugh or a sigh, but he spread his branches.

"Ah, a fine catch," Ssassi said. "Seventy-five cenmarks and it can be yours."

After nearly an hour of haggling, they agreed on fifty cen for the dagger and another twenty for the half-full jug of delberry wine. Duaal handed over what remained of Tiberius' redchip and Ssassi produced some even smaller silver cenmarks from somewhere in his folded bark. Duaal took the change, carefully rewrapped the dagger and picked up the jug of wine. Feeling pleased with himself, Duaal made his way out of the market and back toward the Blue Phoenix.

Xia smiled as she approached the fairies, holding out her open hands. The Ixthian wasn't unarmed, exactly – she had carried her inexpensive but useful laser pistol since her unwilling days as a pirate – but it couldn't hurt to look harmless. The trio of Arcadian men watched her cautiously, but their fear was dull, weary from years of abuse.

One of them stood and bowed as Xia neared. He wasn't wearing much beside a skirt of thin, silvery fabric. It was nearly sheer and hid very little. Xia flushed and kept her eyes firmly on the fairy's face. His hair was long and pale gold in the ruddy sunlight, fanning over his shoulders in unwashed curls.

"Good day, my beauty," he said in a tired voice. "One so lovely should not have to wander this ugly city alone. Ten cenmarks and I will gladly show you my skills with a lance."

Xia was sure the wink he gave her was intended to be suggestive, but she only stared at the bloodshot red of his eyes. Up close, Xia could see just how slender all three of the Arcadians were, and the scars across their skin. Some of those were from knives, others from needles and many were still healing. But even battered and starvation-thin, all of the males were quite handsome... Which, Xia supposed, was precisely why they were out here.

"I don't want to hire you," she said quickly.

The fairy in the silver kilt frowned up at her. "I cannot work for nothing, even for a lady of such beauty."

With his scars and heavily accented, formal Aver, this Arcadian reminded Xia at once of Maeve. She raised her hands again and shook her head.

"No, that's not what I meant," Xia said. "I only want to ask you a few questions."

The prostitute backed away from her, feathered wings half-spread as though ready to take flight. He was broader in the shoulders and more muscular than the other two, but still considerably smaller than Xia. She supposed the Arcadians had to be built light for flying. The other fairies shifted nervously and whispered to one another in their own liquid, lyric language. What were they saying? Xia wished Maeve had come with her.

"Are you... police?" asked the Arcadian. His voice fell to a low hiss. "You have never helped us when we needed it, no matter how we begged. But now that *you* need–"

"I'm not a cop," Xia interrupted. "I'm doing research, that's all."

"Research?" the fairy repeated slowly. He drew back another step. "What manner of research?"

"I just need to know if you've seen some people around Gharib," Xia said. She tried a friendly smile and gestured as casually as she could to the other two Arcadians. "If you can't talk to me, that's alright. Maybe one of them can spare a minute?"

The man shook his head. "Not unless you know our language. Caiwynn and Rillath do not speak Aver. They do not wish to understand the things your people say to us. I have told them that it is safer to learn, to know if their customers mean them harm. But they refuse."

The half-dressed Arcadian closed his wings around his body as though cold, but then seemed to remember his job and spread them again – putting the wares back on display. He looked down at the ground and didn't meet Xia's eye.

"I need to ask you, then," she said. "What's your name?"

"Anthem," the fairy answered. "Anthem Calloren, once favored by the Night... before the fall. Please, ask your questions quickly. Money is scarce and we must return to our work."

Xia wasn't sure what to say to that. When was the last time these three had seen a doctor? God only knew how many diseases they carried and spread to their customers. But maybe they could help her keep Kessa safe.

"Are there any other Arcadians on Stray?" Xia asked.

Anthem nodded.

"Do you know them?" she asked.

Another nod. "Many of them, yes. Those who can speak Aver well are few and I am often called upon to deal with the others of this world."

"Has anyone... preyed on the Arcadians?"

Anthem cocked his head, his bloodshot eyes blank. "Of course."

Xia would have to be far more specific. *Everyone* preyed on the bird-back aliens. She rubbed at her compound eyes. The dust was making them itch. She sighed.

"Has anyone abducted or killed your males?" Xia asked. "I'm looking for a gang that calls themselves the Sisterhood. They target men especially."

Anthem considered that for a moment before answering, but a pained expression flitted across his face and he nodded again.

"I know the women you are talking about," the fairy said. "Some time ago, they took many of our men. We thought them customers at first, but those who went with the Sisters were killed or returned unmanned."

Anthem made a short slicing gesture below the waist of his skirt and Xia clenched her silver hands into fists.

"Damn it," she said. "The Sisterhood is on Stray. We can't leave Kessa here."

Caiwynn and Rillath jumped back from Xia's exclamation, but Anthem shook his head.

"This happened some time ago," he said again. "The loss of our men went on and we mourned for them, but we do not fight the Nameless when she comes for us. Then the black cathedral was built, though, and the Sisterhood stopped."

Anthem shielded his eyes from the bloated red sun and turned, orienting himself. He pointed east across Gharib and Xia squinted. She could just make out a tall building silhouetted starkly against the scarlet glow.

"That... doesn't look like a Union of Light church," Xia said.

"It is not," Anthem agreed. "That cathedral belongs to someone else. But when they came, the Sisterhood's attacks stopped. There has been violence since then, but I have not seen the Sisters' mark in over a year."

"There are a few other large cities on Stray," Xia said. "Do you know if the Sisterhood is hiding out in any of them?"

Anthem spread his white wings. They were impressive, Xia had to admit... Though there were several feathers missing and the fairy could use an hour or so in a shower.

"We sometimes visit the other cities of Stray to do our work," Anthem said, gesturing with his wings. "Much the same happened in them all."

"But what about these other ones?" Xia asked. "You said that church doesn't belong to the Union of Light. Who is it?"

Anthem hesitated. "They call themselves the Church of Nihil. I do not understand the name."

"The church of nothing," Xia told him. "More or less. But that... doesn't make any sense. And what happened to the Sisterhood? Did this Church of Nihil chase them off? Why? Competition? A rival gang, maybe?"

"I have never visited the cathedral," Anthem answered. "But many other Arcadians have. There are speeches... sermons there on most nights."

"Do you know what they talk about?"

Anthem shook his head. "No. I can give you nothing else. Unless you have reconsidered hiring me for the evening...?"

There was a fragile note of hope in the fairy's voice. Xia wasn't sure if he was that desperate for money or just a few hours' work with a client who might not abuse him.

Both ideas made Xia's stomach clench up and she dug a white cenmark chip from one of her pockets. It was worth twice what Anthem charged for his services, and the Arcadian's brow furrowed. He turned the square of plastic over in dirty, scarred hands.

"Ah... thank you for the help," Xia told him. "And you might want to get a medical screening..."

Anthem didn't seem to know what to say, so Xia hurried away to save them both from further awkwardness.

Maeve wasn't in the doorway where Xia had left her. Now the fairy crouched like a gargoyle on the low roof, spear held loosely in her right hand. In the other, Maeve clutched a narcohol bottle. That hadn't taken long... And the bottle was already nearly empty, Xia noted with a sigh.

She waved, but Maeve wasn't even looking at Xia. She stared across the road at Anthem. A tall Mirran woman had approached and was haggling with him. Anthem finally nodded and accepted a few small silver cenmarks from the Mirran. Five cen, only half his asking price.

Anthem turned to say something to the other two – perhaps a farewell or asking them to wait for his return – but the woman grabbed his arm and hauled the fairy prostitute away. The Sisterhood might have been gone, but Xia didn't think the Arcadians' situation had improved much.

There was a sharp hiss of breath and the sound of shattering glass from above Xia. Maeve was on her feet, wings spread and eyes blazing. She gripped her spear in white-knuckled hands and tensed to leap out across the street. The narcohol bottle lay broken on the roof and the last of its contents dripped over the edge of the wall, evaporating quickly in the hot, dim sun.

"Maeve, stop!" Xia shouted.

The princess didn't look at Xia, but instead of launching herself into the sky after the Mirran woman, she landed on the ground next to her crewmate, her spear held once more against her side. A passing human huffed at Maeve as she folded her wings.

"Keep those wings to yourself, little bird-back," he told her.

"*Eira en varii, anai'i!*" Maeve hissed at him. "You seem to find my kind pleasant enough to hire us into your beds!"

The man glanced across the street toward where Rillath and Caiwynn still sat, both looking lost without Anthem to translate. The human's expression turned from irritation to disgust and he shook his head emphatically.

"Not me. I wouldn't hire you to scrape sand," he told Maeve in a low growl. "Not sure why the police haven't taken out that trash over there, but it'll happen eventually. So why don't you fly along, little bird?"

Maeve narrowed her gray eyes and lowered the point of her spear suggestively. "I am given to understand that your local police do not intercede often. Certainly not often or fast enough to keep me from gutting you."

"Maeve, stop!" Xia said.

She grabbed the fairy's elbow and gestured around the crowded Gharib street. At least twenty men and women had stopped to glare at Maeve and Xia would have bet a solid redchip that most of them carried weapons beneath their dusty robes and capes.

"Let's go, Maeve," Xia said. "Getting into fights out here won't help Kessa."

Maeve sighed and pulled her spear back. The human snorted and stuck one of his fingers out toward her in what seemed to be a local rude gesture. A few other humans asked if he was alright, but the man waved them off and stalked away down the sidewalk.

"Go back to your own Goddamn planet," he shouted from a safe distance.

Xia glanced at Maeve, but the furious blaze was gone from her eyes, now replaced with a familiar, sullen discontent. The fairy's shoulders slumped again and she watched the crowd impassively as they dispersed.

"What did you find out?" Maeve asked.

"The Sisterhood used to be here on Stray," Xia answered. "But they were displaced a little while back by some new church that I'd like to learn more about. There are apparently sermons there most nights."

"And you... wish to listen?"

Xia nodded. "It's about sunset, so we're not far off from the next one. Let's call the Blue Phoenix and talk to Tiberius."

Maeve shrugged and Xia pulled a com from her pocket. She selected the captain's frequency and began walking back in the direction of the landing crescent. Maeve followed Xia along the road, grumbling over the loss of her narcohol.

[9]

LOCK AND KEY

"Our lives are only the last thing we give in the line of duty."

– PRIAN POLICE MOTTO

Xyn's shop was considerably further out from the landing crescent than Tiberius remembered. Orphia clutched at his forearm with her sharp talons, watching Gharib with remote disinterest. Grumbling, the old police officer turned down another vaguely familiar side street and shouldered his way through the crowd to get a better look.

"There it is," Tiberius told Orphia, pointing to the shop. The hawk blinked her black eyes and resumed preening one wing.

The name *Unbreakers* floated over the entrance in blue holographics that contrasted jarringly with the sandy yellow-brown of Gharib. The doors hissed open at Tiberius' approach and directed a short burst of air at him, trying to blow away the dust. Inside, shelves of machinery lined the store's walls. The store was full of NI generator parts, FMS relays and more pieces of metal and flashing lights than Tiberius knew the names of, much less their purpose. Unbreakers' ceiling was hidden, utterly obscured by blocky engines and generators too large for display cases. They floated suspended overhead on cloudy orange null-fields.

A bored-looking Lyran boy sat behind the counter, inspecting a small computer in pieces across the top. He frowned at a rectangle of black ceramic no larger than a fingernail. His ears swiveled toward Tiberius and he glanced up with golden eyes.

"Oh. Afternoon, sir," said the Lyran. "Welcome to Unbreakers. What can I do for you?"

His tone suggested that despite his greeting, this intrusion on an otherwise quiet afternoon was anything but welcome.

"Is Xyn around?" Tiberius asked.

"Uh, I think so." The boy pointed a furry thumb in the direction of a closed door in the rear of the shop. "Try the back room."

Tiberius nodded and stroked Orphia's graying feathers as he squeezed between shelves toward the indicated door. She tightened her talons around Tiberius' arm and he grunted. The unfamiliar sounds and lights were agitating his bird, and an upset hawk was the first step on a short road to a lost eye or finger.

"Calm down, old girl. We won't be here long," Tiberius assured Orphia as he pushed the door open and stepped through.

The 'back room' of Unbreakers was twice the size of the shop and entirely given over to Xyn's laboratory. The walls and floor were sterile white, filled with rows of steel tables covered in glass beakers and sample tubes. A pair of huge ceramic tanks dominated one wall, each of them aglow with flickering instrument panels. Those tanks held the phennomethylln protein, Tiberius knew, worth more than its weight in bright plastic color.

An Ixthian man in a pale green lab coat leaned down to scan the tank instrumentation. Like all males of his species, he was considerably shorter than an Ixthian woman.

"Get out of here!" Xyn shouted without looking up. "Chaith can help you with whatever you need. This batch is at a very delicate stage and requires special attention. Out!"

Tiberius snorted. "Delicate? Delicate was getting you a sample to make this blue sludge in the first place."

Xyn straightened and spun to face Tiberius, grinning. The little scientist had gotten fatter, he noted. Business must have been good. Even the Ixthian's short antennae were chubby. Xyn's multifaceted eyes gleamed a pleased white that mirrored his pale hair and he reached up to clap Tiberius on the shoulder.

"Tiberius? Good God man, are you back on Stray already?" Xyn asked. "What did you do?"

"I burnt off my phenno, Xyn. I need a new batch."

"Again?" Xyn asked. "What happened? Or do I even want to know? You would get into a lot less trouble if you would just dump that damned fairy girl. Mauve, Midge... whatever her name is."

Xyn went to one of the tables and began measuring cloudy blue liquid phenno into a large pressure canister.

"Don't start," Tiberius growled. "Without Maeve, you wouldn't even have a redprint for this phenno. She's the only reason we got close enough to the Nnyth to take your sample."

Xyn didn't answer that. Instead, he poured the phenno into a metal drum and filled the rest of the container with another syrupy solution. Tiberius helped Xyn carry it over to a confounding knot of machinery, computers and tubes.

"What is this thing?" Tiberius asked.

"Perpetuating protein folder," Xyn grunted as they heaved the canister into place. "Perfolder. Who needs all those extra syllables?"

Together, the two men fitted the drum into the perfolder and Xyn turned it on, filling the lab with a loud buzz. The machine went to work propagating the phenno's protein structure through the amino acid sludge Xyn had mixed in. When they were done, the stout Ixthian gestured for Tiberius to take a seat at one of the tables.

"How's business?" Tiberius asked as he took a seat. Orphia fluttered to perch on the edge of the table, her claws screeching on the metal.

"It's been good," Xyn answered, wincing. "No one uses as much phenno as you, of course. But I don't have a whole lot of competition, so anyone who needs to carry things discreetly or who doesn't want their systems fried by an EMP pays me a visit sooner or later."

"Emphasis on *pays*," said Tiberius.

Xyn gestured at the tanks behind them. "This batch will be up in a week and should last me for about six months."

"Do you still have the sample I brought from the hive?" Tiberius asked.

"Certainly not. The original genetic strand broke down a year ago. But naturally, I had the foresight to clone a few extras. I'm using the third generation now."

They sat for a few minutes until the perfolder toned and Xyn nodded.

"There's the timer," he said. "Your phenno is up."

Tiberius helped Xyn wrestle the canister out from the mixer. The phenno was heavy and sloshed loudly when they moved it.

"That should be plenty to lacquer your ship again," the Ixthian wheezed. "Good thing for me you don't fly anything bigger than that rusty junker."

Tiberius considered arguing, but Xyn wasn't wrong about the Blue Phoenix. Still, he tipped the phenno canister up and let the short Ixthian scientist take almost half the weight. Xyn groaned and staggered. Tiberius hefted the drum again with a grin.

"What do I owe you?" he asked.

They set the canister down on a steel table and Xyn rubbed his back, compound eyes fading from a pained red to pale blue. He shook his head.

"You know better than that," Xyn said. "I wouldn't have anything if you and your Arcadian hadn't brought me that sample. I owe you my entire business. Not that I intend to give you the *whole* business, but I can part with some phenno from time to time. I really am grateful, you old bird-lover."

"Thanks, Xyn."

The Ixthian scientist pointed to his door. "Well, that's enough generosity for one day. Go on, get out of here. I've got work to do."

Tiberius hefted the canister of phenno up over one shoulder. The handle was wide, designed to accommodate an Ixthian's extra fingers and probably comfortable enough for the walk back to the Blue Phoenix. Tiberius whistled for Orphia with one of his old police commands: *come*. The hawk pushed herself into the air with a single beat of her wings and glided over to land on her master's arm. Together, they left Xyn's store.

But the trip back wasn't as easy as Tiberius had hoped. Weighed down by phenno, it took nearly an hour to return to the landing crescent. Maybe he should have hired a ride, but Tiberius had walked out to Unbreakers and he would sure as hells manage the hike back.

Sweating and cursing, Tiberius finally stumped up the Blue Phoenix's cargo ramp and into the hold. He deposited the drum next to the airlock with a clang and sucked in a few deep breaths. The cool air of the Blue Phoenix was a welcome relief from the thick heat of Stray. Cool air? Gripper must have made some progress on the atmospheric recycling system. Good.

Once he caught his breath, Tiberius would get started applying phenno to the hull. If he could just remember where he put the bedamned compressor...

Tiberius was scratching his rough cheek and pondering when he heard footsteps on the catwalk above. Prompted by instincts born of fifty years on the Prian police force, Tiberius listened before calling out. The steps were too light to be Gripper's, but too heavy and measured to belong to Kessa. No one else should have returned to the Blue Phoenix yet. Tiberius frowned. That left only one other passenger.

The footsteps were closer, ringing on the stairs. There was a soft clink of metal against metal – the sounds of illonium and steel.

Somehow, Logan Coldhand had gotten out of his prison and now he was free on the Blue Phoenix.

Orphia sensed Tiberius' unease and tensed on his arm. The old captain searched frantically around the cargo bay, but they weren't hauling anything and there was no cover down here.

"Oh shit," Tiberius breathed.

Coldhand froze, surveying the cargo bay. He caught sight of the other Prian and burst into motion again, launching himself down the stairs three at a time. The hunter's gun holster was hurriedly belted around his waist – liberated from wherever Xia had stored it – and the long-barreled Talon was already in his hand.

Common sense screamed at Tiberius to dive out of the way, that being between Coldhand and the open airlock to freedom was suicide, but he stood his ground. He swore loudly and reached under his arm for his NI gun. The Blue Phoenix was *his* ship and no filthy bounty hunter was going to cow him on his own bird.

Tiberius raised his hand and whistled to Orphia. *Attack!*

The hawk hurled herself into the air with a screech as Tiberius yanked his weapon free and fired a warning shot past Coldhand's shoulder. The bounty hunter flung himself over the railing of the stairs, slammed hard against the floor and sprang back to his feet. Coldhand swung his Talon around to aim at Tiberius.

"Get out of my way," he said in a flat voice.

Orphia wheeled and dove at Coldhand, talons outstretched. He threw his metal hand up to shield his eyes as she plummeted and caught the worst of her claws on the heavy illonium, but one scrabbling talon carved a red line along his jaw. The wound sheeted blood down Coldhand's neck and stained his borrowed shirt crimson. His face was empty of anger, of fear or even pain. Orphia pumped her wings and circled for another dive.

"Stand down, Coldhand!" Tiberius shouted.

He intended to go on, pointing out that Coldhand's Raptor was back on Axis, that Stray was a harsh world and surely hostile to a bounty hunter, but Tiberius was cut off by the sharp whine of laser-fire. A burst of red bolts burned through the cargo bay and hot pain seared across his shoulder.

Too slow, old man, Tiberius chastised himself.

Most lasers were invisible to the naked eye and deadly silent. Weaponized lasers added visible spectrum light for aiming and were required by CWA law to be equipped with noise generators. For some heavy color, either mechanism could be deactivated by a back-alley chop shop, but Coldhand had done neither. Not that Tiberius was complaining, but why the hells not?

The bounty hunter was circling wide across the cargo bay, but never took his eyes from his goal: the open airlock behind Tiberius. He fired again, forcing the other Prian to press himself against the wall beside the controls. Tiberius tried to close the airlock, but Coldhand shot at his questing fingers as he reached for the button. The old cop snatched his hand back with an oath. How long could he stand his ground against a younger and fitter man?

Tiberius leaned around the panel and fired. Coldhand was on the move again, throwing himself to the side and narrowly avoiding the first few bullets. Tiberius tracked his movement and pulled the trigger, but Coldhand fell back with his cybernetic hand held defensively across his chest. Tiberius' shot rang off the illonium armor and dug deep into the hunter's forearm, which cracked with a scream of tearing metal and hissing of sparks. But it stopped there, buried in Coldhand's cybernetics.

Orphia folded her banded wings, falling through the laser- and gunpowder-heated air, down at Coldhand. The other Prian swiftly juggled his Talon-9 into his metal hand and put his fingers to his lips. He whistled.

Stop.

Orphia responded to the command at once, beating her wings frantically to veer off course. The old hawk wheeled back toward Tiberius, trilling her confusion. The calls used by the Prian police for their birds were subtle by design, one whistle barely discernible from the next and intentionally difficult to learn. After all, weapons that could be controlled by criminals were of little use.

But Coldhand knew the calls. There was always a chance that he was just intelligent enough to have deciphered them on his own, but it was far more likely that Coldhand had been trained in their use. He was a cop, a Prian cop.

"What the hells?" Tiberius growled.

Coldhand didn't answer. His blue eyes remained glacier-hard as he took advantage of the old captain's shock to dash for the airlock. Tiberius raised his gun, but too late. Coldhand was close enough to jam his elbow into Tiberius' arm and the shot went wide. The bounty hunter dropped his gun back into its holster and then his armored cybernetic fist struck Tiberius in the stomach.

Tiberius doubled over and staggered, wheezing obscenities. He straightened and tried to bring up his gun, but Coldhand was already lashing out again. The NI pistol tumbled from Tiberius' suddenly numb fingers and he flung himself back into the hunter's path, between Coldhand and the airlock. If the man escaped now, he would only come after the Blue Phoenix crew again – armed this time. How many of Tiberius' people would this bastard hurt or kill to catch Maeve?

But Coldhand was a cop. Or had been, at least. How the hells could he have become... this?

Coldhand was on Tiberius once more, fists and feet flying. The old Prian barely saw the flurry of blows, but he heard his ribs crunch and felt the sickening pain. A high kick caught Tiberius in the temple, slamming his skull into the orange- and black-striped frame of the airlock. He slumped and fell to the floor of the hold, dazed. Coldhand leapt over him and through the hatch.

Tiberius grabbed clumsily for his fallen gun and rolled onto his stomach, ribs protesting painfully. Coldhand was close enough that his wavering aim wouldn't matter much. The bounty hunter was on the cargo ramp, boots ringing off the metal with each pounding step. Tiberius squeezed the trigger and fired. The shot tore a hole into Coldhand's shoulder and blood sprayed down the back of his shirt. But he didn't stagger or slow as he ran away from the Blue Phoenix, out into Stray's faded sunlight and clinging dust.

Tiberius lurched to his feet and gave chase, but his vision swam with spots of blistering red light and every bellowing breath made his broken ribs scream with pain. He was too damned slow to catch up with Coldhand, even injured. Orphia raced out of the ship after Tiberius, struggling to alight on his shoulder and keening in frustration when her perch swayed again.

He needed backup to catch Coldhand, Tiberius thought wildly. He tried to grab for the com on his belt, but he was holding his gun and Orphia was still trying to land on him. Tiberius could only see Coldhand in staccato bursts between the frenzied flapping of her wings. The bounty hunter ducked beneath the nose of a shiny silver Hyzaari transport and vanished.

"Hells take you!" Tiberius shouted after him. "You took a vow! Come back and face me!"

But Coldhand was gone. Panting, Tiberius shoved his gun into its holster again and held out his arm for Orphia. She sank her talons into his leather sleeve, then settled her wings against her back. Tiberius leaned heavily on a pitted fueling pylon to stroke the old hawk's ruffled feathers. His pulse and his thoughts raced.

Logan Coldhand was a Prian cop...? But that made no sense. Prian police had integrity and honor. They weren't the kind of people who would hunt bounties, who would sell piecemeal justice to the highest bidder. And Coldhand was far too young to have retired like Tiberius. Why wasn't he back on Prianus, serving his planet?

Tiberius was already tired and sore from a long day chasing a Pitch dealer through the alleyways of West Oak. The chase had gone on for nearly an hour before finally making the arrest, but the pain and fatigue didn't matter right now. What mattered was the young woman standing in front of Tiberius in the precinct office, holding up her left hand. It was shaking.

"Here before family and friends, peers and God himself, do you swear yourself to the service of the world and people of Prianus?" Tiberius asked. "To protect the innocent, to help those in need, to be merciless to the unjust? To serve Prianus with devotion and honor?"

The young officer swallowed hard. Today was her very first day in uniform, but the cloth was already worn, handed down from a fallen officer that was about her size. The Prian Police Force just didn't have the money to buy the uniforms new. But every cop wore their threadbare blues with pride.

"I do so swear," she answered. Her hand may have been shaking, but her voice was steady. "I'm ready."

"Then by the authority entrusted to me by the Prian Council," said Tiberius, "rise as Constable Ren Norris of the Prian Police Force. You are assigned to Oak District."

He handed Ren her gun and badge. The old Talon-6 was scuffed and battered, but well made. The gun looked just like the one Tiberius himself carried on his belt, issued only to the police and forbidden to be removed from their service. Seven generations of cops had worn the badge before Ren and it would serve many more until it was smoothed unrecognizable by years of use. Perhaps even longer than that.

"Carry these well," Tiberius said. "Remember those who wore them before you in service to Prianus and bring another generation of honour to them."

Tiberius stood and limped heavily back into the Blue Phoenix, every labored breath making his cracked ribs burn with pain. Xia had said something once about broken ribs puncturing lungs, but Tiberius couldn't remember what kind of advice his medic might have given on the matter.

When he was inside once more, Tiberius sealed the airlock and coaxed Orphia off his arm to perch on the railing of the stairs, then pulled out his com. Before Tiberius could turn it on, though, it beeped in his hand. He frowned and keyed open the channel.

"Tiberius here," he said.

"It's Xia. We're on our way back to the Blue Phoenix. We have some answers and a couple of new questions."

"No," Tiberius said. "Stay right where you are. Coldhand got off the ship and he's somewhere out in Gharib."

"I will find him," Maeve replied at once. Her voice was barely audible over Xia's com channel.

"Like hells you will, princess," Tiberius told her. "You're the one Coldhand wants and I'm not about to just deliver you to him."

There was a moment of silence on the line before Maeve finally answered. "You have never involved yourself in the quarrel between myself and Logan Coldhand. I do not know why that has changed, but I swear to you it is not necessary."

Tiberius snorted. "It changed when you brought Coldhand onto my ship and when I found out he was a cop. A Prian cop."

"What?" Xia asked. "What would a Prian police officer be doing out here? Do you think Coldhand's working undercover on some kind of investigation?"

That hadn't occurred to Tiberius. Could it be? Tiberius squinted at his com. He didn't like to hope, but...

"Maeve, are any of your crimes on Prianus?" he asked.

"I have never been to your homeworld," Maeve answered.

"And there are no Prian colonies," Tiberius said. "No money for them. Damn it. That means Coldhand isn't a cop anymore."

"Are you sure?" Xia asked.

"The force is stretched thin as it is, and they wouldn't dispatch someone off-world just to take a few bounties," Tiberius answered. "I'm moving the Phoenix. If Coldhand comes back for Maeve, it won't put him off the scent for long. But it might buy some time if we're not where he left us."

"Call us when you've landed again, captain," Xia said.

Tiberius ended the transmission and whistled. Orphia fluttered to his arm again and he carried her toward the cockpit, but Gripper waited in the corridor, Kessa cringing behind him.

"What's going on?" the mechanic asked in a shaking voice. "We heard shots."

"Coldhand got out and made a dive for it," Tiberius said. "The bastard got away."

Gripper pointed one big finger at the captain's shoulder. "Are... are you alright?"

"Fine," Tiberius growled. "I need to move the ship."

"Don't you think you should have Silver take a look at that?"

"After we land. Get down to the engines and make sure nothing falls out."

Gripper squeezed past Kessa, going back the way he had come. The Dailon chewed her blue lip.

"What do you want me to do?" she asked.

"Go to your room and lock the door until we know it's safe," Tiberius told her.

Kessa nodded hastily and then retreated. Tiberius hurried to the cockpit and keyed Duaal's frequency into the communications panel. He drummed his calloused fingers on the metal until his copilot picked up.

"Duaal, where are you?" Tiberius asked.

"Just leaving the market. Why?"

"Don't come back to the bird, Duaal. You hear me? Don't come back yet," Tiberius ordered. "Coldhand escaped and he's out there somewhere. I shot the bastard, but I don't think it's slowed him down much. I'm moving the Phoenix in case he decides to circle back. I'll call you when I know it's safe."

"Wouldn't I be more useful on the ship? I can fight if Coldhand comes back," Duaal protested. "I've got spells and a new knife. You can't ask me to just sit this out when you might need help!"

"I'm not asking," Tiberius snapped. "This is an order, Duaal! Stay put until I tell you otherwise."

Duaal cut the transmission and Tiberius sighed. He sagged into the pilot's seat and drummed his fingers across the console again. He hurt like hells, but not enough to want Duaal back on the ship if Coldhand returned. Damn the boy and his pride... Tiberius jabbed at the controls and fired up the Blue Phoenix's engines.

[10]

STRIKING SPARKS

"Sometimes hate and fear are the only weapons we have."

- GREN BARVISS, LYRAN CONSUL (750 MA)

Duaal seethed. Tiberius didn't think he could handle one wounded bounty hunter? Did he think Duaal was some ordinary, helpless little boy? Duaal was the *only* one like him in the entire galaxy. The only human mage... Well, more or less the only one. Could Coldhand say that? Or Tiberius?

Maeve said that Logan Coldhand felt no pain, that he was as tireless and unstoppable as a machine. That seemed... unlikely. And Coldhand was just one man, Duaal reminded himself, with a reputation that surpassed his own only because the young mage had no chance to prove himself yet.

Well, that was about to change.

Stray's fat crimson sun was setting and it would be night soon. Shadows followed their owners home through the darkening streets of Gharib. In the circle of the great central marketplace, vendors hawked their remaining wares with increasing desperation as their business wandered away. As their last customers vanished into the sinking twilight, the merchants unfolded static covers and closed down their stalls for the evening.

How would Duaal hunt a bounty hunter? The excitement of it tasted hot and metallic. Duaal tapped his fingers against the jug of delberry wine, thinking. Gharib wasn't the biggest city on Stray, but it was certainly large enough for a single man to lose himself in.

Tiberius said he had shot Coldhand. Unless some of the wilder rumors that Maeve had repeated were true – that Logan Coldhand had nitric coolant running through his veins instead of blood, or that he was really a robot instead of human – he would be bleeding from the wound. If he was on the run, Coldhand would need to put some distance between himself and Tiberius before he could stop to tend the injury. So he was leaving a blood trail, right?

Pleased with his own cleverness, Duaal made his way back in the direction of the Blue Phoenix. He stopped three landing pads down from where it was berthed, though, and peered over the rounded nose of another ship that – to guess by the liquid lines and its name, *Riptide* – came from Hyzaar. Like Duaal himself.

Beyond, the Blue Phoenix was still grounded, probably waiting for clearance from Stray's automated air control system. Duaal frowned. He would have preferred to start there, but he didn't want to risk Tiberius seeing and stopping him. Duaal circled the landing pad, searching for the telltale signs of Coldhand's blood. It wasn't until he made his way back around to the other side of the Riptide that he found what he was looking for.

Duaal was disappointed by the tiny cinnamon-colored spray. He had expected a great red splash of gushing life-blood. He leaned close to examine the small stain. It wasn't droplets, but smeared fingerprints. There must have been blood on the bounty hunter's fingers. Duaal squinted. His right hand, since there were tiny, whorled ridges in the crusted blood. The cybernetic fingers of the hunter's left hand were smooth and wouldn't have made marks like that.

A moment later, Duaal realized that simply checking which side the thumbprint was on would have told him the same thing, but he was still proud of his clever discoveries and brilliant deductions. What any of it actually meant, Duaal wasn't sure yet. He set down his heavy wine jug and leaned against the Riptide, wondering what to do next.

"Oi, what are you doing back there?" someone asked.

Duaal jumped up and whirled to find a woman in oil-spotted orange coveralls frowning at him. Her skin was dark and lined from the sun, her black hair braided into a long tail. She eyed Duaal suspiciously. He straightened and gave her his brightest, sweetest smile.

"Is this your ship?" Duaal asked.

"Na, not mine," the woman answered, shaking her head. Her accent was distinctly Hyzaari, but much thicker than Duaal's. "I just work on it."

She jabbed a thumb over her shoulder toward a fuel pylon extended above the Riptide and the flashing red light that indicated it was in use. Perhaps Duaal's smile was working because her posture lost some of its defensive rigidity.

"The cap'n is in the city taking care of some business. Maybe I can help you?" she suggested.

"I'll bet you can," Duaal said. "This is a big ship. You must have been fueling for a while, right?"

The woman nodded. "About an hour now."

"Did you see a man running away from that ship over there?" Duaal pointed at the Blue Phoenix.

"Ya, two of them. A man with a cybernetic arm – who has those these days? – and an older fella chasing him. Prian, I think. There was a big bird chasing him. The one with the metal hand ran off and the older man yelled after him for a bit, then went into the ship there."

"Did you see which way the one with the cybernetics went?" Duaal asked. He was getting closer...

"Off that direction," the Hyzaari woman said, pointing north.

"He'd been shot," Duaal told her, indicating the blood on the nose of the Riptide where Coldhand must have steadied himself. "Do you know where he was bleeding from?"

"Na, I didn't get that close. I stayed back behind the fuel pylon until it was well over."

Duaal thanked her. He could find out for himself how badly Coldhand was wounded when he cornered the bounty hunter. Now that Duaal knew which direction to go.

He made his way north, weaving between the ships in search of his quarry. The landing pads formed a large crescent on the west side of Gharib, running in a curve north and south along the city's edge. The Blue Phoenix was just south of the midpoint, so Coldhand had fled further up there, not into the city.

Once Coldhand put some distance between him and Tiberius, what would he do? This close to Gharib, the landing crescent was full of passenger ships instead of the cargo vessels that made berth further out. Most were small starships carrying no more than fifty people. Stray wasn't exactly a vacation port.

As evening crept over Gharib, shops and bars turned on bright holographic signs and neon lights, illuminating the dusty city like a discarded Waytide decoration. Duaal jogged up the main landing road. Vehicles on their null-fields buzzed past and Duaal pulled up his collar against the cool rising wind. Stray's sun was half hidden behind the horizon, sinking Gharib into deep russet shadows. It was getting cold.

Duaal scanned the streets of the landing crescent, full of vehicles moving cargo or supplies to or from ships, but with only a few pedestrians. Most everyone was already in the city, bedding down for the night or else drinking it away. What could Coldhand want in the landing crescent that he couldn't find in Gharib? It wasn't a place for a lone man to lose himself in the crowd, much less one so obviously wounded and deformed.

Maybe Coldhand was looking for a doctor? The hunter was injured, after all. But why go search out a ship medic when he could just go to a hospital in Gharib? The city doctors were almost as corrupt as the police, but could Coldhand find anyone better in the landing crescent?

Or were the rumors true...? Maybe Coldhand didn't care about his injuries. But if he wasn't trying to hide in the city or get medical attention, then where was he going?

To get off Stray, Duaal realized. Back to his starfighter on Axis, equipped with plenty of weaponry to shoot down the much larger but unarmed Blue Phoenix. Coldhand had been chasing Maeve for the better part of a year and never seemed to have much difficulty in finding her. The detour to retrieve his Raptor was probably an acceptable delay.

Now what? Duaal wandered along the street with no idea where to go or what to do next. The entire roadway was lined with ships, crossed by myriad tributary streets leading out to the next rows of landing pads. One by one, the ships and cargo haulers flipped on their nightlights, etching the landing crescent in glaring reds and greens.

Coldhand could be inside any one of those other ships. Hells, he might already be gone, up in the big black and on his way back to Axis. Duaal stopped and frowned through the deepening darkness of the Stray night.

An elegant silver ship sat across the street, all smoothly curving, swooping lines and delicate chromium filigree that threw back the surrounding lights like a broken mirror. A Kahli design, maybe? They were very expensive, all customized by the Narsus shipyards.

A gleaming figure in white stood at the bottom of the extended boarding ramp. The darkening night and layers of pale cloth disguised race or gender from a distance. Their posture seemed all wrong, but their covered face was raised, contemplating the stars. Staring just like Duaal. What if they had seen Coldhand? Maybe Duaal could still bring the hunter back to Tiberius.

Duaal ran across the road to the lowered ramp and grabbed the white-shrouded figure by the shoulder.

"Hey, did you see a man with a metal hand come this way?" he asked. "He would have been bleeding."

It was a woman. She was considerably shorter than Duaal, delicately feminine under his hand. What he had mistaken for a cloak from a distance were long feathered wings, held out behind her and nearly lost against the soft white of her flowing gown.

An Arcadian? On a ship like this? Maybe she was some kind of hired help? The dry desert wind rustled the fairy's feathers and tugged at her dress. It was expensive, too, just like the ship. Layers of silver-embroidered white silk were knotted at the waist with an intricately wrought gold belt, beaded with glass. Her back was straight and her chin held high. Duaal doubted that such a woman would ever serve someone else.

A hood of snowy velvet was pulled up over her face and a white veil affixed across her high, sharp cheekbones. Small silver disks dangled from the edge, chiming in the evening breeze. Duaal was about to repeat his questions, but the words died in his throat. Her eyes were lined in ashy gray makeup that curled down over her cheeks in graceful arcs and vanished beneath her veil. It wasn't the exquisite makeup job that arrested Duaal, though, but her eyes – the only color anywhere on the fairy woman. They were a deep violet, like lilacs at twilight. They were lovely and sad, but proud and defiant.

So beautiful...

Duaal had no idea how long he just stood there, falling into the Arcadian woman's violet gaze, before a loud cry roused him from his reverie.

"Lady Xartasia!"

Two men raced down the boarding ramp behind the Arcadian. They were also robed and hooded, but in fading black cloth instead of white, and not nearly as fine a cut or weave. The one who had shouted was human with unremarkable blond hair poking out from under his hood, but his accent marked him as Cyran, from the old farming colony. A Lyran with singed-looking fur ran close on his heels. Both of them drew worn laser pistols and leveled them at Duaal.

"You, stand back!" the Lyran barked.

Duaal frowned, but he removed his hand from the Arcadian woman's shoulder and stepped back. Both guards bowed to the fairy. Xartasia, apparently.

"My lady, are you alright?" the human one asked. "Is this boy bothering you?"

Annoyed though Duaal was at being treated like any old piece of Gharib trash, Duaal actually hoped he hadn't disturbed her. Xartasia ignored her guard's question and cocked her head toward Duaal, curiosity in her violet eyes. She took in Duaal's clothes, the arcane symbols and strange sigils there.

"I have not seen such marks in a long time," Xartasia said. "You stir memories of my home, if only for a moment. And for that moment, I thank you. Are you searching for someone?"

Duaal nearly swooned. Xartasia's voice was as smooth and sweet as the finest golden mantle syrup. It was the most beautiful thing he had ever heard. And it sounded strangely familiar...

"Um, yes," Duaal said. He wasn't sure how he should address her, but she obviously commanded respect. "My um... my lady."

"A bleeding man with a metal hand, I believe you said. One with blond hair and a rather... stark bearing?"

Duaal wasn't certain what that last part meant, but it certainly *sounded* like Coldhand.

"Yes, he's a bounty hunter," Duaal said. "He's trying to catch one of my crewmates."

Duaal didn't think he would mind if Coldhand hauled Maeve away, but the man had shot at Tiberius. Xartasia regarded Duaal with those luminous, heart-stopping violet eyes.

"And what will you do to this man when you find him?" she asked. "Kill him?"

Duaal blinked. "What? No! I just want to stop him before he gets off Stray. I need to take him back to Tiberius."

Xartasia stepped closer to Duaal, her white skirts whispering. She stroked his cheek with cool alabaster fingers. Her guards still held their weapons at the ready and watched the scene carefully, but didn't say anything.

"This man is a bounty hunter," Xartasia said. "A man who kills for money. One who would kill your friend for nothing more than plastic cenmark chips."

Duaal wished that he could see the fairy's lips, but they were invisible behind her veil.

"She's not my friend," he objected half-heartedly. "I don't think she's really worth killing someone over."

Something flickered in Xartasia's glorious eyes. Why did she care? But Duaal couldn't help the surge of gratitude that she did. Xartasia stepped behind Duaal, trailing soft wings along his arms.

"Kill him," she urged. "This man is a monster. A misshapen destroyer who spreads pain like a plague."

"Have you... met him?" Duaal asked. His head was spinning.

"I do not have to."

Xartasia's words made a dreamy kind of sense. Bounty hunters were fringe rogues themselves, not much better than the criminals they hunted. Coldhand was worse than most. He hunted Maeve, a woman Duaal didn't like, but whose loss would be a painful blow to Tiberius. If Duaal killed Coldhand, the captain would praise his bravery. Maybe Tiberius would finally see that Duaal was a far superior first mate and promote him up over the drunken, chem-addicted fairy.

"To conquer a killer, to conquer death… it takes strength," said Xartasia. "Do you have such strength?"

She smelled like flowers. Xartasia's wings closed around Duaal like a soft white cage. Maeve was a wanted criminal herself, wasn't she? She must have done *something* to earn the bounty on her head. Maeve didn't belong on Tiberius' ship. Logan Coldhand was ruthless and inhuman, but at least what he did was legal. If Duaal killed Coldhand, wouldn't he become a criminal, too? A murderer?

"I can't… kill him," Duaal said. "I just need to find him. Do you know where he went?"

Xartasia withdrew her wings and stepped back, disappointment in her beautiful violet eyes.

"Your heart is sullen and your spirit is placid," she told Duaal. "I have nothing else to offer you."

Xartasia turned away and gestured to her Cyran guard.

"We have business to tend to in this place, I believe," she said.

They were all ignoring Duaal now. He felt small, insignificant, and he hated it.

"Yes, my lady. The cathedral is this way," her human guard said, nodding to the east. "He is waiting for you. I'll escort you there."

"Remain with my ship," Xartasia instructed the Lyran.

The second guard bowed, too, and took up his position next to the shiny silver ship. Xartasia spread her wings and leapt into the darkened sky, her skirts rippling like clouds in the breeze. Duaal found himself gazing after her with the same expression of devoted adoration as the other two men. Her perfect whiteness shone bright against the night for a moment, dwindled and then was gone.

The Cyran man shook himself and holstered his gun. He cursed under his breath, hiked up his black robes, and then jogged out east after the departing Arcadian. So much for escorting her. With a sigh, Duaal turned back to the Lyran they left behind. He had put away his gun, at least.

"Did you see the man I'm looking for?" Duaal asked.

The Lyran growled. "Lady Xartasia didn't tell you, so I don't see why I should. Get along, boy!"

"Then you *did* see him," Duaal said. "Which way did he go?"

"You heard the lady," the Lyran barked. "We're done!"

"Tell me!" Duaal demanded, drawing himself up and glaring at the guard.

The Lyran snarled, his uneven hackles bristling and laying his ears flat against his skull. He bared long, sharp teeth. "Run back home to the bitch that spawned you, pup! Stop whining for a rip or I *will* give it to you!"

He placed his hand over the butt of his laser pistol. Duaal raised his hands before him and laced the fingers together into a jagged star pattern.

"*Na illya ma'naari su,*" he chanted.

There it was, that mix of thrill and terror as the Arcadian words moved through Duaal, the fairy spell turning thought into deadly form. The air around Duaal's hands cracked and flickered with twisting bolts of blue-white lightning. Now the Lyran sank to his knees and curled his tail awkwardly between his robed legs.

"God... what? How did you...?" the man whimpered.

"Tell me!" Duaal shouted.

The blaze of electricity had already faded, but the effect – and the smell of ozone – lingered. Trembling, the Lyran pointed to an empty landing pad just down the road.

"The man with the cybernetics... he went to the ship landed there. It was unmarked. It took off half an hour ago."

"Was he on board when they left?"

"I think so," the Lyran said.

"Damn it!"

He was too late and Coldhand was already gone. Briefly, Duaal contemplated trying to pry a departure vector or flight plan from Stray's orbital control. But what was the point? Duaal didn't have any of the necessary codes or credentials to get that information, and he already knew where Coldhand was going – Axis. Back to his ship and his weapons. There was no way to haul the bounty hunter back to Tiberius now.

"Damn it," Duaal growled again.

Behind him, the Lyran said something and Duaal looked back over his shoulder.

"What?" he asked.

"I answered your question. Will you kill me now?"

"What? No!" Duaal said, aghast.

"I'm ready. Kill me."

The Lyran certainly looked prepared. He was still down on his knees, head bowed and ready for execution.

"What are you doing?" Duaal asked. "If you wanted to die, why did you answer my question?"

The Lyran's ears angled back flat against his skull. "You... know magic. Aren't you...?"

But he trailed off, suddenly looking uncertain. There was something going on here that Duaal didn't understand.

And Duaal had no desire to. He was angry, frustrated at his lack of success and ashamed of threatening the Lyran guard like that. Duaal didn't want to kill Coldhand, much less this shabbily dressed stranger.

The Jinn couldn't even scream anymore. Her delicate amber leaves blackened and smoked under the jagged blue curls of lightning. Duaal's master released the spell and the Jinn pitched forward, twigs and charred boughs snapping as she fell to the concrete floor. He brought his black boot down hard on her branches. Tears streamed down Duaal's cheeks, but he didn't dare leave his master's side.

"Answer me and your pain will end," said the old man. His tone was one of gentle compromise, even as the Jinn's branches crunched under his feet.

"Why are you questioning me? Ask the Arcadians! Or the Nnyth!" she cried.

"The Ivory Spire adepts are all dead. Even the Arcadian princess can't tell me what I need to know. She was never trained in those spells. The Nnyth won't let any ship I hire get close enough to have such a... civil conversation as this. So you must tell me."

Please just answer him, *Duaal wished silently.* Make it stop!

"Why do you want the opening spells?" the Jinn asked. "There are no Waygates in the core to use them on! You've already somehow managed to learn more of the Arcadian's magic than any human before you... Can you not be proud and content in that?"

"If the spells are so useless, then stop fighting me."

"No," the alien tree whispered. She closed her berry-like eyes. "I don't know what you intend to do with those spells, but if you somehow learn to use the Waygates, you could bring your... gentle touch... to any world."

Duaal stared. Would she truly rather die than tell the old man her secrets? But Duaal's master was unimpressed. He grabbed the Jinn by the boughs and hauled her up to her roots, chanting another spell in his rich, powerful voice. The words rang through Duaal's mind and rose in his throat like bile, unwelcome but inexorable. He screamed out his master's words.

To any other coreworlder, they would have meant nothing. Duaal didn't speak Arcadian, but he knew these words. His master had burned them into his memory, forced the boy to understand them, and that understanding lent power and form.

The close air crackled and hissed. Duaal's ears popped as lightning consumed the air in the room and surged at the captive Jinn. Her bark split and cracked, baring soft wood beneath that smoked and splintered. Leaves burned away to drifting ash and the Jinn girl lay still as an ordinary tree.

The monotone beeping of his com brought Duaal back to the present. The Lyran was still on his knees, but pricked his ears toward the sound. Duaal thrust his hands into his pockets and walked the opposite direction as quickly as he could without breaking into a run.

When he had created a little distance, Duaal grabbed his com and swore under his breath. Somewhere along the way, he had lost the jug of delberry wine purchased from Ssassi. He must have set it down at some point and forgotten to pick it up again. Thirty cenmarks thrown away for some Gharib vagrant to drink...

Duaal keyed on his com with a sigh. "Yeah? What is it?"

"The bird's secure now. You can come back," Tiberius told him. "Are you safe? You didn't run into Coldhand, did you?"

"I'm fine. And I haven't seen Coldhand all evening," Duaal said truthfully.

[11]

FULL CIRCLE

"Guilt weighs heavy on the heart, but forgiveness must be even heavier, to judge by how little we give it."

It was well into the night, cold and dark outside the Blue Phoenix. By the time the ship had been thoroughly searched for any nasty surprises Coldhand might have left behind – there didn't seem to be any – it was too late to attend the speech at the black cathedral that Anthem had told Xia about.

"How did this happen?" Tiberius asked. "How did Coldhand get out?"

He was pacing across the medical bay, limping with every step. Xia grabbed Tiberius firmly by one shoulder and pulled him back down to sit on a small operating table. Her surgical instruments were laid out and fixed magnetically into their trays to keep them in place even during bumpy atmospheric flying. Since most injuries were sustained in the air, it was best to be ready to operate even under turbulent conditions.

"Sit *down*," Xia told Tiberius.

The captain frowned. "Why?"

"Those pain chems I gave you aren't helping much if you just make your injuries worse," Xia said. "Do you want to be laid up for the next month?"

Tiberius grumbled and sat. Xia tipped antiseptic onto a disposable pad and resumed cleaning the burn in Tiberius' shoulder. His chest was a rug of gray hair interlaced by a network of pale scars mapping out fifty years of service to the Prian police. If only his people had better medical care... Xia sighed.

Gripper held out an old datadex to Tiberius.

"I think Coldhand used this to pry up the access panel and then rewired the door. It must have taken him days. You can't just rip out a handful of wires like in the shows," Gripper said, then groaned. "And it's going to take twice as long to fix. Coldhand knew what he was doing, but barely."

Tiberius growled and lifted the datadex to fling it across the room, but Xia gave him a stern look until he dropped it into his lap instead. The Ixthian put aside the bloodstained pad and then taped a clean bandage into place over the burn.

"Damnable lasers," Xia sighed. She hated those things. "They cauterize the shot."

"Doesn't that make them easier to fix?" Duaal asked her. "Cauterized wounds don't bleed as much."

"No, but they get infected. Antibodies are carried by the blood and if blood can't reach the burn, it goes septic," Xia said, looking pointedly at Tiberius. "*Especially* if the patient insists on pulling off the bandages. Keep the burn covered. It has to stay clean."

"But laser burns itch," Tiberius grumbled.

"They itch because they're healing."

Tiberius looked down at the datadex in his hands rather than meeting the medic's irritated gaze. Idly, he turned it on.

"I wonder if he ever even read it," Tiberius said. "Maybe it could teach him a thing or two about loyalty. But if he didn't learn it as a police officer back home, I doubt a book would have done it. Damn him to all the hells!"

Tiberius shouted and this time, he did hurl the datadex across the medbay. Xia frowned disapprovingly and Gripper ducked. The datadex hit one of the white cabinets and then fell to the floor. Gripper picked it up by a corner. The broken screen was a muddy spiderweb of cracks.

"I swear I'll kill that bastard!" Tiberius raged. He heaved himself up off the table and out of Xia's grip. "He's betrayed his uniform, his oath to Prianus! And he overwrote my book!"

Desperately, Xia caught Tiberius by his uninjured shoulder and pulled the old captain back down to the padded examination table. Again.

"Calm down, captain," she told him. "I don't have a reconstruction chamber to deal with these ribs. You've cracked three of them and you need to be careful until they heal."

"I'll burn Coldhand so bad there won't be anything left to put on his pyre!" Tiberius said.

The hunter was a deadly opponent... To books as well as to people, apparently. Xia had been treating Maeve long enough to be familiar with his bloody work. Tiberius had told them about his own fight with Coldhand once the crew had gathered again on the Blue Phoenix. Xia suspected that the injury to the old Prian's head – which had driven him to the ground and out of Coldhand's path to freedom – was the only thing that had saved his life.

"Hey, Coldhand wrote something!" Gripper exclaimed.

The mechanic held out the cracked datadex. Maeve took it and angled the screen against the sterile fluorescent lights, squinting to make out the words.

"*The Sacred Temple of Creation*," she read. "*Vanora.*"

"What does that mean?" Xia asked.

"There is a drug called Vanora White," said Maeve. "I injected Logan with it when we last fought, but it failed to affect him. I can see no reason why he would write it here."

Gripper rubbed his bald head, thinking. "Isn't Vanora the old name for Axis? Before it became the capital of the Alliance?"

"He's right," Xia said. "Gripper, you know Alliance history better than most natives do."

"I had to take a citizenship test," the Arboran admitted.

"But what does that have to do with the Sacred Church of whatever?" Duaal asked.

"The Sacred Temple of Creation," Kessa said.

Xia looked back at the Dailon, who was perched on a stool in one corner of the medbay. She had nearly forgotten that the girl was even there.

"It sounds familiar," Kessa said. "I think that I've heard it before. Maybe from Xel, the Ixthian who led us. You met her, Maeve."

"What did she say about it?" Tiberius asked.

His face was still an alarming shade of red, but he seemed to have recovered from his rage enough to rejoin the conversation. Xia took advantage of his distraction to prod at Tiberius' knee with her fingertips. Swollen, certainly... She frowned and pulled an imager over the strained joint.

"I don't remember," Kessa said.

"If I get access to the local mainstream, I'm sure I can find out," Gripper offered.

He grinned. The Arboran loved absolutely any excuse to play with machines or electronics. He was young and relatively new to the technologies of the Alliance, still awed and fascinated by every wire and blinking light. The computer mainstream must have been a candy store.

Xia cleared her throat. "You didn't tear anything in your knee when you fell, Tiberius, but it was a near thing. The tendons are strained and brittle. You're old. I'm going to give you some supplements to help repair the damage."

"I hate taking pills," Tiberius grumbled. "Can't you just give me a shot?"

"No, I don't have any needles strong enough to get through your thick skin," Xia answered, but then sighed. "I'm out of injectors. We were supposed to buy some on Axis before we left, so now you'll have to take the capsules."

Tiberius groaned and turned back to Gripper. "I'll give you the colour for an uplink. But tomorrow. I don't want you out in Gharib in the middle of the night."

"I am certain Logan gave this information to us for a purpose," Maeve said. "Perhaps further planning should wait until Gripper has learned something about it."

Tiberius nodded. Xia handed him a half-full bottle of glucosamine and callosen tablets and then pronounced the old Prian free to go. Tiberius pulled his shirt on and then the crew filed after him out of the medical bay. Once back out in the corridors of the Blue Phoenix, they scattered to find their bunks.

But Xia followed Maeve and caught up with her in the small mess area. She cleared her throat and waited until the fairy stopped walking. Maeve turned on her heels to face Xia, frowning.

"Maeve, what happened to your worlds?" Xia asked.

She was nervous about approaching the temperamental winged woman, but she could no longer contain her curiosity. She had to know. Maeve's frown deepened into a scowl.

"Why do you ask now? It is not a pleasant song."

"You're the only Arcadian I've spent much time with... Until that man Anthem today," Xia said. The memory of the thin, malnourished and mistreated fairy was all too fresh in her mind. "I always figured that you were the only one who was... the way you are. But now I'm beginning to wonder."

"If we are all inebriated and wasted criminals?" Maeve asked.

"Employed under only the faintest façade of legal profession by the graces of a too-forgiving captain?"

Xia sighed, but refused to let herself rise to the bait. She had asked for some of that, maybe, by confronting Maeve like this. But perhaps if Maeve knew that someone cared, she would open up. Maybe even begin healing what was clearly a deep and painful psychological wound.

"The Arcadians' appearance in the core is well-documented," Xia said. "But not what brought you here. That all happened before I was even hatched... So what's the story? What drove all the fairies out of the White Kingdom?"

"All of the fairies out...?" Maeve repeated bitterly. "No, not all of them."

Xia blinked. "What?"

"Most are dead, yes. Less than one of fifty survived, but all of those were of my kind. The aerads."

"Aerads?" Xia asked. "I thought you were called Arcadians."

"That is the name that Cavain gave us, his own species, when he founded the White Kingdom," Maeve said. "The others retained their original names."

"There were other species of fairies?" Xia asked.

"Three of them," Maeve answered, nodding. "Four races before Cavain killed the rebel pyrads to create the White Kingdom. For ten thousand years, the aerads, dryads and nyads all lived in the kingdom that he built. Some aerads escaped to become the Arcadians as you know us now, a shattered fragment of ourselves. But the rest are gone."

"What actually happened? How did they all die?"

"The White Kingdom of Arcadia spanned all the worlds of our stellar system," Maeve answered, tracing a circle in the air. "They were connected by the Waygates. We were not alone in their use – the Jinn and the Nnyth know much about them, as well."

"I've heard a bit about Waygates. They were instantaneous transportation portals, right?" Xia asked.

The Ixthian sat down at the table and then gestured for Maeve to take a seat, too. The fairy reluctantly turned another chair backwards and dropped down into it.

"That is correct," Maeve said. "Waygates are opened as one-way paths to most any destination."

"Opened by what?" Xia asked. "Or who?"

"Each Waygate requires its own skilled operator. The adepts of the Ivory Spire were trained in those arts. Once they mastered their craft, each operator was paired with a knight to guard and protect both the singer and their Waygate. But a century ago, as you count time, one of these knights damned us all."

Xia cocked her head. "As we count time? I thought an Arcadian year was about the same as an Alliance CSY."

"Almost," Maeve said. "But a natural year is two hundred eighty-eight days, made up of twelve months, each three weeks long. So it has been more than a century by our count."

"Oh..." Xia answered. She wasn't sure what else to say to that. "What happened with the knight?"

Maeve folded her arms across the back of the chair and drew a deep breath.

"There was a Spire adept, a young prince of the royal family, assigned to the Waygate in Tamlin, on the planet of Orindell. He was in the city on personal business when his knight companion attempted to open the Waygate alone. She had heard and seen his spells often enough to make the attempt."

"Untrained?" Xia asked. That sounded like a bad idea – she had experience with the mess untrained medics made of their patients.

Maeve nodded. "When her spells faltered, the knight failed to call for the aid of the other priests. In the end, she opened the Waygate, but the songs were terribly wrong, twisted beyond belief.

The Waygate boomed in a strange, terrible tongue. And then what came through the gate... It was nothing less than death Herself."

"What was it?" Xia asked.

"An endless army of monsters that we named the Devourers," Maeve answered in a flat voice. "Wingless and taller even than the Hadrians or Ixthians. But much more of their appearance than that remained a mystery. Each of the Devourers was shrouded by thick black smoke... or perhaps that was a part of their bodies. We never knew. But those dark, swirling clouds were far from insubstantial. The Devourers formed great blades and whips that would dissolve back into smoke when engaged. In concentration, these shadows were able to fire lasers more destructive than anything I have seen in the core."

"Why did you call them *Devourers*?"

For a moment, Xia wasn't sure if Maeve heard her. The Arcadian was staring down at the floor.

"There were only a few in the beginning," Maeve answered at last. "The prince flew to the Waygate, but he could not undo what his companion had done... and he was the first killed by the creatures that she had summoned. They shot him down out of the sky, cut the wings from his back and devoured him."

"They ate him...?" Xia gasped. "A sentient creature? But Maeve, aren't you from the royal family, too?"

"Yes. That singer was my younger brother, Caith."

"Your brother? Maeve, I'm so sorry," Xia said.

Maeve still didn't look up. Her face was hidden behind a curtain of tangled black hair, but tears splashed onto the back of her hands and ran across her pale skin.

"More and more of the Devourers poured through the open Waygate. Hundreds and then thousands of them," Maeve told Xia. "They ate every creature on Orindell. My people fled to other planets of the White Kingdom, but the Devourers followed them through the Waygates. They spread like a plague across our worlds, destroying and consuming all. The Arcadians pulled back in full retreat, leaving the dryads and nyads behind to their fates.

"We fought for three long months as the remaining Spire adepts debated with the king on how to save what remained of Arcadia. Some few argued that the Devourers could be banished from our worlds, that the same corrupted spell which summoned them bound them still to the Tamlin Waygate. If it was closed, they said, the monsters would vanish. But the spell they developed could only be cast from Tamlin, where Devourers streamed through every day.

"But most of the surviving spell-singers agreed that Arcadia was lost and that leaving our home entirely was the only option left to us. They told the king that they could open the remaining Waygates – those in the capital city were the only ones still under our control by then – to somewhere further away."

"The human worlds, right?" Xia said. That was a part of history she had learned in school at least. "The Arcadians all went to Axis, Mir, Hyzaar, Prianus and Hadra."

"The Waygates can only be opened to places that their operators remember. It is a part of the magic built into them. We knew no place besides the planets of the White Kingdom, but I am told that the Waygates had... memory of their own, after a fashion. Whatever happened to summon the Devourers was bound up into that same magic, they said, that same memory. I never understood why, but it no longer matters.

"King Illain decided that our people had no choice but to flee and commanded the Spire adepts to open the way into the galactic core. But the defense of the capital was already crumbling and we feared that the Devourers would follow us across the galaxy. So a bold and fierce knight rallied all that remained of our warriors and flew for the Tamlin Waygate."

"You were a knight back in Arcadia, right?" Xia asked.

"I was a knight, yes," Maeve answered. She finally looked up at Xia with red-rimmed eyes. "But no, it was not me. It was my teacher,

Sir Orthain Fyre, who led the last knights into Tamlin. I flew with him, though, into the heart of the darkness. There were only four remaining Ivory Spire adepts, and all of them stayed behind to hold open the Waygates, to evacuate our people to the Alliance worlds. So since my brother had been such a spell-singer, I was chosen to attempt the closing song."

Maeve laughed bitterly at this and Xia raised a silvery eyebrow.

"It was a dangerous decision," the fairy said. "After all, was it not an unpracticed voice singing to the Waygates that began this catastrophe? But the White Kingdom was lost... we did not think that anything could be worse. So Sir Orthain and the last knights of Arcadia protected me as we flew. It was a long and terrible journey across worlds that I had loved, through ruins of pitted and shattered glass. Five of the other knights died before we even reached Tamlin. When we neared the Waygate, there was little time... The rest fell quickly, buying me precious moments to sing the spell I had been given. I sang as they tore Orthain apart."

"Did it work?" Xia asked. "Did you close the gate?"

"I closed my eyes at the end. But when I opened them again, I was alone," Maeve said. "Sir Orthain was gone... but so were the Devourers. I flew back to the capital with all the haste that I could, but the monsters had overrun the city before I banished them. All who had not yet fled through the Waygates were dead, some still lying half eaten on the glass streets."

"But some of the Arcadians escaped," Xia said. Hundreds of thousands of the fairies had appeared on Alliance worlds. Almost a million of them. "Couldn't they... go home?"

"The Waygates are a one-way trip and the singers who operated them were all dead," Maeve said. "King Illain was gone. I found what was left of my uncle beside one of the dead Spire adepts, his spear in his hand. He had died protecting his people... Our kingdom has spanned five worlds and ten thousand years, but within three months, it was all gone."

"What did you do?" Xia asked.

"I hesitated," Maeve answered. "There was a single Waygate still open, guttering with the last power of its spell. I did not know where it would go, but what else could I do? So I stepped through and joined my people in exile. I appeared on Hyzaar and you have seen what my life became here in the core."

Xia didn't trust herself to comment on that. Maeve was an unhappy woman – for which Xia could hardly blame her – and often seemed intent on making herself even more miserable. But Xia still had a question.

"What happened to the other knight, the one who opened the Waygate in the first place?"

Maeve shook her head. "No one knows, precisely. But her fate will be terrible, if I have any say in the matter."

"You can't blame her," Xia told Maeve gently. "It sounds like the entire thing was a tragic accident."

"She killed Caith and Orthain," Maeve snarled. She jumped to her feet and spread her wings. Unabashed tears were streaming down her reddened cheeks now. "My enarrii... my beloved ones... I will watch her suffer! And then she will finally die in pain for what she has done!"

Xia stood up and placed a careful hand on the smaller woman's shoulder. "Maeve, I'm so sorry for everything that you and your people have been through. But you're here. You can build new lives and new homes..."

Maeve shoved Xia's hand away and turn to stalk off deeper into the Blue Phoenix. Xia briefly considered following, but then decided against it. She sat down again and drummed her silver fingertips on the tabletop. It was hard to blame Maeve for trying to drown such terrible memories in narcohol and chems... But the fairy's depression was dangerous – potentially even suicidal. Xia could never condone that kind of behavior, but she had no idea how to help Maeve.

Xia remained sitting and thinking in the mess for a little while longer, but eventually followed the examples of the rest of the crew and went to her bunk to get some sleep.

Discussion of their plans resumed early the next afternoon. Xia repeated to the others what Anthem Calloren had told her about the Sisterhood on Stray, how they had vanished when the Church of Nihil arrived. Kessa flinched and cradled her belly protectively.

Tiberius was sitting at the mess table, shoveling down a plate of fried minnas from Gripper's garden. The starchy tuber was native to Hyzaar, but early CWA colonists discovered that the minnas thrived on a variety of worlds and it had become a staple of coreworld diets. Duaal was in a bad mood and didn't eat much, but Kessa made up for him. Maeve declined lunch, instead taking long drinks from a bottle.

Gripper suddenly brandished a datadex overhead in his claws and let out a triumphant shout. Orphia – who had been perched on the back of Tiberius' chair – shrieked and vaulted up into the air. She circled twice, but when the hawk found nothing to attack, she finally settled down once more behind Tiberius. Gripper smiled sheepishly.

"Sorry," he apologized to Orphia, who ignored him. He looked at the rest of the crew. "I found them!"

"Found who?" Tiberius asked.

"The Sacred Temple of Creation," Gripper said. He tapped the datadex. It wasn't the one that Coldhand had broken, but a fresh datadex with a screen full of text. "Or, as they're called these days, the Sisterhood."

"What?" Duaal asked. "They're the same thing?"

"Uh, sort of. I never would have found it if Coldhand hadn't given me that hint about Vanora. It's a pretty obscure bit of history,"

Gripper answered. "It was about three hundred years ago, before the Arcadians arrived. When the Central World Alliance was just being created, there was a religion on Vanora – Axis – called the Sacred Temple of Creation. They weren't the dominant faith or anything, but they had a few million followers."

"That's a fairly small religion," Xia said. "The Union of Light has adopted and absorbed much bigger ones."

Gripper nodded. "Yes, but the Sacred Temple of Creation didn't get folded into the Union. They believed the same stuff as the modern Sisterhood – females are goddesses, males are trash. That sort of thing. They had no desire to join the Union of Light and become a part of the official church of the Alliance."

"Yeah, that sounds familiar," Kessa said.

"How did that go for them?" Tiberius asked.

"Not very well," Gripper answered. "They attacked a few Union of Light priests, got themselves declared a heretical cult, and the Alliance shut them down. Most of the Sacred Temple disbanded, but the ones who wouldn't give it up were imprisoned. Unfortunately for the CWA, the stuff they taught was pretty popular in prison. It was rebranded as the Sisterhood of Life – mostly just shortened to *Sisterhood* – and was reborn as a criminal group. It's been a few centuries and the Sisterhood's popularity goes up and down, but you can find chapters on just about every planet in the Central World Alliance."

"So... there's nowhere for me to go?" Kessa asked. "The Sisters are everywhere?"

"Maybe not," Tiberius said, looking at Xia.

"He's right," she agreed with a nod. "They *were* here, but if what Anthem told us is true, the Nihilist church has run the Sisterhood off of Stray."

"We are not yet sure that this new cult is any less dangerous," Maeve objected. "What did they do to the Sisters here? Would Kessa be in danger from them?"

"I'm not exactly an active member," Kessa said.

Maeve balanced her fork between her fingers, as if weighing the Dailon girl's words on it. "That may not matter, if there is a quarrel between the Church of Nihil and the Sisterhood. Your past could be enough to damn you."

Kessa stopped eating and her blue skin paled a shade. "Really?"

"Maybe..." Xia answered. "But maybe not. We just don't have enough information yet."

"We missed the Nihilist's sermon last night, but there should be another one soon," Tiberius said. "Some of us should go get a feel for these hawks, see if they're going to be a problem."

"I'll go," Xia offered.

"So will I," Maeve said.

Tiberius pointed to Gripper. "Will you be finished with those repairs soon?"

"If it means I get some time on the planet, I can have the SL engine singing the Prian anthem by tonight," Gripper answered with a broad grin. "I've never been to Gharib!"

"A functional air recyc' system will be fine," Tiberius told him. "Then you can go with Maeve and Xia. Duaal, I want you here on the ship with me."

"What? Why?" Duaal asked, sitting up in his seat.

"In case Coldhand comes back."

"You want me around so you can win the next fight with him?" Duaal asked, scowling. "Or so I'm close by if you have to run?"

"That's enough, Duaal," Tiberius said.

"Yes, captain," the mage answered sullenly.

Kessa looked like she wanted to say something.

Xia gave her a nod. "What is it?"

"Um, what about Vyron?" Kessa asked. "We still need to get him, somehow."

"I'd forgotten about your man," Tiberius confessed.

But Maeve suddenly grinned at Kessa. There was a predatory glint in her gray eyes that made Xia nervous.

"If I remember the details of your story correctly, Vyron belongs to a rival criminal organization," Maeve said. "The... Steelskins? Tell me what you know of them and I believe that I can bring Vyron right to us."

[12]

HUNTER

"The rainbow in the sky pales in comparison to the one in my hand on payday."

- ESCAI KANNO, ACTOR (173 PA)

"Prian police! Freeze!"

The rest of the criminals fled into the night, but the man in the black cloak stood his ground. Logan couldn't make out his face, but the shadowed hood turned toward him. The man's movements were loose and easy, utterly unconcerned. Even faced with two armed Prian officers, he wasn't frightened.

This man didn't fear death. He feared nothing.

Next to Logan, Lieutenant Zachary Reginald gestured with three fingers pointed off to his left. Flank him. *Logan nodded to his partner and began circling slowly as Reginald whistled to Maria. The fan-tailed falcon launched herself from Reginald's gauntlet and circled high through the clear, cold Prian night.*

The man in the cloak watched Reginald's bird. He pushed back his hood, finally revealing his face and Logan was almost disappointed. They knew him only as the Emberguard, but that was a title, not a name.

With as terrible a reputation as he had built on Prianus, Logan had been sure they were facing some kind of vengeful fairy or unknown alien... But he was only a human man, like Logan and Reginald. He had the dark stripes across his cheeks and curly green hair of a Mirran. Not from Prianus, then, but why would he come to their remote planet just to kill people...?

There was a steely hiss as the Emberguard drew a long nanosword from under his black cloak, briefly revealing the red robes he wore beneath. Logan wondered if those coal-colored robes were the source of the Emberguard's name.

"Put away your weapon and stand down!" Reginald shouted.

The Mirran laughed and Logan shuddered at the sound.

"Who do you think you are to deny me?" the Emberguard asked. "I am the hand of nothingness itself! I fear no man, for I have been enlightened. I am the last cinder of destruction before the blaze that will be true oblivion. I fear no man, no pain, no death! But you, too, will find peace when I rip the life from you."

"Take him," Reginald said.

Logan brought up his Talon and aimed. The Emberguard raised his sword. Smiling and laughing, he charged into battle.

Coldhand woke in a tangle of sheets, shivering despite the sweat pouring down the back of his neck. He raked cybernetic fingers through his damp blond hair and sat up carefully in the tiny bunk. Coldhand couldn't remember his dream – but he didn't have to. It was always the same one. And after five years of reruns, it was growing old. But Logan's computer-regulated heartbeat remained steady and slow, unchanged by his nightmare.

His bunkroom was small, even more claustrophobically close than the one Xia had locked him in aboard the Blue Phoenix. Fare aboard the Temptation was expensive – paid in full up front to the one-eyed human captain – but that was the cost of discretion, not lavish accommodations.

There was a quiet knock at the door.

"Come in," Coldhand said, just loud enough to be heard in the corridor outside.

A thin Ixthian man entered, carrying a bulging medical bag, and called up the lights. He gave Coldhand a studied smile, but his antennae twitched uncomfortably and his eyes glittered red. No one aboard the Temptation asked the bounty hunter his name – they all knew it, and knew to shut up unless they wanted to be his next target. The Ixthian unwound the bandages around Coldhand's right shoulder, inspecting the bullet wound beneath. He probed it gently.

"Does that hurt?" he asked.

"No," Coldhand answered.

The doctor opened up his bag and pulled out a small sensor. He flicked it on and scanned the wound.

"It looks like I managed to get the entire bullet out," he said in a slightly unsteady voice. "The fracture is reweaving just fine."

"How long?"

"Five more days until you can use the arm freely. Faster if you'd let me give you a nanite injection."

"No machines," Coldhand said.

The doctor's colorful eyes were drawn inexorably back down to the cybernetics. The illonium was still twisted and blackened from Tiberius' bullet. Coldhand followed his gaze.

"No *more* machines," he corrected.

"I don't have the facilities here, but once we arrive on Axis, if I could get a redprint to one of the vats, I could take care of..." the doctor began, gesturing gingerly at Coldhand's cybernetics, but the hunter frowned. The Ixthians sighed. "Jumo will come by soon to take a look at it."

His work done, the doctor hastily retreated. Coldhand's body would heal with time, but he needed the Temptation's mechanic to see to his cybernetic hand. Machines didn't heal. He tried to close the metal fingers, but only two of them would respond.

Another man might have been angry. Tiberius was doubtlessly furious about their battle, about the injuries to himself, to his ship and to his pride. The repairs were costing Coldhand high color, too, money that would not hold out forever. He *should* have been angry, but the bounty hunter only noted the rising cost of his hunt and calculated whether he had spent more cenmarks hunting Maeve than he would make from her bounty. Even after a year of chasing her, the expenses were still considerably less than the reward for her live capture.

He would continue the hunt.

Coldhand mentally replayed the fight against Tiberius. Perhaps his tactics had been unwise. The hawk had to be Tiberius' beloved Orphia, and she was dangerous. Tiberius was prone to rage and impulsive decisions, but Orphia wasn't. She was more like Coldhand – a creature of sharp hunter's instinct and no remorse. Coldhand should have shot the bird, not just called her off.

He wouldn't make that mistake again. Coldhand pulled his shirt back on over his bandaged shoulder. The torn muscles strained with even that simple task, but Coldhand finished dressing without flinching.

Tiberius knew that Coldhand had been a Prian police officer back home. Before, the captain of the Blue Phoenix had been entirely reactive, always favoring running away over fighting. But now the fight was personal. The man would stand and bare his talons when he should turn and fly.

That would make tracking Maeve easier. She couldn't fly away as easily if her angry captain was spoiling for another fight. Coldhand's Raptor was a short-range vessel and pushing it all across Alliance space in search of his mark had cost him a lot of color in maintenance. Perhaps Tiberius' involvement would change that... But it would also complicate the fight. A man in retreat only fired shots enough to cover his escape, but now Tiberius would shoot to kill.

Coldhand weighed his options and chances, then shrugged. He could handle the crew of the Blue Phoenix if their captain's personal vendetta put them between Coldhand and his prey. Maybe it would even be... exciting.

There was another knock on the bunkroom door, not the quiet rapping of the Ixthian doctor, but a hard banging on the fibersteel.

"Come in," Coldhand said.

Jumo entered with a few tools in his brown-furred paws. The Lyran was short and wide, like most of his race, with golden eyes and sharp, sensitive ears. The Temptation's mechanic held a cigar clenched between his long teeth.

"You wanted to see me?" Jumo asked.

"Yes," Coldhand answered.

He held out his cybernetic hand. The Lyran engineer examined it and gingerly probed the damage.

"What the hells did you do?" Jumo asked. "This is grade five shielding. How'd you blast it open like this?"

Coldhand said nothing. Jumo furrowed his furry brow, but didn't press the issue. He shined a small light into the twisted rent in the bounty hunter's forearm, leaning this way and that to peer at the cybernetics' inner workings. Chomping on his cigar and grumbling, Jumo turned on and calibrated a scanner not so different than the one used by the Ixthian doctor. He tapped a few buttons, the display flashing amber numbers and symbols.

"Everything's still carrying a signal," Jumo said. "At least, I think that's what this damned piece of fairy drop is telling me. But some of the wiring got clipped. It'll need to be replaced."

"Can you do it?"

"I have a few spare spools for the micro null-generators on the Temptation's weapons that should work. It's not ideal, but no one makes this kind of thing anymore," the Lyran said, pulling the cigar from his muzzle and gesturing with the smoldering tip at Coldhand's cybernetics. "I don't have any illonium shielding that's thin enough and I don't keep particle planers onboard. I can do it by hand, but it'll be a rig job. Ugly, but functional."

"Fine."

"And it's going to be expensive," Jumo warned.

Coldhand nodded.

"I'll have the wire tested and ready in a few hours."

The wolfin engineer gathered up his tools and headed out the door. Three hours later, just as promised, Jumo called to tell the bounty hunter that everything was prepared. Coldhand made his way through the ship to the Lyran's workshop, set up in one corner of the engine room. The Temptation was a cargo vessel, though it was much larger than Tiberius Myles' little bird. But like the Blue Phoenix, the corridors were patched and closed in by extensive modifications.

After overwriting Tiberius' old book with his own message and fighting his way past the other Prian, Coldhand had searched the Gharib landing crescent for a ship to return him to Axis. With its large gun turrets, the Temptation had caught his eye. Contrary to the shows, most ships – including the Blue Phoenix – didn't carry heavy weaponry. Except, of course, for pirate vessels and the warships of the CWA Armed Forces. Crews engaged in legal cargo transportation rarely mounted guns on their craft. It made them look dangerously like the former and drew too much attention from the latter.

Warships saw a lot more action than the average freight hauler, injuries and damage as a result that required skilled doctors and mechanics to mend. It was those assets the hunter was willing to pay for, more than spacious quarters or fine meals. CWAAF ships weren't for hire, so Coldhand had bought passage on a pirate ship heading back to Axis.

The pirates that Coldhand passed in the corridors were largely made up of hulking, muscular specimens of their assorted races. Each of them radiated a sense of violence and confidence, but they all watched the bounty hunter pass in tense silence. Was Coldhand just a passenger? Or was he on the hunt?

Jumo's cramped workshop was hazy with smoke. Every counter, table and stool was covered in a jumble of tools and ashtrays, all full with cigar stubs. He must have disabled smoke detectors, which was a bad idea in an engine room. The Lyran swept the mess from a short cha-gri and pulled the chair over next to a low workbench.

"Have a seat," he said.

Coldhand sat and rested his broken cybernetic hand on the table. Jumo snuffed out his cigar and lit a new one before getting to work. It took the Lyran half an hour to find the seams of the illonium casing on the cybernetics and then pry them loose, exposing the packed bundles of circuitry, sensors and servos inside. Jumo carefully disconnected the damaged wiring and removed it. He inspected the twisted, blackened ends.

"Damn. These wires are basically your nerves," Jumo said "Did it hurt when the casing got blown open like this?"

"No."

Jumo shuddered and returned to the task at hand. He measured and cut new wires, then pinned and tabbed the ends. After pulling a magnifier over Coldhand's exposed circuitry, the mechanic fitted each of the replacements into their tiny ports. Jumo jerked back his paw with a pained yelp as a bad connection shocked his fingers.

"This thing was prefabricated," the Lyran complained. "It was never meant to have parts replaced, so nothing's marked. I'll do my best, though."

"Do that."

The smell of singed fur was almost as thick as cigar smoke by the time Jumo finished refitting the forty-three wires that Tiberius' bullet had damaged. He replaced the illonium casing as best he could, holding the heavy alloy in place with a few temporary welds, and reminded the human that he could only properly replace the shielding on Axis or some other industrialized world.

Coldhand flexed and curled his fingers experimentally. Each of them responded to his nervous system, clicking flatly against each other. He left the workshop without thanking Jumo.

The Temptation was equipped with better SL engines than those on the Blue Phoenix and made the journey from Stray to Axis in only five days. The pirate ship was a fast one, Coldhand noted with satisfaction. Little but pure data transmissions traveled faster.

Coldhand spent most of the time in his quarters. He had no desire to mingle with the pirates and no need for company. The Ixthian doctor returned three times to inspect his patient's progress, pronouncing Coldhand healed after four days.

Beside contact with the medic, Coldhand made only one effort to interact with anyone onboard the Temptation. He followed the yellow stripe painted on the wall of the hallways, marked *mess hall* in stenciled Aver.

It was early in the day and the mess was nearly empty. A pair of burly humans arm-wrestled in one corner, stopping to watch Coldhand as he entered. The bounty hunter dismissed the two sweaty men with a glance. They wouldn't have what he wanted. He raked the room with icy blue eyes. A group of assorted races clustered around another table, watching a svelte Mirran woman with a pale mask of golden stripes on her face performing some sleight of hand for the amusement of her fellows. They laughed and applauded her efforts. Coldhand moved on.

A gaunt human man sat alone in the back of the mess, a small computer open on the table in front of him. The sleeves of his faded black jumpsuit were pulled down low over his arms, but the dark tracery of the man's veins was still visible along his neck. His curly brown hair had been shaved off not long ago, but not maintained and now rose from his scalp in unkempt tangles.

Coldhand took the chair across the table and the man sat bolt upright, staring.

"Whoa, hey! I didn't do nothing," he protested.

The other pirates heard the panic in their crewmate's voice and turned to watch, but none of them made a move to stop Coldhand.

"God, don't kill me," the pirate said. "Don't rip my heart out!"

Coldhand raised one eyebrow, then darted his cybernetic hand out to grab the other man's bony wrist. He pushed up the sleeve to the elbow. The pirate's thin arms were lined with dark needle runs and clumsy punctures in his waxy skin. His eyes were wide, dilated unnaturally.

"What kind of chems are you on?" Coldhand asked.

"What?" the skinny human squealed. "I ain't taken nothing...!"

"What kind?" Coldhand asked again.

The pirate jerked and shook in Coldhand's grip, not daring to attempt an escape but unable to keep his body still. The air of the Temptation's mess hall was taut, every eye on Coldhand and the man he interrogated.

"Cedrophin," the pirate answered at last.

"How much do you have?" Coldhand asked.

"I uh..."

The man reached into the breast pocket of his jumpsuit with his free hand and fumbled out a pair of vials. They clattered off the open computer and rolled in a tight crescent on the tabletop. Each was tiny, no longer than Coldhand's smallest finger. The glass had deep grooves on each side – guide tracks for insertion into a syringe or pneumatic injector.

"I'll take both."

"Yeah, yeah," the pirate said, nodding far too emphatically. "Of course. They're all yours."

Coldhand picked up the cedrophin in his right hand and released the other man. He fished two orange cenmark chips from his pocket and they slid for a mechanical heartbeat in his illonium fingers before Coldhand dropped them to the tabletop. The pirate stared at the money as though it might bite him.

"I'm a bounty hunter, not a thief," Coldhand said.

He pocketed the two vials and left the Temptation's mess hall. Everyone in the room watched him go, but no one stopped him.

Once back inside his rented quarters, Coldhand fitted the first ampoule of cedrophin into a folding injector. He cinched a black strap around his arm above the seam where flesh met metal, and waited. Coldhand didn't bother clenching his fist or otherwise working the muscle to make the veins more visible, as Maeve had on the streets of Axis. It would have been pointless, anyway. Coldhand's organic muscles ended at the elbow. There was nothing but metal and wires to react to his balled fist.

So Coldhand waited. When the tourniquet finally revealed the blue lines of his veins, Coldhand checked the seal on the vial. It was intact. He didn't tap the syringe and nudge the plunger. That kind of thing was for the shows. A century ago, it might have been useful to remove air from the needle and avoid an embolism, but now even the cheapest chems came in vacuum-sealed packaging that made such practices obsolete.

Coldhand put the needle against his arm and pushed, watching the point tear a tiny hole into his skin. The pain was hollow and distant. Coldhand emptied the stimulant into his vein and waited. Nothing. He loaded up the second vial of cedrophin and injected it.

Still nothing.

Coldhand lay down on his narrow bunk and stared up at the blank fibersteel ceiling. The double dose of cedrophin would have most species – even the resilient Hadrians and Lyrans – crawling up the walls. Coldhand touched his right hand to his chest.

He felt his mechanical heart beating rhythmically inside. It would never race with excitement, even chemically induced. Only exertion would speed Coldhand's pulse, and only as much as was strictly physiologically necessary.

The cybernetic organ was already filtering the toxins from his blood, encapsulating them in lipids for safe excretion. Within an hour, Coldhand would just piss out a hundred cenmarks worth of drugs. He would never get sick, never get drunk, never get high off chems.

Twenty percent. Only twenty percent.

The Temptation set down on Axis late the next day. Unwilling to attract unwanted attention, the captain landed her ship in a private Level Two bay. She nodded to Coldhand as he disembarked and offered him no parting comment or well wishes.

An hour's brisk walk brought Coldhand out of the private bays and into the busy Axis streets. He found a public computer terminal with a short line. Looking back over their shoulders at him, three humans and a chubby Dailon decided that their business could wait and left.

Coldhand fed a silver chip of change into the computer and the monitor flickered to life. It displayed the blue and white Starwind logo just long enough to make a subliminal impression and then brought up an Axis mainstream search screen. Coldhand keyed up the records for his Raptor, grounded on Level One, and frowned. His unexpected trip to Stray and back had left his fighter moored longer than expected. The unconcerned monitor informed Coldhand that he owed almost three hundred cenmarks in fees and the Raptor was impounded pending payment.

He brought up his financial accounts. They were all overdrawn. Coldhand had spent most of his money paying for his fare on the Temptation. The color in his pockets was all he had left, and even that was barely enough to cover a few meals and a place to stay. He drummed his cybernetic fingers on the edge of the terminal's keyboard, thinking. The computer flashed up a red-lettered warning, telling the bounty hunter that his credit was about to run out. He gave the machine another silver cenmark.

Coldhand needed work. Almost a year of exclusively chasing Maeve had paid nothing so far and he had spent his entire savings. Coldhand had to find a bounty, a short-term job that would pay the bills until he brought down his Arcadian mark. But with his Raptor grounded, he couldn't take any off-world bounties.

He needed something local, a job somewhere here on Axis that didn't require access to a starship. Coldhand pulled up a third screen – this one branded across the top with the blue, white and green of the Central World Alliance – and scanned quickly through the CWA bounty listing.

It was short, as usual. The Alliance had enough trained soldiers and firepower to bring in its own criminals. Coldhand keyed up another listing, bounties subject to CWA approval, but posted by individual planets or private parties.

A handful of notices caught his attention: Zoen Temple, wanted on Giadeen for illegal chemical shipping; Titania, an Arcadian who failed to appear in court on Kahl for questioning related to a pair of particularly gruesome murders; Toku Mikigawa, a human member of the Sisterhood wanted for five counts of rape on Mir. Interesting, but nothing close enough for Coldhand to chase down without his ship.

Instinctively, Coldhand began swiping past the Stray listing. The ratty fringe world made good money harboring the kind of people that often had bounties on their heads. It didn't pay to hire hunters to kill or arrest their own patrons. Sometimes a personal bounty would crop up on Stray, but usually for some petty crime or vendetta that simply didn't interest Coldhand. This time, however, one listing made him hit a key to freeze the screen and read the details.

The bounty was for a Dailon man by the name of Vyron Fethru. It was posted from Stray, but the mark was here on Axis.

The client gave no name, only a disposable com frequency to contact once Vyron was brought to Stray.

Vyron was wanted for gang-related crimes on Axis, listed as the frontman for the group. He and his gang were under suspicion for several killings, kidnappings and high-color chem running. Vyron was to be taken alive only, unharmed, and brought intact to Stray. His bounty, however, was to be paid out of an Axis account. The amount was an adequate four hundred cenmarks to be delivered upon capture, confirmed by genetic scan. The bounty promised another four hundred on Vyron's delivery to Gharib.

Eight hundred cenmarks. Coldhand pondered the posting. The initial payment would be enough to get his bird off the ground and back into the sky, where it belonged. The hundred left over would cover the cost of repairing his cybernetic casing. Four hundred color would pay for hunting Maeve Cavainna for another month.

Coldhand checked the date on the listing. It was two days old. That was ample time for any number of other hunters to see the posting and begin tracking down Vyron Fethru. Bounty hunting wasn't a popular occupation, but Axis was the most densely populated planet in the core. At least a dozen hunters had surely started on the job by now. He would have to move quickly to reach Vyron first.

[13]

THE BLACK CATHEDRAL

"The cost of war is not measured in blood alone."

A week of food and mooring in Gharib bit deeply into Tiberius' funds, and Xia worried about it over meals. Most of that color would be needed to pay for Vyron when he was delivered to Stray according to the instructions of their anonymous bounty posting. The first payment alone would leave their accounts on Axis practically empty, Xia pointed out. Tiberius only shrugged at dinner each evening and asked if anyone knew when the next Church of Nihil sermon would be held.

One afternoon, Duaal finally nodded. "I hear around the bazaar that the pastor is back in Gharib tonight and going to give another speech."

Duaal had been venturing out to the city's central market every day – but usually came back with nothing – and Gripper wondered what he was up to out there. Whenever he returned to the Blue Phoenix, Duaal always seemed both relieved and frustrated.

Was he chasing a man? Maybe that Arcadian guy, Anthem? Or a woman...

Gripper could never predict who or what might catch Duaal's perpetually wandering eye. Alien mating rituals continued to baffle and exasperate the Arboran and Duaal's eclectic tastes didn't clarify matters one bit. It wasn't for lack of trying to understand... Gripper glanced sidelong at Xia, but then Tiberius demanded his attention again.

"Are you done with the recyc' repairs?" the captain asked.

"Days ago, Claws," Gripper answered. "Does that mean I can go outside and play? Oh please, may I?"

"This isn't a game," Tiberius said. "But you can go with Maeve and Xia tonight."

Gripper scratched his cheek with a massive claw, wondering if the Prian's sense of humor needed repairs, too, or if it had never been installed in the first place. Gripper glanced around the table and found Maeve watching him. Her expression was sad and angry, but distant. Whatever turned Maeve's eyes that stormy, it wasn't in there in the room with her.

Duaal wasn't laughing, either. Whoever sold humor packages, Gripper hoped they shipped in bulk.

But Kessa and Xia were both smiling at him. The Dailon gave Xia a knowing look, then dissolved into gales of laughter. At least *they* thought he was funny. Gripper smirked, flushed and got to work finishing his dinner.

Maeve, Xia and Gripper dressed in layers against the cold Stray night and made their way out of the landing crescent, into the city. The faded red sun slipped below the horizon as they left the jigsaw of ships and fueling pylons behind and joined the evening crowd of Gharib.

The two women had to stop frequently as Gripper stared in wonder around at the city. He had only been away from his home-world for about a year, and half of that time was spent on Kahl, learning the difference between a fern and an FMS relay. Gripper's first glimpses of Stray left him on fire with curiosity. Gharib was nothing like the structured bustle of Axis or the quiet shipyard colony of Merrid. He couldn't wait to see the entire galaxy...

"What's that?" Gripper asked, pointing to the front of a shop.

The storefront was dominated by a flickering hologram of a large insect, about as long as Gripper was tall. It was striped in delicate bands of brown and gold, with a slender stalk connecting a round thorax to a tapered abdomen with a huge, curved stinger. The wasp had six skeletal, triple-jointed legs and two incredibly long pairs of yellow-veined wings.

Best Wasp Traps in the Core, boasted the neon sign beneath.

"That's a Nnyth," Xia answered. "It's not actual size, of course. They're about twice that big, I think."

She looked to Maeve for confirmation, but the Arcadian was glaring at the sign.

"I've never actually seen one, you know," Gripper said, staring at the hologram rotating in the window. "Just amazing! And they can fly through space without a ship!"

"Nnyth traps? That is a brutality," Maeve snarled.

The other two gave her startled looks.

"But the wasps tear apart spaceships that get too close to their hive. Those ships have the right to defend themselves, don't they?" Gripper asked.

He tried to word his objection carefully. Though Maeve stood only about as high as his navel, she could frighten Gripper badly and often did.

"The Nnyth will only defend the Tower, and do not range far from their home," Maeve answered. "Merchants profit from the un-founded paranoia that the Nnyth will someday attack the Central

World Alliance. Traps like those are expensive and ultimately useless fear-mongering."

"The traps make those who live and work on the edge of the core – places like Stray – feel safe," Xia told Gripper more calmly. "The Rynn system, where the Nnyth Tower is located, is out on the end of one of the galactic arms. Ship captains who have something to prove claim to have made the trip, but most of them are probably lying. It's a long flight. A lot of things can and usually do go wrong. Except for Tiberius, I don't personally know anyone that's done it. Or who would want to."

"It was the work of centuries and great diplomacy for the White Kingdom to reach agreements with the Nnyth Tower," Maeve said. She stood next to Gripper at the window and pressed her small fingers against the glass. "The Nnyth are wise. But they are secretive, and slow to trust."

"Trust? You mean they're intelligent?" Gripper asked. "I thought they were just... bugs!"

Xia frowned at him and waved her own insectoid antennae. Gripper blushed for the second time and looked away.

"The Nnyth are the oldest and most skilled Waygate operators in all the worlds," Maeve said. The fury was suddenly gone from her voice. Instead, Gripper thought he heard longing. "If we had only forged a stronger alliance with the Tower, maybe they would have helped us when the Devourers came. Perhaps something of our kingdom could had survived."

"Um... what?" Gripper asked.

He was having a hard time following the fairy's swiftly changing moods, but Xia took his arm and whispered into Gripper's ear.

"Later," she said.

Gripper glanced back at Maeve as the fairy plodded along behind them and wondered what exactly Xia knew that he didn't. Whatever it was, it made Maeve so very sad. Gripper wanted to comfort her, but she was volatile and prickly. Trying to help Maeve was like playing with live wires. Gripper might find out something interesting, but he would more than likely get painfully zapped in the process.

They resumed walking through the dusty yellow city toward the Nihilist cathedral. But Gripper was still distracted by worrying about Maeve and bumped into someone. Two someones, actually – a couple walking hand in hand, Gripper realized. He was acutely aware of how much larger than the other species he was as the pair looked up at him, the streetlights revealing human faces. They both flinched and moved quickly on. Would he ever understand this place? Gripper suddenly missed the Blue Phoenix and wished he hadn't been so eager to join Maeve and Xia tonight.

Gripper barely felt Xia's hand on his arm, squeezing reassuringly. Ordinarily, any attention from the jewel-eyed woman would have made Gripper light-headed and warm. But he was far from home on Arborus, far from his people. Here, the ground was dizzyingly close, and the air was dry and choked with dust. Gripper fought down a wave of panic.

But the new worlds that he had discovered were full of wonders, Gripper reminded himself. They were inhabited by other species that had found and colonized dozens of other planets long before Gripper's arrival. And he was the first Arboran ever to travel off-world. Gripper was a brave explorer, he hoped, if not voluntarily.

By the time they were leaving Gharib's central market, Xia had let go of Gripper's arm. Maeve remained sullen and silent, but Gripper didn't seem inclined to question her anymore, erasing the need for Xia to lead him away. The Arboran was even taller than she was, and Xia had to admit to herself that it was hard for her to adjust. Ixthian males were much smaller than their female counterparts. Large men seemed so very... alien.

Xia looked across the market. Most of the vendors' stalls were closed, all dark and covered with charged sheets of plastic to repel the dust. But tonight, the marketplace was still alive with people, though only a few of the booths remained lit and open for business in the plunging temperature and rising indigo shadows. Most of them sold food, long coats and veils to those who had not thought to bring their own. A few customers hovered around the market stalls, but most of the crowd was making its way to the eastern edge of the plaza, where the cathedral of the Nihilists stood silhouetted starkly against the fading scarlet stains of light on the horizon like a looming giant.

The mood of the gathering was somber. As they followed the rest of the crowd, Xia estimated that about five hundred beings of all species filtered through the bazaar toward the cathedral. But in spite of their numbers, the audience was quiet. Xia's multifaceted eyes widened, whirling a deep, worried red as she and her companions neared the steps of the black church. She doubled her estimate to almost a thousand in forebodingly silent attendance.

At least half of the gathered throng were Arcadians. What were so many of the fairies doing here? They were crowded off to one side, Xia noted, the other species drawing away from the unseemly number of droop-winged Arcadians with disgust and superstitious fear. The dying sunlight painted the forest of rustling white feathers in bloody red.

"*Shae ina Shae!*" Maeve swore.

She pulled her hood further down over her face and tucked back a few strands of loose ebony hair. That mane of black identified Maeve as a princess of the Arcadians' ruling house. Why would she want to hide it?

"Smoke, is this an Arcadian church?" Gripper asked in a hushed voice, staring out across the rustling sea of wings.

"No," Maeve said, shaking her head. "At least... I do not think so. By all appearances, this place could be dedicated to the Nameless, our goddess of death. But none have dared raise a house to her in thousands of years. It is blasphemy."

"Besides, it's illegal to worship the rimworld gods," Xia pointed out. "The Union of Light had the Lyceum outlaw Arcadian temples a hundred years ago."

Maeve gave the looming cathedral a long look, so full of speculative hunger that it made Xia shudder. It might have been blasphemy to worship the Arcadian death goddess, but Maeve seemed to do it anyway.

Distance had disguised the cathedral's true size. It was massive, built all of black basalt and slate. Four needle-like steeples crowned the tall, blank walls. Each of the towers were inset with empty windows that made Xia think of old, open wounds; a dark, bloodless rending of dead flesh.

Xia squinted, trying to take advantage of the swiftly fading light. The entire cathedral looked crude and unfinished. Though most of the Nihilist church was built out of rough siltstone blocks, long stretches of wall were little more than patches of metal bolted haphazardly into place and hastily painted black. The dark rock wasn't fitted and left jagged, broken corners jutting out in all directions and covered in Stray's ubiquitous dust. Xia guessed that, for all its great size, the cathedral had been built quickly and could be torn down just as fast.

A broad set of uneven stairs led up to the gaping entrance of the Nihilist's church. Like the windows, it was open, with no doors or even a plastic static sheet to keep out the sand and dust. A patch of sooty orange light filtered out of the arch from the cathedral, illuminating a robed figure as it detached itself from the deep shadows inside.

The Nihilist that made its way into view appeared to be human, as far as Xia could tell. He was too broad of chest and shoulder to be an Ixthian, too tall to be Lyran, and he lacked the solid, planar build of a Dailon. In fact, he seemed hunched by age or disease, though it was hard to determine which. Like so many other citizens of Stray, the figure at the top of the steps was hooded and robed against the cold and dust. There was no marking of rank or status on his plain robes – just dusty black cloth.

"Listen," the robed Nihilist said in a rich, booming voice.

He raised his hands to the crowd. The man's strong, sonorous voice carried easily across the crowd without any visible means of amplification.

"Listen, you forgotten children of the stars," he said. "Listen, you forsaken exiles of the heartworlds and distant kingdoms. Hear me. I know that you feel alone and forsaken. And you are. The worlds of this universe are only unfeeling stones set to spin mindlessly in the void. The planet that birthed you cannot feel your pain, taste your tears or hear your prayers.

"Our evolution has bred into us the need to eat, to breathe and to breed. Afraid to learn the emptiness of our own existence, we have given myth and meaning to our needs. We eat in celebration, in companionship, to give some meaning and comfort to our base, animal needs. We expel breath in useless songs and prayers to a god who doesn't exist. We have named our rutting needs *love* and drive ourselves to destruction in its tender name. But lies cannot give our lives purpose."

Xia glanced sidelong at her two crewmates. Maeve was listening raptly to the Nihilist's smooth voice, her silver-gray eyes half closed. Gripper was paying attention, too, but his expression was troubled. The audience was silent and Xia shifted her weight uncomfortably.

"In our desperate loneliness, we reached up into the heavens," the Nihilist preacher said, gesturing up at the star-dusted sky overhead.

Stray had only a single moon, and the system's weak sun barely managed to illuminate Stray, let alone its satellite. The moon was a flat, colorless disk in the sky of Stray, outshone by the glittering suns of distant worlds.

"Perhaps we hoped to find our god, but we only found other lonely, hungry species: the five races of humanity, the Dailons, the Lyrans and the Ixthians. In time, we discovered the outer kingdoms, each floating alone in the cold void."

The robed man's words thrummed with almost palpable energy, an electric excitement as though he were making the discoveries instead of merely narrating them. He brought his hand down, closing it into a fist. Xia had to admit a grudging respect for anyone who could make hopelessness sound so captivating.

"We found power in the distant stars, but not answers. Because there were none to find. Though we searched the galaxy, we know no more than we did when we first raised our eyes to the heavens. There is no ignorance, for there is no meaning for us to discover or understand.

"And this struggle, clamoring across the sea of stars for food, for air and space to multiply, ultimately yields nothing. Death finds us all in the end. It finds us tired from a lifetime of ceaseless toil, pain and emptiness. Years of struggle and suffering... all for nothing."

The Nihilist's voice was gentle, like a loving father explaining a sad truth to the child on his knee. Xia felt the weight of thirty years of life like lead in her chest. She swayed, suddenly exhausted by the idea of another seventy stretching out ahead of her. Next to her, Gripper reached out to steady Xia.

"Are you alright?" he whispered.

Xia nodded and waved the Arboran off. Like most Ixthians, she had spent her existence protecting and perfecting life. It would take more than a single sermon to convince her that it was all in vain, but she *did* feel tired. How much harder it must be for Maeve and the hundreds of other homeless and hopeless Arcadians.

"The child who cries over her mother's body, dead that very night of starvation for the food she gave up to her daughter," said the Nihilist on the steps of the black cathedral, his arms open imploringly to the crowd. "The man who stares through the bars of his prison cell, tried for crimes he never committed and dreaming of the day he may return to his lover, unknowing that he has taken his own life in grief. The lost who cradles their father in their arms, knifed by a desperate thief for money he didn't have. They scream out for help, but no one comes. Their tale is that of every tormented soul that screams out in pain and begs for release. But is greeted only by silence.

"Yet there is an end to this pain. Reflect on my words, my children, and if a hot meal, prattling talk or a night in your lover's arms does not soothe you, return to me. I can show you another way. The doors of the Church of Nihil never close."

The Nihilist preacher bowed his head to the gathering, then turned and vanished once more into the crooked cathedral. There was no applause, no hissing or cheering, only a subdued hush.

Xia shook herself and patted Gripper's arm. The big Arboran glanced down at her.

"I... don't know if that told us anything useful," he said.

"Neither do I. Did you get something helpful, Maeve?"

Xia looked around. The crowd had begun to disperse, melting away into Gharib, but the Arcadian princess was already gone.

Maeve crouched on top of one of the cathedral's jagged black spires. The shingles were still hot under her bare feet from the heat of the day, but the nighttime chill was quickly leeching away the warmth. Her boots sat next to her, the dry cracks in the plastihide invisible in the darkness. Maeve pulled her knees up against her chest and wrapped her wings around herself.

The sky was full of Arcadians, all flying back into the city, many to sleep in alleyways and refuse piles. Some would return to cheap apartments and illegal squatters' camps. Maeve's vision blurred and she wiped her eyes with her sleeve.

How the great had fallen. The greatest. The Arcadians had been rulers and protectors of the other fairies for thousands of years, trusted and revered as knights and leaders. Under Cavain's guidance, they had left behind their rings of stone and built beautiful, glittering cities of glass. In time, the Arcadians coaxed other fairy races from their primitive dwellings to join them.

Dominion of their entire stellar system for ten thousand years. No coreworld nation had lasted for a third of that. Even the great Alliance was less than three centuries old. Maeve's father had lived longer than that. But now he was dead, and the White Kingdom was rubble while the rest of the galaxy... well, they didn't thrive, but they survived.

All we have left is death.

The nyads and dryads were gone. In the end, the Arcadians had failed to protect them. Only a handful of Maeve's people remained, perhaps a million across the worlds of the core. She watched the dregs of her race spread their wings and fly away into Gharib. But what of their queen? Maeve was the last of Cavain's blood, wasn't she? What did she owe her people now?

My mother promised me I would never be queen, Maeve remembered as she cried, honking without dignity into her dusty sleeve. *I was only a distant cousin to the throne. Mother swore it to me in the lily gardens of the Sua'ii Na. I was supposed to be nothing.*

And nothing I will become.

Maeve buried her face in her hands, shuddering with ragged, hiccuping sobs. The surviving Arcadians deserved a queen, but it could never be her. Maeve could only give them her death, and even that was long overdue. Maeve's com chirped and she choked down her tears.

"Yes?" she answered.

Xia's voice crackled on the other end of the channel. "Maeve, where are you? We need to get back to the Phoenix and report to Tiberius."

"I will meet you at the ship," Maeve told her. "Do not linger on my behalf."

"Are you alright?"

Maeve didn't answer. Only small knots of the Nihilist's audience remained, drifting slowly through the central market toward their homes. Perhaps half of those who lingered were Arcadian. Maeve pulled her boots back on, then jumped off the rooftop, spreading her wings to catch the turbulent evening air. The Arcadians were vagabonds. Vagabonds had no need for a queen, and she had more important things to worry about, like her own life.

When she was done talking to Maeve, Xia slipped her com into her pocket again. Gripper followed her through the thinning crowd filtering back into Gharib. They walked together in silence, mulling over the Nihilist's speech. He wondered why a church had chased out the Sisterhood, as Anthem had told Xia. In studying for his citizenship exam, Gripper remembered reading about religious wars. Centuries ago, the different faiths had fought one another for dominion of worlds.

Such things had been common in the early days of the CWA. Each of the founding worlds had several religions, warring constantly even before they encountered other species. The discovery of alien faiths had only served to add fuel to an already dangerous flame. The Sacred Temple of Creation had been one such religion, but Gripper couldn't remember the Church of Nihil anywhere on his study list. It must be new.

Thirty years of slaughter back and forth convinced the Central World Alliance that a unified church was vital to their survival. One that was lenient, accepting and could incorporate all other known religions. The result was the Union of Light, a vaguely monotheistic faith generally accepted by the worlds of the CWA.

Gripper watched Xia's shapely backside sway as she walked out ahead of him, then wrenched his eyes upward. The Ixthian was ticking something off on her long-fingered hands.

The Sisterhood was barely a religion anymore, wasn't it? Their priestesses were scattered and practices buried under decades of repression. Kessa hadn't even realized that her family group wasn't a gang, but a congregation.

Something was wrong with this picture. The Sisterhood that Kessa described was all tough, hard women. They wouldn't have given up their hold on the city without a fight.

"Hey, Silver?"

Xia hurried to catch up with Gripper. The stars were fewer and distant on the edge of the core, and shed little light across the city as they walked through it. Streetlamps arced over the walkways, but a thick layer of dust covered them and the lights didn't offer much more illumination than the stars.

"What exactly did that Arcadian guy say about the Nihilists and the Sisters?" Gripper asked.

Xia pursed her burnished lips, eyes narrowed as she struggled to remember. "Anthem told me that the Arcadian men stopped disappearing after the Church of Nihil opened up. They never ran into the Sisterhood again."

Gripper gave Xia a worried look. "We've been assuming that this is some sort of gang turf war, that these Nihilists sent the Sisters packing because they don't like troublemakers. But what if it's something else?"

"What are you talking about?"

"What if it was a religious war?" he asked. "Like in the old days? What if the Sisterhood didn't get chased off because they were another gang, but because they were a rival religion?"

"God, Gripper," said Xia. "I hope you're wrong."

The interior of the black cathedral was barren, but it wasn't empty. There was a little bit of light, provided by a few small lamps with filaments burned down to thin, starved orange lines that barely divided light and darkness. The floor was littered with piles of fallen debris from the cathedral's hasty construction. Nothing here was built to last.

Sitting atop one of the jagged heaps of stone and scraps, the master of the Nihilist order pulled back his hood and squinted into the shadows. The exertion of the evening's sermon had left a thin sheen of sweat on his pale forehead. He was an ancient human man, with short hair like yellowed ivory and sad lines etched deep into his face. Despite the translucent thinness of his time-worn skin, and the tremor of his long-fingered hands, the old man held himself with a subtle poise.

He had a cause, a reason. A great purpose.

In the corners or huddled against the rising evening breeze, the converts to his religion – if it could properly be called a religion – slept or spoke quietly to one another. Like their leader, they wore simple robes of a rough black weave. The clothes weren't comfortable or warm, but the discomforts of the body were useful, a reflection of the greater suffering of life.

A slender figure in white glided across the dusty cathedral floor. Every voice in the church fell instantly silent as she approached its founder.

"Your congregation is devout, Gavriel," Xartasia said in lyrically accented Aver. The white-clad Arcadian had removed her veil and her lips were painted perfectly. "I am impressed."

"And their numbers grow every day," he answered.

For all of his years and frailty, Gavriel's voice remained strong and smooth, the voice that had swayed thousands all across Stray. Xartasia sat down lightly beside him, an exquisite snowy gown fanning out around her. Even in the ruddy lamplight, she was still breathtakingly lovely. The fairy woman wore intricate glass beads in her perfectly arranged ebony hair. They caught the orange light and glinted as Xartasia turned her head to look at the Nihilist.

"You have grown old," she said.

"And you haven't changed at all, princess," Gavriel replied.

"I have changed in more ways than you can imagine," Xartasia said. She looked around the cathedral and the dark horizon outside the windows. "You have chosen a new world, a place to begin our campaign once more."

"I needed to start over again, in a place that could receive my message. The Prians are too damned stubborn and I don't have the strength or time to fight every unbeliever from Prianus to Giadeen. But that's why I've summoned you, Xartasia. I could have done it, once. I need that power back."

Xartasia nodded. There was a rustle as she extended one of her long, soft white wings and then wrapped it intimately around the old Nihilist's shoulders.

"Have you told them?" Gavriel asked. "I've heard rumors about an Arcadian princess. Is that you?"

"Perhaps," said Xartasia. "But I have not called my people to me, no. If anyone recognized who I am, it is merely by accident. There is time yet before I am done and I have striven long in the shadows between worlds to my own ends."

"And what are those?"

"I desire an end to our suffering. You know that," Xartasia said. "This universe has wronged us. You have won the hearts of many to a cause we both hold dear. I believe that once more, we have much to offer one another."

"You're actually *offering* to help me this time."

It wasn't a question, but Gavriel was actually curious. The old human was far too proud to plead like a servile whelp. Even half a century ago, when they first met, Gavriel asked for Xartasia's help, but never begged. He needed the Arcadian princess' secrets, but he would never beg.

"I can aid you, old friend," Xartasia said. "But the skies to which I guide you are stormy indeed. You will need strength and I shall restore to you the power that I gave you once before. After all, it deserted you. When all is sung and done, I owe you the power that you earned. And it will be yours. But there are things we must do to prepare."

Gavriel's eyes burned hungrily. "Tell me."

$$[\ 14\ ]$$

MARK

"Laws are for those who cannot make their own moral judgment."

- ERU ILLITH, PYRAD REBEL (10,100 MA)

Scouring the first four levels of Axis yielded little. No one knew or cared about a Dailon named Vyron Fethru. The lower-level gangs and the dangers they posed were safely beneath the notice of the rich and powerful. CWAAF and the Axis police kept most people safe enough, so why concern themselves with the criminals? Those few who recognized Vyron's name did so only because other bounty hunters had been through before Coldhand. They could tell him just what they had told the other hunters – nothing.

Three long days into Coldhand's hunt, as he moved methodically down through the levels, he finally caught the first scent of his mark. Prompted by the barrel of a Talon-9 against her sunken cheek, a human chem dealer working a street corner admitted she recognized the name.

Vyron had been a local boy in a local gang. But his talents had moved him quickly up the ranks, and eventually, he was recruited – stolen – by another gang that called themselves the Steelskins.

The frightened human chem dealer stumbled over her own words in her rush to tell Coldhand what she knew in hopes of preserving her own decidedly unsteely skin. These Steelskins ran a much bigger and more dangerous game, one in which Vyron was now a key player.

An evening of research over a cheap protein pack and a rented computer terminal on Level Five yielded useful information on the Steelskins that corroborated the charges of Vyron's bounty posting. The gang was under frequent investigation for major counts of drug trafficking, numerous murders and kidnappings against their rivals. Individual members received sentences ranging from fines to life in CWA prisons, but the Axis police had made little progress with the Steelskins as a whole.

It was good to have something to back up the charges listed on the bounty, though. A search through the Axis police records had turned up no prior convictions or even accusations against Vyron. The gang might have run into the police, but Vyron himself had never been one of those indicted.

An archived news story – originally broadcast more than three weeks earlier – recounted a brutal shoot-out between the Steelskins and Axis police on Level Seven. Since then, the gang had been keeping quiet, probably increasing their numbers to make up for those killed in action. Small wonder the police hadn't been able to hunt them to ground yet... The lower levels of Axis were crowded and full of places to hide.

Coldhand frowned as the video clip ended and was replaced by a shiny, rotating Alliance News Network logo. If the Steelskins were in hiding, it would make his task far more difficult. The bounty hunter didn't have the time or inclination to sift through every filthy alleyway of the lower levels. Each moment he spent on Axis only let Maeve get further and further ahead of him.

There were better and more efficient ways. Coldhand would just have to convince Vyron to come to him. It was among the hunter's favored tactics, one that saved him valuable time yet allowed his marks to come at their leisure, full of unwarranted confidence. Easy pickings.

Coldhand brought up and enlarged the map from the shootout story. On a different world, one not covered entirely by a single overgrown city, it would have been in another province. The place was about seven hours away, if he took city transports and made good time. Coldhand tapped his illonium finger on the map, thinking. He knew someone near there.

He drained off the last of the bland but nutritious protein paste from the plastic tube and dropped it into a trash can. The terminal refunded him four cenmarks for the unused computer time, spitting the silver chips into a tray. Coldhand pocketed the change and went in search of a place to sleep.

The bounty hunter rented a small room from a sour-faced man. It was all cheap, sterile white, from the paint on the walls to the stiff sheets. Coldhand lay down on the narrow bed, not bothering to undress or remove his gun. The discomfort didn't bother him and there were more than a few rival hunters and enemies on Axis that wouldn't be above ambushing Logan Coldhand in his sleep. He pillowed his head on his right arm, his left lying motionless at his side. Coldhand counted the beats of his mechanical heart until he fell asleep. Two hundred eighty-eight before he tumbled down into unwelcome dreams.

The hospital gown was made of paper. It crinkled and crunched with every movement, but Logan wasn't listening. He cradled the guitar in his lap while the monitor beeped in time with the steady, even beats of his new artificial heart. Jess sat next to him, politely not looking at his maimed left arm. She rubbed Logan's back through the paper gown and smiled encouragingly.

"Try Bristler's Call," she suggested. "You know all the hawks at the office will want to hear it when you get back. It's one of their favorites now."

Logan closed mechanical fingers around the guitar's neck and pressed down on the strings, strumming with his whole hand. His real hand. But his illonium fingers slipped on the guitar's neck and the note went sour. Jess flinched, but Logan only stared blankly at the instrument. She kissed his cheek and stroked his hair. He knew she was trying not to cry, trying so hard to be strong for him.

But he just... didn't care.

"They're all asking about you, love," Jess said. "The service for Reginald is next week. I helped bring in some of the wood for the pyre. The captain was hoping you'd speak. They all miss Reg, but they are glad you're still alive. It's a miracle, really. I love you, Logan. I don't know what I would have done if... if..."

Logan wasn't listening to Jess. He tightened his grip on the guitar, pushing down on the strings. One of them snapped under the pressure with a weak, discordant twang and curled up around the neck like a dead thing. Logan dropped the guitar to the floor and Jess burst into tears.

The Rusty Frigate looked for all the worlds like an actual crashed ship. The exterior of the crumpled hull was artfully painted to look corroded since the ship had never been exposed to the elements long enough to rust. The nose – smashed and ripped open to form the entrance to the bar – lacked the sharp, ragged edges of a real crash. They had all been smoothed out, probably to avoid injuring drunkenly reeling customers.

At some point – years before Coldhand lost his hand and heart – the bar's owner had purchased the shell of a small cargo freighter. Rather than equipping it with expensive engines and life support systems, it had been meticulously cut and pulled back, the equipment inside rearranged to create a bar. The Rusty Frigate was a popular watering hole for those who had once made their living in the stars, but whom circumstance had grounded on Axis.

Coldhand went inside. A husky Lyran bouncer eyed his Talon, but thought better of trying to disarm the bounty hunter.

It was early in the afternoon and The Rusty Frigate was only half full of customers. Behind a row of dark, powered-down consoles that served as the bar stood Sarah Marcus, the bar's aging owner. Steely gray peppered the Prian woman's blonde hair and her once-curvaceous figure had many years ago become quite plump and matronly. Above her head, a display glowed with a selection of drinks and their prices. She scowled deeply at Coldhand as he approached.

"What the hells are you doing here?" Sarah asked. She reached under the bar, doubtlessly going for the big antique shotgun she kept there.

"I need some information, Marcus," Coldhand said.

"Why should I help you?"

Coldhand said nothing. Finally, Sarah sighed and turned over a glass, then filled it with a colorless liquor that smelled like it could melt lead.

"What kind of information?" Sarah asked.

Coldhand reached for the drink, but Sarah made a rude gesture at him. She finished it off herself in two large gulps, then refilled the glass. After a moment's thought, Sarah poured another and nudged it across the bar.

"I'm looking for a gang called the Steelskins," Coldhand said. "There was a shoot-out with the police a few weeks ago, and now they've gone into hiding."

"Yeah, those boys work a couple levels down from here," Sarah said. "They brawl with the other gangs from time to time, usually the Grinders and the Sisterhood. But they make their color on Vanora White. The Steelskins have a lab somewhere that produces the stuff."

"Do they sell the White themselves, or deal wholesale to someone else?" Coldhand asked.

He took the sharp-smelling drink in his cybernetic hand, the metal of his fingers clanking loudly against the glass. Sarah winced at the sound.

"The Steelskins deal their own White," she said. "Guess they don't want to cut in a middleman. You going to drink that or let me talk it to death?"

Coldhand stared at his drink. Light shone through the glass.

"Twenty percent," he said to himself.

"What? It's on the house. As always, you damnable robot."

Sarah thought he was talking about paying for the drink. Coldhand was silent. His failure with the cedrophin didn't inspire him to try again so soon. Strong drinks, good chems, beautiful women… All of it was pointless.

"Well, no reason to let it go to waste," Sarah said. She reached out and took the glass, slipping it easily from the bounty hunter's cybernetic fingers. The stout bartender threw back the shot and swallowed hard.

"The man I need is named Vyron Fethru. Do you know him?" Coldhand asked.

"Sure. Vyron's their salesman. A smooth-talking Dailon," Sarah answered. "A hawk, I think, but it can be difficult to tell with them. Knows how to cut a deal, that one."

Coldhand nodded. Sarah had given him enough information to hunt his mark to ground and take him. Without thanking her, Coldhand turned away and strode out of The Rusty Frigate.

Sarah watched the hunter leave, still holding his glass. The dregs of kyn were bright at the bottom, clear as the starlight back home. Sarah sighed and tried to relax. It had been four years since she first met Logan Coldhand, and it had never gotten any easier to deal with the ice-hearted young hunter. Even now, he always managed to give her a bad case of jitters.

Afterward, Sarah berated her bouncer for letting the obviously armed Logan Coldhand into the bar and threatened to replace the retired pounceball player if he couldn't handle the job. In spite of all he had done for her, Coldhand was a dangerous man and she prayed that he would never walk into The Rusty Frigate again.

Had it really been four years? It seemed like so much less. Four years since Coldhand had hunted down her husband's killer, the man who had knifed her beloved hawk over a cheap drink. Sarah traced her fingers over the polished surface of the bar she and Durwin had built together. She knew every nick and scratch, every dent Durwin put in the thing. God, how he had loved the Frigate.

But love wasn't money. Fifty cenmarks was all Sarah could offer as a bounty for her husband's killer, not even enough to pay for recharging the batteries of Coldhand's gun. The hunter had taken the single orange chip without complaint, though, informing her in that cold voice that Durwin's murderer was dead and his body in the custody of the Axis police.

Sarah still remembered the tears of gratitude and fumbling for the words to thank him. The young man offered no comfort, pulling away from her weeping embrace with his reward in hand and stalking away without saying another word.

The next day, Coldhand made his way down to Level Nine, pausing in his descent long enough to spend some of his dwindling color on some new clothes. Despite the neutral temperature of the environmentally controlled city, he bought a large coat and full gloves, effectively hiding his cybernetic hand when he pulled them on. No one would recognize Coldhand's face. It was his namesake metal limb that might be recognized, but the hem of the coat reached his knees, concealing his Talon.

By early afternoon, Coldhand had spoken to almost every chem dealer in that part of Level Nine. From each one, he tried to buy fifty vials of Vanora White, far more than any of them kept in stock. About the time that Coldhand's stomach was growling in protest of a second neglected meal – having missed breakfast already – he finally found what he needed. For the last of Coldhand's money, the chemical vendor sold him two vials of White.

"I could put you in contact with someone who can sell you the rest of it."

The dealer was an Axial man with mismatched eyes. One green and one brown, and both focused on Coldhand.

"Down here, only the Steelskins have that much White," he told the bounty hunter. "I could probably get thirty vials from north side in about a week for cheaper, but you're in a hurry. You've got better things to do than wait around, right? Meet me here tonight and I'll have a contact for you."

Coldhand was waiting for the odd-eyed chem dealer later that evening. The man was smirking and rubbing a pair of grubby white cenmark chips together between his fingers. A finder's fee from the Steelskins for bringing in a new customer, no doubt.

"Tomorrow morning," he said. "The Steelskins will send their man here at eight with the goods. A Dailon fellow called Vyron."

"Will you be here?" Coldhand asked.

He would need to know how many combatants to prepare for if things came down to a fight, but the dealer misinterpreted and gave Coldhand a slick smile.

"I've got me some business on the other side of Nine," he said, patting Coldhand on the shoulder companionably. "But don't be nervous. As long as you have the color to pay, you've got nothing to be afraid of."

"Will Vyron bring... friends?" Coldhand tried to sound worried.

He wasn't a skilled actor, but the pause in his question was enough to convince the other man.

"The Steelskins usually send Vyron with a couple of their own for muscle these days," he said, nodding. "Vyron used to deal alone, but I hear he got caught a level down by another gang. They had a Nnyth of a time getting him back."

"I'm surprised they went after him," Coldhand admitted.

"Count me in on that. But Vyron's a damned sweet talker. I guess they didn't want to have to replace him. Be here in the morning with the color and they'll have your White."

Coldhand thanked the other human curtly and left. He was out of money, but it didn't matter anymore. He had what he needed. Once out of sight of the empty fueling station, Coldhand tossed the two vials of Vanora White he had purchased into a rusty trash can. He had no use for a depressant that would only deaden his already artificial nerves. If it did anything at all.

Late that night, when the lights in the distant ceiling of Level Nine had dimmed to a faint approximation of starlight, Coldhand returned to the empty station. He prowled silently through the dark streets, slipping past the vagrants slumbering in doorways without waking them. The chemical dealer was gone, probably gone home to an apartment that far outstripped the homes of his customers. Coldhand suspected that he had stepped over several of those customers as they snored on the sidewalks.

He had hoped that Vyron would come alone tomorrow. It would have made Coldhand's job easier, but the Steelskins apparently deemed his mark a valuable member of their organization. Anyone sent along with Vyron would fight hard to defend the Dailon.

Coldhand examined the abandoned fueling station for hiding places or cover that his opponents might use. The four freestanding fuel pumps were flimsy, the dispensing mechanisms covered only in thin aluminum siding. They were long since decommissioned and wouldn't present a volatile hazard.

Coldhand checked the door to the office. It was boarded over and closed with a heavy padlock. The lock showed signs of violence as Coldhand angled it in the artificial twilight, but hadn't been broken. Circling the small building, he found the same treatment on the rear entry and all of the windows.

Nothing here could be used to much advantage by either side, Coldhand decided. He could take the high ground against Vyron and his companions, but a fire-fight would make it harder to catch the Dailon man. Stuck on the rooftop, he would be irrecoverably behind if his mark ran. Coldhand carried only his Talon-9 and he didn't have the time or color to get his hands on something less lethal. No, despite the disadvantages, Coldhand needed to be on the ground to capture Vyron intact.

He pulled his com off the gun belt around his waist. It had been left clipped to the leather when Xia had disarmed him aboard the Blue Phoenix, recovered when the bounty hunter made his escape. The blocky green letters there blinked 2:38. He still had hours to wait until Vyron showed up.

Coldhand walked a short distance away until he found a recessed doorway, the entrance to a flooring store long since driven out of business. The sign was gone, leaving an only slightly paler smear on the building's façade where it had been. The windows were filthy, inside and out, making it impossible to look through. Coldhand sat down in the niche, positioning himself so that he could still watch the empty station. He pulled up the collar of his coat and leaned back. No one would be able to discern him from the countless local vagrants.

Nights in the lower levels of Axis were timeless, a single, unchanging gray moment stretched from the planet's dusk until dawn. Coldhand looked up. There was no mistaking the ceiling of Level Nine for a sky. The daylights were set at regular intervals to create a predictable, geometric net of dim lights that were nothing like the sea of stars that shone over Level One.

From the first time he saw it, Coldhand had found the glittering sky of the core almost claustrophobic. It was so different than the sparse, diamond-studded black of Prianus; more like some cosmic giant had upended an entire jewelry store over his head. The stars would have been beautiful, Coldhand thought, if he could appreciate beauty at all. But he much preferred the muted lower levels with their pale mimicry, lights dimmed down to twenty percent.

Coldhand waited for the unchanging night to end.

Vyron and the other Steelskins arrived early. They walked past Coldhand's hiding place without glancing down. Vyron carried a metal briefcase scratched all across the ribbed sides. The Dailon was tall and lean, with deep sapphire skin and long, glossy black hair worn in a braid. Vyron's eyes were the same pure obsidian as the rest of his race, but they had a bright, nervous shine to them. They were difficult to read, but Coldhand thought that the Steelskins' frontman wasn't as confident as he should have been.

Vyron glanced back often at his three companions. All four wore denims and shirts in varying shades of the black and gray that seemed to be the Steelskin colors. Two of Vyron's associates were huge, at least half Hadrian. They both towered nearly as tall as Vyron, with dark skin and pale eyes. At their waists, half covered by the hems of their shirts, each carried a holstered laser pistol with tape covering the power indicators.

Those lights were probably flashing orange or red, Coldhand guessed. The gang's weapon resources would have been taxed to their limit by the recent shoot-out with the Axis police. Leaving the lights uncovered would warn their targets as much as their owners that the precious power cells were running low. But with those indicators covered, the bounty hunter couldn't count how many shots each had left.

Walking well behind the other three, the last Steelskin was an Arcadian. He had blond hair shaved close to his scalp and the point of his right ear was clipped off. The fairy man wore a long gray coat, slit high up the back to accommodate his wings. Half-concealed underneath, Coldhand saw a glitter that reflected the artificial sunlight in a hundred tiny rainbows.

Glass.

He would have to be careful of the Arcadian, Coldhand decided. A year chasing Maeve had taught him the dangers of their strange glass weapons. They were archaic compared to laser and nanotechnologies, but were wickedly sharp and very nearly unbreakable. Maeve had come close to gutting him on several occasions with her spear.

Coldhand waited until the four Steelskins had taken up positions at the abandoned fueling depot, all standing around an empty pump. Coldhand crept closer, slipping his Talon free and turned off the safety. The two humans leaned on the derelict pump, boasting and telling stories. Vyron seemed distracted and didn't answer.

Relegated to the only real work to be done for the moment, the Arcadian Steelskin stood at the corner and watched the street for their promised customer. Coldhand circled to the far side, behind the fairy. As the bounty hunter closed, one of the Hadrian men was thumping Vyron on the shoulder.

"Relax, Vy. When we're done here, we'll send the bird–" he said, jabbing a finger toward the Arcadian. "–back to Jainna with the color and then we'll take you out for a drink. You need to unwind."

"You deserve it, Vy," the other Steelskin agreed. "You've been flat ever since the Sisters."

Vyron shrugged noncommittally and craned his head from side to side, searching for his customer with large black eyes. He spotted Coldhand approaching and smiled until he saw the gun in the bounty hunter's hand. The Dailon didn't have a chance to warn his companions before the shriek of laserfire raised the alarm for him.

Coldhand's first shot – fired as he came around the corner of the boarded up office – caught the nearest Hadrian right in the knee. He had been leaning against the pump, but now without half of his support, the man tumbled to the ground. His skull impacted the pavement hard enough to make his eggshell white eyes roll back in his head.

The second human shouted in surprised rage, whirling on the threat as he drew his own gun. Vyron backed away and held up the case of White like a shield. His dark eyes were wide with terror. In an instant, the Arcadian was in the air, beating his wings in a frenzy to gain altitude and yanking a pair of glass daggers from under his coat. Coldhand pulled back behind the corner of the empty station as the remaining Hadrian freed his weapon and fired. His aim was sloppy and the shots burned silently into the side of the office, but the noise generator had been modified into a shrieking scrape of metal on metal.

Coldhand didn't dare stay behind cover for long. Vyron was going to run. Coldhand darted out from the office and tucked into a low roll to minimize his profile. Molten laserfire flew over him before the Hadrian could readjust his aim, but the bounty hunter bounded back to his feet, swinging his Talon around and firing two return shots.

The first laser bolt clipped the enraged human in his gun arm. He screamed and fumbled with his weapon, but it was already on the ground. A shot through his calf laid the Steelskin out beside his weapon. Coldhand kicked the gun into the street, far out of reach, while the injured man howled obscenities.

Vyron turned to bolt, dropping his briefcase. The metal clanged on the pavement and Coldhand heard glass shattering inside. He lunged to tackle the Dailon to the ground, but there was a rush of wind and the Arcadian was on him. Coldhand parried the fairy's first face-seeking slash aside on his cybernetic forearm. The glass blade rang hard off the illonium, but Jumo's welds held. For now.

The hunter ducked a second thrust, letting it glide past his right shoulder. Coldhand tried to grab at the Arcadian's overextended arm to drag him down, but his hand closed on something smoother than skin or cloth and the man slipped from his grasp. Pulled off balance, the Arcadian's wings slapped against the ground, momentarily tangling in the long tails of his coat. The fairy tugged it off and coiled his legs under him, leaping back into the air.

No longer concealed, Coldhand could see the Arcadian Steelskin's suit of armor. It looked a lot like the steel plate mail that he had seen illustrated in books as a boy – worn on Prianus almost two thousand years ago – but this armor was crafted entirely of shining and transparent glass. Tiberius claimed that Maeve had been some kind of knight on her homeworld, but Coldhand had never seen her wear such armor.

He brought his aim up as the Arcadian wheeled through the air. Vyron was running away. Coldhand heard his feet pounding on the asphalt and his sobbing, labored breathing. There wasn't much time left before the Dailon was too far away to catch.

Coldhand fired a shot that should have dropped the Arcadian with a smoking hole through his heart, but the laser dispersed as it struck the glass armor. No wonder the suit of crystal armor glittered so brightly, even in the flat artificial light of Axis' lower levels. The refraction index was probably more refined than diamonds, so low that a couple of angles harmlessly dissipated laserfire.

The Arcadian folded his wings and plummeted again, daggers extended. Coldhand stood his ground as the Steelskin dove. When the fairy was almost on top of him, Coldhand stepped aside and smashed his cybernetic fist into the side of the other man's unprotected skull. No helmet, no head or face protection. The Arcadian crashed into the street hard enough that Coldhand heard bones break, but his armor didn't so much as chip.

Coldhand didn't have time to see if the Arcadian was alive. He whirled and sprinted after Vyron. The Dailon was half a block away

– gasping with terror and fighting for breath – when the bounty hunter caught him. Coldhand grabbed Vyron by the back of his shirt, jerking him to a halt and putting the hot muzzle of his pistol to the man's temple.

"Are you Vyron Fethru?" Coldhand asked.

Vyron was shaking so hard that he could barely stammer out an answer. "Yes, that's me. What... what do you want with me?"

His mark's identity confirmed, Coldhand dragged Vyron away without answering.

[15]

RED AND GOLD

"Better a noble war than an ignoble peace."

- CAVAIN A'SHAE, ARCADIAN MONARCH (10,620 MA)

Xia tried to calm him, but Gripper stumbled over his own words as he rushed to tell Maeve what he feared – religious wars, bloody battles fought right here on Stray! Gripper waved his arms in distress, nearly knocking into Xia several times. Maeve listened quietly until the young Arboran finished. Then she gestured for the other two to follow her inside the Blue Phoenix.

"What're we going to do, Smoke? What if there is some kind of religious war going on here?" Gripper asked, loping along beside her on his big knuckles.

"Do? We will do nothing for the time being," Maeve said.

"But–" he protested.

Maeve cut him off. "The wars of the galaxy are not our concern. Only if the Nihilists' campaign proves a danger to Kessa and her child will this become our business."

Maeve turned toward Xia. The Ixthian doctor frowned, but not at her. Perhaps her caring nature was torn – a war may have been brewing here on Stray, one that might endanger uncounted lives, but involving the crew of the Blue Phoenix would put them in the middle of it, as well as the pregnant Kessa.

"Xia, go wake Tiberius and Kessa," Maeve said. "Duaal is young and so probably still awake. We must discuss Gripper's concern and decide if this is a threat to Kessa."

Xia nodded and hurried out of the hold, but Gripper lingered. He looked frightened. Gripper's expression was not the intellectual worry of a far-off religious war that would have little – if anything – to do with him, but much more like the look Caith had worn the first time he faced his sister across the lists of a tourney field.

"This is not a good idea," the young prince said.

Maeve jumped down from one of the large wooden rings affixed on top of a tall, bright-painted pole. She landed beside Caith and set her spear down. The deadly glass blade was swathed with brightly-colored cloth for training, just like Orthain's when she was a squire.

"Come now, little brother. Are you afraid that I would hurt you?" Maeve asked, putting a wing around him. Caith smiled up at her.

"Of course not. You have always been gentle with me. I fear that I will harm myself. I do not have your grace."

Maeve ruffled Caith's black hair. "You have grace of mind. And that will serve you well if you still want to be a knight, like me."

"I will never be a champion of the tourney field. My only interest in the spear is so I can stay with you when you work, enarri. So... so let us return to our work with no more concern for your clumsy little brother," Caith said with a brave smile.

Maeve blushed and giggled at Caith. He was working so hard to become a knight just so they could always be together. She embraced her brother and picked up her spear.

"Are you... alright?" Maeve asked Gripper.

"What if Tiberius thinks the Blue Church of Nihil is dangerous to Kessa?" he asked in a whisper. "There isn't anywhere else to take her. Will we have to fight?"

"Perhaps. Or perhaps not. We must investigate further," Maeve said. "There may be no danger here at all."

Gripper brightened a little at that. Maeve couldn't help smiling, too. He was so much like Caith.

Kessa was still rubbing blearily at her large black eyes when Xia escorted her to the mess. Tiberius and Duaal were already there, listening to Gripper recount the evening's sermon. Kessa dropped sleepily into the seat that Xia indicated.

Maeve watched Kessa. Her time was close. Kessa's splayfooted waddle was growing more pronounced by the day. Among Maeve's duties – and one of few she actually performed – she monitored the Blue Phoenix's supplies. Since the Dailon had come on board, their food consumption had nearly doubled as Kessa ate for both her taxed body and the rapidly growing baby inside her. But in the past few days, her appetite had plummeted.

Maeve didn't want to ask Xia about it, so she had looked up the issue last night on the Gharib mainstream. After an hour or so of snarling at the slow connection out in the landing crescent, Maeve found documentation on Dailon pregnancy. Their gestation period was short by galactic standard, lasting just four or five months. Mother and child formed an extensive network of interconnecting blood vessels to facilitate the massive flow of nutrients to the baby growing inside her.

When the pregnancy was nearly over, those veins and arteries began to atrophy and separate, maintaining only a bare minimum to sustain to the child. Otherwise, Dailon mothers would bleed to death during delivery. To guess by the way she was eating and the sketchy dates Kessa had provided for the baby's conception, Maeve guessed that the girl was no more than a week from delivery – possibly as little as a few days.

Coldhand would have to work quickly to get Vyron to Stray before his child was born. There was a chance, of course, that some other hunter would take the bounty and deliver Vyron, but Maeve doubted it. It was a paying job that would place Coldhand back on Stray and Maeve suspected that would be too great a temptation for her bounty hunter.

At least, Maeve hoped so. She hoped so hard that it became an ache.

Maeve and Caith darted in, encircling the hart in a cage of wings and arms. With a soft bleat, the white faun sank down to its knees, their fingers tangled gently in its fur.

"We get to make a wish now, right?" the young prince asked.

He began stroking the pale, soft fur. The little hart calmed under his touch, lying quiet on the carpet of fallen leaves.

"Yes, one wish," Maeve said. "We caught but did not harm him. The gods are obligated to hear our wishes."

"Maeve?"

Everyone was staring at her. Maeve realized that she was pacing and clenching her hands. They were shaking. Badly. She wanted a drink.

Tiberius scowled at her. He was still dressed for bed in checkered red flannel pants and a robe whose tattered sleeves bore mute testament to Orphia's affections.

"Maeve? What do you think?" Tiberius asked.

"I think we know too little," Maeve answered slowly. "I think it unlikely, but perhaps the Sisterhood left this city in peace and is no threat to the Union of Light or to Kessa."

"If they're like the Sisters back home on Axis, not a chance," Kessa said, shaking her head. "They've never done anything peacefully and they would never listen to a group led by a male."

"Is it impossible that the Nihilists threatened violence upon the Sisterhood and that they left rather than answer it?" Maeve asked.

"They would have fought," Kessa said.

Maeve nodded, conceding the point.

"How isn't as important as why," Duaal said. "Was it a gang war? Or a religious one? If it was just a territorial spat, then it shouldn't be a problem unless Kessa starts up a new chapter of the Sisterhood."

"Does it matter?" Xia asked. "If the Nihilists are after the Sisterhood, they're not going to be happy that Kessa's here."

"Duaal's right," Tiberius agreed. The young mage preened. "If the Church of Nihil chased the Sisterhood off just to clean up their new nesting ground, I doubt they'll make any problems for Kessa. Anthem said the Sisterhood's been gone a while. No reason they'd be looking for a Sister now."

"If they learn of Kessa's past membership, trouble may find her," Maeve said. "But it is a simple secret to keep."

Kessa blinked as she sleepily tried to follow their conversation. Finally, she seemed to understand and her blue skin paled a shade.

"You mean that they might try to kill me because I used to be a Sister?" she asked. "If I tell anyone?"

Tiberius shrugged. "It's possible."

"We can't let them do that," Gripper said.

"But we don't *know* yet," Tiberius reminded them. "Not for sure. Maeve is right, too – we need to find out what's going on here. Are these Nihilists going to be looking for Kessa or is their business with the Sisterhood over?"

"Our task must be done quickly. Kessa has very little time left," Maeve said.

"Take care of it," Tiberius ordered.

Maeve nodded. "I will go to the Church of Nihil tomorrow and discover the truth of the black cathedral."

"Hey, Smoke?" Gripper asked.

"Yes?"

"Be careful, please?"

"I will not bring harm to Kessa's child," Maeve promised.

"That's not what I meant," Gripper mumbled as she stood and left the room.

Maeve stroked the white hart's ear. "My wish... I wish to do what no other knight has ever done. I wish to see the stars and their worlds. I wish to travel."

Caith gasped, his jade green eyes wide and frightened. "You want to leave the White Kingdom?"

Maeve suddenly felt guilty for her wish, but Caith smiled at her.

"I know what I wish for. If... when Maeve flies into the stars, I wish for her to be safe. Let her be well and happy. That is my wish."

Caith lifted his wings and gave the hart a light swat on the flank. The white fawn bolted back through the forest and Maeve pulled her brother into a tight embrace, gently chiding him for wasting his wish on her. Caith buried his face in her feathers and held his only sister close.

"I just want you to be safe and happy, Maeve," he said. "Promise me that you will be?"

When Stray's ancient red sun rose early the next day, Maeve was already awake. She stood in the semicircle of communal showers, her wings spread to their full length to keep her feathers out of the cascading water. The princess washed her matted black hair and worked a heavy comb through the wet tangles.

Her usual negligence served well enough to pass among the other Arcadians on Stray, and perhaps even work in her favor to convince the Nihilists that she belonged in their cathedral. But her hair was a problem. Maeve pulled the comb through it with gasps and curses until there was no more resistance.

She turned off the water and picked up a bottle of hair bleach from the floor – pilfered from Duaal's personal stores – and poured the contents into her hand. The bleach stank and made her eyes sting, but she lathered it between her palms and rubbed it through her hair, from the roots out to the tips. She carefully applied a little to her brows, as well, and hoped that no one would look too closely at her eyelashes.

When Maeve had washed the bleach away, she inspected the results in the mirror. The dark blonde wasn't quite the pale golden color that marked the rest of her race, but it would have to do. Her natural color was tenacious.

Maeve stared at her reflection. Oh, how her mother would have scowled to see her daughter wash away the mark of her heritage. But did it matter what her mother would have thought? Princess Beltain was dead.

Without bothering to wrap a towel around herself, Maeve left the showers and made her way back through the Blue Phoenix to her quarters. Tiberius passed her in the corridor, yawning and carrying Orphia on his arm.

"Good God, girl!" Tiberius shouted. "How many times have I told you not to prance around my bird without clothes on?"

"More times than the sky has stars," Maeve answered.

She brushed past Tiberius and keyed the door to her room open. The Arcadian was fairly certain she saw him blush a bit, but it was difficult to tell through his stubble and ruddy skin.

There was a half-full bottle of narcohol partially hidden under her bunk. Maeve picked it up and drained it in a couple of swallows, then dropped it unceremoniously onto her unmade bed. She prodded at the clothes littering the floor with her toe, wrinkling her nose in disgust at her own mess.

Maeve went to the tiny closet and picked gingerly through its contents. Some of the clothes hanging inside hadn't been worn for longer than anyone else on the Blue Phoenix had lived. Maeve's half-formed plan hinged on convincing the Nihilists that she was wealthy and powerful enough to be of help to them. She hoped that the promise of a beneficial alliance would loosen some tongues and tell her what the Church of Nihil was doing on Stray.

Maeve passed up a gauzy gown of red and gold with an intricately laced bodice. While parading through Gharib as a princess – albeit of a lost kingdom – might have convinced the Nihilists of her wealth, it also stood a perilous chance of being utterly unbelievable. The entire Cavainna family was said to have died on Illisem, protecting the last of the White Kingdom as their people fled.

But the illusion of wealth was a delicate balance to strike. Arcadians were regarded the worlds over as pathetic refugees. They had escaped their world with little but their lives. Maeve ran her fingers through the crimson ribbons of another dress, also in Cavainna red and gold. How many Arcadians had left their homeworlds with nothing? Less than nothing? Even after their flight from the White Kingdom, thousands died of their wounds or strange alien diseases. And yet Maeve was staring into her closet and contemplating pretty dresses. It wasn't right or fair.

Maeve settled on a simple but elegant dress of emerald green silk. It had been a gift from a pair of young dryads on Maeve's thirtieth birthday. A blue cloak – cut into three panels around her wings – would keep her consistently dressed with the robed and hooded populace of Stray. Maeve clasped the cape and selected a few changes of clothes, then threw them into an empty satchel.

How long would this infiltration take? A lady of station could not be seen wearing the same dress twice. Maeve grumbled and forced herself to pull the crumpled gowns back out of the bag. She folded each one meticulously and replaced it. Maeve had never been skilled at courtly games. She grabbed a handful of multicolored cenmarks from a table beside the door and stuffed them into her supplies.

Leaning against the wall was Maeve's glass-bladed spear, hung with its collection of fading tourney ribbons. Maeve paused, considering. But after a moment's thought, she decided against bringing it with her. A spear was the weapon of a knight, not a lady of the Arcadian court.

When she could think of nothing else to pack, Maeve picked her way through her cluttered room and went down to the hold. There were other airlocks exiting the Blue Phoenix, but those were built for orbital docking and well above ground level when the ship landed. Since no one except the winged Arcadian princess could use them easily while grounded, Tiberius kept them sealed. That left the cargo bay airlock.

Kessa was waiting for Maeve down in the hold, leaning heavily on Duaal's arm. The young mage watched Maeve with a brittle lack of expression, but Kessa waddled a few ungainly steps and threw her arms around the fairy.

"I don't know how to ever begin thanking you for all of this," she said, holding Maeve tightly. "On Axis, I really thought my baby and I were dead. But you saved me. You and your friends are going to find a safe place for me. Thank you!"

"They are not my friends," Maeve objected stiffly. "They are... colleagues."

Kessa giggled as though Maeve had made a joke and tightened her hug.

"You've helped me so much. I have a doctor for my baby. I'm not hungry for the first time in... in longer than I can even remember. I'll have my Vyron back and then we'll be able to live here. It's kind of hot and sandy, but it's better than Level Seven."

"We do not yet know if Stray is safe for you," Maeve pointed out.

Kessa finally let go, her embrace not returned by the Arcadian, but ebony eyes still sparkling with tears of gratitude.

"I know," Kessa said. "But you're going to find out. And I know it's dangerous, so I... I just wanted to thank you. Thank you, Maeve. More than I can ever say."

"I do not need or want your thanks," Maeve told her. "I am no angelic savior, girl. My hands are stained to the bone by the blood of those I have killed, enough to drown you and your baby both."

Kessa flinched. "Then... then why are you helping me?"

"I owe you no answers," Maeve snarled.

Kessa turned away with fresh tears in her eyes. She stumbled awkwardly up the steps out of the hold and vanished into the Blue Phoenix. Duaal crossed his arms and rolled his eyes. There was a new ornament on his belt, Maeve noted – a glass dagger with a hilt crisscrossed in woven ribbons of blue and silver. Calloren colors.

"You know, I can see why Tiberius made you first mate," Duaal said. "You really have a deft touch, Maeve."

"I stole your hair bleach to create this disguise."

"Yeah, I figured that out," Duaal said. "Do you *have* to be such a little witch? Kessa only wanted to thank you."

"You are welcome to take my job... if you can convince Tiberius to entrust it to you."

Duaal glared at her and then turned on his heels to stalk off without answering. Maeve was well aware of the young human's dislike, but he lacked the steel or spite to kill her or even properly torment her, so she didn't bother to cultivate his hatred. Better to spend her time honing a more effective blade.

Like Logan Coldhand.

But Maeve turned Duaal's insult in her mind. He was right, of course. She was a beast, a monster. Perhaps that should have made his words sting all the more, yet Maeve felt only a thin sort of regret that Duaal could find nothing worse to condemn her for than insulting Kessa.

The sun was barely above Stray's flat horizon, but the day was already hot. Maeve stepped through the airlock into a wall of dry heat. She shook out her wings and vaulted into the air, soaring east toward the black cathedral.

[16]
PILLARS OF LIGHT

"The faces of God are as many as the faces of his children scattered among the stars. But the demons of the hells, too, wear a multitude of faces. Open your heart to your fellow children of God, but be wary of a smile that seems too sweet."

- THE BOOKS OF LIGHT (23 PA)

Compared to the vast megatropolises of the other Alliance worlds, Gharib was barely worthy of notice. It was a small city, without a single starscraper or even any buildings over twelve stories tall. Seen from the air, Gharib stretched out in a rough sandy circle, a great blemish against the uniform yellow-brown of the surrounding desert.

A dusty highway encircled the central marketplace, alive with vehicles whose individual styles and builds were invisible from Maeve's altitude. The road was spanned by several footbridges, all constructed of the dun-colored siltstone that seemed to make up most of Stray. The stone was cheap and plentiful here, found all over the planet. It was the perfect building material for the often poor beings who came to Stray for a new start.

The dark cathedral of the Nihilists shimmered on the eastern horizon, wavering and dancing in the hot air like a sickly black flame. Maeve curled her wings into the wind and swooped down to land in front of the church.

A Mirran woman of middling years met Maeve at the door and led her inside the cathedral. She was tall, with dark skin and curly green-brown hair that fell in tangles down around her cheeks. A hood and veil of the same rough black cloth as her robes concealed most of the woman's olive-striped face – except for her downcast eyes. She asked Maeve to wait and then vanished off into the gray shadows.

It was swelteringly hot inside the dark Nihilist cathedral. Maeve heard some hushed conversation and several fits of racking coughs. There was even the thick, wet sound of someone being noisily sick, but no hum of a cooling system. Sunlight filtered down through the windows of the spires and holes in the roof, creating amber pillars of light out of the dusty air.

The church was a single vast room, as far as Maeve could tell. Rusted ladders hung from the uneven ceiling like bones thrust out from the softened flesh of a rotting corpse, leading up into each of the four steeples. Old ropes dangled from chipped and cracked bells, barely within arm's reach of the ladders. For anyone without wings, simply ringing the bells was a dangerous task.

Not that the Church of Nihil had any lack of wings... The huge room was filled with people. Maeve wasn't able to make an accurate count where she stood, but she could take a guess. There must have been nearly two hundred beings huddled around makeshift tables constructed from stones and sheets of metal, sharing small meals or sitting against piles of fallen masonry, sleeping or perhaps simply too weary to move. Most wore the coarse black robes that seemed to be the cathedral's uniform. Maeve caught sight of a Nihilist whose robes had been dyed a brilliant, ember red, but the man vanished into the crowd before Maeve could study him further.

At least half of those sprawled around the church were Arcadians, their pale skins muddy with sweat and dirt. Many of the gathered fairies dragging wings too injured to fly. They were scabrous and sickly-looking, great patches of feathers fallen out from malnutrition. A few of the other Arcadians raised their hands or wings to Maeve in greeting, but none made any further effort to welcome her.

A human of indeterminate lineage approached Maeve. He was quiet, perhaps out of respect for those sleeping inside the Nihilist cathedral, but more likely out of habit. None of them seemed very excitable. They all lay quietly, simply waiting for their deaths.

The man couldn't have been much past thirty years old, but his brown hair was retreating across his scalp and his face was prematurely lined. He moved with a drunken, dreamy sway to his step, weaving between piles of refuse and sleeping bodies. His eyes had a distinct glaze to them and Maeve guessed that the Nihilist could barely even see her.

"Welcome to the godless house," he said. "How may we serve you, child?"

"I am looking for the man who leads this church. Is that you?" Maeve asked.

This man's voice, age and posture didn't match what Maeve had seen the night before, but she wanted to be sure. The Nihilist shook his head.

"No. That was Lord Gavriel," he answered. "He's taught so many of us the true emptiness of being."

"Who is he?" Maeve asked.

The man smiled at her. He was missing several of his teeth and the empty gaps stared like the blank eye-holes of some dead thing lying beside the road, left to rot in the sun.

"Gavriel is the founder and master of the Church of Nihil. His wisdom has brought comfort to many. He travels across all of Stray to spread his message."

"His words have opened my eyes," Maeve said. Convincingly, she hoped. "I would thank him myself."

"Unfortunately, Gavriel left early this morning for Kharnig," the Nihilist told her. "He won't return for a several days."

Maeve swore inwardly. She had already missed him. Whatever this church's agenda was, it was surely the plan of their master, Gavriel. But Maeve made herself smile brightly back at the gap-toothed man.

"No matter," she said. "It is not for pleasant company that I have come. I will thank Gavriel when he returns."

"You're welcome to join the Arcadians here. You and your kind have known so much pain. We can help you find your death."

"I long for such an ending," Maeve said.

The words came easily and naturally.

The Nihilist – who introduced himself as Bren – found Maeve a corner where a piece of siding was propped up against a heap of trash and sand. Bren left her there, pleading some other errand, but assured her that he would return.

Maeve folded her wings along her back to protect her from the heat and leaned against the sand. She needed time to gather her thoughts. Did she need to wait for Gavriel or could Bren tell her if the Church of Nihil was a danger to Kessa? Maeve wasn't sure... Bren's glazed eyes and drunken stagger didn't inspire much confidence. Even if the man had been trusted with important knowledge, there was no guarantee that he could recall it.

Gavriel was already gone, but with only a few hours' head start. Maeve contemplated flying after the Nihilist leader, chasing the man down and wresting his secrets from him. But she discarded the idea. Maeve was not a skilled tracker. Even a century ago, when she was still an honored knight of a flourishing kingdom, her brother had led their hunts. Caith's eyes had been just as sharp as his mind. There was almost nothing clever, sweet Caith couldn't do.

Almost.

Maeve's eyes were dry in the cloying, close heat of the cathedral. She was certain they would shrivel up in their sockets like raisins before long. Maeve rubbed her face. She had to think, figure out what to do next, but memories – more than a century in their graves – wouldn't leave her alone.

"Highness, please. Listen to me!" Orthain said.

He took Maeve by the shoulder and spun her to face him. They were on one of the broad green tourney fields, Aes' brilliant light glowing off their glass armor. Maeve's plate mail was as intricately wrought as lace, covered in delicate scrollwork of deep red and glittering gold. She clasped her spear in white-knuckled fingers.

"Your words are treason, Sir Fyre!" the princess said. Her cheeks were pricked with a dark flush and her voice was shaking.

"Treason? Maeve, I only want to protect you and your brother!"

Orthain's beautiful golden hair was unbound, falling in wild curls that hearkened back to the Arcadians' ancient days as free creatures of the skies. His eyes blazed and his fine fingers tightened on Maeve's shoulders. The glass of his armor clinked against hers.

"Highness, Erris sings a unique song for each of us. Your song – and mine – is that of a knight. But not Caith. He has a keen mind and a sharp eye, but no talent for the spear. He is a danger to himself and anyone around him. Caith is not meant to be a knight and tries only for you!"

"Enough!" Maeve said. "Caith will *be a knight. You just want to take my brother away from me!"*

She raised her hand to hit Orthain and he caught her wrist. He held it firmly, but gently as a bird that he worried would injure itself with its panicked thrashing. Maeve dropped her spear and tried to lash out again, but the older knight easily deflected the punch again. It was not for his beauty that Orthain had been knighted.

"You are a skilled knight, princess," Orthain told her. His voice was thick. "You have not been my squire for years, yet you return to me for teaching and I... would be lying if I said that I do not eagerly anticipate every lesson. It has been my privilege and joy to serve you, Highness."

Orthain pulled her against him. Their crystalline breastplates rang at the contact and Orthain wrapped his wings around Maeve. She was furious, but there was more to her racing heart than that. Maeve had adored Orthain since she was a little girl, watching the handsome young knight in training with her father. Her decades learning under Orthain had sometimes been more than she could bear.

"I would never take your brother away, Highness," Orthain said. "But I fear that is exactly what will happen if his love for you forces him into knighthood. Caith cannot survive on the battlefield, princess, and I would not see him taken from you."

Maeve sagged against Orthain and she rested her cheek on the cool glass of his armor. Orthain was right, of course. She could not make Caith become a knight just for her, and she couldn't be angry at Orthain for telling her so.

"Thank you for your honesty, Sir Fyre," Maeve said. "I am sorry that I did not listen better, but I will speak to Caith. As knights, we might have been able to serve together, but it seems that our paths must part..."

Orthain released Maeve and smiled down at her.

"If you are feeling a little more receptive to my advice, Highness," he said, "I have an idea to let you remain with your brother."

"What is it?" Maeve asked.

Orthain trailed the glass fingertips of his gauntlet along her jaw and Maeve's breath caught.

"I will tell you... if you will please call me by my given name," he said.

The princess blinked. Knights did not call each other by their first names, not unless their relationship was one other than that of professional peers. Did he mean...?

"I will call you Orthain," Maeve said, "if you will call me yours."

Orthain smiled and hooked his finger under Maeve's chin, lifting her face to his. He kissed her.

"Until the Nameless takes me, Maeve," he whispered against her lips.

By that afternoon, Maeve still hadn't decided what to do. When it grew too hot, she rose from her resting spot and wandered aimlessly around the church, pondering her next step.

Bren didn't seem to be the only priest in the black cathedral. Half a dozen other men and women moved about the church with a purposeful stride and spent most of their time with the sickest of their congregation, but didn't administer any kind of treatment that Maeve could see. Instead, they sat beside the dying, giving smiling encouragement as though illness were some great achievement and offering their congratulations.

The Nihilists were friendly... in their way. When Maeve asked, they shared stories of misery, abuse and hopelessness with the heedless, tired cheer of the terminally ill. Most were sick, racked by disease or chemical use. Many of them were dying. A group of other Arcadians invited Maeve to join them around a dented metal bowl. Something inside was burning, filling and overflowing the dish with sweet-smelling smoke. Maeve considered for a moment, then declined and moved on.

As the day wore on, more converts trickled through the cathedral doors. Each was greeted by one of the priests and shown to a squalid patch of their own. Some of them left once they realized that last night's persuasive speaker wasn't there, but most remained and joined the sickly congregation, like Maeve had. Bren visited each who stayed, chatting with the newcomers for a minute or two before wandering away again.

Maeve watched and listened. The priest's eyes weren't quite as glassy and distant as she had first thought. Bren didn't seem wholly devoted to the task of welcoming the new Nihilists, but the princess suspected that his mind was not gone – just elsewhere. Bren was looking at the Nihilist converts with bright eyes, inspecting each of them closely.

Hours passed and the dusty pillars of light began their slanting westward march. Maeve perched on a pile of crumbled siltstone, studying Bren.

The priest spent mere moments with a plump Lyran woman who held a bundle of torn puppy clothes to her breast, but lingered beside a gaunt Dailon with a blood-stained bandage tangled in his ragged black hair. A Hyzaari man with wide, sad green eyes merited scarcely a glance, while Bren stared at a jittery skeleton of an Arcadian woman for almost an hour. Bren eyed the open red sores on her exposed skin with frank admiration.

Bren was gauging their health, separating those who were dying from the ones who were merely ill. Those closest to their final breath were guided to places in the middle of the cathedral floor, laid down on dirty beds and pillows in plain view of the congregation. Was it some kind of... worship? Gavriel had spoken so lovingly of death. It followed, then, that his church would put it on reverent display.

Maeve didn't know how to feel. She had longed for death since the fall of the White Kingdom. Why should the practices of the Church of Nihil bother her? The Arcadian waved her question away for the moment. She was here to perform a duty, one of vital importance to Kessa and her unborn child. Maeve returned her attentions to Bren.

He knelt beside a reclining woman, an Ixthian whose silver skin was so fragile that it bruised and bled at the priest's lightest touch. Radiation sickness? Her eyes burned with a feverish ember light. The Nihilist priest brandished his bloody fingers to the small crowd gathered around the dying woman. He was saying something, but his voice didn't carry to Maeve's pointed ears. The circle of watchers seemed to agree, though, nodding to one another and murmuring.

Maeve turned toward the sound of footsteps. It was the same Mirran woman who had brought her into the cathedral earlier that day. She had removed her black hood and veil to reveal dry lips and a crooked nose, broken at some point in the past. She held a basin covered by a relatively clean towel and carried it with painstaking care across the church's uneven dirt floor. Maeve beckoned to her.

The woman approached slowly, not raising her gaze up from the floor.

"Do you need something?" she asked.

"Only conversation and perhaps answers to some small questions," Maeve said. "May I ask your name?"

"Elsa," the Mirran answered quietly.

There was a moment of uncomfortable silence and then Maeve realized that she was expecting a name in return. No one else in the cathedral had asked.

"I am... Shae," Maeve told Elsa.

It was a common name in the White Kingdom. Translated into Aver, one of its meanings was *night* – though it had many other translations. *Shae* was the reverent form of the word, usually used when demurring to use Cavain's true name. He was said to have carried divine blood, born of Aes Sky-Dancer herself. Stories said that early courtiers were so awed by the half-divine Cavain that they couldn't bring themselves to call their king by his birth name. So for his midnight hair, they called him *Shae*. In the millennia since those days, the title had become a popular name among the noble houses of Arcadia and was supposed to grant good luck.

"Shae?" Elsa asked. Her gaze crept up Maeve's green silk dress. To judge by the covetous hunger in her brown eyes, it was probably the single most expensive thing she had ever seen. "Isn't that name from the rich fairy families?"

"You are very well versed in Arcadian culture," Maeve said with sincere surprise. "Most in the core have difficulty telling us apart, much less remembering our naming traditions."

"Lots of fairies come here," the other woman answered. "And I like them."

"You... do?" Maeve asked, even more shocked.

No one in the core liked Arcadians. But there was something strange and sincere about how Elsa said it, slowly and almost childishly... The Mirran woman nodded.

"They have such sad stories to tell. Your kingdom was beautiful, but now it's all gone. Eaten." Elsa looked curiously at Maeve. "Some of them let us sleep under their wings when it gets cold at night. There aren't enough blankets for everyone, not unless a lot more people die. Some fairies came here with pretty clothes like yours, but I think your world was very warm because the cloth is quite thin. They had to get robes and some of the nice ones gave me their dresses. Lord Gavriel says I'm not allowed to wear them here, but I like looking at them."

"I hoped to ask you about that priest there," Maeve said, trying to get Elsa back on track. She pointed across the cathedral floor to Bren.

The Mirran nodded. "That's Doctor Bren. He's very smart. Bren runs things when Lord Gavriel is gone. He watches the sick and hurt ones, reminds them that the end is good and helps them die."

"How exactly does Bren help? Does he administer medicine to ease their pain?"

Elsa's eyes went wide and she shook her head emphatically, as though Maeve suggested something terrible. "Oh, no. Nothing like that! Death is a release and pain is the gateway, Lord Gavriel says. We don't drug the dying ones here. We honor them."

Elsa paused, visibly rewinding the conversation in her mind to recall Maeve's original question. She smiled when she finally remembered.

"Bren helps us die if we're impatient," Elsa said, setting down her covered bowl and gesturing around the church.

"You mean suicide?" Maeve asked.

"Yes. It's hard to let go of living. I'm not ready yet... But when I am, Doctor Bren will help. It takes time, but when we're ready, Bren is very good at helping us die. He was a doctor in one of the big colonies on Quarrus until he came here."

"But Quarrus is on the other side of the Alliance, far from Stray. How did he end up here?"

Elsa shrugged. "I think Lord Gavriel knows. Maybe Bren is sick, too... His teeth fall out sometimes. I don't ask. I just carry things. I should probably be doing that again."

The green-haired woman picked up her covered bowl with a shy, sheepish expression. She held it carefully in her hands and moved to leave. Maeve hesitated, then called out Elsa's name. The Mirran turned back.

"Elsa, why are you in this place?" Maeve asked.

Timid and kind as she was, Elsa didn't seem much like a death worshiper. There were still joys in her life, if only sad stories and pretty clothes. Elsa thought for a long, ponderous moment before answering.

"I lived on Giadeen most of my life," she said at last. "I grew up there and met a man. He was a traveler and he was beautiful, so we were married. He brought me with him on his ship and we flew away from Giadeen together. But I found out that he wasn't as nice as I thought."

Elsa pushed back her thick, curly hair. There was a terrible scar on her temple, the mark of a blow so violent that it had left an indentation in the skull beneath.

"My husband didn't love me very much. He hit me when he was angry," Elsa said. There was no anger in her voice, just the regret of one remembering something she lost long ago. "Sometimes with his hands, but once with a welder and everything went all red. It took months to heal and... things were harder after that. Bren says he damaged my brain."

Maeve swallowed hard. "I am sorry for what was done to you."

"We flew here, to Stray. When my husband landed and went into the city to buy some things, I ran away. I didn't know where to go, but I thought that sleeping in the sand was better than being hit again. Some fairies helped me. They didn't grant wishes like the stories about the Fair Ones that my mama told me, but they were kind. They gave me food and a warm place to sleep, then they brought me here. They're dead now. Bren helped them die. I miss them sometimes."

"Did your husband ever come in search of you?" Maeve asked.

"Yes, I think so," Elsa said. "I heard him at the door once, late at night, yelling to see me. I was hiding, but then I heard Lord Gavriel talking to him. Gavriel said some strange things in words I didn't know. Arcadian words. There was more shouting, and then nothing. Lord Gavriel came back inside with a pretty silver knife, but it was all bloody. He looked very angry, but he promised that my husband would never hurt me again."

"Gavriel killed him?"

Elsa shrugged again and fiddled with the corner of the towel draped over her bowl. "I... I think so. Now I really need to get back to work."

"I beg your pardon and thank you for your time, Elsa," Maeve apologized.

The Mirran smiled and left with the bowl. Stray's ancient red sun was setting again, turning the slanting pillars of light a ruby color that faded quickly as the holes in the cathedral's ceiling went dim. Maeve pulled her wings around her shoulders against the cold creeping into the Nihilist church and shivered. The remote silver specks of stars were beginning to show themselves through gaps in the roof. They were dimmer and fewer than above Axis. Almost like the deep black skies of her home in Arcadia, so far away from the billions of suns in the galactic core.

What now? Elsa's comment about clothing concerned Maeve. Not because she was worried about the skittish Mirran trying to steal from her, but because Gavriel had forbidden Elsa to wear her gifts. If the Nihilist renounced luxuries like fine clothes, then what good was Maeve's deception? They clearly had no need for money and probably not for anything Maeve could tempt them with.

She spread her wings and flew to an outcropping of corrugated metal. What was there to spend Alliance color on here, anyway? The cathedral seemed to be built from cast-off blocks of stone and ship siding. It was rough and unfinished, but the Nihilists didn't seem to care. And why should they? Death was the only thing of importance in this place. The Nihilists could die on the side of the road just as well as in a lavish citadel. Maeve's façade as a wealthy but morose Arcadian philanthropist would get her nowhere.

But Maeve had no intention of leaving empty handed. If Stray wasn't a safe world for Kessa, it would take time and effort to find another. Maeve wasn't convinced that most of the Nihilists cared enough about anything to pose a danger to Kessa, but what about their shadowy and eloquent leader, Gavriel?

That chapter of Elsa's story didn't sit well with Maeve, either. Gavriel was clearly willing to kill, at least when a problem came shouting to his doorstep. And Elsa said that she had heard Gavriel speaking in Arcadian. But Elsa's husband wasn't a fairy and their language was not widely known. After a century in the Alliance, even Maeve used Arcadian infrequently. She only spoke her native tongue when the Aver word simply would not do. Or when singing a spell, of course.

And why did Gavriel use a knife? Even the endlessly machine-honed nanoblades were fairly archaic weapons by Alliance standards. So why not a gun? Avoiding noise, perhaps? But null-inertia projectiles made almost no sound except a small snapping from the ignition of the powder, and a muffled thump of displaced air as the bullet left the gun and the null-field.

Lasers were silent, though Alliance law required manufacturers to install sound generators. Most models, like Logan's Talon-9, used a high-pitched whine or pulse. Tiberius had told Maeve once that the sound was a silly choice. Lasers had made such noises in their ancient stories and shows, long before the weapons' actual invention. So those were the sound effects the makers gave them.

But the generators could be programmed with other sounds, sometimes intended to make the weapon seem either more or less frightening. Maeve had heard gossip of pirates or bounty hunters remodeling their lasers to emit anything from the mew of a kitten to agonized screams.

But Gavriel had engaged Elsa's mate in a shouting fight. Clearly, noise wasn't a concern. Maeve would have liked to ask Bren about the incident with Elsa's husband, but she didn't want to arouse any suspicion. A devout Nihilist would never question death, only celebrate another life passed into unbeing. But Maeve recalled the scar hidden under Elsa's curly hair and admitted to herself that she was not weeping for the loss of her husband.

The evening was as sharp and chilly as the silver blade in Elsa's story. Sounds of coughing and chattering teeth filled the Church of Nihil. How many Nihilists would die here tonight, of starvation and illness hastened by the cold? Their icy corpses were the altars of the Nihilist's twisted faith and would be celebrated in the morning.

Could Maeve help them...? But she quickly dismissed the idea. These people came here to die, and Maeve was supposed to be one of them. She pulled her wings around her and fell into uneasy sleep.

[17]

BARE NECESSITIES

"The real beauty in chaos is the opportunity to create order."

- GENERAL CIERRA, CWAAF 12TH FLEET (62 PA)

Vyron's wrists were bound in steel handcuffs. Coldhand kept his Talon free and powered up, but no longer against Vyron's temple. Such obvious force would only attract attention from the gangs and other criminal elements of the lower levels. The Dailon was terrified and didn't need reminding that he was one untimely twitch away from death. As they exited the lift to Level Three, Coldhand finally put the gun away.

The CWAAF testing and collection station was a simple, tidy white building on Level Three and was made of a sturdy, functional plastic. Wood was a hard-to-grow luxury, available only to the very wealthy of the city-world, and fibersteel was generally reserved for spacecraft. Microwoven steel or aluminum was durable but flexible, making it uniquely suited to the constantly changing pressures and stresses of interstellar travel. For most cheap buildings, plastic and ceramic sufficed.

Uniformly shaped green marsona bushes skirted the station and to judge by the sparse sprinkling of lavender flowers, Axis' long summer was finally coming to an end. Reinforced white plastic doors hissed open at their approach and Coldhand marched his bounty through. There was a metal sign inside with black letters etched into it.

Identity Testing and Bounty Collection Center
CAID #45K93-288D-5VS
Please have your license and identification ready

The reception and waiting area was small and currently empty, with a gray plastic floor scuffed by numerous escape attempts. In the center, the flooring was stamped with the auroch emblem of the CWA. Another set of sliding double doors stood closed at the other end of the room. There were no handles on this side of the entry – they could only be opened from inside.

A fat, bored-looking human sat behind the square window next to the vault-like doors. He wore the dark green uniform of the CWA Armed Forces, which he filled almost to overflowing. The bars on his collar identified him as a first lieutenant and a name tag on his lapel read *P. Darson*. He looked up from his computer as Vyron and Coldhand entered.

"License please," Darson said. His voice was rendered hollow by the speaker set into the window.

Vyron stared around the room with wide, frightened black eyes. He twitched, but didn't make a run for the door.

"I don't have it," Coldhand said. His bounty hunter's license was stowed on the Raptor with the rest of his gear.

The lieutenant rolled his eyes at the obvious incompetence of any bounty hunter who couldn't keep track of their license.

"Print scan, then," he said.

Darson flipped open a panel at the bottom of his window and out slid a flat scanner with the outline of a hand on it, the thumb pointing off to the right. Coldhand held up his cybernetic left hand to Darson. Despite the thick window between them, the CWAAF officer went pale and recoiled.

"Oh." Darson seemed unable to tear his eyes from the illonium hand, morbidly fascinated. "Right, we'll have to… to take a retinal scan, Coldhand, sir. For the records."

Coldhand heard a few soft beeps as Darson entered an access code into a keypad somewhere out of sight. With a low clank, the secondary doors unlocked and slid open. Vyron whimpered as the Prian hunter grabbed him and shoved him roughly through and down a short hallway that opened up into a much larger room. It was lined down one side with scanning stalls and a bank of computer terminals along the other.

A pair of Ixthians in green scrubs sat at a table, a tall female and smaller male gossiping over plastic coffee cups. The man's antennae twitched in his white hair and he turned to see Coldhand pushing Vyron into the room. The Ixthian stood quickly, dropping his drink. His cup bounced off the tabletop and fell onto the floor, spilling lukewarm coffee in a brown puddle at his feet. The woman gave her counterpart an annoyed look, but then followed his whirling red eyes to Coldhand. She raised her multitude of fingers to her mouth. Darson jogged around the corner after the hunter, his pudgy face quite pink. He skidded to a stop.

"It's Coldhand," Darson announced unnecessarily. Anyone who worked in an identity center knew his name.

Darson approached the pale-haired hunter gingerly, as though expecting a blow. His fingers twitched nervously against the automatic laser pistol holstered under his arm.

"I'll scan you in," he said, pointing to one of the booths along the side of the room.

Coldhand nodded. He shoved the cringing Vyron into the arms of the waiting Ixthian technicians.

"Get his ID confirmed," he instructed. "I've got verbal only."

They pulled the Dailon toward a stall. Coldhand turned and followed the CWAAF lieutenant to another one. A collection of scanning equipment, each attached to a central core by folding metal arms, hung from the ceiling like an immense steel spider.

Darson hesitantly asked the hunter to sit on a narrow bench jutting from the wall. He pulled down a mechanical arm that terminated in a fist-sized box and lined up a circular lens with Coldhand's icy eyes. Darson pressed a button and a network image of the nerves and blood vessels flashed up onto the screen behind Darson. The computer high-lighted key points and accessed the CWA database, blanked and then brought up a name. Darson turned to look.

Centra, Logan A.

"Uh... what the hells? Sorry, I'll get another one," Darson said, frowning nervously.

"Don't bother. It's correct," Coldhand told him. He tapped a key on the computer console. The screen flashed and changed again.

Centra, Logan A.

    Known aliases: Coldhand, Logan

    Bounty hunter: License class E3 (full exemption)

    Species: Human

    POB: Prianus, New Empyrean, district C

    Age: 26.23 CSYs

"You didn't think my family name was actually *Coldhand*, did you?" he asked without the faintest trace of a smile. The hunter tapped another key and the screen blanked again.

"Class E3?" Darson said. "Full exemption... You don't see many of those outside the Alliance forces."

"And you won't tell anyone you did, certainly not one named Logan Centra," Coldhand suggested in a frosty voice.

The flush drained from the other man's face and he nodded vigorously. "Yes, of course. I absolutely understand. Discretion. Let me get you the datawork."

Coldhand doubted that Darson actually understood, but he didn't press the lieutenant. Logan Centra was a dead man, a stupid young police officer back on Prianus that vanished six years ago. His marks knew Coldhand only as a ruthless killer, remorseless and inhuman. The story of a one-time cop turned to bounty hunting would undermine his reputation. Prian police respected the laws. They protected people. Coldhand didn't.

It wasn't a part of his life he had any desire to advertise. Or to think about.

Lieutenant Darson led Coldhand out of the scanning booth and then to the table where the two Ixthians had been seated a few minutes before. He motioned for Coldhand to sit and vanished back to his office to retrieve a few forms. There was an indignant yelp from another stall. The privacy curtain was drawn, but behind it, Vyron was being subjected – and loudly objecting – to a full-body scan. Advanced though Alliance medical equipment was, it couldn't take an accurate enough image through clothing and no one wanted to risk that some bounty hunter might have caught the wrong man.

Darson returned a moment later with a slender silver datadex and held it out to Coldhand.

"Just the standard forms. Mark identity confirmation and auto-nomous authority. Uh, these ones here. I need your signature on the last line of each," Darson said, and offered a stylus. "In the event that you apprehend or execute a person found to be innocent, you will be held responsible for criminal acts including, but not limited to harassment, assault and unlawful death in the second degree under CWA law."

"This is a privately posted bounty."

"Oh, right," Darson said. He pressed a key at the bottom of the datadex. "Then please sign the PBP-19 on page forty-seven. Both you and the party responsible for posting the bounty will be subject to investigation if the CWAAF receives any complaints pertaining to this arrest."

Coldhand quickly signed his assumed name to the forms and then passed them back. Darson keyed through the screens to check over the datawork, nodded to Coldhand and went to one of the computers on the opposite wall to file it.

A few minutes later, Vyron was led out of the scanning stall. His sleek black hair was disheveled and his angular blue face was contorted by embarrassment and fear. His handcuffs had been replaced around his wrists and the tall female Ixthian was holding Vyron by the shoulders.

"Are we keeping him?" the male asked from the booth.

"Nope, it's a private bounty," Darson said. "Xed, send over your confirmation."

"Sure." There were a few soft tones from the Ixthian's computer. "Got it?"

"Yeah. Thanks."

Xed waved to the lieutenant, but hesitated in the doorframe of the scanning stall. He stared at Coldhand for an uncomfortable moment, then stepped back into the booth and let the curtain drop. Darson returned to where Coldhand was waiting.

"The bounty has been transferred to the account we have on file," he told the hunter.

"Good."

Coldhand held out his cybernetic hand for the receipt. Darson shuddered visibly and pressed the plastic strip into his metal palm. Coldhand scanned it for a moment, reading, frowned thoughtfully and dropped it into his pocket. He took Vyron by the shoulder and led him from the building.

The Dailon hadn't said a word since Coldhand captured him. Vyron stared sullenly at the ground, not meeting any of the curious stares in the streets of Axis, as Coldhand hauled him to a lift and pushed him inside. Once the curved doors sealed shut and the lift's machinery hummed to life, Vyron hesitantly lifted his eyes to the bounty hunter's.

"A private bounty? Did I hear that right?" he asked. "But who would pay for me?"

Coldhand could understand why Vyron was the frontman for his gang. Even nervous and dispirited, he spoke in a musical tenor and his words were crisp, far more educated than a typical lower-level thug. By his accent, Coldhand guessed that he was from Tynerion, one of the oldest colonies of the CWA. Tynerion had a reputation for being a world of great culture, a cradle of literature and education.

"You're wanted in connection with drug trafficking, kidnapping and murder," Coldhand said.

"What?" Vyron shook his head and sagged hopelessly against the wall of the large lift. "I should have guessed. They think I'll break and incriminate the other Steelskins, don't they? Great."

Coldhand didn't answer.

The lift chimed to let the occupants know that they had reached their destination. The doors hissed open, and Coldhand and Vyron stepped out onto Level One. It was midmorning and bright light poured over the city from Axis' brilliant white sun. The pale blue sky blazed with millions of twinkling stars.

The lifts were all clustered together into a clover shape and let out into an expansive plaza. Space commanded a premium price on Level One, but this was the capital world of the Alliance and even the public works had the money to build whatever they wanted. The courtyard was paved in a mosaic of blue, green and white; the colors of the CWA. A fountain rained endlessly glittering water over a brightly enameled Alliance crest.

A great crown of starscrapers circled the plaza, majestic spires of ceramic girders and tempered glass. Their points soared up so many hundreds of stories that the summits were lost in the silver-blue brightness of the sky; monuments to the power of Axis, the center of the galactic Alliance, thrusting toward the sun and stars with possessive, crystalline grandeur. Whoever had the color to afford buildings like this, though, remained concealed behind the polarized glass.

Roads paved in hardened white sancrete led out into the rest of the city and were packed with all manner of vehicles, from archaic bearing cars – ironically collected as a status symbol by the wealthy of Axis – to wide bulk transports, humming on their null-fields, all pushing bumper to bumper through their daily business. The side-walks were no less crowded, alive with pedestrians of all species. On this megalithic altar to commerce and progress, personal space was sacrificed for the chance to work and walk on the surface of the most popular and populous world of the Alliance.

Many years accustomed to the dark lower levels of Axis, Vyron's eyes watered in the bright light of Level One and even Coldhand had to squint a little until his vision adjusted. He prodded his prisoner into motion and they began walking down the shining, busy streets.

And kept walking. Corporate starscrapers and manicured business parks gave way to high-rise residential spires and expensive department stores that sold only the galaxy's best clothes, food, and electronics. At least, that was the boast in every elegantly designed holographic display.

Vyron stared. In stark contrast to the lower levels, everything here was fastidiously clean. Despite the heavy traffic on the streets, the air remained cool and clear. Coldhand knew it was recycled, cleaned and pumped back into use by vast overclocked industrial machinery somewhere in the bowels of the massive city-world. Booming population and development at the dawn of the CWA had choked out the plant life that would naturally have done the job. There wasn't so much as a stray blade of grass or sprout of moss in sight. Nothing that wasn't part of a garden or sculpted topiary.

Vyron fidgeted, trying in vain to find a comfortable way to walk with his hands bound in front of him. The passing denizens of the Axis' upper crust stared in frank curiosity and Vyron studied his feet. They stared at Coldhand, too, but the hunter ignored every glare or shocked start.

Finally, the apartment spires faded into the distance and Coldhand led Vyron into a network of small private airfields and communications towers.

"Where are we going?" Vyron asked at last. "Did someone on Level One put the bounty on me?"

"No. I'm here to pick up my Raptor. My bird."

Vyron gave him only a blank stare.

"My ship," Coldhand said.

"You actually keep a ship up here?" the Dailon said. "That's got to be expensive. Does bounty hunting pay that well?"

"Sometimes. The bounty out on the woman I'm hunting now is twenty thousand cenmarks dead. Thirty-five if I can take her alive," he replied.

Vyron's black eyes bulged. "But you could live for years on that! What did she do to be worth that much color?"

Coldhand shrugged and didn't answer. He wasn't particularly inclined to discuss Maeve's crimes with a petty gangster. A private party wanted the fairy for sixteen counts of premeditated murder, all verified with the CWA Armed Forces records office. Most of them had been committed before Coldhand was even born, but those weren't why he chased after the fairy princess. Every one of Maeve's victims had been themselves wanted beings, all guilty of murders and rapes so terrible that the details were never released to the news networks. If Maeve hadn't killed them, Coldhand would have taken each bounty himself. They must have been worth thousands of colour, though the Arcadian princess hadn't collected their bounties.

Far more interesting was the final charge on Maeve's bounty posting, listed all on its own and with no explanation: genocide.

Since Coldhand found her bounty a year ago, he had hunted no one and nothing else. With the exception of Vyron... but that was only means of returning to the *real* hunt.

How could one woman commit such a crime? Maeve Cavainna was an experienced and deadly fighter, but she couldn't have wiped out an entire species with her spear. So what happened?

Vyron cleared his throat. He didn't seem to like the silence. There was a reason the man made his living talking.

"So... what am I worth?"

"Eight hundred cen."

The Dailon looked a little crestfallen. "That's it? Damn. You can't be taking me very far for that much money."

"I'm delivering you to Stray," Coldhand said.

Vyron jerked to a halt. The hunter stopped, too, and eyed the blue-skinned man with chilly curiosity. A human woman in an exquisitely tailored burgundy suit brushed past, glaring at the men in rushed irritation.

"Stray?" Vyron asked. "You can't take me there!"

"You live on Level Nine, Fethru, and run with a gang known for brutality."

"Yeah, and I got roped into dealing chems for them. I was abducted by a rival gang, you know."

Coldhand didn't answer. Vyron raised his cuffed hands in an imploring gesture.

"I only made it here because the Steelskins protected me," he said. "They can't help me on Stray!"

The bounty hunter shrugged. "Keep moving."

"But–"

"Move," Coldhand said.

Vyron turned away and resumed walking slowly through the city. But not silently.

"Why do you keep your ship up here?" the Dailon asked. "It's got to cost a fistful of color. It'd be cheaper a level or two down."

"Level One aerofields have priority for takeoffs and landings. Any ship leaving from a lower-level port may have to wait several hours, but I can be off the ground in under five minutes. That's worth the extra colour."

Vyron stumbled down the busy sidewalk, glancing frequently back over his shoulder at Coldhand. His mouth worked and he tried to find another question to fill the silence, but found none. Coldhand didn't offer one.

The bounty hunter finally directed Vyron to turn left down a quiet side street that eventually led to an arched wrought iron gate. It was set into a colorful wall high enough to cramp the neck of the tallest Hadrian trying to see the top. An elegantly austere etched silver plate affixed to one of the gateposts read *Haven Field*. The wall's shiny tiled surface was an almost impenetrable layer of ceramic armor that covered the entirety of the tall barrier, all painted with a graceful and colorful geometric pattern. The decoration might come close to convincing a casual observer that they were looking at something more welcoming than an airfield so secure that it bordered on being a fortress.

At Coldhand's approach, a hologram appeared from a hidden projector and displayed a young Lyran woman with glossy white fur and golden eyes. She smiled warmly, if toothily.

"Good afternoon, sirs, and welcome to the Haven Field airbase. My name is Arianna. How can I help you?" she asked. Her voice was pleasant and transmitted with almost no mechanical buzz over expensive fiber optics from wherever she was.

"I'm here to get my Raptor," Coldhand said.

Arianna tapped a few keys not picked up by the holo-feed. "Ah, Mister Coldhand?"

He nodded.

"You have a balance due of two hundred eighty-four point three cenmarks before we can release your vessel," Arianna said.

"I have it."

"Will you be paying in cash?" the Lyran asked.

"No, the money is in one of my accounts."

"Please enter your account information, Mister Coldhand, and we can release your craft."

A keyboard slid out from under the screen. Coldhand typed in the account number and the keyboard withdrew. The Lyran receptionist glanced at her computer again.

"Thank you very much, Mister Coldhand. Your funds have been verified and your Raptor has been released for takeoff. Will you require any additional assistance?"

"I'll need some grade five illonium shielding and the use of one of your mechanics for about fifteen minutes."

"We can have a technician report to your hangar immediately and bill your account. Will that be all, sir?"

"Yes."

"We thank you for your continued business, Mister Coldhand," Arianna said. "Haven Field looks forward to serving your needs in the future. Safe flying and have a nice day."

The hologram of the Lyran vanished and with a buzz like the release of a prison cell door, the heavy gates unlocked. They swung smoothly open on mechanized hinges and Coldhand pushed Vyron through ahead of him. The gate clanged shut behind them.

Vyron stared around this latest prison. Hangars and repair bays were all arranged in straight rows of the same stark military design.

A more corporate building sat in the southeast corner, sided with the polarized glass popular all across Level One. A pair of blast-phalt runstrips – both vacant for the moment – dominated the rest of Haven Field.

Coldhand took Vyron toward one of the hangars. The doors were equipped with a massive computerized lock, but true to her word, the Lyran receptionist had released it. The entry was wide open by the time the two men reached the hangar.

Inside, taking up less than a quarter of the available space, was the Raptor. Afterward, Vyron certainly would not have said that Coldhand relaxed when he saw his ship, but some of the steely tension seemed to bleed away and the hunter's glacial eyes softened just a little.

Raptors were far from the most beautiful, fast or deadly fighters in the galaxy, but they were tough and could take one hell of a beating. Much like the Prians who made them, some said. The fighter had a standard conical body with long, backswept wings and short tail fins, all plated in a thick layer of illonium armor.

And Coldhand's Raptor could clearly give as good at it got. The small ship bristled with weapons: missile launchers slung under the wings, an NI chain gun mounted on the right side of the cockpit and a double-barreled laser in the nose of the armored fighter.

Vyron swallowed hard. How often did his captor need that kind of weaponry?

A pair of elongated pods were fitted over each of the Raptor's wings, connected over the ship's body by an arch of fibersteel. The pods looked like extra engines and the name *Long Wings* was stenciled on the side above a serial number.

PPFC LWAP 2144-23VA

Coldhand unlatched the Raptor's canopy and flipped a switch, turning on the computer inside to begin a prelaunch diagnostic.

The computer beeped at him and began scrolling rapidly through text and numbers. Vyron noted unhappily that between all of the sensor panels and controls, there was barely room in the Raptor for a pilot, much less a passenger.

"We're not flying all the way out to Stray in this, are we?" Vyron asked.

Coldhand ignored him as another Lyran trotted into the hangar wearing a mechanic's jumpsuit and produced a plastic case filled with sheets of silver-white illonium.

"Is this what you need?" he asked.

Coldhand glanced at the rectangles of metal. "Yes. Now I need you to install it."

The Lyran looked at the Raptor. "Grade five isn't used on hulls, sir. Do you have some system repairs to make?"

"It's not for my ship." Coldhand extended his cybernetic hand.

The Lyran inspected the damaged illonium skin and probed the welded joints with a thoughtful frown. "I can fit and fix replacements in about fifteen minutes."

"Do it," Coldhand said. He looked at Vyron. "Don't run. Haven Field is completely enclosed. There's nowhere to go."

"I wasn't going to," Vyron answered.

He hadn't been, but now it was all he could think about and Vyron wished Coldhand had said nothing at all. Fifteen minutes later, the Lyran mechanic pronounced his task complete. Coldhand flexed his cybernetic fingers and curled them into a fist. A faint mechanical whirring came from the servos.

Vyron flinched. Why didn't he buy a real hand?

Apparently satisfied, Coldhand dismissed the mechanic and opened a small cargo area in the side of the Raptor. He pulled out a dark blue flight suit, rolled up around the helmet. It looked heavy in his hands. Vyron guessed that like his cybernetics and his ship, the hunter's suit was armored, meant to keep him alive when someone else wanted to make him otherwise.

Unabashedly, Coldhand stripped to put on the suit and his pale skin prickled in Axis' artificially brisk air. Vyron could make out scars across his chest, most old and white, but overlaid with a few fresh, livid ones. One of the new stripes was nearly the length of his arm, stretching from shoulder to navel. Whatever had made it was a long weapon, to judge by the straight length of the scars.

Vyron turned quickly away and stared at the notice posted on the hangar wall until Coldhand tossed his discarded clothes back into the small cargo hatch.

"Get in," he said, pointing to the Raptor.

"But… it's only a fighter," Vyron objected, even as he obeyed and pulled himself into the tiny seat behind the pilot's chair. "Tell me you have a larger ship in orbit…"

"No. The Long Wings pods each contain superluminal engines," Coldhand said, gesturing to the augmentations fitted over his fighter's wings. "They're just as fast as the bigger birds. We should be there in four or five days."

"Five days? In this?" Vyron asked.

Coldhand leaned in as he situated himself and handed Vyron a pair of small hoses that attached to the side of the cockpit. Vyron took them awkwardly in his cuffed hands.

"Um… what are these?" he asked.

"Waste collection. Put them in."

"You can't be serious," Vyron said. He regarded the tubes as though they were live snakes.

"I won't have you pissing yourself inside my bird. Put them in yourself or I will."

Vyron's face went hot and he did as Coldhand instructed. The human climbed into the pilot's seat, affixed another pair of hoses to his blue flight suit and set his helmet on the instrument panel. The Raptor thrummed as he powered up the engines and steered the fighter out onto the runstrip. He radioed Axis control to request permission to take off, and was immediately granted clearance.

Coldhand pulled back on the throttle and the fighter accelerated down the runway. Speed shoved Vyron into his tiny seat hard enough that he struggled for breath. The Raptor angled and then shot upward, arrowing through the pale blue sky of Axis and into the star-studded black of space. Through his blurred vision, Vyron almost thought he saw the bounty hunter smile.

[18]
BLIND EYES

"No matter who you try to take with you, death will always remain
a cold and lonely bed."

- NOMUSA UDO, MIRRAN WRITER (230 MA)

*Maeve lay in a slanting ray of golden sunlight with her head pillowed in
Orthain's lap, her ink-black hair spilling over his thighs. The garden of
Morningfire Court was full of singing birds, but Maeve was only listening
to one song.*

> *"Time lay in its cradle quietly*
> *Once upon a day long ago*
> *Not the song of Erris is heard*
> *Yet voices carried on the wind faintly."*

*Orthain sang the ancient ballad of her family in a smooth, sweet
voice that wove seamlessly with nightingales trilling in the apple tree, the
velvety drone of bees humming from flower to flower, and the whisper of
the distant sea.*

Laughing spring winds come whispering
To find that Aes lays no longer
In her high, heavenly bower
But in a mortal wing's embrace so loving

Two hundred eighty-eight days of light
Will be desired by a Night
If you would dare lay claim to the right
To ask a gift of the White..."

Orthain brushed a strand of Maeve's hair back from her face and she felt the heat there in her cheeks. After seven years, it was still so strange. The lightest brush of Orthain's fingers made warmth surge through Maeve, but he had pushed the bounds of their new romance no further. The knight would bide his time. One did not rush the courtship of a princess, after all, even a princess as far removed from the birchwood throne as Maeve Cavainna.

Orthain's dark green eyes sparkled in Aes' bright sunlight and Maeve's heart skipped a fluttering beat. He sang the ancient story of Cavain's birth, his victory over the fiery pyrads and the early founding of the White Kingdom. Finally, the last chorus faded away into the garden's song.

"You have paid your respects to me for more than the promised year, enarri," Maeve said. "We have shared three oathsongs. You are within your rights to make at least one request of me!"

Orthain smiled. He wasn't wearing his glass armor here in Morning-fire Court. There was no duty here in the garden, only songs and gentle touches. So Orthain wore a flowing skirt of House Fyre red and purple, leaving his chest and feet bare. His wings and long blond hair were damp from bathing, drying slowly in the sun.

"There are few things that I desire which we have not yet shared, Maeve," he said. "And I would never use the rules of the Lay of Cavain to obligate you, enarri."

Orthain's eyes lingered on the princess. She wasn't wearing her armor either, but her soft golden silk dress covered more of her body than Orthain's skirt. Yet Maeve blushed under his scrutiny.

"Will you come with me to Caith's initiation tomorrow?" she asked.

"Of course, enarri," Orthain said. "It was, I admit with the utmost modesty, my suggestion that he study spell-singing at the Ivory Spire. I would not miss his graduation, and your father would never forgive me if I did. It has been half a century since I was Sir Arlinn's squire, but I still fear the man's spear."

"My father? What about my mother's reproach?" Maeve asked. "She is the king's sister, you may know."

Orthain laughed and plucked a small blue flower off a nearby bush. He trailed the star-shaped bloom over Maeve's lips.

"Princess Beltain is a standard of grace and diplomacy the worlds over, enarri. I do not know that I would even realize if she were actually angry with me."

"And what of me, my enarri?" Maeve plucked the sky-colored flower from Orthain's fingers and tucked it behind one of her pointed ears. "Do you have such confidence that you could face my wrath?"

"None," Orthain said with a grin. "I have taught you too well. I would not risk battle against you."

But the knight sobered quickly and Maeve sat up, frowning.

"What is it?" she asked. "I was only playing..."

Orthain sighed. "I know, Maeve."

He reached out to trail his fingers through her black hair, then down her cheek.

"You will be leaving soon," Orthain said. "Caith will be assigned to the Waygates and you will go with him. That is all both of you ever wanted."

"I love my brother."

"More than you love me?" Orthain asked. "No, that is an unworthy question. Caith is blood. I love you and would see you both happy, enarri. But I will miss you."

Maeve could think of nothing to say.

Maeve woke with a groan, trying to push away the clinging threads of her dreams and memories. The past could never stay quiet, even a century gone. It was no enemy that Maeve could fight or flee. Or even endure.

She unfurled her sweat-sticky wings and arched her back. Her spine popped, protesting a night spent on the ground. By the dim light filtering through the glassless window, Maeve guessed that it was not long after dawn, but it was already swelteringly hot inside the black cathedral.

Perhaps more accustomed to the cloying heat, the rest of the Church of Nihil's congregation still slept. Only a few others were awake at this hour, milling aimlessly around the cathedral. Elsa was up, carrying servings of thin porridge on a tray. The Mirran woman offered one of the bowls to Maeve. Even though her stomach rumbled, Maeve declined. She needed to think.

Her com was still aboard the Blue Phoenix. It was programmed with the ship's frequency, as well as the crew's personal channels and those of some of her more often frequented chem dealers. If Maeve's fraud was uncovered, it didn't seem like a good idea to give the potentially violent Church of Nihil such an easy way to find her co-conspirators, so she had left it behind.

Maeve couldn't call back to the Blue Phoenix to report her few findings or request help. If she left to go speak with Tiberius or Gripper in person, it might arouse suspicion from the Nihilists. Maeve was on her own for now.

Bren was also awake, checking on those who lay too still and smiling when he found an old man who would never rise again. Maeve picked her way across the church to stand beside the Nihilist doctor.

He smiled at the fairy as she approached and gestured toward the body of the dead man, already stiffening in the morning heat.

Maeve resisted the urge to cover her mouth and nose. In death, the man had messily emptied his bowels and bladder in the dirt. The stinking mud oozed across the cathedral floor.

"All that remains is a husk," Bren said. "Empty and perfect."

Perfect? Maeve had to disagree. The corpse was dressed in the same robes as everyone else in this place, but in his final convulsions, the man had raised his hands, perhaps in supplication or merely the misfiring of his failing nervous system. His ragged black sleeves had fallen back to reveal sores, old and crusted with blood, and dark veins extending down his forearms. Maeve looked reflexively at her own arms, at the sleeves covering similar discolorations.

"He is beyond pain and sorrows," Bren said.

Bren took her hand and pressed it to the dead human's chest. Maeve's skin crawled and she wanted to shriek in disgust. But she was supposed to be like him now and Maeve made herself remain still.

"Listen to the perfect silence of death," Bren told her. "Have you ever heard anything more beautiful?"

A thousand things, Maeve thought. The songs of the nyads as they beckoned men to them from the water's edge. The crystal bells of the Ivory Spire rung at golden dawn. Orthain's voice singing to her in the gardens of her home. Caith's laughter when she told him a joke.

But Maeve shook her head at Bren. She gagged on the stench of excrement, felt the Nihilist holding her hand to a dead man's still chest. But she deserved this, she knew. The core races believed in a multitude of hells, but not a one of them was deep enough for Maeve's sins.

Finally, Bren let go of her hand and stepped back. The Nihilist's gaze swept over Maeve, looking deeply disappointed at her health. He sketched a mocking little bow, turned and left to continue his morning's work. Maeve stood beside the corpse, not knowing what else to do.

Not much later, the rest of the congregation had roused themselves. Most of the Nihilists seemed no busier than Maeve, simply sitting or lying wherever they had slept the night before.

There was a polite cough behind her. Maeve turned and looked up to see Elsa, a bundle of folded cloth in her arms.

"To wind him," Elsa explained, hefting the fabric and pointing to the body.

Elsa found a relatively clean patch of dirt and worked with surprising speed and care, winding the corpse in three long sheets that covered him from head to toe. On her knees, she was about eye level with Maeve.

"Can you help me get him out back?" she asked.

Out back...? The Nihilist church was on the very outskirts of Gharib. What could be behind the cathedral other than empty sand? But Maeve nodded and took the dead man's cloth-swaddled feet. Elsa grabbed his shoulders and together, they dragged the corpse off the stone and away to the back of the cathedral.

The waking congregation in the crowded church cleared a path for Maeve and Elsa, standing aside and watching the tiny mortuary procession pass. One by one, then in a huge huddled group, the Nihilists began to follow. Many prayed aloud, some to the god of the Union of Light, others murmuring to themselves in other languages to other deities, grasping at the forgotten psalms of religions that predated Aver.

The Arcadians fell in at the back of the procession and sang a hymn to the Nameless. The fairies always sang. Even as the Devourers ripped their wings off and split bone in their fanged maws, the Arcadians sang.

By the time Maeve and Elsa reached the back of the cathedral, about half of the Nihilists were following behind them. Though most eyes were on the body they carried, Elsa seemed to enjoy the attention. Maeve kept her head bowed behind a curtain of bleached blonde hair, hoping that no one studied her too closely.

Elsa paused, set down her burden and peeled aside a sheet of fibersteel from the back of the church.

If Maeve expected to see a door cunningly concealed behind the metal, she was disappointed. The jagged piece of fibersteel *was* the door, bolted inelegantly above a roughly rectangular hole in the cathedral wall. Elsa hefted the limp weight of the dead man's shoulders once more. No one else had come forward to take up the burden. Maeve and Elsa carried him out of the cathedral.

At first, Maeve wondered if the Nihilist congregation intended to just heave the body out into the desert dunes that forever lapped at the edge of Gharib like the waves of a dry, hungry ocean. The ground behind the Church of Nihil was a rocky, flat expanse that covered at least an acre. Gavriel must have chosen the stoniest ground in all of Gharib on which to build his ramshackle black cathedral, Maeve reflected sourly. Dust had blown up over the rocks, obscuring them from sight. But the sandy mounds were laid out in ordered rows.

Tombstones.

There had to be five hundred or more headstones, but it was almost impossible to count them beneath the sand. Rows of dusty graves stretched off in every direction. The wind whipped up clouds of sand, unhindered by the windbreaks surrounding Gharib, and stung Maeve's eyes.

Anthem had told Xia that the church wasn't very old, or at least had not been in Gharib for long. Where did so many graves come from? Surely one or two deaths a night couldn't account for such a vast graveyard. Who else lay buried by Nihilist hands in the dry dust? The Sisterhood? Not unless the Sisterhood was far larger on Stray than the vast city-world of Axis. Kessa's gang wouldn't have filled more than a corner of the Nihilist graveyard. Was Elsa's husband out there, too? How many had the Church of Nihil killed?

Nihilists poured out of their church like maggots from a corpse. At Elsa's instruction, they found a tiny plot of unmarked ground and began to dig. None of the Nihilists had shovels or even cruder digging implements. They tore into the loose dust, then the hard-packed ground with their bare hands. It wasn't long before there wasn't room for more than a single digger to work in the deepening hole. They scrambled one by one down into the ground to dig in the dirt their hands were bloody.

Every Nihilist who took a turn in the ground did so with religious zeal, tearing away at the last bonds of life with fingers bruised and bleeding. What was this to them? Punishment? Worship?

When her turn came, Maeve couldn't risk refusing the Nihilists' twisted honor, so she squeezed down into the hole. The other death-worshipers had been at their business for hours and the grave was deep enough now for the crumbling lip to rise up over her bleach-blonde head. Maeve held her wings close to her back, but there simply wasn't enough room. Stones jutting out from the wall of the narrow grave caught at her long feathers, bending and breaking them. The close air stank of blood and sweat.

Maeve scratched and clawed at the rocky ground until her back and fingers ached. The prayers and songs of those outside of the hole above were muted and echoed in the narrow grave. Down under the sand and stone, time stretched like the spun sugar that Maeve had loved so much as a child. She couldn't see the dim red sun as it measured out minutes or hours.

Her hair, her eyes, her mouth were full of choking dust. Caith had been less fond of candy... right? He always gave Maeve the larger share of any treat. But he would have done anything for his sister. Maeve would have done anything for Caith... and had.

Maeve dug her fingernails into the ground to pry up thin handfuls of dry dirt, which she flung up and out of the hole. It wasn't long before her nails were torn raggedly and blood oozed from beneath them.

Maeve kept digging, surrounded by the dead. Only thin walls of brittle dust separated her from the next grave, from the corpses all around her. From their staring eyes and slack jaws, open to ask horrid, idiot questions.

What happened?

Why am I so cold on this hot world?

Maeve dug faster. Sweat poured down the back of her neck and between her wings. Maeve should have been down here, too. She deserved it. Eight million other Arcadians lay dead in the broken remains of the White Kingdom. Ten million dryads and thirteen million nyads all consumed, eaten raw like carrion. Every life in the White Kingdom was gutted and torn apart by the Devourers. All dead... Maeve hurled fistfuls of salty mud from the grave with wordless, sobbing cries of rage.

"Maeve! Enarri, listen to me! I have to go! I have to close the Tamlin gate!"

Orthain was shouting over the whine of laserfire and screams of dying knights. There were dead among the Devourers, too, but so few. The monsters didn't scream when twenty knights finally managed to bring one down, or even leave a body behind. They faded into shadows of shifting black dust and vanished like something out of a nightmare.

Orthain was flying close enough to Maeve that she could feel the brush of his wings against hers. His hair was tangled by wind, sweat and blood, and Orthain's left eye was darkly bruised. Both knights' armor was smeared with gore, some once belonging to Devourers and some to fae, and the glass was webbed with fine cracks. The rainbow of tourney and questing ribbons hanging from their spears were stained red and black by battle.

"No!" Maeve cried. "Get through the Waygate! Evacuate with the others!"

They circled the westernmost Waygate plaza. The mosaic below was laid out in the crimson likeness of a setting sun, but the design was lost under the storm of white wings as Arcadians pushed and shoved their way through the Waygates. The gates flickered with blue light as fairies fled through them. The smells of blood and smoke were thick in the air.

"Go with them," Maeve said. "Get away from here!"

"The Devourers will follow us!" Orthain shouted. His spear was broken in half and blood ran down his face. "If we let those monsters into the core, trillions will die! But the Spire adepts have an idea... If we can close the Tamlin Waygate, it will banish the Devourers."

"But there is no way to get one of the spell-singers close to the Tamlin gate. It is suicide! And they are needed here, to get our people to safety."

"You are right," Orthain said.

Maeve could barely hear him over the screams and sounds of battle surging through the streets of Arcadia. But she saw the resolve in his expression.

"Orthain, no!" Maeve cried. "You cannot think to go to Tamlin! You are no Spire singer. You will die and for nothing!"

"I will die trying to save what is left of our kingdom," Orthain said. "The Spire adepts have told me what to do. I can only hope it is enough, but I have never worked a Waygate protection."

Maeve's heart turned to ice inside her.

"But I have," she said. "I will fly to Tamlin with you, Orthain. I will close the Waygate."

"Maeve, no! You are a princess of the House of Cavain. You are needed here, with your people! Get through the Waygates!"

"I am not their queen!" Maeve shouted.

Orthain wheeled through the air and caught her by the arm, pointing to the closing lines of roiling black moving through the city below. Glass and blood shone in the sunlight.

"King Illain is wounded and we cannot locate the crown princess," Orthain said. "My enarri, your mother and brother are dead. Before today is done, you will be all that remains of the royal house. Your people are frightened and lost. You will be their queen and they will need you!"

Maeve pulled her arm out of Orthain's grasp and beat her wings hard to regain altitude.

"Whatever else I may be, I am a knight of Arcadia," she told him. "If you are right, and if there is ever to be anything left for our people to *return to, then I am going to the Tamlin Waygate. Tell me what it is the Spire adepts instructed you to do."*

"No, I will not!" Orthain shouted against the hot, fetid wind. "I cannot send you to Tamlin to die! I love you!"

"If I am to be your queen," Maeve said, "then consider it a command."

Orthain's eyes flew wide and his steady wingbeat faltered, but he bowed his head. "Yes, Your Highness. I will tell you all that I can, but you will never reach the Tamlin gate alone."

"No," Maeve agreed. "I will need your help, Sir Fyre, and any knights that can be spared from the evacuation."

"We will die," Orthain said.

Maeve wiped the tears out of her eyes and nodded. "Yes, we will."

[19]
WORTH OF A STONE

"Killing time poisons eternity."

— ARCADIAN PROVERB

"Shae?"

For a potentially fatal moment, Maeve didn't recognize her false name. Elsa leaned over the rim of the grave and touched her wing.

"Shae, you can stop now," she said. "The hole is plenty deep."

Maeve straightened and looked down. Sure enough, her frenzied digging had considerably deepened the pit. How long had she been clawing at the hard-packed sand? A skinny Arcadian man reached down to her, helping Maeve scramble up out of the grave.

The swollen Stray sun was already dipping down toward the eastern horizon. It had been mid-afternoon when Maeve climbed into the ground. She frowned at another day almost gone without enough information to take back to the Blue Phoenix. Elsa took the princess' hands, squinting critically at the bloody scrapes there.

"You'll need some cold water and bandages on these," Elsa said. "Or you're going to get an infection."

"Is that not desirable?" Maeve asked.

The tall Mirran shook her curly green hair and led Maeve back toward the church.

"Oh no," Elsa said. "The dirt here is full of bad things. They can turn your nails black and peel off some of your skin, but none of them will kill you. Come inside and I'll clean them up."

More pain wasn't the point of the church, Maeve supposed. Anything short of death was just a petty annoyance. Maeve glanced back at the graveyard. Four of the Nihilists – three humans and a Lyran with matted calico fur – lifted the cloth-wrapped corpse and lowered it feet first into the grave. The dead man thumped and then sagged against the walls. Everyone picked up heaping handfuls of dirt and threw them down into the hole, quickly refilling it. The calico Lyran trotted off into the desert in search of a new headstone.

Elsa whistled and Maeve turned away. Back inside the church, Elsa sat her down on a bench made of a gray siltstone slab propped up on a pair of stout cargo canisters. The other Nihilists gave Maeve a wide berth, perhaps out of respect for her recent endeavors, or maybe just trying to avoid the stink of the dead man still clinging to her. Elsa left for a few minutes and then returned carrying a cup of water with some precious cubes of ice floating in it, and a strip of clean cloth. Elsa wetted the fabric in the cold water and dabbed at Maeve's fingers.

"Should you not use hot water?" she asked.

A knight's training involved a little field medicine, not much more than splinting broken bones, patching up wounded wings and a few basic pain-killing charms. Maeve recalled Orthain telling her to use water as hot as possible to wash open wounds, preferably steeped with willow bark for the pain and starkroot to help clean out any potential infections.

"Not for things that grow in the dirt here," Elsa said. She fanned herself somewhat theatrically with one hand and smiled at the fairy. "Germs on Stray like the heat, yeah? They stay warm at night in the ground because the cold kills them off."

Maeve wasn't a doctor and she accepted Elsa's explanation with a shrug. It sounded reasonable enough and Elsa appeared trustworthy. Despite the foreboding church that had become her home, Elsa was a gentle and kind woman and her devotion to Gavriel and his teachings seemed a waste.

She deserved better. Elsa's open innocence had cost her dearly. Maeve remembered the terrible scar hidden by the Mirran's hair. Her husband had done that to her and Maeve found herself hating the dead man.

"The Church of Nihil keeps an extensive graveyard. I confess to being surprised," Maeve said. "I am humbled by the many dead in this sacred place."

She was worried she might have overdone it a little bit, but Elsa just bobbed her head in agreement as she dabbed cold water onto Maeve's cuts.

"There are many in the ground here," Elsa said. "I've buried a lot of them. Some die here at night. Some die from being sick. Some die from fighting."

"Fighting? Like Gavriel's battle with your husband?"

"Yes."

"And the police of Gharib do nothing?"

"No," Elsa answered. "Lord Gavriel tells us they're just another problem. They are scared and lazy, so we have to do it."

"Cleansing the city?" Maeve asked. "Did your people fight the Sisterhood?"

"Sisterhood...?" Elsa gave her a blank look.

"A group of women. They would have worn armbands marked by an elongated red triangle, the symbol of their faith."

Elsa nodded. "Yes, that was their sign."

"When did this happen?"

"When I first came to Stray... Two or five years ago."

So the Nihilists *had* hunted the Sisterhood. The Sisters fought back and lost. How did one fight opponents who didn't fear death?

Battling these Nihilists would be like warring against a legion of Logan Coldhands. A shudder worked its way down Maeve's spine. The story was probably much the same all over Stray. Anthem told Xia that the Sisterhood had vanished from all of the major cities and it was now clear why.

"How many of the Sisters did Gavriel have killed?" asked Maeve. "How many are buried out there?"

"Not a lot. There weren't very many. Maybe twenty?"

That was just here in Gharib... but it wasn't nearly enough to fill the graveyard behind the black cathedral. Unhindered by lazy and corrupt police, Gavriel and his Nihilists had killed hundreds more. This world wasn't safe for Kessa and her child. Even if the Nihilists believed that the Sisterhood was gone and no longer hunted them down, any perceived transgression against the Church of Nihil would place Kessa in mortal danger. Gavriel's people worshiped death in all its forms...

"Thank you, Elsa," Maeve said. "You have helped me more than you can know."

Maeve took the Mirran's striped hands in hers and squeezed gently. Elsa gave her a grateful – and confused – smile, then gathered up the water and unused bandages. She hurried off to find other tasks in service to the cathedral.

The last two days of work had paid off and Maeve finally had her answer. The Church of Nihil was a twisted cult, too dangerous to Kessa. Maeve looked up through gaps in the cathedral ceiling. The sky had darkened and the air was rapidly cooling to an icy cold that made Maeve think of Logan.

Once full night fell, Maeve would slip out of the church and return to the Blue Phoenix and report the news to Tiberius. They would have to begin the search again.

Xartasia had condescended to walk beside Gavriel instead of flying back to the Gharib cathedral. She wore her white cloak and veil once again, covering her black hair. Xartasia walked gracefully next to him, floating like cotton down on a breeze. One of her small, perfectly smooth hands rested delicately on Gavriel's arm. He moved slowly and couldn't support much of the fairy's diminutive weight. The years had robbed him of so much strength...

Gavriel had covered himself, too, layered in the black robes of his order with the hood pulled up. His withered old body couldn't withstand the cold of the desert night. Xartasia leaned close, deceptively intimate for the benefit of the few who still roamed the streets at such a late hour.

"You must learn greater patience," she told him.

"I'm an old man, princess. I don't have time to be patient anymore," Gavriel said with disgust in his rich voice. "I'm not really interested in keeping my enemies alive. I want them dead. I want *everyone* dead."

"Death holds a place of high honor and divine purpose for both of us, but there are moments in which *life* can better serve our needs. You should not have killed those men so quickly. We might have been able to make use of them."

"I don't need anything from anyone, Xartasia."

"Do not be a fool, Gavriel. You have for many years needed me. I was your teacher not so long ago..."

"And I paid my respects for a full year, just as your traditions demanded. You gave me no charity. What I had, I earned," Gavriel said. "I've taught your magic to students of my own since then. But *you* have an undischarged debt to me, princess."

Xartasia dismissed his objection with an airy flip of her feathered wings.

"You have taught one, old friend, and that boy was no student. He was an accident," Xartasia said. Her intense violet eyes caught Gavriel's sunken gaze. They burned with an almost palpable flame.

"That boy learned from you only because he was a part of your charms. He felt every spell you had to direct through him and discerned how to wield your spells for himself. We should not have used a living vessel for your magic. You lost everything when the boy ran away."

"The boy?" Gavriel asked. "He had a name. Duaal Sinnay."

Gavriel peered at Xartasia suspiciously. He couldn't read her expression behind the white veil, and her twilight eyes were always mysterious. Of course, even if she were standing naked before him, Gavriel wasn't at all certain he could discern the fairy's mind. For a princess of her people, Xartasia seemed to have many enemies and hid herself from them well.

"If it was such a bad idea to use a living tool like Duaal, then why are you lecturing me about killing that streetwalking trash?" Gavriel asked.

"Only for killing them too soon," Xartasia said. She might have smiled behind her veil. "There are ways to retrieve the power lost when the child left. But taking it will require effort."

"What kind of effort, exactly?" Gavriel asked. "I'm not getting any younger while you wait to make your point."

"Taking your power from one place – even such a wellspring of energies as Duaal – is inherently weaker," Xartasia answered. "You must hold your power within yourself, so it cannot be taken from you once again. I will teach you to take what you need."

They were nearing the Gharib cathedral. The quiet marketplace was behind them and even the scant shops and homes at the edge of the city were becoming fewer and far between. Against the darkness of the night sky, the deeper blackness of the cathedral reached up toward the stars like a skeletal hand.

Xartasia seemed about to say more, but then she stopped and watched the sky with wide violet eyes. Gavriel followed her gaze just in time to see a white-winged shape soaring overhead, away from the Church of Nihil. He squinted. It had to be an Arcadian – there was no bird on Stray with a wingspan like that.

Why was Xartasia staring? There were fairies all over this dustball planet. The princess watched the departing shadow long after the night had swallowed even the faintest trace of white feathers.

"Eru nai'i Shae…" she murmured. When Xartasia turned back to Gavriel, she was smiling. He could see it there in her sparkling eyes. "Patience. Remember the worth of a stone."

"Yes. A boulder will sit on a mountainside for centuries without complaint until the landslide comes, carrying it away down the mountain to crush what lies below," Gavriel said, nodding. Decades ago, he had told the Arcadian princess that story himself, a parable from the treacherous mines of his dismal gray homeworld. "Damn it, alright. Show me what to do and I will have the patience to do it."

They walked in silence again as Xartasia gathered her thoughts. When they finally arrived at the cathedral, Bren roused himself from his sleeping pad beside the door. He bowed deeply.

"Are you thirsty, Holy One?" Bren asked.

Gavriel nodded, but Xartasia was carefully removing her white veil and paying no attention to the glassy-eyed Nihilist doctor. She watched the slumbering shapes scattered across the cathedral, but none of them approached. Most slept fitfully in the cold, ragged blankets pulled up around them as they shivered. A few of the Nihilists remained awake, but there were no lamps lit and no one of them seemed to have noticed Gavriel's return.

Bren called out for Elsa to bring them something to drink. The Mirran woman delivered three glasses of water, and Bren handed them to Gavriel and Xartasia, then took the last for himself. Elsa bowed and retreated into the darkness.

"What brings you back to us so soon, my lord?" Bren asked Gavriel.

"Have any other Arcadians come to the cathedral since we have been gone?" Xartasia interrupted.

Bren jumped, startled at the sudden attention from the striking fairy woman. He thought for a moment before answering. "Ah... Yes, Lady Xartasia. Twelve of them in the past two days."

"Did any of them have black hair?"

Bren blinked and then shook his head. "No, my lady. All blonde. Except for you, of course."

"Are you certain of that?" she asked.

"Yes, Lady Xartasia," Bren answered.

Gavriel knew from long experience with Xartasia that there was deadly importance in that question, but he didn't know what it was. He scowled.

Elsa waited in the darkness of the cathedral with her head cocked, listening. Lady Xartasia was a new arrival to the Church of Nihil, but already second only to Lord Gavriel in authority. Still, Elsa didn't quite trust the pretty Arcadian. Most of the fairies Elsa had met were sad. It made her sad, too, but nothing she did or said ever seemed to help. Lady Xartasia wasn't sad, though.

She was angry.

Even Lord Gavriel was different since Xartasia arrived. Elsa had always been scared of him, but at least he ignored her. Gavriel freed Elsa from her husband, but that did little to make her less frightened of the intense old man. She loved him – all of the Nihilists did – but figured it was better if she admired him from far, far away.

When Xartasia looked at Elsa, there was something frightening in her purple eyes. It was a sort of easy, casual dismissal, as though Elsa were some small, disgusting thing on a floor she was scrubbing. Something that, while annoying and inconvenient, was easily overlooked because it would soon be gone. Not that Lady Xartasia would ever clean a floor... Just thinking of it made Elsa giggle to herself. She put her hands over her mouth to keep quiet.

She wasn't doing anything wrong, not really. No one had ever expressly forbidden Elsa to listen to church business, but it was probably better if Lord Gavriel and Lady Xartasia didn't know.

Xartasia must have been asking about the new girl, Shae, who had come in yesterday morning. Shae's hair wasn't as golden as the other fairies. Some of the parts closest to her head were still black, as though Shae had been in a hurry coloring her hair yellow. Why did it matter if Shae had black hair?

Elsa didn't know why Xartasia was looking for Shae, but it was a bad idea to make the great lady wait. It would be best if Shae went to her now instead of waiting until morning. Elsa tiptoed through the cold, restless darkness to where the new fairy had lain down for the night, but when Elsa reached Shae's flat slab of gray siltstone, it was empty.

The Mirran searched around the church, wondering if Shae had moved. There was no sign of her anywhere, though. Elsa contemplated telling Lady Xartasia that Shae had left, but that didn't seem like a good idea.

Instead, Elsa slipped silently away to go get some sleep. Shae seemed smart. She would know what to do when Xartasia finally found her.

[20]
AERIE

"I have seen other worlds of the Alliance, with all their blessings and gifts. And I can only say that I love Prianus all the more for what we have given ourselves."

- MARCUS VERA, PRIAN CONSUL (35 PA)

There was little in the way of conversation in the Raptor. Superluminal speed shift turned each star into a streak of dazzling rainbow, scattered spars of color with violet tips tapering off into invisible spectra. Vyron didn't seem inclined to talk anymore and the Dailon man spent most of the four-day journey staring out of the canopy, chewing miserably on the tasteless nutrition rations that his captor provided.

When he was tired or simply too bored to stay awake, Vyron slept. He shifted uncomfortably in his sleep, sitting upright in the small, cramped seat in the back of the Raptor's cockpit. By the third day, all sense of time had been erased by endless hours of star-striped monotony. Vyron's neat black braid had long since come undone and with no external ears to tuck the loose strands behind, his hair hung over his face.

Now he was asleep again, leaning his blue forehead against the inside of the canopy and leaving Coldhand alone with his thoughts. Memories, really, that so often came unbidden in the darkness, either behind closed eyes or between the stars. Waking or sleeping, they would not leave him be.

"Sorry I'm late, dove," Logan said.

He kissed Jess on the head as he came into the room. Her hair was still damp from the shower and smelled of her shampoo. Jess sat in the worn old armchair that dominated an entire corner of their tiny apartment, wearing her favorite red robe. Their battered copy of The Still Wind *lay open in her lap. She frowned at Logan with mock seriousness, but her eyes sparkled mischievously in the lamplight.*

"You're always late. Comes with the territory," Jess said.

But she smiled as she closed the book and set it aside, then stood and put her arms around his waist. Logan hadn't taken the time to change out of his police uniform and his badge reflected the light from its scratched, worn surface. He brushed the fingers of his left hand over it, feeling the cold, scarred metal.

"Prianus needs us, dove," Logan said. "Illius died yesterday and we all have to take turns covering his beat."

"Not that territory, hawk. Being engaged to a musician," Jess told him. She pointed at the guitar case in his right hand. "You stayed late playing, didn't you?"

"A little," Logan confessed. "They wanted to hear Bristler's Call... It was Illius' favorite. Reginald made me play it three times before he would let me go."

Jess kissed Logan soundly, letting her hands roam over parts of him that made the young police officer blush. "I don't think I believe you, my hawk. I'm not sure you even know Stickler's Call..."

"Bristler's," he corrected mildly.

"...So I better make certain that's what you were really doing. For all I know, you might have been picking up some tail trying to get her talons into a cop. Prove it and play the song for me."

Logan chuckled as he took the chair Jess had vacated and opened the guitar case. She sat at his feet, resting her cheek against Logan's knee as he laid the instrument across his lap and began to strum softly. Jess smiled as he sang.

"Caught in the lowlands in the dry season
Flying on fire's wings
Found what I'm looking for
For years gone, I searched beyond reason

After climbing for days a score
Gambling for my quest a life, a love, and a treason
Searching in stone's clasp and under sea's shadow
At long last, to seek never more

On his mountain, Bristler waited with unblinking eye
Waited until, by wind's tempest
I came to the old one's claim
'For a summer, I have searched,' cried I

'To find through soul's desire
'A sire to match my true-blood dame...'"

Logan didn't even get through the second verse before Jess was pulling the guitar out of his hands. She yanked him to his feet and toward the bedroom, fingers already working at the fastenings of his faded uniform. Logan fell into Jess' ready embrace and returned her youthful passion in kind.

Vyron mumbled unhappily in his sleep. Coldhand ignored him until whatever nightmare that chased Vyron seemed to catch up to him and the Dailon cried out. The bounty hunter ducked a flailing fist and Vyron's sleepy punch bounced harmlessly off the pilot's chair.

"Wake up. You're dreaming," Coldhand said.

He spoke loud enough to rouse the other man, but not angrily. Coldhand didn't care about his mark's comfort or peace of mind, but neither did he bear the Dailon any particular malice for disrupting the quiet journey. Vyron was a prisoner. A certain level of disquiet was to be expected.

Vyron woke with a start, cracking his head against the rear wall of the cockpit.

"And now I'm having a nightmare," he groaned. Vyron rubbed his face with his cuffed hands and looked around the Raptor with bemusement. "I'm dying of thirst."

Wordlessly, Coldhand tossed a sealed packet of tepid water over into Vyron's lap and the Dailon tore the corner off the envelope. He sucked down the contents gratefully and then handed the empty package back to Coldhand, who pushed it into a small waste receptacle.

"Do you ever have nightmares?" Vyron asked after a moment.

"No," Coldhand lied.

"I do," Vyron said. "I dreamed that I was back with the Sisters. The other Steels just laughed at me when I told them about what those women did to me. They said it sounded like a free trip up to the entertainment district. They were wrong."

"You're male. You were bound to be mistreated."

Vyron shuddered and combed trembling blue fingers through his hair. "It was horrible. It made me feel so dirty, you know? No, I guess you don't. I can't even imagine anyone trying to rape a man like you."

Coldhand thought back to the Level Seven alleyway, pressed up against the filthy wall with Maeve pointing his own weapon at him. It seemed so long ago now, but only a few weeks had passed. That had been a ruse and nothing more... No man or woman or anyone else had been able to stir his interest since Jess, when he had still been Logan Centra.

Coldhand's first bounty after leaving Prianus had been an Ixthian surgeon with the unsavory habit of stealing organs from his patients while they were under anesthesia. Bringing the man down had earned Coldhand enough money to visit the entertainment districts of Level Three. A few high-marked chips of color bought him two women for the entire night. Less than an hour later, the striped Mirran had stormed out in frustration at Coldhand's lack of response. She had kept his money in her plastihide purse as she stalked out of the rented room.

Coldhand had been so certain that the second woman would be able to seduce him. She had been a stunning Arcadian – bought significantly cheaper than the human prostitute – with golden hair that fell in perfect ringlets nearly to her waist and wide green eyes that reminded him of Jess. And surely her wings would catch his Prian fancy. Coldhand didn't ask the fairy her name, but she had tried all night to please him, never complaining at his unresponsiveness. She even sang a few bedroom charms in a sweet voice, but nothing could rouse Coldhand's unfeeling body. At dawn, the Arcadian woman finally departed, leaving Coldhand lying naked on a cheap bed and wondering why he couldn't even feel ashamed of his failure.

Twenty percent.

"Whoever you're taking me to must be better than the Sisterhood," Vyron said. "That makes me feel a little less awful, but not by much. I wouldn't go back to the Sisters for anything, even if they would protect me from whoever is waiting for me on Stray."

He paused looking out at the elongated stars.

"I guess that's not true, really," he added, voice softening.

"Why?"

"It was horrible, don't misunderstand, but I did get one thing out of the hells with the Sisterhood. When I was there, I met this girl. I don't know what she was doing running with the Sisters. She was sweet and kind to me. I wouldn't have survived without her, and I don't just mean the food and water she brought. She was the only thing that reminded me that people could touch each other without violence or violation. I wonder what happened to her."

"You don't know?" Coldhand asked with sterile curiosity.

"No," Vyron said. He shook his head and immediately looked ill. Artificial gravity played havoc with the equilibrium of those un-accustomed to it. Vyron swallowed and went on. "The Steelskins broke me out of the warehouse where the Sisterhood had been holding me. I wanted to bring her with me, but the Steels didn't really have anything more to offer and there was a damned good chance she would've gotten shot or stabbed for being from a rival gang. I wanted her to be safe. But I miss her sometimes. I hope she's alright."

Coldhand said nothing.

Duaal paced back and forth through the hold of the Blue Phoenix. It was the middle of the night, but no one on the ship slept.

Tiberius sat on top of an empty cargo canister and stared up at the hydroponic garden suspended from the ceiling with a stunned expression. Gripper wasn't far away, hanging off a planter and dis-tractedly eating a red-skinned somato. Another moaning shriek echoed from deeper inside the ship and made the Arboran flinch. Juice dripped down Gripper's rough-boned, brutal-looking face and he looked like he might faint.

Why was this happening now? Kessa wasn't supposed to go into labor for at least another three days. Not until whatever bounty hunter had finally found Maeve's listing returned Vyron to Stray and the fairy herself came back to make her report on the Church of Nihil.

And where the hells was Maeve? Passed out in a dusty alleyway from one drug or another...?

The charms dangling from the hem of Duaal's vest chimed as he paced back across the cargo hold. Over dinner, the Dailon girl's face had gone a pale sky blue as her water broke. Gripper panicked, of course, overturning chairs and nearly the table in his terrified haste. Tiberius had been even more bloodless than Kessa – Duaal didn't know if he had *ever* seen the old Prian looks so terrified. With an effort, Xia restored order, banishing the men to wait in the hold while she led Kessa to the medical bay. Duaal didn't have to be told twice.

That had been at least five hours ago. Tiberius still hadn't said a word, but Gripper wouldn't shut up. He jumped at every wail from the medbay, wringing his claws – huge enough to crush a human skull to splinters – like a fretting grandparent.

"Do you think everything is alright?" Gripper asked the other men. Again. "Maybe I should go find out."

"Xia told us to stay out of her way," Duaal answered. "And we're going to do just that."

"I know, I know... But what if Silver needs some help? Maybe I should ask. I mean, she doesn't have anyone to fetch us, right? I can go check."

"Xia will call us if she needs something," Duaal said, pointing to his com.

"Oh, right."

Gripper seemed more worried about Xia than he was about the Dailon actually giving birth. Duaal didn't wonder at that. Gripper was not skilled at subtlety and his infatuation with the Ixthian doctor was no secret aboard the Blue Phoenix. The only one who never noticed was Xia herself.

While interspecies romances weren't expressly forbidden, they were quite rare among her race. The Ixthians prized genetic purity and pursued it with a society-wide zeal. They couldn't fruitfully breed with any of the other known species and couplings that could not produce offspring were generally considered a waste of time.

As a result, Ixthians were largely unconcerned with the mating rituals of other races and ignored romantic overtures by anyone with less than six fingers on each hand.

The Arboran engineer swung to the next planter on his long arms. He looked down at Tiberius and opened his mouth to ask a question, but was interrupted by a tone from the airlock. All three men jumped as the seal indicator cycled and the door hissed open. Duaal chanted up some elemental lightning between his fingers. What if it was Coldhand? They were expecting a bounty hunter, after all. Duaal would prove his effectiveness against him...

But Duaal was disappointed to see Maeve stepping through the door. She stared around the hold and blinked her gray eyes in surprise at finding everyone awake and apparently waiting for her. Maeve looked like hells. The Arcadian's bleached hair was even filthier than usual – despite being washed only two days ago – and her expensive gown was stained darkly.

The airlock slid shut behind her and sealed. Duaal waved away the crackling lightning and put his hand over his nose and mouth. Maeve reeked of something unclean.

"By God, did you come back through a sewer?" Duaal asked.

Tiberius was up on his feet in an instant, striding in a few long steps to Maeve. The fairy ignored Duaal's question and saluted the captain with her right wing swept across her chest.

"Report," Tiberius ordered.

"This planet is unsafe," she replied promptly in a crisp voice. "The Church of Nihil killed the Sisterhood here on Stray, as well as many others."

"Damn it. Are you sure?"

Tiberius seemed a little more comfortable now, but there was another cry from the medical bay and Maeve's head snapped in the direction of the sound.

"What is happening?" she asked.

"Kessa's gone into labour," Tiberius answered.

"Silver's with her and told everyone to stay out," Gripper said.

But Maeve was already in the air. She ignored the stairs entirely and vaulted up onto the catwalk that led to the rest of the ship. The Arcadian vanished down the hall toward the medical bay.

Duaal leaned against the wall, crossing his arms. It was hot in his brocade and velvet – the cold Stray night was sealed safely away on the other side of the airlock – but what else was new? Nothing. Duaal was uncomfortable and Maeve was taking off on her own personal errand while he sat idle. Tiberius looked frustrated and Duaal couldn't blame him.

"Maeve should've finished her report," Duaal said. "She might have misinterpreted something. She could be wrong."

"I trust Maeve's judgment," said Tiberius, then added: "On this."

Gripper dropped to the floor with a resounding clang. "Smoke has her problems – not that she ever talks much about them, really, though that's beside the point – but she doesn't let them interfere with work. You know, most of the time..."

"Have you already forgotten that she brought Kessa in the first place?" Duaal asked. "And when she did, she dragged Coldhand along for the ride!"

"I haven't forgotten," Tiberius answered. "Do you really think we should have left Kessa to the Sisterhood?"

"Of course not, but..."

"Maeve made the right choice bringing her here," Tiberius said. "Coldhand followed and that wasn't her fault. He wouldn't have let her leave him behind without a fight and that would put Kessa at risk. Maeve may have made some questionable choices in the past and she's just as unpredictable as the rest of you, but I've never regretted making her my first mate."

How could Tiberius actually defend Maeve even now? Even if he was right about Kessa – which Duaal had to admit inwardly that he probably was – how did that excuse Maeve's many past sins? The Blue Phoenix had to flee a lucrative salvage operation in the Hadra system only weeks ago because Maeve's pet bounty hunter found them again. Before that, a shipment to Jormaan was days late because they had to detour into a nebula to shake Coldhand's tail.

Aside from the many dangers of being constantly chased by a bounty hunter, Maeve was often too drunk or low to perform her duties on the ship. She barely bothered to show up for meals, much less report for duty each day. Duaal balled his fists at his side, so tight his brown knuckles were turning white.

"Tiberius, that woman..." Duaal's eyes stung, but he refused to cry. He was a man now, not a frightened little boy to run away and hide. "Maeve is the worst thing that ever happened to this ship. She's going to get us all hurt or killed!"

"Are you questioning me?" Tiberius asked.

"No, sir," Duaal mumbled.

"Still..." Gripper said. "It might have been nice of Smoke to tell us more before she took off. I guess we could follow her and pry the rest of the story out of her."

Another loud cry echoed through the bay. The men looked at each other.

"It can wait," Tiberius said.

Gripper whimpered.

[21]
RELEASE

"Love is the strangest alchemy, able to make even the most leaden heart as light as air."

- XIE, IXTHIAN CHEMIST (856 MA)

It was just as well that Xia didn't keep strong pain medications stocked in the Blue Phoenix's medical bay. The baby was coming early and Kessa screamed with the effort. If Xia had any chemicals more potent than the basic blockers that Tiberius often pilfered, she would have given them to the wailing girl hours ago. They weren't good for the baby, but it was hard to watch Kessa suffer.

She lay on the examination table, her borrowed denims and shirt replaced by a pale green surgical sheet. For the moment, the sheet simply preserved Kessa's modesty, but Xia feared that she would have to use the sheet for its original purpose if the child did not come soon. She hadn't performed a surgical birth in years, not since her intern days, and wasn't eager to test her memory. Xia held Kessa's sweaty hand in her smooth silver one and mopped the Dailon's blue brow with a sponge.

"Push," Xia urged.

"I can't! It hurts so much!" Kessa cried. She flopped back on the table. "Oh God, it's too soon. I'm not ready! I can't do this, Xia!"

Xia released Kessa's hand and dropped the sponge into a tray of cold water. With both hands free, she levered her groaning patient back into a half-sitting position and rubbed her bare shoulders encouragingly.

"You're not doing any of this alone," Xia said in what she hoped was a soothing voice. "I'm here with you. And Vyron will be here soon, too."

"Vyron doesn't know! What if he's angry?" Kessa panted.

"What? He'll be so happy for you both," Xia said. What male wouldn't be thrilled to learn that his genetics had been propagated? "Now push, Kessa! This child won't be born on its own. He needs your help."

"He? Is it a boy?"

"It's a good thing you ran from the Sisterhood," Xia told her. "This little man wouldn't have been safe with them."

Kessa smiled weakly.

"I did something right," she said. "Just once."

Xia hadn't thought to close the door behind her after bringing Kessa to the medical bay. Through the open hatchway, she heard footsteps rapidly approaching. Xia grabbed her laser pistol, the weapon left over from her involuntary service on the Caitiff. Xia hadn't stopped carrying it since Coldhand's incarceration on board the Blue Phoenix. Kessa leaned heavily against Xia and was holding breathlessly still.

"Breathe, girl!" Xia hissed. Depriving the baby of oxygen would only put him in further danger. "I'll take care of this. You just breathe and push."

Xia almost shot Maeve as the fairy came running through the door. Xia barely recognized the princess. Duaal had warned her about the blonde hair, but Xia had no idea the change would be so drastic. Kessa let out an explosive breath and sobbed with relief.

Maeve didn't seem to notice Xia's gun. She dropped to one knee at Kessa's side with her head bowed and took the girl's sapphire hand in her tiny white ones. Xia blinked at the strange scene. She had *never* seen Maeve act like this.

"I humbly beg for your permission to be present at this sacred moment," the Arcadian said.

Maeve actually sounded as though she meant it. If Kessa said *no*, Xia had little doubt that she would leave without another word. Kessa hesitated, but she smiled and nodded.

"Of course," she said. "If it weren't for you, I would still be back on Axis with the Sisterhood. I... I'm really glad you're here."

"You need to clean up first, Maeve," Xia told the fairy. She wrinkled her nose at the smell. "I won't have you dragging infections in here."

Maeve looked as though she wanted to argue with both women, but she nodded once and rose, already stepping from her ruined dress. She wadded up the cloth and shoved it down a disposal chute. Maeve strode naked out the door, presumably down to the showers. Kessa stared, wide-eyed and startled at the Arcadian's immodesty. Xia only chuckled, long since accustomed to it.

She put her gun away in its holster. Maeve wanted to help? That was a first. But it seemed to soothe Kessa, so how could Xia refuse? Finally, something was going right.

The Raptor dropped out of superluminal flight at the edge of the Bannon system, just outside the orbit of the fourteenth planet. The blue-white little ball of ice was on the near side of the system's aging sun, represented by a green sphere of glowing lines on the navigational computer's screen.

Coldhand had flipped a pair of switches to engage the sublight engines. Alerted by the change in the SL drive humming through the hull, Vyron stirred from his half-doze as the higher-pitched Raptor systems fired up. He blinked his black eyes and yawned.

"So this is it," Vyron said. The Dailon heard his own voice still raspy and thick from slumber. "The Stray system."

"Bannon system," Coldhand told him. "Stray is just the third planet."

"Great. Bannon, Stray… whatever. It's all just a graveyard to me." Vyron leaned forward, handcuffs clinking. He squinted at the navigation computer readout. "Third planet? We're still a ways off, then. Maybe I can pray for a comet to smash into us or something."

"Unlikely."

Vyron looked up from the display at Coldhand. The blond human wasn't watching him. His mismatched hands were on the yoke of the fighter as he guided the Raptor past the outermost planetary orbit of the Bannon system. Maybe Vyron could use the handcuffs to choke Coldhand out and fly away. But Vyron sighed and slumped in the cramped confines of the cockpit. There was no way he could fight a trained bounty hunter like Coldhand. The Prian had made short work of the other Steelskins back on Axis.

A twitch, that's all it would take for Coldhand to kill Vyron. He had gotten half of his bounty, after all. If Vyron tried anything, the hunter might well just kill him and forget the rest. Even if Vyron somehow incapacitated the Raptor's pilot, he would only condemn himself to a slow death, suffocating when the air ran out. Vyron had no idea how to fly a ship.

He couldn't escape Coldhand… No one ever had. It was impossible.

"So, how long until we land?" Vyron asked.

"A few hours," Coldhand said.

"Where on that dirtball am I going? Are you dropping me in a city, or just the middle of the desert so whoever it is that wants me can kill me away from prying eyes?"

"I'm delivering you to Gharib."

There was a subtle edge to Coldhand's voice at that. If Vyron had been Lyran, his ears would have visibly pricked, but his black Dailon eyes only widened. What was going on? Was Coldhand actually annoyed about something?

"What's wrong with Gharib?" Vyron asked him. "Is that a city or what?"

The bounty hunter said nothing, leaving his prisoner to worry. The two men flew on in silence.

Vyron wasn't sure how long he had been staring out the canopy at a tiny speck of orange. It radiated no light, but was distinctly visible. It had to be close, a planet growing rapidly larger as the Raptor approached. On closer inspection, the world below wasn't actually the amber color it had first appeared, but a uniform sandy yellow. Even the red light of the sun could not disguise the dismal, drab beige of Stray.

An ugly little place to end Vyron's ugly little life. They were approaching rapidly, the planet filling the canopy. Coldhand adjusted his grip on the controls and skimmed the fighter through the thin film of Stray's atmosphere. The ground below darkened to a chocolate color, then into black as the hunter circled around to the night side of Stray. He pulled up another map on the navigational computer display and verified his coordinates. Coldhand toggled a few more switches, firing reverse thrusters to slow the fighter's descent. Entering the atmosphere at the speeds needed to travel across the stellar system would rip his ship apart, Vyron supposed.

A green light blinked on the controls, accompanied by an insistent chirp. Coldhand pressed a few buttons and a previously blank monitor lit up. It displayed the staticky image of a frowning Ixthian woman surrounded by instrument panels much like those in the Raptor, but far more modern and expensive-looking.

She had to be young, not long into maturity. Her silver face was still rounded and had a distinctive pale sheen to it, not yet with the sharp features and darker silver-gray skin tone of a mature Ixthian.

Despite her apparent youth, one of her short antennae was gone, leaving only a puckered scar above her right eye. The other pale stalk thrust up through white hair pulled tightly back away from her face.

"Coldhand?" Her voice was firm and ringing. Whether she was asking a question or just confirming his identity wasn't clear. "I've got my guns trained on your ship. Power down and prepare to hand over Fethru."

"What? Who is that?" Vyron asked.

Apparently, the Ixthian heard him.

"My name is Xoe," she said. "I'm a bounty hunter, too. You might have heard the name."

"No," Coldhand replied.

Xoe looked a bit crestfallen, but her compound eyes were a determined blue color. "I'm taking Fethru."

"Why?" Coldhand asked her. "I've already collected half of the bounty. There's only four hundred cenmarks left. Hardly worth dying for."

"Half the bounty for less than half the work. Four hundred cen will keep me going for weeks. Well worth fighting for, I think," Xoe said with a smirk.

Vyron knew that over-confident smile all too well. He practiced it in the mirror every morning. Or had until Coldhand caught him and threw him in the back of his Raptor.

"A few weeks?" Coldhand asked flatly. "Four hundred cenmarks should keep a bird in the air for months."

"I must be used to a more lavish lifestyle than you," Xoe said. "It comes with success, I suppose."

Vyron had worked the streets of Axis long enough to recognize the verbal swagger of someone just trying to make a name for herself. He had watched the other Steelskins do it a hundred times – pick a fight with some other street tough that already had a reputation. If you can win, suddenly you have one of your own.

Xoe had probably cut off her own antenna to give herself the look of a battle-hardened veteran.

Great, I'm in the middle of two bounty hunters' pissing match.

Coldhand looked away from the Ixthian huntress and tapped at the keyboard of another panel. Sensors, Vyron guessed, as a grid of the nearby planet lit up. It was too dark in Stray's shadow for him to see much, but the Raptor's sensors were far better than Vyron's eyes. Coldhand highlighted a point on the screen and the view magnified to display a sleek, top-of-the-line starfighter with hooked wings and all of the latest weaponry. Coldhand glanced over a list of numbers and abbreviations that scrolled across the monitor beside the image of Xoe's ship.

"A Starstalker, model C. Expensive," Coldhand said. "But your registry is still out of Narsus Shipyards."

Xoe flushed. "The ship is new. I haven't had a chance to change it yet. But you should be worrying about the missiles I've got trained on you, not reading my data."

Vyron almost bumped into Coldhand as he stared at the nearly incomprehensible jumble of instruments. Xoe had to be bluffing, right? Coldhand's entire demeanor was uncaring and casually dismissive. Surely the hunter would be panicking – or at least mildly concerned – if some hotshot hopeful had a weapons lock on the Raptor.

Coldhand brought up another screen on his display, replacing the scan of Xoe's ship. It was full of blinking red warnings. Vyron stared in horror.

"God, she's serious?" he gasped.

Coldhand ignored Vyron entirely, but the Ixthian huntress was still listening.

"Very," Xoe said. "Hand over the bounty or hand over your life. I'll burn you out of the sky, Coldhand."

The ultimatum sounded like something out of a bad show. If the circumstances had been less dire, Vyron would have laughed.

He wondered how she would turn in the bounty if she shot the Raptor down and killed both pilot and passenger, but the color was doubtlessly secondary to making a name for herself. If Xoe could kill Coldhand – or at least bloody his nose – she would certainly have that.

The hunter turned back to Xoe. His eyes were like ice. Vyron was glad that look wasn't leveled at him.

"Are you threatening my bird?" Coldhand asked.

Did that mean that Coldhand was going to give him to Xoe? Vyron felt like a color chip, traded from hand to hand at a whim, with no control over his own fate. At least he was a high mark one, expensive enough to buy off Xoe's missile locks. Vyron was a career move for the Ixthian huntress, if only because of the infamous hunter who had caught him first.

But what was he worth to Coldhand? Probably not much.

Xia didn't waste time on exasperated guesses at how Maeve had gotten her hands on a set of scrubs. They were thin, disposable and the same antiseptic green as the surgical sheet draped across Kessa. The top was tied above her wings, leaving her entire back bare, and the pants were so loose that they threatened to fall off the fairy's narrow hips at any moment. Maeve had picked up the skills of a thief at some point during the century since her homeworld's fall and Xia didn't want to reflect on her friend's less savory pastimes.

Maeve's currently blonde hair was damp from the shower, all of her exposed skin scrubbed pink. Xia was surprised. The Arcadian never worried about her personal hygiene. Xia had expected Maeve to wash her hands, maybe her face. Two showers in as many days was practically unheard of.

Maeve stood next to the examination table, her hands clasped through Kessa's. The Dailon was clinging to her with the iron grip of someone drowning and her short, ragged gasps did nothing to dispel the illusion.

"Pain is but a messenger," Maeve told Kessa in a soothing tone that Xia had never heard her use before. "It is only your body reminding your spirit that something important is happening. Let this pain move through you, scream out its message, but then let it pass."

Xia really wished Maeve wouldn't encourage Kessa to scream. Her ears already ached. But when Kessa did cry out, her nails biting hard enough into Maeve's hand to draw crescents of blood, there was release in the sound. Kessa sagged against Maeve, panting, but some of the tightness had drained from her face. If it helped, Xia couldn't really fault Maeve's methods.

"Push," Xia reminded the girl.

Kessa nodded, gritted her teeth and obeyed. She wailed again. She was still in pain. Maeve bowed her head and sang softly.

"Aes eru nai'i illitha vernae isha,
Cerra nai esha arae ilvae loe,
Shie'i junno sen."

Maeve's short song seemed to sever whatever bound Kessa to her pain and she relaxed visibly, staring down with an expression of wonderment.

"There's so much blood," Kessa said. There was worry in her voice, but no pain.

"That's normal for your physiology," Xia assured her.

Maeve nodded with a smile. "You are in no danger, Kessa. This dance is sacred and natural, and you move through it with grace. Xia will protect you and your baby."

Xia could hardly believe that this was the same woman she had been flying with for the last three years, but she didn't have time to wonder about it.

"Push, Kessa," Xia urged. "I can see his head. It won't be much longer now. Push!"

Kessa pushed.

Vyron caught a glimpse of rage on Xoe's face before the screen went black as Coldhand cut the transmission. The bounty hunter ran his cybernetic fingers over a row of switches. Each one clacked loudly as he toggled them and the panel lit up with blinking red indicators. He grabbed a brightly painted handle marked *LWAP Release*, yanking down hard. The entire Raptor shuddered. Vyron's stomach rose into his throat.

"What are you doing?" he choked.

For a horrible moment, Vyron wondered if the label on the lever somehow meant it would release him into space for Xoe to pick up at her leisure. That was impossible, of course, but the realization did little to dispel his fear.

Coldhand was paying no attention at all to his prisoner. His eyes moved between half a dozen displays, each flashing with readouts all in urgent-looking red and orange. Vyron craned his neck to look around and got his answer. The Long Wings pods had detached, becoming a pair of rapidly dwindling silhouettes against the stars. There was no reason to drag heavy superluminal engines into a firefight, Vyron supposed. Coldhand flicked a toggle next to the release handle and a yellow light flashed. Vyron could just make out a matching emerald spark on the Long Wings – a transponder to find the pods again when this was all over.

In the emptiness of space, there was no sound as Xoe's fighter descended on the Raptor. Vyron was still staring at the Long Wings when her silver ship eclipsed the view. He barely had time for a startled breath before Coldhand slammed the Raptor into motion and the air came wheezing right back out of Vyron's chest, unused.

The artificial gravity, localized in the flooring of the Raptor, lessened the sickening sense of motion, but the inertia of his own mass hurled Vyron back into his seat.

Coldhand shot the starfighter forward, skimming the nebulous haze of Stray's outer atmosphere. Behind them, Xoe responded almost too late, vanishing momentarily from sight. But then she gunned her engines and hurtled after the Raptor. Coldhand pulled back with a feather light touch, firing reverse thrusters so gently that they barely glowed. He was subtly slowing, letting her catch up. Xoe swooped in on his tail, taking the bait.

But the Prian's metal cybernetic hand slipped, jerking too hard and sending the Raptor into a dizzying roll. Lips pressed together into a tight line, Coldhand wrestled his ship back under control. He flipped the fighter over, reversing direction. For a hammering heartbeat, Vyron stared through the canopy of the Raptor and into Xoe's Starstalker as it flew past. The Ixthian huntress stared back, eyes an angry ruby while she struggled with her controls.

Xoe wasn't fast enough. Coldhand fired maneuvering jets again and dropped in on Xoe's tail. He flipped up the cover on his right control stick and pressed the red button underneath. Molten light bloomed from the nose of the Raptor as the twin-barreled lasers fired, burning deep black lines along the Starstalker's shiny hull. One of Xoe's engines sparked and went dark. The silver fighter dipped toward Stray, wavered and recovered. Xoe wheeled the Starstalker sharply, zigzagging wildly as she tried to shake Coldhand. He tightened his grip on the yoke and matched her move for frenzied move.

Vyron groaned and closed his eyes, fighting the urge to vomit all over the cockpit. The press of a body's own inertia was hard on all races and was one of many reasons for the great popularity of null-fields. But when those generators were in use, a single bullet or meteor could tear a ship to pieces, making them infeasible for use inside a stellar system or in combat.

How was Coldhand keeping his protein paste lunch down? Xoe was probably faring better... The Ixthians' insect heritage didn't quite give them an exoskeleton, but silvery skin that was reinforced with a rigid collagen mesh. The same stiff fibers ran through their entire bodies, strengthening organs and blood vessels. Their biology made Ixthians more resilient fighter pilots than any other species, capable of executing maneuvers that would cause hemorrhaging in humans, Lyrans or Dailons.

When Vyron cracked his eyes open, Xoe had stopped fishtailing wildly. Her Starstalker climbed out, away from Stray. Coldhand was still close behind her. He fired a volley of the Raptor's missiles and four long bullet-shapes spiraled toward the other fighter, their stabilized acylium propellant freezing instantly in the vacuum and leaving an icy vapor trail in their wake.

Xoe pulled her Starstalker up, nosing at a sharp right angle that would have been impossible in atmosphere, but the missiles stayed on her tail. She fired off several bright flares from small bays on either side of the darkened engine that Coldhand had shot out moments before. They erupted into yellow and white light, then balls of crimson and orange fire as the missiles homed in on the decoys and impacted. With no fuel to consume, the flames vanished as quickly as they had kindled.

Coldhand was already moving in again. He had hung momentarily back in anticipation of his missiles explosive radius, but now he fired the Raptor's engines to close in on the Starstalker's tail once again. Xoe was ready, armed with the best and most expensive armaments offered by Narsus Shipyards.

The flare bays closed, but an under-wing carrier snapped open, dropping a scattering of hemispherical metallic objects. Coldhand grunted and pulled back on the controls. The hunter's blond hair was plastered to his forehead with sweat and the knuckles of his right hand were bloodless and pale. He shot up and over most of whatever Xoe had just unleashed, but one of the things clipped the

Raptor's wing and flashed with green light. It was a mine, Vyron realized, and cringed as he waited for the explosion.

But it never came. The glow faded silently, though the Raptor shuddered around him. Vyron looked over Coldhand's shoulder. His control panels flickered, went black, then flared back to life. Xoe's weapon must have been an EMP mine, made to take out an enemy's electrical systems. The pulse should have shut down everything in the Raptor.

"You have phenno on your systems?" Vyron gasped. "But you work for the Alliance!"

The black market Nnyth protein coating – favored by pirates and smugglers the galaxy over – was the only thing he knew of that could protect against an electromagnetic pulse, but it was expensive and illegal.

Coldhand didn't answer. Xoe fired her engines, spun and then charge toward them again, sharp and shiny needle-nose first. No longer forced to use her few rear-mounted defenses, Xoe's superior weaponry gave her a clear advantage over the worn old Raptor. Coldhand tried to get back onto the Ixthian's tail, but had to swerve to avoid a heavy scatter of laserfire from the Starstalker.

Coldhand spun the Raptor at the same time Xoe came around for another pass. She fired again, but it was not the glowing red of lasers. Coldhand consulted his instruments in a split second and gripped the controls with his cybernetic hand, tensed to swerve out of the way, but seemed to reconsider.

Instead, the human bounty hunter turned his tail to Xoe. Coldhand was stiff and still, waiting. A short cannon fired a mute pulse of dim green light. Another EMP, exactly like those carried by Axial police vessels. The Raptor's phenno-protected electronics flickered and then surged again, but Coldhand made no move to evade Xoe's next shot. Vyron watched in stunned horror as the Prian hunter swiftly powered down his fighter.

"What are you doing? She's going to get us!" Vyron shouted.

"Quiet," Coldhand panted.

Sure enough, the Raptor shook as Xoe launched a pair of grappling harpoons, attached to her ship by long metal cables. The spars buried themselves deeply in the fighter's illonium plating and then began to pull them in toward the Starstalker.

"Do something!" Vyron cried.

Coldhand powered the Raptor back to roaring life and gunned the engines. The harpoons squealed and grated against the hull, but did not release. With the Starstalker in tow, the Raptor leapt forward. Xoe fought, but with only one remaining engine, she couldn't match the Raptor's pull. Coldhand scanned the dark void until he found what he needed and began dragging her toward a patch of faint stars.

No, not stars, Vyron realized, but something much closer: Xoe's EMP mines, the ones that had failed to disable the Raptor. As they closed, the mines flared with a flash of jade-colored light. Coldhand turned his fighter, slicing between most of them. One or two bounced off his illonium shielding, making the cockpit displays waver. Towed by her own cables, Xoe slammed full into the minefield. The Starstalker's fashionable silver hull sizzled and sparked with green light, then the whole thing went dark.

Coldhand regained control of his Raptor, reversed to create a little slack in the harpoon cables and turned. He sheared through the tethers with a couple of laser shots and left Xoe spinning slowly, helplessly alone among the spent remains of her mines. Coldhand wheeled the Raptor back toward Stray.

"How... how did you know that she wouldn't be able to fly right through those mines?" Vyron asked, shaky but curious. "You did."

Coldhand pushed his damp hair out of his eyes and ran a diagnostic to gauge the damage done to his ship in the fight.

"Xoe said her Starstalker was brand new," he answered. "If she'd ever stopped at a shop for phenno, she would have been able to change the registry."

"Oh," Vyron said. He guessed that made sense, but it seemed like a leap. Not much more than a hunch and Coldhand had risked both of their lives on it. "Are you just going to leave her out there?"

"Yes."

"Will someone come up from Stray to find her?" Vyron asked.

"Probably not."

"But she'll die! She'll run out of food or water or air! Or she'll burn up in the atmosphere!"

Vyron certainly didn't like the huntress, but he didn't particularly want her to die. She was just trying to make a living, like Vyron had been back on Axis. But in the pilot's chair, Coldhand shrugged, unconcerned.

"No one's going to cry over a dead bounty hunter," he said.

Coldhand doubled back to retrieve the Long Wings pods. Vyron slumped and wondered if he was really better off with Coldhand than he would have been with Xoe.

Kessa collapsed back against Maeve, pale and sweating. Xia lifted her wet, crying son for her to see. Kessa sobbed as she reached out to hold her baby. Xia swiftly cut and tied his umbilicus, then deposited the baby Dailon into his mother's waiting arms.

Maeve and Xia were nearly as bloody and sweaty as Kessa, but both women wore satisfied smiles. Xia pulled the Arcadian off into a corner of the medical bay as Kessa and her new baby fell asleep together.

"Thank you for the help, Maeve," she said. "What was that song you sang?"

"It was a simple battlefield charm that Orthain taught me when I was a squire."

"Magic, hm? Would there be a point in asking how it works? Or is the answer just... magic?"

Maeve gave Xia a strange look. "You are a doctor. The spell functions merely to stimulate the production of endorphins. There are charms to deaden the nerves entirely, but those are beyond my skill. I was a knight and taught only a few basic spells."

"What?" Xia asked, blinking. The fairy's explanation seemed so... ordinary. There were thousands of medications that did exactly that. "But it's magic!"

"It is the same as the science you studied," Maeve told her. "The manipulation of biology and physical forces. Our tools are different, but the effects are the same. The rules of the universe cannot be broken."

Xia shook her head. She didn't understand. But both women fell silent to let Kessa sleep in peace.

[22]
REUNIONS

"I love not the stones less, but the skies more."

- PRIAN SAYING

A deep red dawn smoldered on the western horizon by the time Xia finally told the men that they could come see the new baby. Gripper followed Tiberius and Duaal up the stairs and back through the close corridors to the medical bay, groggy but grinning.

Kessa was propped up on pillows and covered by a blue blanket scavenged from Xia's quarters. The Ixthian was *always* trying to help, Gripper thought with pride. Kessa looked tired but happy and cradled a wrapped bundle in her arms. Xia and Maeve lingered protectively on either side of the new mother.

Tiberius hung back by the door, looking uncertain, and Duaal remained near his captain, but Gripper knuckle-walked carefully closer. Swaddled in the cloth was a tiny blue-skinned baby with huge, curious black eyes and a shock of startlingly un-Dailon white hair. Xia caught his look.

"His hair will darken in a few weeks," she said.

"What's his name?" Gripper asked.

Kessa blushed and caressed her son's blue cheek with a tired, trembling finger. "I'd like to name him Baliend... if it's alright. It means *fire bird* in old Dailois. After this ship."

Tears shone in Xia's white eyes. Gripper's eyes were tearing up, too, and he sniffled. Even Duaal – well-groomed and proud Duaal – grinned proudly. Tiberius was looking rather red in the face, but he nodded. Even Maeve smiled and Kessa beamed, hugging her infant son to her.

"My little Baliend," she crooned to the baby boy. "My son."

He cooed in answer, reaching for his mother with short, chubby blue arms.

When Coldhand landed the Raptor down on a dusty sancrete pad, Gharib was stirring to life after the long, cold desert night. The bounty hunter unsealed the canopy, climbed out and stripped off his flight suit. Vyron was watching, but that wasn't why Coldhand hurried to redress.

"Get out," he told Vyron as he pulled on his pants and buckled his gun belt.

Still handcuffed, the Dailon took longer to clamber from the Raptor. Coldhand didn't offer to help.

"Where are the people who want me? You didn't call anyone," Vyron asked.

Coldhand just motioned for him to follow. Vyron sighed and did so with shoulders hopelessly slumped. The hunter led him north through the landing crescent, past other fighters and small cargo haulers.

Coldhand paused briefly as he escorted Vyron by an extravagant silver ship etched with delicate red and gold designs. It was another Narsus model, this one far larger and even more expensive than Xoe's Starstalker.

The name *Oslain'ii* was painted onto the yacht's shiny flank. In the year chasing Maeve, Coldhand had managed to pick up a little of the Arcadian language.

Vengeance.

Despite a certain curiosity, Coldhand didn't linger. A fairy with the money to buy any ship – much less an extravagant yacht like this – was strange. Maybe the Oslain'ii simply belonged to someone fascinated with the fallen White Kingdom, but Coldhand doubted it. The Arcadians were by and large viewed as vermin, frail and sickly creatures that swarmed uninvited into the core worlds. It was a mystery, but not one that was interesting enough to stop Coldhand from finishing today's business.

In the stifling heat, Vyron had opened his shirt to the waist in a vain attempt to cool himself. The sun would burn the Dailon's exposed blue skin within hours. But by then, Coldhand's job would be done, so he didn't say anything.

The hunter made his way to an empty landing pad not far down the row from the Oslain'ii. As he neared, the hunter reached for his Talon-9. Vyron jumped back, holding up his cuffed hands.

"Wait, no! I didn't do anything!" he said.

"This isn't for you."

Coldhand pulled the laser pistol free and switched off the safety. He circled the dusty square of blastphalt, his glacial blue eyes frequently flickering toward the sky. Satisfied that the landing pad was safe, he reholstered his Talon-9.

Coldhand knelt and touched his fingers to the blastphalt. It was already warm under Stray's fat red sun. The landing pad had been empty for a while. Without a ship to shade it, the pad was just as hot as the surrounding ground. Vyron watched Coldhand curiously, but he seemed to have finally given up on asking questions. Coldhand stood.

"They've moved their ship," he said. "I need to find a computer, one connected to the mainstream.

Coldhand took Vyron by the shoulder and propelled him back out into the street. A veiled Hadrian man in the white garb of a Union of Light priest averted his filmed eyes from hunter and mark as he passed.

"What're you talking about?" Vyron asked. "The ones who put a bounty on me? Is this where they said to deliver me?"

"No."

Xartasia seemed preoccupied. Gavriel rested his tired body on one of the very few chairs in the black cathedral. It was a high-backed mahogany seat that had doubtlessly been expensive many years ago, but was now so splintered and worn that it had been thrown out. Beside him, the black-haired princess paced restlessly.

At least, it *looked* like pacing. Xartasia flew from one wall to the other, perching delicately on a piece of jagged stone jutting from the church wall and then fluttering to another outcropping. In years of association with the Arcadian – first as her student and then as an ally – Gavriel had never seen her like this.

"Princess, get down here," he said.

Even aged and annoyed, his rich voice was smooth as cream. Xartasia turned, her eyes bright and almost feverish. She said nothing, but soared down from her most recent roost on silent white wings. She bowed gracefully to Gavriel and knelt.

"You are lord of this house and so due the proper respects, my old friend," Xartasia said.

"Tell me what I need to reclaim the power Duaal took from me."

The Nihilists were waking as the sun rose high enough to shine through the gaps in the wall, but they maintained a respectful distance from Gavriel and his guest. Two more had died during the night: a young human woman who declined blankets and let the cold Gharib night kill her, and an Arcadian man who *looked* young, but who was probably at least twice the age of the dead woman. A mottled red and black infection had finally spread to some vital organ and killed the fairy.

Gavriel watched his congregation lift the corpses up and begin the nearly daily ritual of burial, singing discordant hymns of praise and gratitude. Xartasia watched, too, with some unknowable rage blazing in her glorious twilight eyes. They waited in silence until the two bodies were carried away.

"You will find what you require in the mind unmade," Xartasia answered at last.

"Damned riddle. Very well. Unmade? That's why you want me to use the dying, isn't it? When the brain is coming apart and unraveling."

Xartasia nodded and smiled, her perfect white teeth flashing in the pale morning light. She took Gavriel's liver-spotted hands.

"Yes," Xartasia said. She stroked his papery skin. "There shall be a death. But what you require is the blooming of a new mind, like Duaal was when you began your work through him."

"A child."

"As fresh from the womb as can be had, a mind unformed and as malleable as fire-called glass," Xartasia said. "Bring me such a baby and I shall do what must be done. When our task is finished, I promise that you shall regain the power you lost when the boy ran away and more."

Gavriel stood, towering over the kneeling Arcadian princess. He clenched his withered hands into fists. "It will take some work. I've forbidden my congregation to breed. There is no greater sin than creating life here. But one will be found. Bren!"

The doctor appeared instantly when Gavriel called.

"Yes, Holiness? How may I serve?" he asked.

Gavriel told him. Bren bowed again and hurried away with purpose burning in his eyes.

That afternoon, Tiberius leaned against the railing of the catwalk that ran high across the cargo hold. Orphia was perched on his arm, preening her fading feathers. Down below, Gripper and Xia had drawn a pair of semicircles onto the floor in chalk for a game of pounceball.

They had attempted to coax their crewmates into the game, but Duaal stiffly declined and Maeve just stared blankly. They hadn't even asked Tiberius to participate. The game wasn't made for one-on-one competition, to judge by the frequent breaks in play for spirited arguments between Tiberius' medic and engineer.

At the foot of the stairs, Kessa leaned on Maeve's arm, cradling tiny Baliend to her breast and watching the game. Maeve had not left Kessa's side since the birth and still had not given a full report on the Church of Nihil. The short Arcadian used her spear like a staff to keep herself upright under Kessa's weight.

No one wanted to press Maeve for the uncomfortable details of her time with the Nihilists. They all knew what they needed to do – as soon as Vyron was delivered, they would move on to find Kessa and her new family a safe home. But until then, all they could do was wait.

The pounceball game seemed to be an even pairing. Gripper's far superior size and reach were undermined by his tendency to stumble and blush any time Xia got close. The score – kept with tic marks around the edge of their respective circles – was nine to four in the Ixthian's favor.

At the request of the two athletes, the cargo door was closed up against the hot Gharib afternoon. Gripper and Xia had stopped to argue again, the Ixthian defending her tenth and winning goal. She was punctuating her points with wild sweeps of her long-fingered hands while Gripper tried not to stammer. Kessa giggled as she watched the debate.

Tiberius watched his crew play. He was too old and too damned tired from decades on the Prian police force for silly games... but he had to admit it was good to see them relaxing. Everyone on the Blue Phoenix had been on edge ever since Kessa's arrival. They were the crew of a cargo ship, not heroes from one of Gripper's shows.

Tiberius stroked Orphia's back. She nipped his fingers and he rapped her on the beak. The hawk stared at Tiberius with gleaming black eyes, then flipped her wings and decided that it wasn't worth the effort to draw her master's blood.

There was muffled laughter from behind Tiberius. The captain turned to see Duaal in the hatchway, leaning out just far enough to watch the game below but not be seen himself. Duaal felt Tiberius' gaze on him and looked up, sobering instantly. The young Hyzaari turned on his booted heel to leave.

Tiberius wished he wouldn't go. Duaal was a boy, too young to have picked up the worries of an old hawk like him. Duaal should have been down in the hold, playing games and flirting. But then, life had been hard on Duaal even before the mage had stowed away on Tiberius' newly salvaged ship.

"I'm sorry, I'm sorry," the child sobbed, words almost unrecognizable through his tears. "I won't hurt anyone. I won't, I swear!"

Tiberius held the scrawny boy up by the scruff of his neck, staring. He was just a hatchling, and a half-starved one at that. He didn't look capable of strangling a stonemouse, much less harming the battle-scarred Prian cop. Retired cop, Tiberius reminded himself.

"What are you doing on my ship?" he asked, tightening his grip on the child.

"Hiding," the boy whimpered. "Don't send me back to Gavriel! I don't want to sing anymore. Please!"

A loud clang interrupted Tiberius' memory. The thick hatch of the airlock beeped and slammed open, crashing noisily against the bulkhead. Xia and Gripper backed away as the door was filled with ruddy light.

It was Coldhand. His Talon-9 was drawn and ready, swinging the gun in a low, searching arc. Maeve pushed Kessa and the baby behind her. She spread her wings to shield them and whirled her glass-bladed spear, leveling it at the hunter in the airlock door. Xia ran past the cowering Gripper for her gun, hanging in its holster from the corner of an empty cargo container. Coldhand aimed the laser at Xia.

"Don't. Hands up and back off," he said.

Xia froze with her hand a breath from the slick plastic grip of her weapon and then turned slowly away. Coldhand pointed his Talon-9 at Maeve, the only one left armed. Her fingers tightened on the haft of her spear.

Tiberius went nova-hot with fury. Orphia shifted uneasily on his sleeve as the captain pounded his fist on the catwalk railing. Damn him! Damn Maeve! Of all the bounty hunters in the galaxy, why was Coldhand here? How had he known? Maeve had assured Tiberius that the chances of Coldhand taking Vyron's bounty were remote, too small to even guess at.

"Where is Vyron?" Maeve asked.

Duaal was frozen in the doorway behind his captain, still out of sight of anyone in the hold below. Coldhand reached into the airlock with his metal hand and yanked another man into the light.

"Vyron!" Kessa cried.

She pushed past Maeve and ran to her lover. Vyron stared, black eyes wide and disbelieving.

"Kessa? Oh my God, Kes..." he gasped.

Coldhand released Vyron and he stumbled forward, awkwardly putting his handcuffed arms around Kessa and holding her to him. Both of their cheeks were wet with tears.

"Kes, I never thought I'd see you again!" Vyron said.

He kissed Kessa, then sobbed choked, half-formed apologies and confessions of love into her tousled black hair. Kessa answered Vyron's desperate kisses with her own and assured her frightened, harried mate that all was well, that everything would be better now that they were together again.

"Vyron, look," Kessa said. She nodded down to the little blanket-wrapped bundle cradled between them. "We have a son."

Baliend burbled happily and then sucked on his stubby fingers, staring up at his father. Vyron burst into fresh tears and kissed both mother and child.

[23]

SOWING SALT

"It's easy to praise the glories of war when you're not choking on the blood and tears."

- ILLMA MUJAMBI, MIRRAN JOURNALIST (119 MA)

Elsa didn't want to go. She hadn't left the Nihilist cathedral in years and being so far outside the cracked black walls, she felt exposed.

"Bren ordered us to keep to the edges of Gharib," Seon growled quietly. "Lord Gavriel wants to avoid police entanglements."

"But the knights of this city are stretched thin, Burning One," Alainna said with a dismissive flip of her wings. "They are motivated only by their lust for money. They will do nothing."

"Even a half-dead bitch will get up and tear out your throat if you piss in her den," Seon told the Arcadian. "We're not risking it. And they're called *police* here, bird-back."

Alainna shrugged her narrow shoulders and followed Seon out toward the edge of Gharib. Elsa thought the gesture looked strange, but she remembered Bren telling her once that Arcadians had two sets of shoulder blades – one for their arms and one for their wings – that changed how the fairies moved.

Bren had pointed to the bones as he described them to Elsa, almost visible through the thin, waxy skin of an Arcadian man who had recently starved to death.

Elsa hurried behind the other two Nihilists down a dingy residential street that led out of the city and she smiled secretly. Both Seon and Alainna were much smaller than her and it made Elsa feel momentarily powerful.

A few silhouettes moved in the dusty windows, but most of the curtains had been drawn. Seon pricked his furry gray ears. A high, keening wail wafted out through one of the windows, but Seon shook his head, growling.

"No."

Alainna was a hard-eyed fairy woman with long blonde hair she kept in a braid that fell between her wings nearly to her waist. Before joining Lord Gavriel, she had worked in an illegal Gharib brothel and used the profits to drown her old pain in narcohol. When Alainna had first arrived at the cathedral, Elsa had helped Bren splint a wing broken by her final customer. It was still a little crooked, but Alainna could fly well enough. The man who had snapped the delicate bones was buried in the stony field behind the Church of Nihil.

Seon was a tiny Lyran with steely gray fur over numerous scars and bulging knots of muscle. Elsa didn't know much about him, but instead of the rough black worn by his female companions, Seon was dressed in robes of blood red. They marked him as someone special within the Church of Nihil. The red-robed group had a name, though Elsa couldn't remember it just then. Seon's brilliant, flowing robes almost hid a curved nanosword on one hip, a well-worn NI gun on the other.

Almost.

"That one?" Alainna asked.

"No. Too old," Seon said, pointing his grizzled snout toward the window.

Elsa was impressed that Seon could tell how old the baby was just by hearing it cry. She wondered what else the Lyran could hear with his big, fuzzy ears, but decided not to ask.

The city street ended abruptly as the small, single-story houses stopped. Dry desert dust drifted in over the low curb, filling the cracks between homes and spilling out in miniature dunes over the sidewalk. Alainna spread her wings and leapt up into the air. The Arcadian wheeled overhead, vanishing from sight occasionally as she spiraled outward into the pale sky. The streets were busy, filled with men and women coming home at the end of a long, hot day. But no one paid any attention to Elsa and Seon.

Elsa wondered if she should try to talk to the Lyran, but decided against it. She was only there to take care of the baby that her companions were looking for, not to contribute to their plans or tactics. Elsa wondered what Lord Gavriel needed a baby for... Whatever the reason, Elsa would be glad for a chance to hold one, if just for a little while.

Seon leaned against the wall of a nearby house as they waited for Alainna to finish her survey. Despite the heat of the day, he fished a cigar from somewhere in his red robes and lit it. The acrid smoke made Elsa wrinkle her nose. It wasn't the thick, organic scent of tobacco. Whatever the Lyran was smoking, it smelled poisonous – and probably was.

Alainna finally landed beside Seon and a pile of dust puffed out from her bare feet. The Lyran snuffed out his cigar on one of the thick black pads of his palm and Elsa flinched. That probably hurt, but if it did, Seon didn't seem to care. He regarded Alainna with gleaming yellow eyes.

"There are a few other homes beyond these, Burning One," she reported in her accented Aver. "But they are all empty. West of those is the... the place where starships land."

"The landing crescent," Seon growled.

"Are we likely to find a child there?" Alainna asked.

"No," the Lyran answered. "But Lord Gavriel told us to cover this part of the city. All of it. The others are searching the rest of Gharib. You're not questioning him, bird-back."

"Of course not, Burning One," Alainna said.

"Let's go, then."

"You owe me four hundred cenmarks," Coldhand said.

"How did you know we wanted him?" Xia asked.

Gripper was still cowering, but even he looked curious. "Yeah, good question. We posted that bounty anonymously."

"When I was paid back on Axis, I recognized the account suffix," Coldhand answered. "I've been following you and your ship for a long time now."

Vyron looked up from where he was tearfully embracing Kessa and his newborn son.

"What...?" he asked. "You mean you *knew* about this? And you didn't tell me?"

Coldhand just shrugged. Vyron's face went purple with rage, but he didn't seem to trust himself to say more. Kessa stroked his cheek and he turned back to her, fury easing in his black eyes. Coldhand kept his gun trained on Maeve.

"I don't work for free," he said.

Tiberius' jaw clenched so hard that his teeth ground together. The traitor was standing in *his* bird demanding money in return for reuniting a hawk with his family. But Coldhand *had* brought Vyron. Whatever the hunter might be, Tiberius was a man of honor and would pay the bounty as promised. He would have to get the color from the small safe in his quarters...

But Maeve had already pulled four red cenmark chips from her pocket. She threw them down at Coldhand's feet and the money clattered loudly against the fibersteel floor in the sudden silence.

Where had Maeve gotten that kind of money? Just one of those red chips was months of her pay.

Not taking his eyes off Maeve, Coldhand crouched and scooped up the money in his cybernetic hand. The plastic slid through his artificial fingers, but he tightened his grip. Coldhand threatened to crush the color chips, but quickly stood and slipped them into his own pocket. In return, he tossed the key to Vyron's handcuffs on the floor.

"You've got your damned money," Tiberius snarled. He pointed to the open airlock. "Now get off my bird!"

"Not yet," Coldhand said. "There's one more thing here I need: Cavainna."

"Only in death, Logan," Maeve answered.

There was no anger or defiance in her voice. It sounded like a long-practiced ritual. Maeve hefted her spear and settled into a fighting stance, half crouching with wings spread behind her. The bounty hunter's eyes flickered over her blonde hair, her clean face and clothes. It was a wonder Coldhand even recognized her.

Duaal was still hidden in the hallway, taut and ready for a fight. Tiberius leaned over the railing.

"Get the hells away from her!" he shouted. "I'm not letting you take anything or anyone, Coldhand. You've been paid. Now get your traitorous tail the hells off of my ship!"

"Cavainna's a criminal and I'm taking her in."

Maeve circled the hunter slowly, her spear held low. The rainbow of streamers tied onto it rippled in a searing breeze blowing through the airlock. She was already sweating in the rising heat, making her shirt cling to her skin and revealing the lean lines of her muscles. Maeve moved smoothly across the cargo bay, graceful as a hunting hawk as she closed on Coldhand.

"Maeve, stop! Let him go!" Tiberius said.

But his first mate continued her side-stepping prowl, gray eyes bright with anticipation.

"Listen to him," Gripper whimpered. "Smoke, please! Come on, what about Kessa and the baby? We need to get them out of here. Away from the Nihilists, remember?"

Maeve turned toward Vyron, who still held both Kessa and his son awkwardly in his arms. Baliend's round blue face was unhappy, bunching up in preparation to cry. With a bare foot, Maeve sought out and found the key Coldhand had dropped. She kicked it across the floor toward the Dailons.

"Unbind your hands," Maeve told Vyron. "Take your family into the ship. Tiberius will keep you safe. He is a good man and worthy of your trust. Go."

"Damn it, Maeve! Stand down this instant!" Tiberius shouted, banging his fist on the rail. Orphia squawked indignantly at him.

Coldhand took advantage of Maeve's inattention to slip around behind her. The Talon whined in his hand and a ruby bolt of laser-fire hurled through the air, aimed at the fairy's feathered wings. She cocked a pointed ear at the sound of his footsteps and leapt aside. The laserfire scorched several of her white feathers and burned a molten hole through a cargo canister.

Kessa ducked out of Vyron's arms and grabbed the handcuff key. With one arm clutching Baliend, she fumbled, dropped the key and then finally managed to unlock Vyron's manacles. He pulled Kessa toward the stairs, away from Maeve and Logan.

Baliend began to cry.

As the three Nihilists stalked through the landing crescent, Seon's ears suddenly twitched. The red-robed Lyran had stopped in front of a small starship coated in yellow dust, the grit stuck to a layer of damp-looking lacquer on the hull.

There was a name painted beneath the dirt: *Blue Phoenix*. Elsa wondered what a phoenix was.

At the top of a lowered cargo ramp, the airlock was open. Elsa caught only a flash of glittering glass inside and the angry glow of a laser being fired. There was shouting coming from the ship, and the hammer of running feet. But over it all, she could hear the thin wail of a crying baby. Seon pointed at the Blue Phoenix.

"That's the one we need," the Lyran said.

Alainna looked through the open airlock. "There is a battle being waged in there."

"Then we'll find another way in."

Seon gestured with one sharp claw to Alainna. She nodded and then leapt into the air, searching.

"Elsa, stay here," Seon instructed.

Duaal held his breath. It was one thing to chase Coldhand's tracks through Gharib. Hunting the Prian after his escape from the Blue Phoenix had been exhilarating. But now the hunter was *right there* and Duaal's knees felt like water.

Tiberius' face was bright red and twisted in fury. But there was something else in his expression – fear. Tiberius was frightened for Maeve. Duaal still didn't like the fairy, though he had to admit that he didn't really want to see her dead. But more importantly, the loss would wound his captain deeply.

Kessa and her family ran, Xia and Gripper close on their heels. Tiberius waved them all past, deeper into the Blue Phoenix. Duaal stood aside, out of their way, and turned to Tiberius.

"I can stop this," Duaal said. "Coldhand won't even know what hit him."

His heartbeat pounded deafeningly in his ears, echoing a heavy crash below that he hoped wasn't Maeve's body hitting the deck. Tiberius grabbed the front of Duaal's shirt in a fist almost as big as the younger man's head.

"No!" he said. "You stay away from those two, Duaal! I'll call for you when it's safe."

Duaal's jackhammering heart sank. Tiberius told him the same thing when Coldhand escaped their ship before. Why would the old man *never* let him help? Duaal was a mage, one of only two that existed in the entire core! He was better suited to breaking up the deadly fight raging below than anyone else on the ship.

Still, the great mage had to admit that he felt very young and very small. Coldhand's Talon whined again, answered by a screech of glass on metal. Tiberius let go of Duaal and shoved him after the others.

"Stay with Kessa and Vyron," the captain ordered. Something in his voice made the Prian's accent thick and heavy. "Please."

Duaal wanted to protest, but he only nodded.

"What about you? What will you do?" he asked.

Tiberius stroked Orphia, his face set in a grim mask. "I'm going to protect my bird."

Duaal had no idea if Tiberius meant the Blue Phoenix, his pet hawk or his winged first mate. Duaal ran after Xia, Gripper and the Dailons. He looked back once at Tiberius, at the old man who was the only father he had ever known. With the rest of his crew and passengers safely out of the way, Tiberius untethered Orphia and drew his gun.

The dim, hot sun was beginning to fall down out of the sky behind Gharib as Alainna landed on the small freighter's wing. Elsa stared after Seon, chasing the Arcadian in a pair of powerful bounds on his reverse-articulated legs.

Seon climbed and Alainna flew along the dusty hull of the Blue Phoenix, along a ledge between sensor and communications spars. They paused like hunting beasts just before pouncing, and then slipped out of sight into some unseen opening. Elsa waited across the street, clenching her hands and tugging nervously at the sleeves of her black robe.

Maeve clung onto the edge of a planter swinging from the ceiling. Coldhand dashed across the hold below to get a better angle on her. The fairy was favoring one wing, her feathers ruffled and scorched by his opening shot. Maeve's forearm oozed blood from a deep burn that dripped down her arm and along the haft of her spear.

The glass spear blade, too, had tasted blood. Coldhand's leg was slashed across his left thigh and blood painted every other footstep in red. But Maeve had hit nothing vital. The pain was remote, as distant and dull as ever, a regular throb like someone playing music far away. Coldhand could barely feel the other cut, a flaying wound along his lower back. Pain or pleasure, Maeve's spear or the failed seduction of the Arcadian whore... None of it mattered.

Maeve tracked Coldhand carefully. Something was wrong with this... Coldhand's boots pounded across the fibersteel floor and she dove from her perch, her wounded wing trembling with the effort of holding her aloft. The spear whistled over Coldhand's head as the hunter tucked his legs, dropping and rolling under the stairs that led down from the catwalk. Maeve caught the railing with her toes, spun and then was back in the air. Coldhand crouched, aimed and waited.

What was wrong? Perhaps it was just Maeve herself. After over a year of chasing the Arcadian princess, Coldhand was accustomed to finding a dirty woman, wired and alert to his presence only be-cause of addictive chemicals injected into her veins. But this time, she looked different. The needle runs in her arms were fading. The Vanora White she bought on Axis had never been used except as a weapon. When was her last hit?

Maeve landed, forced to the ground by the confines under the stairs where Coldhand had retreated. As soon as she came into sight, the bounty hunter lowered his aim and fired. The laser found its mark, burning deep and hot into Maeve's right leg. The shot was painful but not fatal, meant only to cripple. Coldhand wanted her alive, after all.

Maeve dropped to one knee with a pained cry, but she was close enough to stab her spear at him. The glass blade hissed against the fibersteel stairs, but fell short of striking flesh. Coldhand darted in a wide circle around Maeve, out of spear reach. Blood ran down her leg, but the fairy made no move to staunch the flow. If Coldhand could hobble either her other wing or leg, the fight would be over.

The Arcadian took to the air again, thrusting her spear toward Coldhand. That glass blade could shear even through the illonium of his cybernetic hand if he wasn't careful. Coldhand retreated and brought his metal forearm down across the flat of the blade to parry the swipe. Maeve recovered, spun the spear and cut a bloody line along his shoulder.

It could easily have been a deadly blow. The fairy was far more dangerous with a spear in her hands than a needle of White. Had Maeve adjusted her aim only a little, she could have slashed open the arteries that carried the blood from Coldhand's computerized heart to his brain. He would have been dead in less than a minute.

That's what was wrong. Maeve wasn't fighting to kill Coldhand. Why? Why fight Coldhand at all, if not to kill?

He took advantage of his superior size, kicking at the haft of Maeve's spear to deflect the blade. Colorful ribbons tangled around his boot, but Coldhand turned his hips into the kick, wrenching the spear from Maeve's hands. The glass chimed off of the floor plating as it spun away. Maeve offered the hunter a mysterious smile.

"Do not wait for my surrender," she said. "You know that I will only refuse. Too many good men have fought for my life to give it up willingly."

What did that mean? Coldhand brought up his Talon, drawing a bead on Maeve's uninjured wing. Was that guilt in her voice? She wasn't trying to kill Coldhand – she was trying to force him to kill her. The hunter had no intention of granting her suicidal wish, but couldn't help wondering why the deception, why the chase? Maeve could kill herself easily enough.

It didn't matter. Whatever the princess wanted wasn't important to Coldhand. He would capture her and capture her alive. Maeve crouched, ready to leap on him and Coldhand tightened his finger on the trigger.

A shrieking brown blur struck Coldhand and a dim line of pain burned along his skin as talons dug into his natural arm. His shot went wild, blackening a section of bulkhead. Coldhand lashed out with his illonium hand, connecting solidly against his attacker. Orphia screamed and wheeled back up into the air.

Tiberius was on the catwalk overhead, his NI pistol drawn and pointed at the younger Prian, but he hadn't fired. Yet. Maeve stared up at Tiberius with her lips pressed together in a tight, bloodless white line.

"Stop!" she cried. "I do not need or want your help!"

Tiberius wasn't listening to his raging first mate. He glowered at Coldhand from under bushy gray brows.

"Get the hells off my bird, traitor," Tiberius said. "Or I swear by the First Feathers that I will burn you down where you stand."

The old pagan Prian oath rumbled like an approaching storm. Tiberius hated Coldhand, hated him with a passion that the bounty hunter could never imitate with stimulants. And Coldhand couldn't say he blamed Tiberius. He had brought disgrace and dishonor to the gun he carried. His uniform and badge were probably gathering dust in some back closet, too unclean to pass on to a new officer. Coldhand should have felt shame, pain, or anger to know his name was slandered on his homeworld. Something. Anything.

But Coldhand felt nothing.

Even in his fury, Tiberius would never shoot Coldhand in the back. He still honored the Prian code of chivalry, but the hunter didn't. Not anymore.

"Cavainna is a criminal," Coldhand said. "Let me remove her from your ship."

"This isn't about her. This is about you, traitor!"

Coldhand swung his Talon-9 around to fire off a quick shot at Tiberius, forcing the older man back behind cover. He brought the laser down again, ready to fend Maeve off, but she hadn't moved, not even to retrieve her fallen spear.

Tiberius ran down the stairs and his NI gun popped quietly, but it hurled a slug as thick as a Lyran's claw from the barrel that only narrowly missed. Coldhand whirled again and fired at Tiberius' feet. The retired cop jerked to a halt, a smoking hole in the floor just in front of his boots.

"Stand down, you stiff-necked old fool," Maeve shouted. "Logan will kill you!"

The fairy stood rooted to the spot, her hands curled into fists. Coldhand could see the terror in her wide silver eyes. What did Maeve have to fear? She wanted to die – that much was clear – so she couldn't be afraid for her own life. For Tiberius? No, that made no more sense. If the bounty posting was right, Maeve Cavainna had killed off an entire species. What was one old Prian beside that?

"I was a cop back home for fifty years," Tiberius said, still barely glancing at Maeve. He ducked behind a stack of cargo canisters. "You left Prianus, Coldhand. You abandoned her. And for what? To become a bounty hunter? Whoring justice for Alliance cenmarks?"

"You left, too," Coldhand pointed out. He circled the cargo pallet on sure, quiet feet.

"Tiberius, stop!" Maeve shouted. "This is justice!"

"I'm not about to let that traitor haul you off my ship," Tiberius said. "If someone wants to arrest you, I'll damned well see a proper badge first!"

Coldhand leapt toward Maeve. She was still unarmed and made no move to defend herself – Maeve was too busy arguing with her captain. Coldhand yanked a pair of handcuffs from his belt and they slipped in his hand, metal against metal, but he held tight and flicked them open.

"You do not need a badge to know what it right," Maeve told Tiberius. "Please, go!"

She caught sight of Coldhand advancing on her and leapt back, beating her wings furiously and spraying droplets of blood from her injured wing and leg. Maeve kicked out and her bare foot connected with Coldhand's jaw. He recovered quickly, dropping the handcuffs to catch the Arcadian by her ankle. Unbalanced, Maeve tumbled from the air and her breath whooshed out painfully as she landed on her wounded wing.

"Let go of her!" Tiberius shouted.

He came around the stack of cargo containers and fired a series of rapid shots to force Coldhand back away from his mark. Tiberius reached out to help Maeve stand, but she pushed herself to her feet.

"I have chosen my end!" she said. "Leave me to face it!"

Tiberius kept his gun pointed at Coldhand. "You'll follow my be-damned orders, Maeve! Now get the hells out of the way so I can remove this filth from my bird."

"This choice is mine to make!" Maeve said.

"Wrong," Coldhand corrected. "It's mine."

A scream drowned out Maeve's reply.

[24]
REAPING TEARS

"It's young hearts that pound the drumbeat of revolution."

- LYRAN PROVERB

Gripper's heart hammered inside his ribs so hard that he wondered if it was trying to break out and run ahead. Xia, Vyron and Kessa – clutching her infant son tight in her arms – raced in front of him through the cramped corridors of the Blue Phoenix. Gripper had to duck and squeeze through tiny doorways, leaving behind scraped skin and tufts of painfully pulled fur as he struggled to keep up. Duaal ran after him, swearing hotly.

Gripper could imagine Coldhand right behind them... He ran faster, grabbing onto bulkheads and swinging on long arms where he could. When they reached the mess, Xia signaled a stop. The kitchen sink was still full of dishes left over from lunch.

Vyron and Kessa crouched behind the table, huddled protectively together around Baliend. Doors at either end of the room led back the way they had come, past the engines and crew quarters, but the other opened into a hallway that went up to the little ante-chamber of acceleration couches and the cockpit.

"That fight may not stay in the cargo bay," Xia said. "Maeve and Tiberius might have to fall back. There's enough room to move in here, if it comes to a fight. But if we go much further, we're going to run out of space."

There was something wrong that a doctor had to know anything about fighting, Gripper thought.

Duaal positioned himself near the door. "I'll handle Coldhand if he makes it this far."

Xia nodded. "Gripper, whatever Tiberius says, Duaal can take care of himself. So can I. Let us do the fighting. Just keep an eye on Kessa and Vyron, alright?"

"I... I'll try," Gripper said. He wasn't sure how he was supposed to keep the Dailons out of trouble. "I'll do my best."

"I know you will."

Xia smiled at Gripper and patted his huge, furry arm. He really, really hoped that he wouldn't let her down.

They all waited in tense silence. It took every bit of Gripper's self-control not to swing nervously from the supports. Shouting and arguing voices drifted up from the cargo bay, but he couldn't make out the words. Duaal and Xia were closest to the door, leaning through as they braced for trouble. Gripper hung back, the Dailon family cowering behind him. The top of his head and points of his ears brushed the ceiling.

Gripper could still hear the shrill of a laser weapon and raised voices, but there was something else.

"Hey, what's that?" he asked.

Duaal shot Gripper a look and Xia shushed him absently, but the noise continued – a groaning, tearing sound. Gripper strained to listen.

The other sound was sharper and higher pitched than he had first thought, but the upper registers were completely washed out by the noise from the hold. It reminded Gripper of a time just a few months before when the ISR junction had fused shut. None of his drills or microsaws had been powerful enough to cut through the melted metal, forcing the Arboran to simply rip through the plating and tear off the fibersteel covers.

Whatever Gripper heard now, it was similar to that buckling of metal. And it was getting louder.

"Um..." Gripper said.

But no one was looking at him. All attention was on the corridor that led down to the hold, everyone poised and waiting for trouble to come tumbling through that door.

The grating sound suddenly stopped, and Gripper let out a sigh of relief. So it was nothing after all.

Gripper didn't realize that they were no longer alone until Xia was stumbling back, reaching for her gun. But it was still down in the hold and she swore hoarsely, invoking the names of demons Gripper didn't recognize. Baliend was crying again, screaming with lungs that seemed far more developed than the rest of his tiny blue body.

Was it Coldhand? And why was Maeve flinging herself at Xia in a furious whirlwind of feathers? Gripper realized a second later that this Arcadian wasn't his friend. The new fairy was taller than Maeve, with butter-yellow hair swinging in a long braid. Her face was far sharper and looked older than Maeve, too. Only her sad, red-shot eyes were anything alike.

Something hard and furry hit Gripper in the stomach, painfully knocking the wind out of his lungs and sending him reeling back into Kessa and Vyron. They stumbled and fell under him.

A snarling Lyran in bright red robes stood over them, a nanos-word in one paw, curved like a fang and running with a shifting oil-on-water rainbow of colors. The blade whistled over their heads as Gripper and the Dailons struggled to untangle themselves. Vyron and Kessa threw themselves out of the way, Baliend clutched between them, but the sword's molecule-thin edge sheered through the tip of Gripper's long left ear.

He howled in pain and clapped his huge claw to the wound. The Lyran in red smiled as Gripper screamed, and spun the nanosword effortlessly. His blade flicked out again, quick as a striking snake and cutting deep, bloody gashes across the Arboran's mottled hide.

How did they get onto the ship? Every lash of the sword sliced a burning line of pain into Gripper's body, over his knotted shoulders, thick arms and wide chest. He tried to wriggle away, but Vyron and his little family were too close and Gripper was just too big. His pained thrashing could kill them almost as easily as the Lyran's nanosword. Blood dripped into his eyes and the Arboran brought up his huge hands, trying feebly to fend off the blows, but each slash slid past and cut free another howl of agony.

The mess was suddenly alive with crackling electricity. Gripper shouted and the Lyran went stiff, his exposed fur bristling. Curling fingers of lightning leapt from the empty air, surrounding him in burning energy. The Lyran fell to one knee with blackened burns smoking all across his gray pelt.

"Hey there, pup!" Duaal called out. "Why don't you come dance with someone who knows the steps?"

He touched fingers to a symbol embroidered on his coat and sang alien words. The Lyran jumped to his paws and whirled on Duaal, red robes billowing. Duaal stepped back, snapped a word and released his spell. The air sizzled and then burst into flame all around the Lyran. He howled as the fire enveloped clothes and fur, blazing and filling the mess with the stomach-churning smell of burning hair and flesh.

But the flaming Lyran pounced on Duaal, sending both combatants skidding across the floor. The smaller and more muscular man slashed out with his nanosword – still clutched in one smoking paw – at Duaal's unprotected face.

Duaal gasped a word and splayed his gloved fingers. The sword rang as though it had impacted steel, crashing off the apparently empty air in front of Duaal's face. But the force of the blow shoved him down, cracking the back of his head against the deckplates. Duaal blinked slowly, eyes glazed.

"Magic!" the Lyran growled.

There was something in his voice, a respectful, even reverent tone. But he didn't get off of Duaal.

Where was Xia? Gripper hauled himself back to his feet, trying not to crush Kessa and her family. He bled from a dozen painful wounds, and the stickiness running down into his ear made it hard to hear.

Xia was struggling to disarm the Arcadian of a dagger that the fairy had pulled from somewhere in her rough black robes, but not faring well. Xia sported fewer cuts than Gripper, but not by much. Her silvery skin was spotted with blood and her jeweled eyes whirled a frightened red. Her fairy attacker had Xia pinned in a corner and was bearing her blade inexorably down on the Ixthian. The medic had one of her six-fingered hands wrapped around the Arcadian's slim wrists, warding off the knife, but she was tiring quickly.

"Silver!" Gripper cried.

He jumped at the Arcadian and grabbed her wings in his huge claws. Delicate bones snapped like twigs in Gripper's hand as he yanked her off of Xia. The fairy screeched sharply in agony and Xia sagged against the wall. The strange Arcadian dropped her knife and twisted treacherously, lashing out behind her with a slender leg and landing a kick right between Gripper's legs. Tears sprang into his eyes. He released her and fell to his knees with a groan.

Alainna staggered but managed to keep her feet, even as her broken wings trailed out uselessly behind her on the floor. Seon straddled a dark-skinned human man, who was shaking his head and trying to focus glazed eyes. She retrieved her fallen dagger and made an off-balance dash at the great ogre that had destroyed her wings.

"Alainna, no!" Seon growled. "Take the baby and return it to the cathedral."

Gritting her teeth, Alainna veered off course. It wasn't wise to disobey orders from an Emberguard. Seon regarded the human boy beneath him, who was struggling to stand.

"What of these life-clingers?" Alainna asked.

She didn't like the idea of leaving anyone alive. What right did these land-bound creatures have to breathe when the White Kingdom was gone? And there were practical considerations, as well – survivors now might make enemies later.

"I'll finish them," Seon answered.

The Lyran's yellow eyes smoldered with a banked flame, a mad spark of burning need. Blackened fur around his muzzle and ears still smoked. Seon pointed his nanosword at the human who had burned him.

"Except this one," he said. "Lord Gavriel will want him. I think he's a mage. I'll kill the rest, but then bring the human prize to our master myself."

"You want all of the glory for yourself, Emberguard."

"Take the baby and go!" Seon growled.

But at the sharp end of the Emberguard's sword, the human boy whimpered like a beaten dog, his sea-green eyes wide.

"Gavriel...?" he asked. "Gavriel Euvo?"

Seon whipped his eyes back to the mage, who raised his hands, lips already moving in song. Alainna recognized the focus-words of a lightning call, but Seon struck the boy across the face hard with the guard of his nanosword, shattering the caster's attention. Blood ran from the boy's mouth.

These people were all dead, whether they knew it or not. And when Seon was done with his bloodbath, he would take the mage to Gavriel himself.

The huge ogre-thing was clambering back to his feet, but both the Dailons still cowered in the corner of the mess, cradling their child between them. Alainna stalked across the room.

"Give me the baby," she said.

The Dailon woman hugged her child to her ample blue breast, weeping and shaking her head. Her man stood up shakily between the two women, arms held out and black eyes wide with fear. A pair of handcuffs dangled from his right wrist.

"Leave us alone," he said almost bravely. "Please, I just found my family. Don't take my son!"

Alainna smiled thinly. How tight the living clung to their pointless lives and their empty loves.

Alainna brought the bloody knife down on the male Dailon, opening a gash from his collarbone to navel that gushed red down his blue chest. He fell to the ground and the woman screamed in horror as blood ran across the floor. Alainna sheathed her blade, stepping over the man and grabbed the wailing baby from his mother's arms.

[25]
SCREAM

"Even the greatest mountain is made up of mere pebbles."

- HADRIAN PROVERB

Coldhand bounded up the stairs, shoving his way past Tiberius to follow Maeve deeper into the ship. Fibersteel mesh clanged under his heavy boots. Maeve had recovered her fallen spear and soared somewhat unsteadily into the air on her injured wings. She landed on the catwalk and raced toward the sound of screams. Coldhand gave chase. He wasn't finished with her yet. Chest heaving like a smith's bellows, Tiberius brought up the rear, laboring to keep pace with the younger Prian and light-footed fairy.

Even before Coldhand chased Maeve into the mess, he smelled the metallic tang of blood – much more than had been shed during their battle down in the Blue Phoenix's hold. The air was tight with violence, pulled as taut as a drumhead. Up ahead, Maeve vanished through a narrow door and her white wings eclipsed his view until Coldhand sprinted after her.

Mess hall would have been too generous a term for the small room. There was barely enough space for a tiny countertop kitchen, to say nothing of the table, assorted chairs and a ratty brown couch crammed inside. And there was even less room now – the table was overturned and shoved back against a wall, with chairs scattered in every direction.

The floor was red and sticky with blood. It clung to Coldhand's boots and painted Maeve's bare feet red. Gripper was scrambling away, clutching the limp shape of Duaal in his arms. The young human whimpered and more blood ran from his split lip.

Xia crawled laboriously toward Vyron, who lay crumpled in a spreading pool of blood. Kessa was on her knees beside him, her mouth still open in the scream that had drawn Maeve. Something was missing from the scene, but Coldhand couldn't immediately identify what it was.

"*Vaeli'i la!*" Maeve shouted hoarsely.

Coldhand knew what the insult meant: *Honorless one.* She had said it to him enough, but now she was leaping on a figure in the center of the mess, lunging in with her spear.

Coldhand stopped dead in the door when he saw what she was fighting – a Lyran man robed all in red, his sword flashing in one paw, raised to fend off Maeve's blow, a gun clenched in the other. The burnt gray fur was different than the olive Mirran stripes, the curved nanosword from a different culture than the gleaming long-sword. But there was no mistaking the red robes or the way the Lyran fought: mad, zealous, with no thought of anything but pain and death. Icy sweat ran down Coldhand's skin. The hunter staggered and clutched at his chest.

"Put away your weapon and stand down!" Reginald shouted.

The cloaked Mirran smiled, a flash of teeth barely visible in the dark Prian night. Logan had never seen such a cold smile before, like a sliver of white ice. The Emberguard laughed and he shuddered at the sound.

"Who do you think you are to deny me?" the Mirran asked in a clear voice. "I am the hand of nothingness itself! I fear no man, for I have been enlightened. I am the last cinder of destruction before the blaze that will

be true oblivion. I fear no pain, no death! But you, too, will find peace when I rip the life from you."

"Take him," Reginald said.

Logan raised his Talon and aimed. Backup was on the way. They only had to hold him off for a few minutes.

The Mirran shrugged out of his coat and raised his sword. His red robes were like a bloody wound in the very fabric of the night. The Emberguard held his shimmering nanoblade almost casually, waving it in light, lazy circles, a conductor striking up his deadly orchestra.

Reginald braced himself and fired his Talon-5 at the Mirran, the wide bolt momentarily lighting up the alleyway, but his target was already darting toward the two police officers, so fast that he was a blur of scarlet. Logan never knew if Reginald's laser landed. If it had, the Emberguard showed no sign of slowing down.

"I am the ember that burns in the darkness before the final night," he cried. "Do not fear the pain! It is a gift to deliver you into blessed nothingness."

The Emberguard was on Reginald before the cop could squeeze off another shot. The lights of the squad car illuminated the Mirran's delicate stripes and the excited flush in his cheeks. He gracefully swept his long nanosword in a swift, deadly arc, beheading Reginald in a single blow.

"No!" Logan screamed.

Reginald's body fell limply to the cracked cement. The young cop's vision was blurred with angry tears as he opened fire. What kind of monster laughed as he killed? Could any man be that heartless? Logan shot at the Emberguard again and again, but the robed Mirran slapped aside the Talon-9 with the flat of his blade.

"A gift," he whispered like a secret.

A flick of his wrist brought the nanosword down on Logan's left arm, shearing through the limb just below the elbow. Blood sprayed and was lost in the dark night. Logan dropped his gun, staring in dumb horror at where his arm used to be and a scream welled up inside his chest.

The Emberguard spun his blade again, flashing in the thin starlight.

It looked just like his smile – cold, pale. And then the Mirran thrust his sword into Logan's chest, running him through the heart. The glistening nanoblade trapped his scream in place, pinned like a brightfly to a card.

Logan fell, dying in silence.

In the bloodstained Blue Phoenix mess, the Lyran Emberguard jammed the barrel of his laser into Maeve's stomach. Accustomed to a year of fighting against Coldhand, she spun away and his shot burned through empty air.

Tiberius ran into the room after Coldhand, shoving the bounty hunter out of his way. Orphia swooped in after her master.

"Who are you? And what the hells are you doing on my bird?" Tiberius shouted.

The Lyran didn't say anything, but Maeve gasped an answer as she twisted out of his grasp.

"Nihilists! From the cathedral!"

Nihilists? Coldhand heard the word, but it made no sense. The Church of Nihil was a small-time cult on Stray with narrow power in a handful of cities and perhaps half a dozen patchwork cathedrals scattered over the entire planet. There was no way that this bloody-robed Lyran could be of the same sect as the assassin who had taken Logan's arm and heart...

His life.

But... the red robes, that wild fighting. Coldhand remembered them all too well from his last night as a whole man.

"What the hells is he doing on my bird?" Tiberius asked.

Kessa's wail made it hard to hear even the old captain's booming voice. Maeve said something, but it was lost in the din. Tiberius was still holding his NI pistol.

"Stand down, Nihilist!" Tiberius shouted. "Put up your gun and get off my ship!"

The words eerily echoed Reginald's. This Emberguard was less interested in talking, though, and answered Tiberius with blood instead of words. He kicked out at Maeve, who recoiled but grabbed a handful of fur and managed to stay close. She slammed a sharp elbow into the Lyran's chest.

Tiberius waved his gun, but then appeared to think better of firing it in such tight confines. He was just as likely to hit one of his crew as the Emberguard. He dropped the weapon and brought up his fists.

Coldhand couldn't move. Was this fear? No, it couldn't be. Fear was a feeling, an emotion like passion or happiness. That required a heart to seize in terror or to race with joy. All he had now was a computerized pump.

Then why was Coldhand still standing in the doorway, staring at the Nihilist and shivering?

Logan opened his eyes and immediately closed them again. He was somewhere white, lying on something soft. The air was sterile and thick with the smell of chemicals. A hospital.

"He's awake."

Logan tried to open his eyes again. The silhouette of a man blocked out the bright light. Logan wanted to ask a question, but his lips were dry and stiff.

"Welcome back, Lieutenant Centra," the doctor-shadow said. Logan squinted, but still saw only blackness haloed by scrubbed, too-clean light. "You had us all worried for a while there, but you pulled through. With a little help, of course."

The shadow's gentle laugh hurt his ears, grating on his raw nerves. Logan tried to sit, but only his right arm would obey him as he struggled to push himself upright. The left one was heavy, unresponsive, unfeeling. There was a weight in Logan's chest, holding him in place.

"What...?" The question was just a whisper on his cracked lips. Logan couldn't see the expression on the doctor's backlit face.

"The nearest Ixthian cloning facility is out on Kynfarr. We put in a request for help, but the parts would have taken more than a week to arrive. We just didn't have that kind of time, so we had to use what we had here."

"What did you do to me?" Logan asked.

"Both your left arm and heart have been replaced with cybernetic equivalents, Lieutenant Centra," the shadow answered. "I'm sorry to tell you that though we gave you the best computerized replacements available, they are able to reproduce only twenty percent of your natural nerve sensitivity."

"Twenty percent... feeling?" Logan asked. "That's all I have left?"

The darkness nodded. Logan closed his eyes and waited for tears, but none came.

What the hells was wrong with Coldhand...? The traitor was just standing there, unmoving in the door of the mess.

But there wasn't time to wonder. Tiberius leapt on the Nihilist, grabbing fistfuls of red robes and trying to pull him off of Maeve. The Lyran stumbled and grunted under the added weight, but he was a powerful fighter. He twisted out of Tiberius' grasp, giving up his hold on Maeve. Tiberius swore, dropped clumps of sooty fur and lunged in again.

There wasn't room for Orphia to fly in here. The old hawk was perched on the leg of a toppled chair, watching intently and flipping her wings in agitation.

There was something satisfying about it all, about fighting the good fight after years of retirement. Tiberius' broken ribs creaked in protest, but he didn't care. Age may have dulled his eyes and slowed his body, but the blood thundering in his ears was just as glorious a song as ever. There were innocents to protect and to avenge. Vyron was dying and Kessa was crying. Tiberius' clenched fist connected solidly with the Nihilist's side. Gripper and Xia were bleeding. Tiberius lashed out again, harder. Duaal was hurt. He hammered a punch into the joint of the Nihilist's arm and the gun tumbled out of his dark paw.

The Lyran whirled on Tiberius, his lips peeled back from long, yellowing teeth in a feral snarl. He patted the human's hands aside with the hardened pads of his paws and then came in for his own claw swipes. The gun was too far away to recover, but the Nihilist scrambled for his nanosword, seizing the hilt before Tiberius could stop him.

Tiberius circled behind the Lyran and wrapped one of his thick arms around the shorter man's shoulders, trying to pin him. The Nihilist writhed like a demon, but Tiberius was ready this time and used his superior size to maintain the hold.

Snarling and spitting, the singed Nihilist twisted in his grasp. But the Lyran didn't seem to be trying to escape anymore. Tiberius tightened his grip to prepare himself for... whatever he was about to do.

Tiberius' determination very nearly killed him. The Nihilists feared nothing, death least of all. Unable to strike Tiberius behind him with claw or weapon, the zealot in red reversed his hold on the curved nanosword. Without hesitation, he drove the long blade through his own belly until the point sheared through his back and into Tiberius, just above the hip.

The old Prian stumbled and released the Nihilist with a pained shout. He thumped against the kitchen counter and sank to the floor, grunting. A cold pain seeped through his body and Tiberius clutched his stomach. Blood ran from between his fingers.

Coldhand still hadn't moved. Orphia hopped along the deck, over scarlet puddles and splintered chairs to land on Tiberius' foot and chirp sharply at him. Her talons bit into his boots.

A stain of deeper red bloomed across the Nihilist's robes. He was bleeding badly, but he wasn't on the ground. He would die, but not before killing his enemies.

Maeve let out a furious shriek and rushed in once again. She swept her long wings – one still stained by blood from fighting with Coldhand – around the Lyran, blinding him in a storm of feathers.

Her spear was on the floor at Tiberius' feet, useless and forgotten in the close quarters. Maeve raked at the Nihilist's with her fingers, but he snapped his sharp teeth and drove the princess back.

Damn it, Maeve was going to lose more than a few fingers if this didn't end now. Tiberius forced himself up and staggered toward the combatants, but his vision was getting gray at the edges and he toppled to the floor again. Orphia nipped at the back of his hand, keening in worry.

The Lyran threw Maeve off him. She beat her wings as she fell, trying to fly, but there wasn't enough room and she crashed into the wall with a loud thump.

Robes billowing around him like a crimson cloud, the Nihilist leapt at Maeve, holding his curved nanosword high. His left eye was a mess of viscera and blood, dripping down his muzzle and soaking into his burnt fur. Maeve struggled to rise, but her wounded leg – another gift from her bounty hunter – buckled and wouldn't hold her weight.

Tiberius slumped in a rapidly growing puddle of blood, trying to make his heavy, cold limbs obey him. Trying and failing.

Maeve lashed out with her wings and fists, but couldn't keep the powerful Lyran at bay. His one good eye smoldered as he brought the nanosword down on her unprotected head, but Maeve didn't scream. Her silver eyes were wide and bright as death came for her.

"Smoke!" Gripper shouted from where he stood cradling Duaal, but there was nothing he could do.

Metal rang on metal and the Lyran tried to pull his nanosword back, but Coldhand held the blade fast in illonium fingers.

"Cavainna is *mine*," he said.

Coldhand tightened his cybernetic fingers around the sword as he kicked the Lyran in the center of his bleeding chest. The Nihilist staggered, releasing his weapon and Coldhand dropped it to the floor with a clang. A deep groove cut into the hunter's palm, but the illonium shielding was intact.

Coldhand's Talon was reholstered at his hip. Not much point in saving Maeve only to accidentally shoot her in the close brawling, Tiberius supposed. Dirty dishwater was dripping down onto his' shoulder. It was cold and smelled like eggs.

Maeve clambered back onto her feet, limping heavily. She and Coldhand circled the Nihilist together. He retaliated with a swipe of short, bloody claws across Maeve's injured forearm. The Lyran spun, aiming the same blow at Coldhand, who already had several deep gashes along his right arm from Orphia's talons. The Lyran's claws sliced deeply into the torn flesh and a muscle in Coldhand's jaw twitched, but he took advantage of the proximity to grab one furry wrist. He twisted and yanked the Nihilist's arm up until the shoulder popped loudly.

Maeve rammed her small foot into the Lyran's chest, pushing him against Coldhand, but there was no way the pair could keep him restrained. Coldhand alone wasn't strong enough to hold back the frenzied Lyran. Maeve was a skilled and savvy fighter, but she was too small. She just didn't have the mass to control the man.

Tiberius groaned. Where was Xia when he needed her? She could have the damnable hole in his hide stitched up in a minute. But the Ixthian was busy elsewhere – she had rolled Vyron over onto his back and now straddled his chest, eyes wide and red. Kessa clutched at her mate's hand and sobbed as Xia tried to explain something.

Tiberius waved Orphia off and pulled a damp dish towel down off of the counter, stuffing it into the hole in his stomach. It hurt like hells, but it seemed to slow the bleeding.

Good enough. Tiberius forced himself to his feet and jumped into the fray. The Lyran recoiled, but Maeve and Coldhand were too close, blocking off his retreat. Tiberius grabbed the Nihilist's free arm and yanked it up behind his back the same way that Coldhand had. Tiberius leaned heavily on the interloper, using his bulk to maintain the hold, but more to keep himself upright.

Coldhand shot Tiberius a look that might have been surprised or grateful, but the old captain was concentrating too hard on just standing to worry about it much. Together, they swept the Nihilist's paws out from under him and pulled him to his knees. The Lyran finally pitched forward onto the floor, both men on top of him.

"What are you doing on my ship?" Tiberius panted.

"I'm executing Lord Gavriel's will."

"Who's Gavriel?" Coldhand asked.

"And why the hells did he send you to my God-damned bird?" Tiberius asked at the same time.

The Lyran grinned wolfishly but said nothing.

"Tell me!" Tiberius demanded.

"I am an Emberguard," the Nihilist said. "I answer to no one but Lord Gavriel. Not to you, not to your impotent god. I have done as my master commanded and now claim my reward!"

The Emberguard lifted his head up as high as he could in his awkward position and then smashed it down onto the floor. There was a sharp crunch. Tiberius and Coldhand moved quickly to stop him, but the Nihilist raised his head again and slammed it down a second time. The sound was softer, a sickening squelch, but then he lay still.

[26]

PRAYERS UNANSWERED

"We only live that the gods may enjoy from us all manner of songs, from the most comical to the most tragic."

- ARCADIAN PROVERB

Everyone stared at the body of the dead Lyran Emberguard. And then chaos erupted once again. Maeve closed her eyes, but couldn't block out the sound. She had survived. Again.

"Anslin, will you never answer my prayers?" she asked quietly.

She opened her eyes and looked around the shambles of the mess hall.

"He killed himself!" Gripper shouted, hopping from one huge foot to the other and clutching Duaal against his chest like a child. "Look, he just bashed his brains out on the floor!"

"Kessa, I need you to get down to the medbay and bring me my kit," Xia said. "It's in the blue locker with the cross and circle on it."

"But–!" Kessa objected.

"Go get the kit or Vyron will die!" Xia said.

Kessa nodded, tears streaming down her cheeks, and jumped to her feet. She stepped fearfully over the Nihilist's body, as though frightened it might bite her, then vanished down the hall toward the medbay. Tiberius staggered over to Gripper, staring at Duaal in his arms.

"What happened?" the old Prian asked. "Is he alright?"

"I think so," Gripper answered. "Just passed out."

Gently, the Arboran laid Duaal on the floor and wiped his claws on his shirt. Tiberius sat down heavily beside the boy and took his cold hand.

"Damn them," he said in a voice thick with rage. "Damn them all. What did they want?"

"Power," Duaal whimpered. His eyes fluttered open. They were haunted and terrified, drained of the bravado Maeve was so used to seeing there. "Gavriel needs another one… to replace me."

"What?" Tiberius leaned close to catch the words. "Power? Find out if they took anything, Anandrou."

"Yeah, on it," Gripper said.

The big engineer limped to a wall-mounted computer terminal, grimacing in pain. Xia looked up from where she was holding together the halves of the great rent in Vyron's chest.

"That can wait, damn it!" she hissed. "First, you all need medical attention."

Gripper looked uncertainly between Xia and Tiberius. Kessa ran back into the room with a large plastic case tucked under her arm. She held it out to the Ixthian doctor, who opened the case and pulled out a hypodermic needle as long as Maeve's hand.

"Hold here," Xia instructed.

With tears streaming down her cheeks, Kessa obeyed, replacing the Ixthian doctor's hands with her own. Xia ripped the cap off the syringe with her teeth and plunged the needle directly into Vyron's wounded chest. Kessa closed her eyes and sobbed, but she kept steady pressure on her mate's severed blood vessels. Xia jammed the plunger down and Vyron convulsed.

"Hold him!" Xia said.

Kessa leaned all of her weight onto Vyron. Xia peeled back his eyelids and inspected the Dailon's glassy black eyes. Apparently satisfied, she nodded to Kessa and went to work swiftly suturing up the long cut.

"He'll live," Xia said. "Which is more than I can say for the rest of you if you tear yourselves open any more. There's a lot of blood on the floor and not all of it is from that man there."

Xia pointed her sharp chin in the direction of the dead Nihilist.

"Sit still until I can get to you," she ordered.

There was a cold, hard touch on Maeve's arm. Coldhand had closed his cybernetic fingers around her bicep. The Arcadian tried to pull away, but it was like trying to break free of a vice and she was so tired.

"I have what I came for," Coldhand said and pulled Maeve toward the door. They both left red footprints on the floor.

"Not so fast."

It wasn't Tiberius who had objected, but Xia. The bounty hunter stopped, glancing back at the medic. Xia had finished stitching up Vyron and was regarding Coldhand with determined aqua eyes, hands on her hips.

"You're bleeding just as bad as anyone else here," she said. "You won't get far before you pass out."

"I don't feel it," Coldhand answered.

"Even a mechanical heart needs blood to pump and it can't do that if you've bled out," Xia said. "Sit down before you fall down."

Slowly, Coldhand released Maeve's arm. He pulled the Talon-9 from his hip as he leaned against the wall, ready to shoot any member of the Blue Phoenix crew who might try to take advantage of his wounds. Maeve sagged beside Coldhand. Neither one looked at the other.

Xia went to Tiberius and made a noise of disgust.

"A towel?" she asked. "Do you have any idea what kind of infections you could have picked up?"

"Better than bleeding to death," Tiberius retorted.

"Not by much."

Gingerly, Xia pulled the dishrag from the wound in Tiberius' stomach and went to work washing it out. He grunted in pain. She pulled a can from the supplies, shook it and filled the wound with disinfectant foam, then began stitching Tiberius up.

Maeve risked a sidelong glance over at Coldhand. The man was reputed to be as unstoppable as time and just as ruthless. They *had* fought hard, first against one another, then against the powerful Emberguard. She couldn't really fault him for bleeding.

But she did. Maeve's eyes fell shut. She was ready. She wanted to die and wanted Coldhand to do it.

"Genocide?"

Maeve's eyes snapped open.

"How can one woman commit genocide?" Coldhand asked.

Maeve pulled her wings around her. The feathers were stiff with drying blood.

"By terrible accident," she said. "Not by breaking of any law, but out of love. I turned love into death, Logan. And for that, there is no forgiveness."

Coldhand considered Maeve's non-answer. What did she mean? And did it matter? She certainly implied guilt. The fairy's voice and her silver eyes were full of self-loathing and horror. That seemed answer enough.

Coldhand probed the deep gash left by Maeve's glass spear. It was so close to a killing blow, but she had restrained herself. Blood welled up around Coldhand's prodding finger, but still he felt only the most distant, dull throb of pain.

After tending to Tiberius and then Gripper's numerous cuts, Xia crossed the small room. She looked between Maeve and Coldhand.

Deciding either that the Arcadian was in more need of care or else that the hunter was expendable, Xia began applying a sticky yellow bandaging spray to Maeve's many cuts and burns.

"You're lucky to be alive," Xia told her.

"Bad luck," Maeve said.

Gripper made his way back over to the computer terminal and brought up the internal sensors. "Engine room checks out. Everything's still there. The fore starboard airlock is blown, though. I guess they cut it to get in."

Tiberius nodded absently, still watching Duaal. The boy lay on the floor of the impromptu medical ward, eyes squeezed shut and shivering.

Duaal wasn't the job, Coldhand reminded himself. And neither was Maeve's guilt or innocence. He was just a bounty hunter and Maeve Cavainna was worth high color to someone. He would let nothing stop him from taking her in, not even an Emberguard bent on destruction.

The Emberguard... Coldhand had always assumed there was only one, that it was a singular title for the Mirran man who had taken his arm and his heart. But if what the Lyran had snarled was true, there was an entire faction of them within the Church of Nihil, all serving its leader, Gavriel. Duaal seemed to know Gavriel, and was terrified of him.

So what was the Emberguard doing on Prianus five years ago?

Selling illegal chems...? Maybe. The death-worshipers didn't seem to care much about breaking the law for their own needs. But Coldhand's homeworld was a remote planet, too far away from the main trade routes to be a lucrative market.

The questions didn't matter. Not because Coldhand was afraid. It was simply a useless line of inquiry. That was all.

There were more important things to think about. Maeve was closer than she had ever been in the past year. Close enough that Coldhand could smell the sweat beaded on her pale skin, as salty as a human's, but mingled with something sweet, like honey or vanilla. Close enough to see the imperfections of her bleaching job, the shadows of hair as black as a Prian night. Close enough to touch, to reach out and seize her again or press his Talon to her temple.

But Coldhand *was* wounded and needed Xia's attention. But once she had administered her care, what was to stop him from simply grabbing the tired fairy princess and leaving? Only Maeve herself... For all of her dove-white feathers, she was more like a hawk or falcon, bred and blooded to fly and kill. More like Coldhand. Logan had lost his arm and his heart to juvenile sentiment. He knew better now.

Maeve's head suddenly snapped up. "Wait, where is Baliend?"

Xia blinked, startled, and then an embarrassed expression crept across the Ixthian's face. Kessa had been following her around the mess, handing out supplies as asked for. But now the new mother's fragile composure shattered and she began to cry again.

"That little bird-back stole him!" Kessa sobbed. "The... the one who tried to kill Vyron!"

"It was another Nihilist," Gripper said. "She was wearing those black robes. She took Baliend and ran off while the Emberguard stayed to fight."

Tiberius swore loudly, though he held Duaal gently. Maeve leapt to her feet, eliciting a shout from Xia. The princess scooped up her spear and bounded in the direction of the exit.

"Sit your tail down this instant, Maeve!" Tiberius said.

Maeve paused at the door leading toward the front of the Blue Phoenix. "No, I am going to find Baliend. You have seen the work of the Nihilists and they are not to be trusted with a child."

"I'm not saying that–" Tiberius began, but Duaal struggled to sit up. His ordinarily dark Hyzaari skin was pale and his eyes were wide with terror.

"Maeve, no! You can't go," Duaal said. "You have no idea what Gavriel's like. We have to get off this planet!"

Coldhand didn't think he had ever heard Duaal speak to Maeve. There seemed to be no love lost between them, but there was real fear in Duaal's voice now.

"I have to retrieve Baliend," Maeve argued.

"We... we have to run," Duaal said. "Don't let him take me again, Tiberius! Please! I'd rather be dead...!"

Tiberius' mouth opened and closed, but no words came out. His face was so flushed with fury that he looked like he might actually explode at any moment.

"You mean this man abused you?" Xia asked. "Sexually?"

Duaal shot her a withering look. "What? No! Believe me, I wish it was... just that. He used me... I don't know how else to describe it. Since I was a little boy. Gavriel said he needed me for his spells. I felt them, I sang them for him. He was in me, in my head!"

Duaal trailed off in helpless horror. He clenched his hands into fists and tears ran down his cheeks in shining streaks.

"I don't understand," Tiberius said at last. "Gavriel needed you for... what? A component of his spells? Like virgin's blood and unicorn horns? That kind of thing?"

"No. Magic does not work that way," Maeve told him. She still held her spear and hadn't moved from beside the door. "It obeys the same rules as science, as any truth. The gestures and symbols that Duaal uses are tools given to children to help them learn. They are meant to be put aside when the time is right."

"You said you didn't know much about magic," Xia accused.

"I am no adept of the Ivory Spire, but I am of the royal line of Cavain. I have been to school!" Maeve snapped. She tapped a finger against her temple. "Ultimately, all that matters in magic is the *thought*! The words, the songs, are used to give structure and meaning, to aid in memory."

Duaal was staring down at his clothes, at the dangling charms and the symbols embroidered into his expensive velvet coat, now ruined with dark stains.

"What?" he gasped. "All this...?"

"Is unnecessary," Maeve said firmly.

"I don't need all of this?" Duaal asked, gesturing with a trembling hand.

"Physical foci are for children," Maeve told him. "You should have outgrown them years ago."

Coldhand was listening closely to the conversation and almost shot Xia when she approached. The Ixthian tensed and held still until he lowered his gun again. The case of medical supplies in her six-fingered hands was nearly empty.

"You can listen while I patch you up," Xia told Coldhand.

"Gavriel needed me for his magic," Duaal said. "He always kept me right there beside him, even when he was sleeping. Whenever he started a spell, ever since I was a little boy, I felt it in my head, every word... but he was never talking to me, not like we are now. The songs ran through me and then... things happened. Lightning, fire, whatever Gavriel needed. I understood what he was thinking and I... said... it the right way to make it happen."

"You *thought* it the right way," Maeve corrected.

Duaal nodded. "I hated it. Eventually, I was more scared of the things Gavriel made me do than anything he might do *to* me. So I ran."

"That's why you were stowed away on my bird," Tiberius said. He rubbed his face. "You could have told me, Duaal. You've had plenty of time to do it!"

Xia was almost finished. She had cleaned the wounds left by Maeve and Orphia. Coldhand watched Duaal. The fear was naked in his green eyes and he pulled his knees up against his chest like a much younger boy trying to hide.

"I learned something from the Nihilists that I did not think important," Maeve said. "But perhaps it is. There was a woman there named Elsa. She went to the church seeking refuge from an abusive husband and when he came looking for her, Elsa said that Gavriel shouted Arcadian words. Perhaps a spell. But he killed the man with a silver knife. There is a graveyard of dead enemies behind the cathedral."

"Is that what they're going to do to Baliend?" Kessa asked in a trembling voice.

"I... do not think so," Maeve answered slowly. "And if they knew you were of the Sisterhood, you would be on the floor, not Vyron. No, I mean that Gavriel stabbed a man, perhaps with one of his old ritual implements."

"Is there a point to this story, Cavainna?" Coldhand asked. So far, this all sounded like a waste of dwindling time.

"That's the power he needs to replace," Duaal said. "I was older than Baliend when Gavriel took me, but only by a few years. I... I don't even remember my parents. Just him."

Maeve regarded the young human with a glittering silver-gray gaze. "It would seem that Gavriel lost much when you escaped him. I do not understand why... No Arcadian relies so heavily upon an artifact that they can no longer sing their spells properly when it is lost."

Xia looked up from suturing a long, bloody gash across Cold-hand's left shoulder.

"Why didn't they take Duaal back?" she asked.

"He'd better not try it," Tiberius growled, cracking his thick, gnarled knuckles ominously.

"I don't think they knew about Shimmer," Gripper said. "They were just after Little Blue."

"Is Gavriel going to hurt my baby?" Kessa asked.

"Yes," Duaal answered.

"I will not let him," Maeve said.

Orphia perched near Tiberius, glaring balefully at Coldhand from time to time as if to remind him that, though Tiberius might have been distracted by talk of Kessa's child and Duaal's history, she had *not* forgotten about the bounty hunter.

Coldhand flexed and then balled his right fist experimentally. Xia did good work. She was at least as skilled as the Temptation's medic had been. Better, probably. The skin pulled tight across his bicep, but Coldhand was no longer slowly bleeding out.

The questions being asked were interesting, to be certain, but they weren't important. There was no bounty on Gavriel, regardless of his crimes. Coldhand's injuries were tended to and Maeve hadn't taken advantage of his wounds to get away from him. If she trusted that Coldhand was an honorable man who would not fight the people who had healed him, she was very wrong.

"What can we do?" Gripper asked, wringing his huge claws and worrying at the hem of his shredded *Better FMS than FAO!* shirt. "I mean, we don't know where they're taking him."

"There are several Nihilist cathedrals across Stray," Maeve said. "Gavriel was not at the Gharib church, but his people came *here*. I was told that Gavriel had gone to Kharnig, but I believe that he has returned."

"But we don't know that for sure," Tiberius argued. "We should com the police."

"That is your answer to everything," Maeve said.

"What's the point of cops if we can't call them when something goes wrong?" Duaal asked.

"Maybe we could check the local mainstream and see if this is happening in Kharnig, too," Gripper suggested. "The Arcadian who took Little Blue could be anywhere by now if she had a ship or some other vehicle. Maybe we can find out."

"We have already wasted too much time," Maeve announced. "I am going!"

"We've got to play this carefully," Tiberius told her. "How many of those Nihilists are there? How many more of them are Amber-guards or whatever they are? It took everyone on this bird to take down just one of them. You won't do the kid any good dead."

"You will just stand by while Gavriel threatens a child?" Maeve asked.

"Good God, girl, I'm not saying that we do nothing–" Tiberius shouted.

"Whatever you decide, you'll be doing it short one princess," Coldhand said.

Against her captain's orders, Maeve was already moving toward the door of the mess. Coldhand grabbed her wrist in his cybernetic hand and hauled her back. Maeve stared at him with shocked silver eyes.

"What are you doing?" Xia asked. "I just stitched you up!"

"Your mistake," Coldhand said.

"I would gladly die by your hand," Maeve told him. "But not right now. I need to find Baliend!"

"That's not the job," Coldhand said. "You are."

"Have you no honor?" Maeve asked.

"No."

Coldhand holstered his gun loosely and pulled another pair of handcuffs from his belt. Maeve stood up on her toes, but still didn't reach Coldhand's shoulder. She raised her hand and he braced himself. He had learned long ago not to underestimate her skill and they were both badly injured.

But Coldhand wasn't ready for the sharp impact across his left cheek and a loud crack resounded in the suddenly silent room. A slap? Maeve hadn't even hit him hard, but Coldhand took a stunned step back and raised his hand to his face. After a year of battling for her life and freedom, Maeve... slapped him like a badly behaved child?

The princess spun away, her cheeks as red as though she were the one who had been hit, and grabbed her spear. Without another word, Maeve ran out of the mess hall. Coldhand drew his Talon and gave chase.

[27]

FLIGHT

"The finer the point of the spear, the more easily it is broken off."

- AI'RU VALLAIN, PYRAD REBEL (10,142 MA)

Coldhand chased Maeve down the hallway, his feet hammering on the fibersteel flooring. His computerized heart beat loud and fast in his chest. The hunter had lost a great deal of blood and his body struggled to compensate. There was a sharp tightness in his ribs that Coldhand recognized as pain, muscles cramping from lack of oxygen.

Before Coldhand could take aim with his Talon, Maeve turned sharply, bolted down a short side corridor and vanished out a darkened doorway. Almost too late, he saw the broken locks of a hatch that had been forced open and darkness beyond. Coldhand jerked to a halt as one foot came down on nothing.

The huge, flat pewter disk of Stray's moon did little to illuminate the world far below. Maeve soared away on outstretched wings, not looking back at the hunter she left behind. The door was an airlock, located high on the freighter for orbital docking. The casing had been pried open and the interior wiring ripped out until the hatch finally opened. Not unlike Coldhand had done when he first escaped the Blue Phoenix.

Maeve was already a dwindling spark of white vanishing into the east. Coldhand leapt from the ruined airlock at an angle, landed with a resounding clang on the Blue Phoenix's wing, and jumped again. He rolled with the impact, but when the bounty hunter stood again, he had torn free several of Xia's neat blue stitches and was bleeding again. Coldhand raised his glacial eyes back to the sky, but Maeve was gone.

He didn't waste energy on fuming or swearing. This chase was far from over, if Coldhand could figure out where Maeve was going and get her into custody before one of those Emberguard gutted her. Thinking of the red-robed creatures made Coldhand's stomach clench.

Maeve had talked about several Nihilist cathedrals and guessed that Vyron's baby was probably being taken to the closest one, at least temporarily. She knew where she was going and wasn't restricted to the roads of the city. Maeve was flying east, so that was the direction Coldhand would go, too.

He considered following on foot. The princess was wounded and would be flying slowly. Maybe he could catch up. But Coldhand rejected the idea. Maeve was a creature of passions that ran as hot as stellar plasma. Her injuries wouldn't slow her down. If the fairy was determined to retrieve Baliend, nothing short of death would stop her.

He needed the Raptor. The detour would cost him precious minutes, but it was a necessary gamble. Coldhand turned north and headed toward the landing pad where he had left his ship.

"Damn that girl! Damn her to the deepest hell!" Tiberius shouted. "We need to get that little hare-brain before Coldhand does."

"Those Nihilists will kill Smoke!" Gripper whimpered. "Unless Coldhand catches up first. We have to help her!"

"You can't leave!" Kessa protested. "Vyron still needs Xia!"

"Neither of them is going to make it very far in the shape they're in," Xia said. The medic was pacing and waving her hands in the air. "Tiberius, we have to get Vyron and Maeve to a hospital. Probably Coldhand, too."

Tiberius ignored them both. Duaal had taken his hand again and the boy's grip was cold. His voice was so choked with terror that Tiberius had to lean close to catch the words.

"Don't chase her," Duaal said. "Please, Tiberius. She's going to him, to Gavriel."

"We can't just let this happen," Tiberius told him.

"No!" the boy whimpered. His eyes were wild and wide. "You don't understand. If Maeve tries to fight Gavriel for Baliend, she will die. And if you go after her, he'll kill you, too. Please, don't go!"

Tiberius wasn't sure what to do and the feeling was irritatingly disorienting. Disobedient and often suicidal though Maeve was, he couldn't just leave her to Coldhand or the Nihilists, but Duaal was so frightened.

By all the old gods, birds were easier! They never needed anything but a shred of food and a long leash to fly on. People had demands, strange emotional and psychological needs that Tiberius couldn't afford to simply ignore.

"Please!" Duaal begged.

Maeve was a capable woman, Tiberius reasoned. She had been a knight back in Arcadia and had more experience in battle than any of them, Tiberius included. And after a career in the Prian police, that was saying something. Maeve's wings gave her a significant advantage in a fight. Even birds couldn't match an Arcadian's soft, silent wings for a stealthy approach. If anyone could survive this, it would be Maeve Cavainna. She would make it back to the Blue Phoenix... right?

But Maeve was injured and even a cheap gun all too easily eliminated the advantages of flight. She would be fighting a battle on two fronts, against the Nihilists and against Logan Coldhand. If she somehow managed to get into the cathedral to rescue Kessa's baby, the bounty hunter was right on her tail.

Without help, Maeve would die. Tiberius wasn't like Coldhand. He didn't just walk away from his responsibilities. Something of his decision must have shown in Tiberius' face because Duaal covered his eyes with his shaking hands and whimpered.

Tiberius stood up, his back protesting loudly. He was too old and too tired to go off chasing a crazy dove, but what choice had Maeve left him? Still, getting the rest of the Blue Phoenix crew killed in the process seemed a stupid way to help her, if Gavriel was as dangerous as Duaal claimed. Tiberius wasn't an overeager young fool like Maeve. He would think this thing through.

"Alright," Tiberius said. "We're going to get Maeve and the baby back in one piece. Two pieces. Whatever. Shove up and listen! We can do this, but we'll need some help."

"Do we have to run so fast?" Elsa asked. "It's making the baby cry!"

She had bundled up the tiny Dailon child as best she could in her dark robes and held him close. Still, the baby hadn't stopped crying since Alainna thrust him into Elsa's arms and told her to run. Elsa was Mirran, born on a world of wide, open grass plains and sharp-clawed predators. She had long, strong legs quite capable of running for hours without tiring. But the baby didn't like it and was screaming loudly.

"Close your mouth and run, woman," Alainna panted.

The Arcadian was struggling to keep up. She had slender legs never meant to spend so much time laboring on the ground, especially dragging the weight of her broken wings.

It was getting late and the streets were swiftly emptying as the nighttime chill came on. Elsa eyed the occasional passing vehicle enviously, sealed up against the night. She might be able to run for hours, but she was cold and so was the baby. But sweat ran down Alainna's white skin, washing away the blood until it was only pale pink ribbons. The fairy was panting so hard that Elsa wondered how she managed to keep her lungs from bursting like a corpse in the sun.

What did Gavriel want a baby for? Maybe the great man was just lonely. He spent a lot of time with the black-haired Arcadian, Xartasia, but Elsa supposed even her beauty wasn't quite the same as the tiny warmth of a baby. Gavriel would be a good father to the little boy, Elsa told herself. She hoped it was true.

A low-slung car with peeling paint slowed on its spluttering null-field beside them. The driver blared his horn and made several gestures that Elsa didn't understand, but he was laughing. One of the sealed windows hissed down and a young human man leaned out. His eyes were bloodshot and he reeked of narcohol, even from this far away. Their vehicle easily kept pace with the two women.

"Hey, little 'Lainna. Haven't seen you around here in a while," he shouted at Alainna.

The fairy continued running, not looking at him. Another man appeared behind the one in the window, also leering at her.

"We've missed you, sweetie. Bet you've missed our money, too," he said. The second man's eyes lingered disapprovingly on Alainna's rough black robes. "What the hells is that thing you're wearing? Stop running and let us give you a ride!"

He made another gesture that Elsa couldn't interpret. The first man laughed raucously and grinned at his friend.

"Looks like someone messed up those wings bad," he called out. "Well, you won't need them for us!"

"Oh, we'll take nice care of you," the second man agreed, "if you take care of us!"

Alainna still didn't turn toward them.

"Hey!" shouted the first man. "Don't you dare ignore me, you bird-back little whore!"

Alainna stopped in her tracks and Elsa stumbled to a halt next to her. The Arcadian's chest heaved and her eyes were narrowed to furious, dangerous slits. The car swerved wildly at her sudden halt, spinning around to face the two women.

"Stay here," Alainna hissed.

She stalked toward the vehicle and one of the men opened the door, beckoning to her. Alainna smiled, but Elsa saw her fingers close on the handle of a knife tucked into her robes.

The baby was still crying and Elsa tried to comfort him as the men inside the car screamed. At least they wouldn't be running the rest of the way to the cathedral.

The wind raked icy fingers over Maeve's skin as she flew and her injured wing cramped in the cold, but she was hot with rage and clutched her spear tightly. Gavriel's Nihilists had stolen Baliend and would turn the boy into another Duaal – or worse – unless Maeve stopped them.

Maeve didn't try to fight the stab of guilt. She was no better than Gavriel, but she swore by Anslin that she would return Baliend to his parents before she went off to face final justice. Nothing could ever repay the lives Maeve had taken, but she would at least do this one thing...

The jagged black Church of Nihil loomed up suddenly out of the night and Maeve beat her wings hard, pulling off just before she crashed headfirst into a warped strip of painted fibersteel. She caught her balance again and pushed her fingers between cracks of siltstone and metal, probed with her toes until she found purchase. The cathedral was still warm from the blistering Gharib day.

Maeve clung to the wall on one of the open steeples. She lifted herself high enough to peer over the uneven sill, down into the cathedral. Everything was dark and silent. No lights shone below and nothing moved. Maeve squinted in the starlight and could just make out the massive single room of the church beneath her, but there was no one inside.

Where were the Nihilists? Only a day ago, this place was full of desperate people. Maeve spread her wings and caught an updraft, spiraling skyward and then coming down on a pile of stone left over from the cathedral's construction. Had the Nihilists gone?

A lone dilapidated car was parked outside. It was long and low, with paint peeling off in curling strips. The null-inertia field was powered down and the dented undercarriage rested directly on the ground.

Maeve caught a whiff of something coppery on the rising air. She jumped down from the rocks and tried the car door, surprised to find it unlocked. The interior of the vehicle was stained and torn, probably cheap even before its hard use. It stank of sex and sweat, but those scents were almost overwhelmed by the smell coming from several large, dark wet patches. Maeve touched one of the sticky puddles and rubbed the substance between her fingers.

Blood.

Maeve climbed out of the car. Now what? Where were Gavriel and Baliend? Were they even in Gharib? Maeve closed her eyes and tried to calm herself. Her rage would gain her nothing. Anger sped the hand but slowed the mind, as Caith often said. Any skills Maeve's brother lacked with a spear, he always more than made up for with words. And love...

"Maeve, please...!" Caith begged. "If I do not see Karrian tonight, I swear before Aes herself that I shall die!"

Maeve sighed at her little brother. He looked like such a child on his knees down there in the grass, staining his pristine white spell-singer's robes green.

"I have been away from Orthain for weeks, too," Maeve told Caith. *"No one ever died for lack of their lover's kiss."*

Caith hid a smile of his own. He knew he had already won the argument. His sister's resistance was only a part of the game. Maeve could deny Caith nothing.

"It is sung that Cavain could kindle flames with only the passion of his heart," Caith said, folding his delicate hands over his chest. *"And I am one of his descendants! The heart that could set the dryad's wood ablaze could surely break in two when such love is denied."*

"You have no respect for our blood, little brother," Maeve answered with a laugh. *"Except to get what you want!"*

"Please, I must see Karrian tonight! I swear by the gods my heart will shatter if I do not!"

"That will be nothing compared to our punishment if we are not at the Tamlin Waygate tonight," Maeve said. She sat in the emerald green grass beside Caith. *"Princess Titania herself is coming to the blooming fields this month. We are only the king's niece and nephew – she is his daughter. Titania will be well within her right to thrash us if she finds the Waygate closed!"*

"Our royal cousin is only coming to Tamlin to be with Sir Calloren," Caith said. He caught Maeve's eye and winked. *"She is not denied the chance to see her enarri. Why should I?"*

"She will see no one if you do not open the Waygate."

Caith laid his head on Maeve's shoulder, his black curls brushing her cheek.

"I have an idea," Caith said. *"You can open the Waygate!"*

"What?" Maeve asked. *"No!"*

"You have been watching me do it for years!" Caith told her. *"I have heard you humming the songs. You can do this!"*

"I am only a knight."

"You are my beautiful, brilliant sister. There is nothing you cannot do... if you wish it."

"You are a menace," Maeve said.

She swatted her little brother lightly, then smiled at him.

"Very well. Go see your love, Caith. I will open the Waygate tonight."

Maeve swiped hot tears out of her eyes. Reliving old wounds and sins wouldn't help her now. But what would? She circled the leaning black Nihilist cathedral twice, but found nothing. Maeve stopped in the stony graveyard and wrapped her wings around her against the cold, staring up at the colorless moon and silently demanding answers of the darkness.

It took just minutes to fly the Raptor across Gharib. The central hub of the city was brightly lit, but that illumination tapered off as Coldhand soared east until the ground below finally went dark. Thermal imaging showed nothing but flat black flecked only occasionally by the heat signatures of a few lifeforms below.

It was impossible to tell which one was Maeve Cavainna. Coldhand switched over to the spectrum densitometer and scanned until he found what he was looking for – a large, rectangular patch with higher density than the surrounding sand.

Coldhand investigated the display more closely as he slowed the Raptor. A rectangle with a thin black border – that was the wall of the church and then lighter in the center where the room opened up. Coldhand saw no interior walls, just the irregular gray mottling of stone and dirt. Nothing moved inside.

But behind the cathedral, Coldhand could discern dark blurs laid out in uneven rows. Something was buried there… many somethings. A graveyard? Maeve mentioned one and Coldhand could think of nothing else to explain the scan results. The bounty hunter frowned at his display. There had to be hundreds of graves beyond the Nihilist cathedral.

Coldhand inspected the sensor readouts carefully. There was something else superimposed over the cemetery. Or beneath it…

A network of intersecting lines crossed each other and turned at strange, sharp angles underground. A star? One with eight points. Coldhand had seen that symbol somewhere before, but where?

His questions would have to wait. The proximity alarm blared, warning Coldhand that he was perilously close to the ground. He pulled back on the control yoke, bringing up the Raptor's nose and evening out. The fighter's roaring engines churned dust into the air, boiling in low clouds across the graveyard.

The Church of Nihil jutted up from the murk. It was a towering yet decrepit thing, a massive, graceless piling of dark siltstone and riveted metal that looked as though it would topple at any moment. Coldhand switched back to thermal.

He didn't have to look far to find Maeve. The Arcadian princess stood on top of an abandoned car in front of the Nihilist church, waiting with her spear in hand. Coldhand flipped a switch and a brilliant spotlight bathed his mark in bright white light. Maeve held her ground and didn't run. Her long bleached hair whipped wildly about her, her wings laid flat behind her to avoid catching the wind churned up by the Raptor's thrusters.

The fairy's chin was raised proudly, silver eyes defiant and her mouth set in a grim line. Coldhand couldn't help admiring her, just for a moment. Maeve looked like an angel from Prian legend – sad, lovely creatures of grace and power that carried out God's will. But they were only stories. *This* angel was perfectly capable of killing.

Coldhand brought the pointed nose of the Raptor around to face Maeve. He trained his guns on her and turned on his loud-speaker.

"There's no one left to help you, Cavainna. Stop flying and give yourself up."

Maeve shouted something in reply, but the hunter couldn't hear her over the rumbling of engines and inside the cockpit sealed for flight in the vacuum of space. The fairy shielded her eyes against the spotlight and shook her head emphatically.

No.

"If you fly off chasing Vyron's kid, you might get yourself killed by Duaal's demon mage and I'll lose a very valuable prize," Coldhand said. "I'll kill you myself and take the smaller bounty before I let you out of my talons again, Cavainna."

That was no idle threat. Maeve had trapped Coldhand and, unless she gave herself up, he had little choice. He had poured too many hours and cenmarks into hunting the princess to let someone else kill her.

A bright, impossible hope lit up Maeve's face. How long had she pushed and pulled, trying to manipulate Coldhand into killing her just like this? Now chance and circumstances far outside her control had finally cornered the bounty hunter. But Maeve shook her head again.

No.

No? Coldhand was incredulous. He was offering Maeve what she wanted most in the worlds, and now she was saying no.

Well, it was no longer her choice. Coldhand thumbed the cover off the trigger of the Raptor's lasers. He always got his mark and the bounty hunter felt no regret for killing such a lovely creature. No horror at gunning down the tiny winged woman, for stopping the only one trying to save Vyron's infant son, no terror at the shell of a man he had become, no loss for the death of Logan Centra.

All he wanted was Maeve. All he cared about was the bounty.

Maeve held her arms up to her chest as though cradling something, then pointed imperiously at the darkened Church of Nihil behind her.

The baby. They have Baliend.

Coldhand's mechanical metal fingers hesitated over the weapon controls. His cold blue eyes darted of their own volition over to the densitometer display. That star-shape... he *had* seen it before.

It was on Duaal's coat, embroidered in golden thread across the young man's back. A symbol of power. A focus, Maeve had said.

Coldhand switched to thermal imaging and traced the interlocking lines with his cybernetic hand, unable to feel the smoothness of the screen under his numb metal fingers.

Twenty percent... But if Duaal was right, Baliend would have even less than that. Unless someone rescued him from Gavriel.

The Raptor landed on the uneven ground in front of the cathedral. The canopy clicked and unsealed, then slid back. Coldhand leapt out, already slipping his Talon-9 from its holster, and stopped outside the reach of Maeve's spear. But not out of his laser's range. The bounty hunter stared at her before speaking.

"They're underground," Coldhand said slowly. Each word was a clear struggle. "I picked up a network of tunnels running under the graveyard. At least two hundred heat signatures down there."

Maeve gritted her teeth. Underground, beneath the cemetery. It made sense now. Where else would death-worshipers feel more at ease and powerful than among the graves of the dead? She hadn't even thought to look there.

"How do we get into the tunnels?" she asked.

"According to the Raptor's sensors, one of them comes up inside the church," Coldhand said. "It's likely hidden, but I know where to look."

Maeve turned away and hurried into the darkened Church of Nihil. Coldhand followed warily.

[28]

STAR AND STONE

"Bravery and cowardice are only a single step apart – one toward the thing you fear or one step away."

- SERRA DUSTON, HADRIAN PHILOSOPHER (451 MA)

Coldhand was right. The tunnel entrance was concealed behind a heap of rubble inside the cathedral and covered by a sheet of metal. Maeve helped the bounty hunter pull it slowly aside and tensed at every shrill scrape of steel on stone. Maeve scowled as they worked – the tunnel mouth wasn't far from the slab where she had slept only nights ago. How had she overlooked it?

Beneath the metal sheet was a rough hole that opened out into darkness. Coldhand unclipped a flashlight from his belt, switched it on and shined it down into the ground. The entrance was braced with the same stone and metal that made up the rest of the black cathedral.

It was a sheer drop, but not a long one. Coldhand motioned toward the hole with his Talon-9. Maeve nodded and held her wings tight against her as she dropped down into the tunnel. She came down on dirt flattened by the weight of uncounted Nihilist feet.

Then Maeve stepped back and gestured for Coldhand. He jumped in after her and landed softly in a crouch, shining his light down the passage.

They stood at the top of a sloping ramp of packed dirt and sand. Maeve and Coldhand followed the incline down, where it opened out into a broad tunnel. The passage was surprisingly large, twice as tall as a human and just as wide. The walls were lined with uncut rust-red stone, rocks that had probably been dug up in the process of excavating the tunnels.

The only illumination down here was the narrow beam of Coldhand's flashlight and the air was stale. There was a faint stench like rot and Maeve shuddered.

"Let's go," Coldhand whispered.

Maeve nodded and crept along the tunnel, the bounty hunter close behind her. She weighed his tone as she made her way down into the ground. It seemed impossible that the machine-hearted Coldhand might feel fear, but even his voice was tight around the edges. The Prians were almost as avian a race as the Arcadians. Their world was one of open skies and high mountains and Maeve doubted that Coldhand was any more comfortable underground than she was.

At the bottom of the ramp, the tunnel split, opening up into one side of the underground star. Coldhand led them down the tunnel on the left. He stalked beside Maeve, his hands full of weapons and light. The passage angled back toward the graveyard where Maeve and Elsa had buried a man only a day before. The floor was strewn with rocks, some fallen from the walls and ceiling, others simply never pulled up in the first place. Footing was difficult, and both Maeve and Coldhand moved slowly.

A sound wafted up from the depths under the graveyard. Music, hundreds of voices raised in song, discordant but eerily beautiful. Maeve stopped Coldhand with her uninjured wing.

"Do you hear that?" she whispered.

Coldhand listened, but then shook his head. The hunter's blond hair was dark with sweat and stuck to his skin.

Maeve strained to make out individual voices, but the tunnels distorted the sound, bouncing it back and forth from stone to stone. Coldhand had detected two hundred or more in the catacombs. How many of them were Emberguard?

"What are they singing?" Coldhand asked quietly.

Maeve listened again before answering. "I cannot hear the exact words. Only that they are singing in Arcadian."

"Why?"

"I have no idea," Maeve answered. "There are Arcadians among the Nihilists, but not that many."

They continued down into the darkness. The tunnel was dropping down again. They moved in silence, but the faint song grew louder as Maeve and Coldhand descended. The discordant melody made Maeve's ears buzz and there was a dull pain throbbing just behind her eyes. It was hard to concentrate.

"I hear it now, too," Coldhand said.

"Can you make out the words?" Maeve asked.

The Prian nodded and sounded out the syllables slowly. "Ish-ah shay vah-ree lay mar-na-veh. Ear-ah air-oo en-are-ee."

"Isha shae varii lae Marnavae. Eira eru enarri," Maeve repeated. *"In the darkness, the Nameless Lady waits. In the stones lie those she loves.* But... that song is profane! It is a prayer to the death goddess. Her worship has been forbidden since the days of Cavain."

"Just because it's illegal doesn't mean it doesn't happen," Coldhand said. "The Church of Nihil *is* a death cult, after all, and probably not the first one."

"We are not here to debate the rule of law," Maeve hissed. "We need to find Baliend!"

The look Coldhand shot back quite clearly accused Maeve of starting it, but he said nothing. Instead, he turned off his light and shoved Maeve against the suddenly unseen tunnel wall.

She began to protest, but the bounty hunter clapped his metal hand across her mouth. Since he was still holding his flashlight, Maeve mostly ended up with a mouthful of plastic. She could have switched it on with her tongue.

Silently, Coldhand pointed down the burrow with his drawn Talon-9. Maeve realized that she could see the gesture and followed it with her eyes. Ruddy flickering light glowed around a corner far ahead and grew steadily brighter. Maeve had been too busy arguing with Coldhand to notice, but the bounty hunter was not so easily distracted. She nodded her understanding and Coldhand released her.

A human man rounded the bend in the tunnel, struggling with a dented lighter. The inconstant flame illuminated a deeply seamed face, worn black robes and a large rifle slung over his back. A flashlight had been taped to the top and shined up at the tunnel ceiling. The Nihilist was trying to light a bent cigarette held clenched in his teeth. Finally, it caught and the man slipped the lighter into his pocket. He took a long pull and exhaled a cloud of smoke.

"God love ya, Lord Gavriel," he rasped hoarsely. "God love ya."

The man continued down the passage toward them. Coldhand raised his laser, but Maeve put her hand lightly on top of his and shook her head. Since he had never disabled the sound generator, the Talon would be loud. Coldhand cast a significant glance at the princess' spear and she nodded. It would be quick and silent, giving the Nihilist no chance to raise an alarm.

Maeve bounded through the shadows and leapt on the unprepared human. Too late, he reached for his rifle, but Maeve brought her spear around in a glittering slash. Gurgling and clutching his slit throat, the Nihilist sank to the ground. Blood sprayed from between his fingers for a moment as he thrashed, then went still.

Maeve and Coldhand continued down the tunnel. The singing grew louder as they made their way toward the heart of the Nihilist catacombs.

Kessa was still in the medical bay with Vyron, watching helplessly over her mate. Up in the Blue Phoenix's cockpit, Xia and Gripper crowded in close together to look over Tiberius' shoulder. Duaal slumped down in the copilot's chair, looking pale, frightened and very young.

Tiberius leaned over the communications console, trying to stare down a human man of middle years on the screen. The old Prian banged his fist on the panel, making Xia jump. His stubbled face had gone purple with rage and the Ixthian doctor worried that his blood pressure would split the hasty stitches in his stomach.

"Look, I'm sorry, Captain Myles. But we just can't do anything until CWAAF mobilizes a team," the other man said. He adjusted the collar of his sand-colored uniform. "If these Nihilists are as dangerous as you say, then they're more than the Gharib police department can handle alone. We need military backup."

"Listen here, boy," Tiberius snarled. "Those bastards kidnapped a baby less than a week old! My first mate is trying to get him back – with a bounty hunter on her tail! If you don't help her, she's going to die and that baby will be under the care of the Nihilists! Do you have any idea what they'll do to him?"

"Captain, please try to understand," the police officer said. He sat back from his screen and spread his hands, fingers splayed. "Our budget has been cut again and we've got less than a hundred officers to cover this entire city. There's nothing we can do. But CWAAF can have four squads here from Jharna in two hours. We'll move then, but not before."

"You gutless coward! Didn't you hear me?" Tiberius shouted. Gripper gave an audible squeak of fear. "Maeve is out there right now! In two hours, she'll be dead. On Prianus, we had one cop for every three thousand citizens, but we never – *never!* – backed down from a fight when civilian lives were at stake!"

The Gharib police officer finally looked annoyed. "In case you hadn't noticed, Captain Myles, this isn't Prianus. This is Stray. We've got our own problems, what with all the rubbish floating our way. Including self-righteous old Prian cops. This isn't your backwater little hellworld and I'm not about to send my people out to answer for your primitive sense of honor!"

The other man leaned in so close to the screen that Xia could count the veins throbbing in his neck. Tiberius jumped to his feet and would have overturned the pilot's chair if it weren't bolted to the deck. He hauled back his fist in preparation to punch the console, but Duaal grabbed his arm. Tiberius grunted and lowered himself slowly into his seat again, holding his stomach and grimacing in pain. The police officer on the other end of the video link seemed to realize he had gone a little too far and spread his hands in a pacifying gesture.

"Captain Myles, I can't do anything to speed up the Alliance army. But if it would make you feel any better, in light of your... admirable... work for the Prian police, I could let you go in with our men once CWAAF arrives. I know you want to help keep your crewmate safe."

"Please listen to him," Duaal begged in a small voice. "You said yourself that we need to slow down and do this rationally."

"We know what those Nihilists are like," Tiberius objected. "We can't just leave Maeve to die!"

Duaal hesitated. For an uncharitable moment, Xia wondered if that wasn't exactly what the young mage wanted. But Duaal stared up at Tiberius with nothing but raw fear in his wide green eyes.

"No, Gavriel's there!" Duaal said. "I don't want to lose you!"

Tiberius was silent, hard-faced and resolved. At last, Duaal sat down once more and the old Prian turned back to the officer on his display.

"Come as soon as you can," Tiberius said. "You've got the coordinates of the cathedral. I'm going to get Baliend and Maeve."

"Godspeed. You'll need all the help He can give you," the other cop said and then the screen went dark.

"Get to your posts," Tiberius told his crew. "We need to get this bird in the air. That means you, too, Duaal. Light up your controls."

The bleach-blond Hyzaari hesitated. His hands shook and Xia could see his pulse racing at his throat.

"Duaal, now! Not when I'm burning on a pyre! Now!" Tiberius barked.

"Yes, sir!"

Duaal spun in the copilot's chair and turned on his instruments. Gripper hurried down the corridor toward the engine room and Xia followed him as far as the medical bay. Kessa jumped as the Ixthian stepped inside.

"Gharib police aren't helping," Xia told her. "They're waiting for CWAAF backup, but Maeve and Baliend might not be able to wait that long. We're moving now."

Kessa's black eyes went wide, but she nodded. "What do you need me to do?"

"Secure Vyron."

The Dailon began untangling the straps affixed to the side of the examination table, pulling them tightly across Vyron's chest and legs. Xia prepared her surgical equipment, laying implements out on one of the magnetic trays. She doubted that her work was done for the night.

— • • • —

"The time is near," Xartasia hummed in Gavriel's ear. "My debt to you is about to be paid."

They stood together in the center of a huge underground chamber with crumbling walls that threatened to tumble down on their heads at any moment and stank of carrion. Pale shapes dotted the uneven cavern ceiling where diggers had scraped away the dirt too close to the graves above, revealing flaking dead skin and bloated, rotting limbs that dangled into the cavern like ghastly, overripe fruit. The air was thick and hot with the heat of so many Nihilists crowded inside. And the whole chamber vibrated with the sound of their voices.

Xartasia stood just behind Gavriel on a raised mound of dirt, the fairy robed and hooded in fine ivory silk, stitched in silver. Her white wings were spread, arcing over her head in taut anticipation. All around them, the Nihilists sang the words she had taught them, a song of power from the ancient days of Arcadia.

In front of Gavriel stood a huge, waist-high block of black stone carved on each flat side with an eight-pointed star, chiseled deeply into the dark basalt. It had taken fifteen sweating, grunting Nihilists to carry the altar from Xartasia's ship and one had crushed his leg under the great weight of the stone before finally delivering it to the catacombs.

"Carried she within her a new life," Xartasia sang into Gavriel's ear. "To the halls of the All-Singer with a plea…"

He knew the words of her song well. They were newer than the praise to the Nameless being chanted by his congregation, but still far older than any prayer of the core races. This song was no spell, yet held great power – a refrain that told its singer how to make a request of Arcadian royalty.

> "Two hundred eighty-eight days of light
> Will be desired by a Night
> If you would dare lay claim to the right
> To ask a gift of the White.

"You paid your respects for an Arcadian year, in accordance with the Lay of Cavain," Xartasia said, running her porcelain fingers down Gavriel's sunken cheek. "For two hundred eighty-eight days, you gave me songs and gifts."

"Yes," he said, his back straight and chin held high. "But I never begged."

"You never begged," the twilight-eyed fairy agreed. "And when your year was done, you made your request, as was your right. You wanted power, and I taught you the secrets of our magic."

"But I was too old, a grown man who had learned to think for myself," Gavriel said. "I could repeat all of the songs, but nothing happened when I sang them."

"You needed a malleable mind as a conduit, one that could be raised to think like an Arcadian spell-singer," Xartasia agreed.

Gavriel grabbed the fairy's hand and pulled it from his face.

"Duaal," he said. "It took us years to find him, to mold him into a proper tool for my will. And then he ran away. He shouldn't have had enough of his own will for that!"

Xartasia nodded. "We shall not make such a mistake again, old friend. This time will be different. We will take the power from this child and give it entirely to you. You can never lose it again."

"Yes," Gavriel said.

He gestured toward Elsa. The tall Mirran knelt on the other side of the dark stone altar and cradled a squalling, squirming bundle against her chest. The infant's blue mouth was open in a scream, but the Nihilists' song drowned his cry. Elsa held out the baby and an Emberguard in red took him from her arms, then handed the child to Gavriel.

A smaller Arcadian woman with a disheveled yellow braid was trying to push forward, as well, but two more Emberguard shoved her back toward the other Nihilists.

"Lord Gavriel!" she shouted. "I carry news from Seon..."

"Be silent, *anai'i*," Xartasia commanded, pointing a perfect white finger at the other fairy. "Greater words than yours will be spoken tonight. Your news can wait."

The blonde Arcadian fell immediately quiet, bowing her head and melting once more into the crowd of other black-clad figures.

The Emberguard took Elsa by the shoulders and led her away, too. She glanced back at Gavriel.

"You won't hurt the baby, will you?" Elsa asked.

"I will deliver this child into the same blessed fate I wish upon the rest of creation," Gavriel told her truthfully.

Elsa smiled trustingly at her master and let herself be escorted back to the other Nihilists. Gavriel laid the crying baby on the black stone altar and Xartasia sang instructions into his ear.

[29]

RUNE AND RUIN

"Love is the name we give to the exquisitely nameless."

- ALANDER LISALLE, KAHLI ARTIST (165 PA)

The tunnel widened again as Maeve and Coldhand turned down one passage and then another. Only the hunter had seen the layout of the catacombs on his instruments. He wordlessly pointed left, right, and left once more.

Without Coldhand, Maeve would have been lost. But for the last year, she had been the one playing games with him, taunting him and luring him to her own ends. That he had only realized it tonight almost irritated Coldhand.

Almost.

He should have seen it before. How had he missed it? Because Maeve played on his emotions, insulting him and trying to make him angry enough to act rashly. Not that those kinds of tactics ever worked against him... Which was exactly why he had missed them.

It was never difficult to ignore the taunts, to pass them off as a mark's final act of bravado. The criminals that Coldhand hunted down often begged for their lives, insulted him, cried or screamed.

And the marks he would take after the Arcadian princess would do the same. Coldhand expected it from those he hunted, and it was easy to overlook Maeve's passionate ploy. So why did he see it now?

Coldhand's flashlight was switched off now and clipped to his belt again. Another light source illuminated the tunnel, probably reflected out from the same place as the strange, broken Arcadian song. The chanting had risen to a roar. Whether because they were approaching the singers or because they were singing louder, Coldhand didn't know.

Though there was plenty of room, Maeve walked so close next to Coldhand that her wing brushed his shoulder. He could feel it trembling and the skin of her arms was prickled with goosebumps despite the growing heat.

The tunnel ahead suddenly opened up into a massive central chamber – the heart of the huge star. Maeve and Coldhand pressed themselves back against the wall, behind a pile of discarded tailings. They peered together over the jumble of dirt and rocks.

The cavern was smaller than the cathedral, but not by much, and it was filled with people of every species. Hundreds of them, all standing and swaying as they sang. A few recent converts were still dressed in more ordinary clothes, but most wore black Nihilist robes and almost half had white wings extending from slits through the rough, dark cloth.

No... there were a few not wearing the ubiquitous black Nihilist robes. Eight figures in red waited in a ring around a raised mound in the center of the room. Emberguard.

With an effort, Coldhand wrenched his gaze up the little underground hill. Two more Nihilists stood on the top, but he didn't recognize either of them. One was dressed in a flowing white gown and hooded cloak that didn't disguise her slight but distinctly feminine curves.

The other was a very old, very skinny human man of indeterminate lineage. Despite his fragile-looking body, he held himself with rigid poise and pride. That had to be Gavriel, founder and leader of the Church of Nihil. His long hair was a yellowed white, like old paper, and his skin was sallow. Unlike his fairy companion, Gavriel wore the same faded black robes as the rest of his followers. He raised one hand and the singing died away.

"We have gathered here in the sight of those already blessedly dead," Gavriel said in a surprisingly resonate voice. "We are here to make another sacrifice, to take the next step toward ultimate peace for the galaxy."

"An end to all suffering," the crowd murmured.

Gavriel pointed up to the cavern ceiling. "Out there, the rich and privileged of the Alliance live in decadence that they do not deserve, while the poor and unlucky live in pain that *they* do not deserve!"

"Deliver us!" a Nihilist shouted.

"Deliver them!" cried another, raising hands that were covered in scars.

"I am only one man," Gavriel said. "An old man bent by age and loss, with little to offer you. But tonight, that changes!"

The Nihilist gestured down to a smooth black stone and Coldhand felt Maeve tense beside him. A bundle of dark cloth squirmed on top of the altar and a tiny blue face peaked out between the fold. Baliend's cheeks were already purple from crying, but the infant Dailon drew another breath and wailed.

Maeve gathered her legs beneath her to leap over the heap of stones that concealed them, but Coldhand grabbed her wrist. She whirled on him with gray eyes blazing.

"Release me," she hissed. "I am going to get Baliend!"

"Everyone here is watching that baby, including the Emberguard. They won't let us get anywhere near him," Coldhand whispered. "We have to wait until we have a clean shot to grab the kid. Is this what Gavriel did to Duaal?"

"No, this appears to be different," Maeve admitted. "But what does it matter? We must stop this from happening."

Coldhand was saved from having to answer that by Gavriel's booming voice.

"Behold! Behold the instrument of our destiny," the old man said. "Before I came here to Stray, I was a mage of great power. The first human ever to master rim-world magic! But that power relied upon a tool, a tool which I lost."

Coldhand didn't know where Gavriel was going with all this. Was this just some kind of speech or rally, some way to pump up the troops? When he was finished, they could recapture Baliend. But Gavriel was still surrounded by his Emberguard... Sweat ran down the back of Coldhand's neck.

"Is this it?" Tiberius asked.

The Blue Phoenix was hovering over the Church of Nihil, a brilliant spotlight illuminating the frayed cathedral. Duaal checked his displays.

"According to Gripper and Xia, yeah," he said. His voice cracked. "This... this is it."

"Where is she? Where the hells is Coldhand? Where are those be-damned Nihilists?" Tiberius shouted. He banged his fist on the console. "Find Maeve!"

"Xartasia has come back to repay her debt," Gavriel said, sweeping his hand toward the woman in white. Behind Gavriel, the angelic Xartasia bowed her hooded head. "To return the power that I lost and more."

There were a handful of angry cries from the gathered Nihilists, but the roar of approval drowned them out.

Maeve spat onto the dusty ground. "Xartasia!"

"What?" Coldhand asked. "Do you know her?"

"No, but *Xartasia* is not a name. It is an oath, and a terrible one. *The Dream of Death*."

That sounded fitting, given the company that the fairy in white kept. Coldhand watched, but Gavriel showed no signs of being finished or even slowing down. In fact, the Nihilist seemed to be building up momentum.

"This child will never know the pain of life," Gavriel said over Baliend's ragged infant cries. "But with the gift of his blood and his unformed mind, my power shall be restored!"

"No!" Maeve whispered.

Xartasia pressed a slender glass knife into Gavriel's outstretched hand. They had run out of time. There was no chance of catching Gavriel alone, away from his guards and followers. Maeve yanked her wrist from Coldhand's grasp and sprinted for the mouth of the tunnel.

"Cavainna, no!" Coldhand snarled. "Stop!"

There were too many Nihilists and far too many Emberguard. Maeve was going to get herself killed. But the fairy didn't look back. She spread her long, feathered wings and leapt into the hot air, soaring out over the crowd. Cultists turned and looked up, gasping as Maeve flew over them. Her feathers almost brushed the crumbling, decaying roof of the graveyard chamber.

"Gavriel!" Maeve cried. "Give me the baby!"

The leader of the Nihilists and his own fairy companion spun and stared. Maeve folded her wings and dove at the central mound.

But all around the cavern, Emberguard were moving. A huge Hadrian man flung himself between the descending fairy and his master, drawing a nanosword from his belt. Another Nihilist in red – a Dailon with a ragged pit where her right eye had once been –

placed herself between Maeve and Xartasia. The rest formed up on the small hill, braced for battle.

The Emberguard weren't the only ones armed or who wanted to defend Gavriel. Most of the Nihilists were holding lights or a few torches aloft to illuminate the proceedings, but several were freeing weapons from their robes. Knives flashed – both ordinary steel and the oily gleam of nanoblades – and all manner of guns rose up to take aim.

Maeve wasn't going to reach Baliend if a cultist shot her out of the air first. She had moved in too soon. Coldhand yanked his Talon from its holster and fired – not at one of the gun-wielding Nihilists, but at a gaunt woman holding her torch high and shrieking obscenities at Maeve. His laser cut a charred black line into her skin and the woman dropped her torch, clutching her wounded arm and screaming a new batch of oaths. The torch tumbled to the dirt floor, but not before smearing flaming oil all down the back of the robed Nihilist beside her.

The fire caught quickly in the crowded room. Those who were not burning were shoved out of the way as their companions flung themselves to the ground, trying to smother the flames. Some of Gavriel's followers simply stood still, their eyes glazed even as they steamed in their sockets, and let the spreading flames consume them. The chamber was filled with screams, prayers and thick, acrid black smoke.

"I've got something on thermals," Duaal shouted, pointing at one of the displays. The image was hazy and distorted, but Tiberius could make out a red bloom of heat. He jabbed his own instrument panel.

"Behind the church," Tiberius said. "I don't see anything down there. What's that interference?"

"It's underground. That's why it's so indistinct," Duaal told him.

"There must be something pretty damned hot down there for us to be picking up anything at all."

"Underground?" Tiberius asked. "How do we get down there?"

"I have no idea."

Gavriel grabbed the glass dagger from Xartasia's hand and brandished it at Maeve.

"I don't know who you are, child, and I don't care," he said. "But you will meet the same fate as all life!"

Maeve was almost on top of the old Nihilist, but a Mirran Emberguard leapt at her with long, powerful legs and bowled the princess out of the air. They tumbled together to the ground and Coldhand lost sight of them in the sea of Nihilists.

Gavriel's congregation hadn't overlooked the bounty hunter. A large group was splitting off from the crowd and closing in on Coldhand. At least seven held knives and swords, half again that number leveling laser weapons and NI guns at him. Coldhand ducked a few badly aimed shots, returned a few of his own that dropped three of the death-worshipers, and fell back behind the pile of rubble that had been his hiding spot.

Coldhand waited until the first few Nihilists were running up the sloped side and then kicked a pair of large rocks off the mound. The stones rolled down the heap, smashing into legs and sending Coldhand's pursuers sprawling in the dust. The bounty hunter put a single red blast of laserfire through each of the prone targets, then pressed his back against the wall as return fire filled the tunnel mouth with flying laser bolts and bullets.

All around the chamber, the Nihilists were in chaos. Many were screaming in terror, fleeing the still-burning fire and unknown assailants, bolting down tunnels that spoked out from the central cavern. But a dangerously high number of them surged forward to protect Gavriel. Several of the Emberguard were fighting back the overzealous throng, spilling at least as much blood as Maeve and Coldhand.

Xartasia slipped around the one-eyed Emberguard, as smoothly as flowing water. She snatched Baliend off the altar and wrapped the baby in her white robes. There was a burst of feathers from the edge of the crowd, and Maeve shot out of the sea of red and black robes. She landed in a splay-winged crouch on top of the dark stone block, bloody spear in hand and her lips skinned back from small white teeth in a furious snarl. The Mirran who had brought her down was chasing her through the congregation, but the Nihilists were packed together into a wall of flesh. Blood glinted dully as the Emberguard cut his way through fellow cultists.

"Give me the baby, *vaeli'i la!*" Maeve cried.

"You will have death! Which is more than you deserve," Gavriel thundered. He pointed to her with a long, bony finger. "Kill her!"

The massively muscular Hadrian and smaller Dailon Emberguards advanced on Maeve. In the tunnel, Coldhand almost swore. It had taken the entire crew of the Blue Phoenix and the hunter to kill just one of the Emberguard. Now Maeve faced two – with a third tearing its way toward her through the crowd.

Coldhand raked the toe of his boot across the tunnel floor and kicked loose red sand up into the faces of three Nihilists charging at him. A shot from his Talon through the chest of each one as they recoiled and pawed at their eyes ensured that they would not rise again. Coldhand snatched up a fallen torch before the churned dust could snuff the fire out. Burning oil seeped down onto his cybernetic hand.

The bounty hunter charged into the ranks of shouting Nihilists, swinging the torch like a club and catching one across the temple. An Ixthian woman with silvery skin darkened by disease fell to the ground with blank eyes. Her white hair sizzled and smoldered in the dirt.

Coldhand swung again as a pair of Lyrans grabbed for his arms. One fell away, howling as his fur caught fire, but the torch tangled in his robes and jerked out of the hunter's hand. Coldhand seized the other Lyran by the front of his robes. Another knot of Nihilists was screaming for blood, pointing at Coldhand.

"Catch the life-clinger! Kill him! For Lord Gavriel!"

Coldhand shattered the Lyran's shoulder with a single hard blow of his cybernetic fist. He kicked the crippled man aside, but more Nihilists trampled him as they closed on Coldhand. Blood turned the dirt floor to dark, sticky mud.

Up on the central mound, Maeve was faring badly. The Dailon Emberguard held her off the ground, blue arms wrapped around the fairy's tiny waist. The Hadrian swung his nanosword and red shone on the mottled edge. Maeve was fending them off with her wings and spear, but barely. Her feathers were flecked with blood and every time the sword rang off her glass spear, the princess raised it a little slower to fend off the next blow.

Coldhand brought up his Talon, aiming just above the Dailon Emberguard's aural hole, where the ear would have been on another species. Icy sweat dripped from his damp blond hair, stinging in his eyes. The Nihilists were a breath away from closing in around him again. Coldhand pulled the trigger. The laser whined and a bolt of red light burned through the underground chamber. The Emberguard dropped to the ground like an empty sack.

Maeve staggered back away from the dead woman, shaking her bleached hair out of her eyes, but didn't have long to recover. The Hadrian stepped over the other Emberguard's body without even sparing a glance for his fallen comrade, and thrust his nanosword at Maeve's exposed belly. She leapt over the carved altar, narrowly avoiding the molecule-fine point.

But Maeve was tired and injured. Her heel caught on the corner of the stone and she fell, sprawling on the sandy ground at Gavriel's feet. He brandished his wicked glass dagger and smiled grimly at the princess as she struggled to rise. Maeve tried to kick the glittering knife from his hand, but the Mirran Emberguard had finally cut his way through the other Nihilists and pounced on her. He held Maeve as Gavriel brought the dagger down, burying it to the hilt between the fairy's ribs. He twisted the blade in Maeve's chest and she screamed.

[30]
SHARED BLOOD

"In honor of Cavain's divine call
    Of Aes the cloud-veiled Sky-Dancer
    White Kingdom was named the new land
    To Cavain was given lordship over all."

- THE LAY OF CAVAIN (9,333 MA)

"No!"

The cry rang across the high-ceilinged chamber, freezing everyone in place. Coldhand thought for a moment that it was him who had shouted, but the voice was high, clear and feminine. Xartasia took Gavriel by the shoulder. He shoved her hand away, but the fairy in white would not be so easily dismissed. She held Gavriel's arm and fixed him with her violet eyes.

"No," she said. "Please."

Every eye in the chamber was riveted on the hill. Slowly, Gavriel stepped back, but he didn't remove the knife. It jutted from Maeve's pale skin like a slender glass tombstone. Blood welled up around the blade and ran down her ribs.

"Maeve?" Xartasia asked.

Her soft, musical voice carried through the hushed room. Even the baby in her arms was no longer crying. Baliend stared down at Maeve with wide black eyes.

"By all the gods, Maeve... is that you?" Xartasia asked. "What have you done to your hair?"

Maeve coughed and blood ran from the corner of her mouth. "Give... give me the child. Give me Baliend."

Xartasia held Baliend in one arm and pushed back her white hood, freeing long black braids of hair. Her eyes were a shockingly vivid violet and wide with shock.

Coldhand blinked. It was like seeing Maeve in front of a mirror. The two Arcadians had the same cheekbones, the same sharp chin and full lips. Maeve and Xartasia could have been sisters... Or maybe mother and daughter. There wasn't a single wrinkle on her face or strand of gray in her hair, but Xartasia appeared somehow older, her features more refined.

"Titania?" Maeve gasped. "Cousin... you live? But the Devourers killed the entire royal family when the White Kingdom fell! All of them except... except me..."

"Not *all*, blood of my blood."

Xartasia stood over the fallen princess, regal and poised in a way that Maeve had never been, not in the year that Coldhand had known her.

"While you flew to Orindell, the House of Cavain fought to protect our people as they retreated into the core," said Xartasia.

"I know," Maeve wheezed. "Your father... the king... charged our family to fight for Arcadia."

"And so I do. I followed our people through the Waygates and to the worlds of the core," Xartasia said in a gentle voice. "Someone must protect them."

"Protect them?" Maeve asked. "This does not protect anyone..."

"How did you survive, cousin? You, too, were ordered to fight for the White Kingdom. To the last."

Maeve's skin was chalky white, her lips pale and bloodless as she spoke. "I flew to the Tamlin Waygate. Orthain died holding the Devourers at bay as I closed the gate that had summoned them."

"You... banished them back to whatever dark place they came from," Xartasia said. "But you were a knight, cousin. How did you know the songs to close the Waygate?"

"Because I... I am the one who opened it," Maeve answered in a voice thick with tears and blood. "Titania, it was me. My brother and I were bound for Tamlin, where I would stand guard while he sang open the Waygate there. As we had so many times. But Caith begged to see his lover. And I... let him go. I went to the gate and sang the spells, but I did not know what I was doing."

Xartasia nodded slowly. "That was the spell. The twisted spell that summoned the Devourers."

"I did it," Maeve whispered. "It was all my fault. I brought them into our world, Titania. I destroyed Arcadia."

Genocide. Coldhand understood the final charge listed on her bounty posting. The dryads and nyads were all gone, two entire species of fairies dead in the rubble of the White Kingdom. Nine out of ten Arcadians dead in the battle with the Devourers, thirty million deaths... and Maeve claimed guilt for it all.

A strange sound filled the underground chamber, rising in pitch and volume until the rotting ceiling seemed to shake with it.

Xartasia was laughing.

"You? You destroyed the kingdom of my father? One knight with one song?" the princess sang in her sweet voice. "You are arrogant, cousin. The Devourers killed our people! Those monsters destroyed our home and when we ran, the Alliance turned us away. They cast us into their gutters to suffer and die all over again!"

"You cannot think to forgive my sins," Maeve said. Blood pooled beneath her in the dirt. "I am... I have..."

She drew a shuddering breath and Xartasia smiled beautifully, holding her hand out to Maeve.

"I can absolve your guilt," she said. "I can end this pain."

"Titania... Xartasia," Maeve whispered. She plucked weakly at the glass knife buried in her chest. "Why do you call yourself by that cursed name? Why do you hide here under the graves of the dead and serve the Church of Nihil?"

"We can yet repair what has been broken, cousin," Xartasia said. "Join me, Maeve. Join Gavriel as he brings death to the worlds that turned their backs on us. I did not think I had any family left, but you are here. Help me return beauty to the universe. There is so much to do."

Maeve stared up at her, a feverish light in her eyes. She let go of the knife and held out her trembling hand to Xartasia. In the older princess' arms, Baliend squealed and reached toward Maeve.

"Just let me take the baby back to his parents," Maeve said. "And then I will do whatever you ask, Titania."

Xartasia glanced at the infant Dailon and shrugged her slender shoulders. "Very well, cousin. It does not matter, we shall find another baby."

Maeve blinked slowly and her hand lowered to the knife again. "What? Titania, no! Whatever it is you are doing, it cannot be worth killing an innocent child!"

"How little you understand," Xartasia said. "Maeve, do not stand against me. Do not stand against the Church of Nihil."

"Titania, there must be another way!" Maeve cried.

"My name is Xartasia! I am your queen, cousin, and I command your obedience!"

Screaming in pain, Maeve wrenched the knife from her ribs and lurched to her feet. She pressed the bloody point against Xartasia's white gown, leaving a smear of shockingly bright red against the pristine cloth. Xartasia gasped as Maeve dropped the dagger and snatched Baliend from her arms.

"This is wrong," Maeve said. "I am taking Baliend home to his family."

She staggered a step and grabbed her spear from where it had fallen on the mound. Maeve leaned on the weapon like a cane as she struggled to remain upright.

"You have betrayed your people yet again," Xartasia told Maeve. She turned away to face Gavriel. "Kill her and then we may finish this."

"Your debt to me will deepen for this," Gavriel said.

Xartasia nodded and Gavriel's Emberguard advanced on Maeve again. She clutched Baliend against her and angled the point of her spear out at the Nihilists, but she couldn't lift the weapon. There was more of her blood on the ground than in her body. Maeve was dying, and quickly.

Coldhand raised his Talon up over his head. "Maeve!"

He couldn't just call her *Cavainna* anymore, not with two of the Arcadian princesses.

Maeve spun toward the cry and launched herself up into the air. She flew crookedly and low over the Nihilists as they shouted and tried to shoot her down. Maeve banked and landed in front of Coldhand so hard that the impact snapped the haft of her spear like a twig and the broken pieces fell into the dirt.

Coldhand put his cybernetic arm around Maeve to support her and she leaned heavily against him. Her blood ran hot and wet over his hand. Baliend gurgled as Maeve held him close.

"You will *live* for this!" Gavriel shouted. "Take them both!"

Emberguard and black-robed Nihilists alike charged at Coldhand. The bounty hunter kept his Talon-9 pointed at the chamber's rotten ceiling, pulled the trigger and held it down. The laser sliced into the crumbling sand and rotting bodies. A few rocks fell, but not enough. Coldhand raked the red beam across the roof and the whole huge room shuddered with a low, grumbling groan. Stone grated on stone, screaming as dirt gave way and decaying flesh tore apart.

"Move!" Coldhand shouted.

He heaved Maeve upright and hauled her toward the closest tunnel. She staggered and Coldhand had to hold her up. The river of red pouring down her side was growing weaker by the second. They were running out of time. Maeve stumbled along beside Coldhand as fast as she could. She tripped with every other step, but her grip on Baliend was sure and she ran.

The chamber lurched and grated with another deafening roar. Sand and stone and decaying corpses collapsed onto the Nihilists, pouring down from the ceiling. Huge rocks boomed as they fell, crushing bodies beneath them and throwing up great clouds of choking dust. Nihilists wailed in a chorus of rage and fear as they flooded out into the star of tunnels, fleeing the destruction. Gavriel and Xartasia stood in the center of it all, and then vanished under sand and stone.

The catacombs were coming down, burying the Nihilists alive, but not as quickly as Coldhand had hoped. All too many of them ran down the tunnels behind him. Most of them only wanted to escape, but plenty more were still trying to carry out Gavriel's last order to catch Maeve and Baliend.

The tunnels were plunged into darkness and the Nihilists were running too hard to make effective use of their guns. They fired off a few shots, but most just burned or buried themselves in the sides of the sand. Coldhand ducked them easily and Maeve came away with only a few singed feathers, but the cultists were closing in fast on the hunter and his swiftly fading mark.

"If you don't run faster, Maeve, you won't have to try to trick me into killing you," Coldhand grunted, pulling the fairy along with him. "They'll do it for me."

A faint, furious blaze kindled in Maeve's eyes, but faded quickly. She hugged Baliend to her chest and nodded mutely.

They ran together through the tunnels, the crowd of Nihilists close on their heels. A hurled stone whistled toward Maeve's head.

Coldhand swiped the rock from the air. It shattered against the illonium and fell to the ground in pieces.

There! The tunnel bent around one of the angles of the star and angled slightly up toward the surface.

"Faster, Maeve!" Coldhand told her. "We're nearly out!"

But Maeve's eyes were falling closed and the blood from her wound had slowed to a trickle. There wasn't enough left to keep up the pressure. Her heart would begin skipping soon, its last spasms before death. Coldhand remembered the feeling all too well.

He rounded the sharp bend in the passage, supporting Maeve's negligible weight with his left arm. There was the dusty ramp that led back into the cathedral. Light flooded through the hole above, but how? Up on the surface, his Raptor was powered down.

Coldhand nearly missed the three shadows that reared up like ghosts behind him. He had to drop Maeve to get his metal arm up in time and turn the Nihilist's nanosword aside. It flung sparks into the darkness and across Maeve on the ground, wings and body curled protectively around Baliend.

"Titania..." she whimpered. "Stop..."

A pair of humans and an Ixthian surrounded Maeve and Coldhand. The shadows had hidden them and their black robes until almost too late. Coldhand stood over Maeve, firing off rapid laser shots, but the power warning was flashing on the side of his Talon. The weapon wasn't meant for the kind of sustained fire he had used to collapse the main chamber and with a quiet whine, the gun went dark in his hand.

The Nihilists lost no time leaping on their prey. Hissing and spitting in fury, the Ixthian pounced on Maeve. The fairy opened her dim eyes and raised her wings to ward off the heavy club in the cultist's hand. The cudgel cracked hard and feathers flew into the air. Maeve groaned weakly. She was managing to defend herself and the baby, but she wouldn't be able to keep it up for more than a few seconds.

The two human Nihilists circled Coldhand and he shoved the Talon away into its holster. The gun would do him no good now – all of his spare battery packs were still on the Raptor. One of the Nihilists swung his nanosword at Coldhand. He jumped aside and smashed his cybernetic forearm down across the blade. The blow sent the sword skidding back down the tunnel and the man staggered away, holding his hand against his chest.

The other Nihilist leapt at Coldhand with a chunk of stone held high. He grabbed and twisted her arm until the woman screeched, then pitched her at the first cultist, who was scrambling to retrieve his sword. They sprawled together into the dirt, but more Nihilists streamed up the tunnel toward them. There were too many, and Maeve could barely move. All Coldhand could do was run.

He jumped up over Maeve, lashing out with his legs. His boot smashed the Ixthian in the shoulder, not really hurting her, but Coldhand succeeded in shoving her away from Maeve. He rolled to his feet, scooped up the Arcadian and held her tight against his chest. Baliend lay still in her arms, his black eyes huge and trusting. He giggled as one of Maeve's feathers drifted down to land on his tiny blue face.

Coldhand ran toward the light.

"I'm detecting a tunnel that leads to the surface, but it's full of people," Duaal said, frowning at his readouts. The Blue Phoenix's spotlight turned the Church of Nihil into a slab of blinding yellow radiance.

"Is one of them Maeve?" Tiberius asked.

"I don't know. There are a few Arcadians down there, but I have no idea if any of them is Maeve. Our sensors aren't that accurate." Duaal pointed out at the Raptor, grounded not far from where the Phoenix hovered. "At least we know Logan's here."

"Who?"

"Coldhand."

"I hope they kill that honorless son of a… cat!" Tiberius ranted. "I swear, if I ever see Coldhand again, I'll…"

Tiberius wasn't quite sure what he would do, but Duaal stood suddenly, pointing through the ports at the ground below. A man was bolting out from the cathedral. He held something cradled against his chest, something with long, drooping white wings.

"There he is!" Duaal shouted. "That's Logan!"

"He's got Maeve!" Tiberius snarled.

Nihilists poured out behind the hunter, most robed in black, but Tiberius saw at least one spot of blood red.

"We don't have the time to land," Duaal said. "They'll be all over him in a second!"

Tiberius searched wildly for something, anything they could do to help Maeve. If only he had put some kind of weapons on the Blue Phoenix… That Nihilist church looked about ready to fall in on itself at the slightest nudge. Tiberius stared at the control yolk in his hand, then turned on the ship-wide intercom.

"Everyone get strapped in," he said. "We're making an unscheduled landing and it's going to be a rough one!"

"Why? Is Shimmer flying?" Gripper asked, his voice sounding very small and scared from the speakers.

"No. If something's going to happen to my bird, I want to be the one flying her," Tiberius said.

"What's going to–?" Gripper began, but the captain turned off the sound.

"What are you doing? We don't have any weapons!" Duaal cried.

Tiberius reached up and flipped the ignition switches. "I told everyone to get strapped in and that includes you, Duaal. I'm taking the old lady down and that church is coming with us!"

He pushed the ship's nose down, hit the throttle and gunned the engines. Duaal shouted as the cathedral rushed up at them and scrambled for his safety harness, snapping the buckles in place just as the black stone eclipsed the ports and filled the world with stone and thunder.

The Blue Phoenix smashed into the base of one of the steeples with a deafening noise. The nose crumpled with a shriek of metal, but wreaked equal destruction on the cathedral. Stone and fiber-steel crumbled, falling over the ship and through the ceiling of the church. All across the Blue Phoenix, lights blinked, warnings flaring in bright reds and oranges.

Tiberius' head cracked against one of the panels and blood ran down his face. He fumbled blindly until he felt the ignition switch under his fingers again. Tiberius cut the engines and the Phoenix creaked, and then the scream of tearing metal reverberated through the ship as it fell. Suddenly unsupported by the engines, the cargo ship's aft end crashed through the ceiling of the Nihilist church, sending tons of rock and steel tumbling down to the ground.

Finally, the whole world stopped falling. Tiberius grunted and unbuckled his harness, then grabbed Duaal's shoulder.

"Duaal!" he shouted.

The boy groaned and opened his eyes. "That... was awful."

Duaal stood up, a little shaky but unhurt. Tiberius switched on the intercom again.

"Everyone who can still fight, get down into the hold," he said. "We need to get Maeve back on this bird and she'll probably be bringing uninvited guests."

Tiberius made sure his NI pistol was still in its rig and turned to leave the cockpit, but Duaal moved to follow him. Tiberius stopped, scowling.

"Where do you think you're going?" he asked.

"To fight. You told everyone...!" Duaal protested.

"Not you."

"What? That's not what you said when you were busy crashing our ship into a church!" Duaal shouted.

"Forget what I said and listen to what I'm saying," Tiberius told him. "I need you to make sure those engines still work. As soon as we get Maeve back on board, we have to be ready to fly the hells out of here!"

"Check the engines?" Duaal asked. "That's Gripper's job! Let me help you!"

"No," Tiberius said. "You stay here and that's an order!"

Duaal's eyes filled up with tears and he choked on his answer, slumping into the copilot's chair as Tiberius left the cockpit.

[31]

INTEGRITY

"Death is the end to all roads."

- CORRIEN MARKAV, PROFESSOR OF DAILON STUDIES, AUM

(212 PA)

Tiberius rushed down the stairs and down into the cargo hold. Xia was already there, retrieving her laser from where it had hung since Coldhand delivered Vyron. Had that only been a few hours ago? It seemed like days. Grimly, the doctor belted her gun back into place.

Kessa stood up on the catwalk, gripping the railing tightly and favoring one of her legs, probably banged in the crash. To Tiberius' amazement, Gripper wasn't back with Kessa, but waiting, trembling next to the airlock. He had a welder clutched in his shaking claws. It wasn't much of a weapon, but it was all he had.

"So, are... are we going to save Smoke or what?" Gripper asked with an almost impressive display of quavering bravado. "I checked the airlock and it's mostly working so let's go do... whatever it is we're going to do!"

Xia stood beside the Arboran. "What's out there? I'm assuming there was a good reason for ramming the ship into a building."

"Nihilists," Tiberius answered, nodding. "I'd guess there's about twenty of them left outside. The rest are trapped inside the cathedral or tunnels we collapsed on them. Coldhand's out there and he's got Maeve... She wasn't walking on her own. Let's get her out of his hands and onto the bird. The Gharib police and CWAAF can mop up later. We're just here for Maeve."

"Got it," Gripper squeaked.

Xia nodded. Tiberius punched the release on the airlock. The inner door hissed open, but the outer one creaked and grated for a moment, straining against fallen rocks and metal. Finally, it slid out of the way too. The three made their way out of the Blue Phoenix, weapons held at the ready.

The world outside was all tumbled, broken black masonry. The spotlight mounted onto the underside of the Blue Phoenix was smashed and dark. Only the gray moon and a sprinkling of stars lit the ruined church. It looked like an overturned cemetery. Shattered slabs of stone lay everywhere and two of the walls had fallen outward in the collision, leaving just one corner of the cathedral still standing. It towered over the wasted scene like a cruel alien god. For a moment, Tiberius feared that Maeve had been caught under the toppled walls.

"Gods..." Xia whispered.

A new shape appeared, silhouetted against pale sand and dust. It was Coldhand, his monstrous metal hand glinting red. He ran toward them, Maeve limp in his arms. There was a dark stain across her breast. Tiberius charged at Coldhand.

"You killed her, you bastard!" he shouted, ripping his NI pistol free. "There isn't a hell deep enough for you, but I swear I'll send you to every single one!"

Coldhand didn't flinch. Tiberius pointed his gun at the younger Prian, but the dark shape on Maeve's chest wasn't blood – though there was plenty of that smeared across her skin. It was Kessa's baby boy cradled safely in Maeve's arms, somehow fast asleep.

"Uh, why didn't you just take your fighter and get out of here?" Gripper asked as Coldhand ran toward them.

"Because your little ramming trick buried it under an entire desert's worth of sand and rock," Coldhand answered.

He handed Maeve over to Gripper. The Arboran dropped his welder at once and took her, staring fearfully at her colorless skin and shallow breath.

"She's not dead, Tiberius," Xia said. "But she's close."

"Oh, Smoke... What happened to you?" Gripper asked.

"The same thing that's going to happen to the rest of us if we don't get up in the air," Coldhand said.

The crash had bought them only a temporary reprieve. Nihilists were already pushing their way through the rubble, those who had managed to get out of the tunnels before Tiberius collapsed the entrance or found shelter against the remaining walls. One of them wore the same bright red robes as the Lyran Emberguard that still lay dead in the Blue Phoenix mess.

There had to be at least thirty Nihilists charging toward them. Coldhand yanked Tiberius back as a glowing line of white laser scorched the sand at his feet, followed by half a dozen bullets that shattered stone and sprayed the Blue Phoenix crew with gravel. Only distance saved them and that was quickly dwindling.

"Get back!" Tiberius shouted, gesturing over his shoulder to the open airlock. "Get into the Phoenix!"

Gripper and Xia were already running away into the ship, the two Prian men close on their tails. Tiberius yanked out his com.

"Duaal! Duaal, get those engines up and ready to take off!"

"I can't," the boy said. His voice hissed over the channel. "The engines won't come back up!"

"What? Why not?" Tiberius asked, huffing.

"You ran the Phoenix into a church!" Duaal said. "That might have something to do with it!"

"Damn it!"

Tiberius dove through the outer door of the airlock as swiftly as his old, aching hips would allow, turned and then slammed it shut. The light beside it cycled from green to red. Sealed. The rest of his crew was inside, but so was Coldhand, Tiberius noted ruefully. Xia already had Maeve laid out on the deck, snapping her long fingers impatiently while Kessa ran to get her kit.

"The bird took some damage in the landing," Tiberius said as calmly as he could manage, but his deep voice cracked. "We've got the Phoenix sealed and the CWAAF is on their way. We should be safe enough until they arrive."

Everyone jumped as a hiss issued from the airlock. A burning smell filled the tense air and the lock began to glow faintly.

"My torch!" Gripper cried.

"They're cutting down the hatch," Coldhand said.

"How long until CWAAF gets here?" asked Xia.

"They said two hours," Tiberius answered. "And that was about twenty minutes ago."

"But there's no way we can hold out for over an hour!" Gripper said.

Kessa ran down the cargo bay stairs, taking them a pair at a time and threw the medical kit into Xia's waiting hands. Duaal was close on the Dailon's heels, ignoring a furious look from Tiberius. Xia flipped open the kit and began spraying the deep wound in Maeve's ribs with antiseptic. The canister hissed, sputtered and died. Xia shook it angrily and tried again, but the can remained stubbornly empty. She frowned and filled a syringe with something Tiberius didn't recognize.

Kessa lifted her baby from Maeve's limp arms, weeping openly. Baliend yawned and opened his large black eyes to regard his mother. He burbled happily and held out his chubby blue arms.

"My baby, my boy. My little Baliend," she said between kisses. She knelt and whispered to the unconscious Maeve. "Thank you. Thank you for bringing my family home to me."

"It's bad," Xia said. "Maeve's lost a lot of blood and I can't close up the wound or the air will collapse her lung. If we don't get her to a proper hospital in the next thirty minutes, she's going to die."

Coldhand snarled. "No!"

"Why do you care what happens to Smoke?" Gripper asked.

"I called the Gharib police," Duaal interrupted. "Again. They won't move any faster, though. They're still waiting on the CWAAF and griping about budget cuts."

"Won't anyone come to see what's going on?" Gripper asked. "I mean, there's been a crash! Surely everyone in the city heard it!"

"This is Stray," Tiberius said, shaking his head. "Half the people on this planet are on the run from something – either criminals or those hiding from them. No one is running *toward* trouble. Not unless there's something in it for them."

"So we're on our own until the CWAAF arrives?" Gripper asked.

"Yes," Tiberius answered.

The airlock sparked and smoke began to rise from the burning fibersteel. Tiberius closed the inner door. It would buy them only minutes, but he wasn't ready to die so easily. Kessa held her son tightly to her and stroked his tiny thatch of white hair.

"What do we do now?" she asked.

"We can't get this old bird off the ground," Tiberius admitted. "So we sit tight and defend ourselves until the CWAAF comes to bail us out."

"Wait, why can't we fly?" Gripper asked. "We hit with the nose of the ship, right? But the fuel and engines are all in the aft."

"I don't know, but the engines won't engage," Duaal said.

Gripper frowned and rubbed his shortened ear, gasped in pain and stopped. "There are only sensors and stabilizers in the front. We should be fine to fly, if kind of wobbly and blind."

"Nothing is working," Duaal insisted. "The computer said something about a null-field integrity compromise and shut everything down."

"What?" Gripper asked. "Why didn't you tell me that in the first place?"

"Does it matter?" Duaal asked.

"*Does it matter?* By the Green, yeah, it does! It means something happened to the null-field lines."

"Those fields don't matter unless we're in SL," Duaal said. "They shouldn't be stopping us now!"

"But trying to engage superluminal drives with compromised null-fields would tear a ship into atoms," Coldhand said. "Any ship's computer system is designed to lock everything down and prevent that from happening."

"Can't you tell the computer to just ignore it?" Tiberius asked. "We don't need to fly all the way back to Axis, just out of here!"

The air in the hold was thick with the smell of burning metal. The Nihilist must have gotten through the outer doors and were working on the inner ones.

"That's a hard-coded safety system," Gripper told Tiberius. "The whole point is to keep people from dying just because they're too impatient for null-field repairs."

"But the null-inertia control lines don't run to the beak of the ship," Coldhand said, frowning. "They shouldn't be damaged."

Gripper nodded, clenching and unclenching his huge fists. He kept glancing at the airlock door. "Yeah, yeah. But like I said, the computer core and sensors are all up there. One of them is probably damaged and reading the data from the NI generators wrong."

Tiberius stared at the airlock, too. The inner door shuddered in its frame and Tiberius could hear voices screaming for blood on the other side.

"Can you fix it?" Duaal asked.

"Maybe..." Gripper said. "There's an access hatch on the outside of the nose. If I can get to it, I might be able to fix the sensors enough to get the computer to release the lock. But that's if it's even a sensor problem... If the computer itself is busted, it's going to take weeks to repair."

"Can you get to the hatch?" Tiberius asked.

"Yeah. I can use the same airlock that old Red-and-Dead broke in through. That Emberguard guy," Gripper said. "I... I need someone to cover me. I'm not sure I can do it quiet enough to keep the guys outside from noticing and I really don't want to die."

Coldhand and Tiberius looked at each other.

"I don't trust you, boy," the captain growled. "You're staying right next to me."

"Fine," Coldhand answered with a shrug. He looked at Maeve lying still and pale on the floor. "I'm not letting her out of my sight, anyway."

"Well, someone needs to go," Tiberius said. "And I–"

"I'll do it," Duaal interrupted.

"No," Tiberius snarled. "No way in any hell!"

"There's no time to debate this," Duaal told him. "I'm going with Gripper. You two should be here, with Kessa and Vyron and the baby. And Maeve. Better to keep our best fighters here where there are more lives to defend."

Coldhand narrowed his eyes, but the hunter didn't argue.

Tiberius did. "Xia can go!"

"She's the only doctor we have! She needs to stay with Maeve. I'm going!"

"I'm ordering you to stay!" Tiberius shouted.

Duaal turned away and gestured to Gripper.

"Let's go," the boy said.

With an apologetic glance back at Tiberius, Gripper followed Duaal up the stairs and out of the hold.

"That boy! Why do I have a bird full of hard-headed young chicks?" Tiberius shouted, shaking his fist after the departed Duaal.

"You hired them," Coldhand reminded him.

The old cop was getting himself entirely too worked up over a single stupid teenage boy. If Duaal was as overconfident and foolish as he seemed, he would die. If he didn't, then what was the point of all that shouting?

"Get that gun ready," Coldhand told Tiberius. "They're almost through the airlock."

"I didn't hire Duaal," Tiberius said, but drew his weapon. "Let's make this good and loud and pray those Nihilists bastards will be paying more attention to us than Duaal."

Coldhand shrugged. "Pray all you want, but no one's listening."

"How can you say that?"

The question came from Kessa, standing behind the two Prians. She held Baliend against her shoulder and cocked her head toward Coldhand.

"I prayed every day on Axis for help," Kessa said. "And He sent me a miracle. I met you and Maeve there."

"That wasn't a miracle," Coldhand told her.

"Wasn't it?" Kessa asked. "But maybe the even bigger miracle, I'm learning, is that you two didn't carry on merrily killing each other instead of bringing me here. And you brought my Vyron back to me, Coldhand. I thank God every day for you, for Maeve and for what you've done for me. In spite of yourselves."

Coldhand narrowed his eyes. "I'm starting to regret that choice."

Kessa stared back defiantly. A loud clang came from the airlock and a blackened scrap of fibersteel fell to the floor, edges glowing red with heat. It would be only moments before the Nihilists were inside. Kessa and Xia jumped.

"Shouldn't we move Maeve?" asked Kessa.

Xia shook her head. "No. There's already air in her chest and it's putting pressure on her lungs. She shouldn't have been running around like that, but I suppose there wasn't any other choice. If we move her now, we risk tearing the wound wider or getting more air in there."

"But what if someone... you know, steps on her?" Kessa asked. "Or hurts her?"

Xia wiped bloody bubbles off of Maeve's lips with a folded piece of gauze. The Ixthian closed her medical case and stood, resting her six-fingered hand on the grip of her gun. It was shaking, Coldhand saw, but none of that quaver made it to the doctor's voice.

"We'll just have to keep that from happening," Xia said.

"We?" Kessa asked.

"Me and Xia," Tiberius answered, and then indicated Coldhand with his out-thrust jaw. "And that traitor over there, I guess."

"I'll need a new cell for the Talon," Coldhand said, ignoring the insult. "Mine's dry."

"I don't keep batteries for those things around here. I passed my Talon on when I retired," Tiberius snorted. "Like any proper officer would."

The hunter nodded once, but his blue eyes were on the airlock. There was a spit of blazing white as the Nihilists finally cut through the lock, followed by a heavy *thunk* as the bolt pulled back. Kessa took a step away, clutching her baby.

"Get Baliend up to the medbay with Vyron," Xia said. "Close the door and lock it. Hurry!"

"But I want to help," Kessa protested.

"You can help by getting out of here," Xia said. "Go be with your family."

Kessa turned and ran up the stairs, vanishing into the ship. Xia turned to Coldhand, flipped the slender laser pistol in her hand and grasped it by the refraction chamber. She held it out toward the bounty hunter.

"You're a better shot than I am," Xia said.

"Yes," Coldhand agreed.

He took the offered gun. It was a light weapon, but it was something. Coldhand stood protectively over Maeve as the airlock grated in its tracks and then ground open.

"Hurry!" Duaal hissed.

"I thought you said to be quiet," Gripper whispered.

"Hurry *and* be quiet."

The Arboran crept gingerly along a narrow fibersteel ledge that led up to the nose of the crashed Blue Phoenix. It was barely wide enough for Gripper to stand on, much less try to scamper over behind Duaal.

It was a long drop down to the ground, but that wasn't what frightened Gripper. He was born on a world of trees that towered like starscrapers and never fallen. Not until the sycona that ended up sending him through a strange gate and into Alliance space.

But the Nihilists swarmed beneath Duaal and Gripper, charging through the shattered walls of the cathedral to claim vengeance from those hiding inside. They were all shouting to one another, screaming that their master was dead, others that he was still alive and demanding the heads of his enemies. Duaal flinched and paled with every cry of Gavriel's name, but he kept moving.

Worst of all were the Nihilists who laughed and grinned and promised to join the gloriously dead soon. Gripper held tightly onto the hull of the Blue Phoenix, willing himself to climb silently. Tiberius would be just furious when he saw the new claw marks... Gripper just hoped he would still be alive to get yelled at.

Up ahead, Duaal edged around the ship slowly, too. Everything was slippery with a fresh coat of phenno and even the nimble Hyzaari was having difficulties climbing it. He carried Gripper's tools in a battered box balanced on his shoulder and struggled to maintain his balance.

Gripper held his breath. How long before one of the Nihilists looked up and saw them?

The footing grew more treacherous as they neared the front of the Blue Phoenix. The nose of the ship was crumpled and smashed like paper. Gripper and Duaal had to duck in between sensor spars, many broken or badly bent. Their ledge walkway was torn away in several places, requiring both the mage and mechanic to leap the gaps. After what seemed like hours of climbing, Gripper crouched beside a ruined fibersteel panel and gestured for Duaal to stop.

"Here it is," Gripper said.

"Doesn't look too good," Duaal whispered.

"Neither does the rest of the ship, Shimmer."

The fibersteel was cracked and crumpled alarmingly. Gripper tugged on the handle of the access hatch and it groaned, but didn't open. The two young men froze, but the Nihilists below didn't seem to have noticed – they were too busy cutting their way through the larger airlock below.

Gripper bit one huge knuckle. There was no way the panel was opening in a civil manner. He took a steadying breath, then sank his claws into the fibersteel and tore the cover free. Gripper winced as it shrieked in loud metallic protest, but he still heard no change in the commotion below to indicate that the Nihilists might be swarming up to kill them.

Duaal balanced the toolkit on a pair of sensor spars and leaned over the ledge, staring down.

"Gripper, hurry!" he hissed. "They've cut the airlock open!"

The Arboran risked a glance downward and gasped. How could they possibly survive this? Even if Gripper managed to get the NI lines straightened out, Tiberius would be taking off with a ship full of Nihilists who outnumbered them ten to one. Duaal snapped his fingers at Gripper.

"There's no time to worry. We have to do this, Gripper."

"Right," Gripper said and turned back to the now open panel.

"Aim for their legs," Coldhand said as the airlock opened to reveal a sea of wild eyes and black robes. "Make them climb over each other to get in. It will buy us some time."

Xia winced at his brutal advice, but said nothing. Tiberius only nodded in agreement. Most every being in the worlds was ready to throw principles to the wind to survive, Coldhand noted with chilly satisfaction. The doctor and the honorably retired officer were just as willing to maim the oncoming Nihilists as the loathed bounty hunter was. They had dropped their ship on top of hundreds of them. Honor meant nothing in the end, like the countless men and women who had fallen defending it.

Coldhand couldn't stop himself from glancing down at Maeve. She had gone underground to save Baliend from the Nihilists, to save a baby boy that wasn't even Arcadian. And both Tiberius and Xia could have retreated, locked themselves behind more doors like they told Kessa to do. But they remained here with Maeve and would fight to the death to protect her.

Maybe these people actually had honor.

Coldhand brought his eyes and gun back up as the swarm of Nihilists screamed for blood and charged into the Blue Phoenix cargo bay. It had been a strange day.

"No!" Gripper cried.

Duaal shot a look down at the sea of Nihilists seething below.

"Quiet!" he hissed. "What's wrong?"

Gripper pointed to a bundle of red and white wires running through a bracket inside the hatch. A small light set into the metal glowed a contented green.

"Green is good, right?" Duaal asked.

"It means the lines are fine," Gripper said. "It means it's the computer. Either the core is busted or the cables aren't connected to something in the engines!"

"You said that would take days to fix!"

Gripper banged his head against the hatch and Duaal didn't tell him to stop. It was all over. In spite of everything they had tried, it was over.

Kessa tiptoed quietly into the cockpit. She could hear shouts and shots echoing up from the cargo hold now. Tiberius and Coldhand were fighting for their lives. For all of their lives. Xia was supposed to be hiding, locked away with Vyron and Baliend.

But she couldn't do it. These people had risked so much, given up so much for her. Kessa wanted to cry, but even more, she needed to help. And what was the point of everything Coldhand and the Blue Phoenix crew had done if Baliend and Vyron died now?

No one is running toward trouble, Tiberius had told them all. *Not unless there's something in it for them.*

Kessa sat down in the big pilot's chair. Tiberius was a large man and Kessa sank down into his seat. In her arms, Baliend seemed to sense her fear and cried in tiny, hiccuping sobs. Kessa rocked him absently and read the message flashing in red on most of the control screens.

NI field integrity compromised

Engines disengaged

Kessa didn't understand what the glowing message meant, but it wasn't the engines she needed now. The young Dailon mother searched the maze of controls and sensors, readouts and displays, chewing her lip until she found what she was looking for. Kessa found with relief that the communications system was still set to the Gharib police frequency. She switched it on. The video was turned off, but she had sound.

"Hello...? My name is Kessa," she said. "Can you hear me? I'm a passenger on board the Blue Phoenix."

"An hour at least and that's the best we can do!" said a harried-sounding male voice on the other end. "Just like the last time you called. We don't have the resources to expend on this!"

Kessa swallowed hard and hoped Maeve wouldn't be too angry with her when this was all over. If she lived.

"I know," Kessa answered. "There's someone here on this ship. Her name is Maeve Cavainna. Look up her bounty."

She gave the man on the other end a moment and was rewarded with a gasp. "Thirty-five thousand cen? Oh my God. And you say she's on board the Blue Phoenix? And she's alive?"

"For now. But she'll be dead inside ten minutes," Kessa told the cop. "If you want the full bounty, you'll have to hurry."

"But why would you turn in someone on your own ship? I don't understand."

"You don't have to," Kessa said. "Just do it!"

[32]
PAID

"Freedom isn't only about the things we can do, but those things we *must* do."

- LYRAN PROVERB

"Titania was right," Caith said. "You played your part in the destruction of the White Kingdom, but you cannot claim responsibility for it all."

Maeve's brother smiled gently at her to soften his words. They sat together in the west garden of the Blooming House, surrounded by delicate pink roses. Maeve couldn't smell them in the dream, but bees striped in gold and black hummed their way between the blooms, harvesting pollen with gentle precision. In the fall, the dryads would have gathered the rich amber honey to make mead for the Snowmelt Festival. There was no sweeter drink in all the worlds.

"The fault was mine, too," dream-Caith said. He draped a soft white wing around Maeve's shoulder. "Opening the Waygate was my duty and I abandoned that. We both made mistakes... but they do not make us monsters."

Caith was fading like the silvery morning mist. Maeve reached for him, but her fingers closed on nothing.

"Caith... I miss you," she said. "Please, do not go...!"
"Sister, I am already gone."
Maeve wept.

There were two shadows leaning over her. Maeve tried to speak, but there was something in her throat – a ribbed tube. The silhouettes glared at one another across her bed and the room seethed with violent potential.

"She'll live," said the one on the right. "But it was close."

The larger shadow nodded. "You got her out of that place alive. It couldn't have been easy. You could have died, too. Why did you help her?"

"She was my mark."

The shadows were quiet for a long time. The tube in her throat pushed scrubbed air into Maeve's lungs and needles pumped liquefied nutrients through her veins. One of the dark, faceless shape spoke again in a voice thick with barely restrained rage.

"If I ever see you again, there's going to be blood, traitor. Saving Maeve once will never make up for everything you've done."

Coldhand's shadow said nothing.

The oxygen pump hissed and fed sterile air into Maeve's lungs. The plastic bags hanging beside her bed gurgled quietly as they emptied their dissolved contents into her blood.

Do not go, she wanted to say. But Maeve's eyelids were so heavy. She fell back into uneasy sleep and let the machines live for her.

"I was ready to die at the Tamlin Waygate," Maeve said. "I wanted only to die beside you, my enarri."

Maeve's eyes were dry now, but the sandy feeling behind her eyelids told her that they hadn't been that way for long.

"But then it... worked. I closed the Tamin Waygate and the Devourers vanished from our worlds," she said. "But by then, it was too late. You were dead. My brother was dead and our people were gone. Our kingdom was gone."

The grass had disappeared. Maeve and Orthain stood atop one of the tall crystal spires overlooking the city, a mosaic of ivory and silver that glittered in Aes' bright light. The citadel – the hereditary seat of Cavain's line and the heart of the entire White Kingdom – burned with blinding golden radiance in the distance. Maeve slitted her eyes against the brilliant glare. Something was wrong... There was a dark stain in the heart of the city, like a bruise upon the perfectly wrought glass of her home.

And it was spreading.

"Princess Titania was right, enarri," Orthain told Maeve. "We still do not understand how the Devourers came to our world, not truly. You know that the Waygates lead only one way. Nothing should have been able to come through the gate. What happened was a terrible mistake, but a mistake only."

Maeve leaned against the cool, unyielding glass of Orthain's armor. "I should not have opened the Waygate."

"No," Orthain agreed. "But you did not create the monsters that came through, and you did not command them to destroy our worlds. All of this, all of the death and smoke... It was not your doing."

"I love you, Orthain."

"And I love you, Maeve. But I am not the only one."

Gripper's voice was the first thing Maeve heard when she finally drifted up out of the darkness.

"Smoke? Smoke? She's awake! How're you feeling?" he asked.

The huge young Arboran leaned over her, blotting out the light.

His left ear no longer matched the one on the right and the short-ened tip was still a shiny, healing pink.

"Your ear..." Maeve rasped.

Gripper struck a comically dramatic pose. "Yeah, I could have gotten it cloned, but I think it makes me look rakish."

Maeve lay in a bed of rough white linens, her wings wedged in awkwardly under her. Flexible plastic needles were taped into her forearms and connected by tubes to hanging bags labeled in Aver. Maeve's entire body was stiff and sore, swathed in thick bandages under a blue hospital gown.

More shapes crowded around her bed to join Gripper. Tiberius was scowling, as usual, but there was joy and relief in his eyes. Xia smiled at Maeve, nodding approvingly as though simply waking up was some kind of major accomplishment.

Maybe it was.

Kessa waved from the foot of Maeve's hospital bed and Baliend burbled happily while Vyron leaned on her shoulder. Even Duaal seemed happy to see Maeve awake.

"What... what happened?" she asked. Maeve's voice was quiet and rough from disuse. She coughed painfully. "How long have I been asleep? Where are we? I recall little after Logan carried me from beneath the graveyard."

"You're at Kharnig Unified Faith Hospital," Tiberius answered. "Racking up another medical bill for us."

There was something strained in the old Prian's voice at that, but Gripper interrupted.

"When Coldhand brought you out, there were all these Nihilists chasing you both!" the Arboran said with an excited sweep of his arms. Duaal ducked just in time to avoid being hit. "We couldn't convince the Gharib police to help without CWAAF backup, so we crashed the Blue Phoenix right into the cathedral and smashed it all down on top of them."

"Didn't work quite as well as I'd hoped," Tiberius grumbled.

"It busted the ship up pretty bad," Gripper agreed. "Shimmer and I went out to fix it while the Nihilists were trying to cut open the ventral airlock. But then we... we couldn't make the repairs and I thought we were all dead."

"How...?" Maeve asked with fragile curiosity.

"It was Kessa's doing," Xia said. "And yours. At least, it will be."

Maeve shook her head in confusion and quickly regretted it. The whole world swam for several seconds before coming back into focus. When Maeve could open her eyes once more, Tiberius had crossed his arms over his chest.

"It's your bounty," Tiberius said. "The Gharib police are desperate for money and they came running when Kessa told them about the price on your head."

Maeve frowned. "Then... why am I in a hospital instead of an Alliance prison?"

"Well, it's a private bounty," Kessa said, clearing her throat. "Not an Alliance one. And they can't collect it if you're locked up in jail."

"Why not?" Maeve asked.

"Because *you* posted it," Kessa answered. "You put the bounty on yourself."

"What? No," Maeve protested, but her mouth was dry.

"You know how to post a bounty," Kessa said, bouncing Baliend in her arms. "You created the one for Vyron and paid Coldhand when he delivered. You threw the money on the ground like it was nothing, like you're used to having plenty. Maybe you could pass that off as part of being a princess, but then Coldhand asked you something about... about genocide after the Emberguard attack."

"There hasn't been a genocide committed in hundreds of years," Vyron said. He put his arms around Kessa and stroked his son's hair. "Not since the old religious wars. Something like that would have made the news all across the core. So whatever you did, it must have been back in the White Kingdom, at least a century ago. That's ancient history for most of us, but not for you."

"I… I…" Maeve stammered, but she could think of nothing else to say.

"There wasn't much to figure out after that," Kessa said. "We all know the fairy kingdom fell apart, even if we don't quite understand why, and most everyone died. And you're always so angry, so guilty… Guilty enough to put a bounty on your own head."

Maeve sagged back into the white sheets and closed her eyes, but that didn't stop the hot tears from spilling down her cheeks. She nodded.

"Yes. I created the bounty, summoned my executioner to punish me for bringing the Devourers to the White Kingdom."

"You?" Xia asked. "In your story… you were *that* knight? But you swore you'd kill her!"

"And that is precisely what I hired the bounty hunters to do," Maeve said.

"You did this? You brought Coldhand down on yourself and on my crew with that damned bounty?" Tiberius asked. "God, I hoped Kessa was just being a twit!"

"I wanted to die," Maeve answered. She opened her eyes to look at her captain. "More than anything. I did not care what it cost. I… I am sorry."

"Damn it, Maeve," Tiberius growled, but he didn't seem to have the heart to argue further.

Vyron shook his head. "I know what you went through for my son and my mate. I know there's more to you than just an elaborate death wish. So… thank you. I don't think I've gotten to say that yet."

"Where did you get the money?" Gripper asked. "I mean, Claws doesn't pay us that much."

Maeve swallowed against a hard weight in her throat. "I brought it from my home. When I closed the Tamlin Waygate, I was alone in the White Kingdom. The Devourers were all gone, but so were my people."

"Why didn't you just… stay?" Gripper asked.

"How could I remain in the home I had destroyed? The world I loved was lost and the Waygates are a one-way journey. The gates used for the evacuation were still open. I had a day before the spells that held them collapsed. I could not stay, but I gathered clothes and a few precious items that had escaped the Devourers' destruction. It was not much, not compared to the riches of Arcadia, but it was enough to sell off and offer a bounty for my life."

One of the instruments monitoring her beeped a warning at Maeve's rising blood pressure.

"A bounty that I will pay to the Gharib police," Maeve managed to whisper. "As agreed. What happened to the Church of Nihil?"

"Well, the police showed up and dealt with the ones that were overrunning the Phoenix," Tiberius answered after a moment of uncomfortable silence. "Brought a medic to take care of you, then held the place until CWAAF arrived. The Alliance wasn't too happy about the Nihilists' graveyard, so they rounded up everyone still trapped in the tunnels."

"They raided all of the other Nihilist churches," Gripper said. "But most of them were already empty. Someone warned them that the Alliance was coming."

"The Church of Nihil seems to have left Stray, near as CWAAF can tell," Xia told Maeve.

"Gavriel and Xartasia? What was their fate?" she asked.

"Gone," Duaal answered. There were deep, dark circles under the young human's eyes.

"Allied forces excavated the Gharib cave-in and found plenty dead," Xia said. "None of them were Gavriel or your cousin."

Coldhand must have informed them of the blood Maeve shared with Xartasia.

"The Nihilists are still out there, then," Maeve said.

"That's not our problem," Tiberius told her firmly. "Those bastards are gone from Stray and it's safe for Kessa's family now. We did our job."

"They didn't find Gavriel or Xartasia," Xia said. "Or even that altar. It was all gone. But they did find this."

The Ixthian picked up something carefully from a table beside Maeve's bed and held it out to her. It was a glass blade the length of her hand with a broken piece of wood jutting from the base, wound all around by the torn, burnt remains of once-colorful ribbons.

Xia handed Maeve the blade of her spear. The princess sat up slowly in the hospital bed, wincing as the tubes in her arms tugged, and took it gently. She twined her fingers through the ruined ribbons and laid it in her lap.

A spear was the weapon of an Arcadian knight. It was meant to be wielded in defense of innocents and the cause of justice. But what had Maeve done with it? How much shameful blood had this blade spilled over the century since her fall? In Maeve's hands, it had become a weapon of despair and disgrace.

Titania... Xartasia had fallen to the soul-broken hopelessness that ruined Maeve. It drove her to join the Nihilists in their zealous search for death. How many had suffered and died for the pain of two women?

"Where..." Maeve struggled to find her voice. "Where is Logan? He had best be ready to fight me when I can leave this bed."

"That's one part I never did figure out," said Kessa. "If you want to die so badly, why hire a hunter to do it? Why didn't you just kill yourself? Or at least post a dead-only bounty? You could have died years ago."

Maeve covered her face with her hands, tangling her collection of tubes and sensors.

"My brother was in Tamlin when I opened the Waygate," she said. "He was among the first to fly for the gate when it... when it all went so wrong. He was trying to close the Waygate when the Devourers killed him. Trying to fix *my* mistake. And my Orthain... he died protecting me from those monsters. The men I loved best fought too hard for me to give up my life easily."

"You were making them earn it," Duaal finished slowly. "The hunters... and you. Because you thought you deserved the pain."

"Logan was not the first to hunt me," Maeve said. "But he came closer than anyone else. Where is my hunter?"

"Coldhand's gone," Tiberius answered. "He left three days ago. He said the mark had been caught and the hunt is finished."

"Then it is over," Maeve said. She closed her eyes and wondered if she would ever be done crying.

Repairs to the Raptor had been expensive and now he needed to find work. On the second level of Axis, Logan Coldhand sat at his rented computer terminal, keying through bounties. They flashed up onto the screen in rapid sequence, one after another as he dismissed each listing with a glance.

Some were worth more than Maeve. Two or three might even be more dangerous than the princess. But none of them were half as interesting.

Logan brought up another list, reading through and then forgetting each of the bounties. Maeve was a skilled warrior, trained as a knight for longer than Logan had been alive. From what Xia told him about the White Kingdom's destruction by the Devourers, most of the other knights died defending the remaining Arcadian people. How many had managed to escape? Maeve may well have been the only knight of Arcadia left in the universe. Fighting her had been a challenge that he would not likely find again...

Not outside Gavriel's Emberguard, at least.

Maeve was cunning, too. Logan had to admire how cleverly she crafted her own bounty and how deftly she had manipulated him. The Central World Alliance might have posted a bounty for the crimes she had committed, but there were millions of killers across the worlds.

No, that would never have been enough to catch the attention of an infamous hunter. She needed the genocide charge for that.

Logan wasn't sure that Maeve was actually guilty of that crime, but it had certainly been an imposing accusation. Only the most dedicated or fearless bounty hunters would ever try to take in a mark with that kind of record. That way, Maeve was sure to attract a deadly tool with which to commit her elaborate suicide.

Even the rewards listed on her bounty were cleverly planned. She offered enough money to entice, but not so much that greed would tempt the desperate into a dangerous hunt. Was she trying to protect the weak bounty hunters from a job too difficult for their limited skills? Or just making sure she didn't end up confronted by an inept hunter? Maeve wanted someone who understood what they were getting into and who was prepared for a fight.

And Maeve wanted a fight... That was why she posted the live bounty. Yet the lesser but still considerable sum offered upon death meant that even Logan had been willing to kill her in the end.

He remembered the pain in Maeve's silver eyes as she confessed what she had done to Xartasia. The guilt, the loss. Maeve wanted to suffer, but then she wanted to die.

But Maeve threw it all away to fly off after Vyron's stolen son. A moment of impulsive passion had unraveled what had to be years of work toward her own end. There was only one thing left in all the worlds that she wanted, but she saved Baliend instead. Logan felt the mechanical beat of his computerized heart and knew he could never entirely understand Maeve Cavainna.

Logan keyed up more bounties. She had been a perfect mystery: eloquent and unfathomable, full of strange contradictions, terrible, deadly skill and inhuman patience. There would never be another mark like Maeve.

She was gone and Logan almost managed to convince himself that he didn't care.

Almost.

[EPILOGUE]
CRUCIBLE OF STARS

"Ichi, Eru, Cavain, Kael
  Catch a white hart by the tail
  If she is smiling, a wish she will give
  But if you harm her, she will not forgive."

- ARCADIAN RHYME

The darkness pressed in on Elsa like collapsing stone, smothering her. She tried to scream, but the gag turned her cry into a strangled sob. It tasted of sweat and blood.

There was dirt beneath her bare, aching feet and red-clad arms reached out from the black to grab her by the wrists. They pulled her down, arching her back painfully over the flat stone altar. She struggled against them, but the Emberguard's grip was like steel. A dry hand caressed her forehead.

"Elsa," Gavriel said. "My child. You have what I need."

Elsa ached to scream at him. Whatever she possessed, she didn't want to give to Gavriel. He had tried to kill the little Dailon baby. Elsa thought he was better than her husband, but they were the same, just hurting her to get what they wanted.

"Why take another child when I have you, my dear?" Gavriel asked. "Those parts of a child's mind that are unformed by age can be undone by injury. Thank you, Elsa. And I suppose I must thank your husband, too."

Elsa screamed furiously into the gag.

Another shape glided out of the darkness, luminously white as an angel. The feathers of Xartasia's wings trailed gently along Elsa's shoulders and bound arms. In a voice sweet and clear as spring water, the fairy princess began to sing.

Elsa didn't understand the words, but she felt them crawling over her skin like spiders, pushing and cutting through her very being, as sharp as glittering shards of Arcadian glass.

"In the mind unmade lies power fallow," Xartasia said, "waiting only to be harvested."

Elsa writhed and howled in defiance, but Gavriel's bony hand remained on her forehead. He seeped into her... No, that wasn't it. Elsa was dissolving, her brain coming undone and he was drinking it up. She couldn't think anymore, couldn't put words to the horror as Xartasia unwove Elsa's mind, picking apart her already frayed memories and thoughts into threads. And then as Gavriel gathered them up and rewove them in the darkness of his own mind.

Screaming silently, everything that was Elsa fell away into nothingness.

Eight million years ago.

Captain Rhyan expected to find darkness. Here on the edge of the galaxy, she thought there would be only blank blackness, for the emptiness of space to eat up and flatten the vastness of distance. But even here, there was pale light in the black – entire galaxies, so distant that they were single pinprick sparks barely discernible to the naked eye.

Entire galaxies just waiting to be devoured.

"We're ready, ma'am," a voice said behind her.

"Bring us about," Captain Rhyan ordered, not bothering to turn away from the viewport.

Ponderously, the huge warship turned. She felt a deep regret as her vessel maneuvered to face back toward the galactic core, back toward that dense sea of stars. The captain of the VSS Pioneer had nothing but contempt for that twisted mass of glittering suns and planets. That scattering of lights and rocks had once made up a great empire, but been long since stripped of most usable resources. Work crews left behind only barren rock, incapable of supporting life much more complex than single-celled organisms.

The old galaxy was a hearth, Rhyan decided. Once it had blazed with brilliant, glorious life, but only dying embers remained now. It was time to leave. There were flames to kindle elsewhere.

A colossal ring floated in front of the ship, a massive circle constructed in eight segments, each one larger than the entire Pioneer and made of a different elemental metal. Some of the older devices were built from stone, but only the great space gates were powerful enough to transport starships.

The VSS Pioneer flew toward the Waygate. First one section and then the next began to glow, swimming all across its surface with the same swirling radiance. The Waygate lit up in red and faded to green, then a soft, permissive blue.

"They're ready for us, ma'am."

"What sector did the Guides select?" Rhyan asked, turning to face the pilot.

"One nineteen by two eighty-eight," he answered, reading the number from a nearby display. "Probability is thirty-nine, sir."

"Thirty-nine?" Rhyan asked.

"Yes, ma'am."

"We're getting closer, then," she said. "Are the ground reinforcements ready?"

"They are."

"This galaxy is useless to us now," Rhyan announced, turning back to the viewport and gesturing out at the stars that had served as her people's home for eons. The captain smiled and displayed her sharp predator's teeth. "Those worlds are only shells, broken bones hollowed of marrow. But new worlds await us. Forward!"

The VSS Pioneer vanished through the Waygate, leaving the old galaxy behind.

[APPENDIX]
THE LAY OF CAVAIN

Professor Xil:

The Lay of Cavain is the oldest recorded song in this galaxy. There are some sociologists who theorize that the hive-mind of the Nnyth might know several older ones, but they share less with the CWA than the Arcadians do. And even if Professor Massir is right, I respectfully submit that Nnyth droning would hardly be recognizable as music.

The Lay seems to describe the rise to power of the first Arcadian king, Cavain a'Shae, and his conquest of the other races of fairies, including the genocide of the pyrads and subjugation of the nyad and dryad species.

The factual accuracy of the story is unknown. It was recorded several hundred years after the events it recounts and whether or not the historical Cavain even existed is something of a mystery. The Arcadians seem convinced that he did, however, and that his direct descendants still lead their kingdom.

Of note, the term *spell* seems to refer to law in this context, not fairy magic.

- Dr. Ellan Markav, Dean of Outland Studies

Time lay in its cradle quietly
Once upon a day long ago
Not the song of Erris is heard
Yet voices carried on the wind faintly

Laughing spring winds come whispering
To find that Aes lay no longer
In her high, heavenly bower
But in a mortal wing's embrace so loving

[Chorus:]
Two hundred eighty-eight days of light
Will be desired by a Night
If you would dare lay claim to the right
To ask a gift of the White

To every blossom, its season
Autumn caresses laid to rest
The goddess to the sky returned
Yet from Erris, she could not conceal her treason

For when the petals fall from the tree
The wanton branches swell with fruit
Carried she within her a new life
To the halls of the All-Singer with a plea

[Chorus]

Erris, the first god, burned with anger
That his bride had strayed from him
For the innocent she carried
The rage that tore worlds asunder did waver

For the life of her child, Aes pleaded
For the love in his divine heart
Erris agreed with his lady
But his realm never with mortal blood seeded

[Chorus]

In the fullest turning of a year
To Aes was born a baby boy
With hair black as the deepest night
Cavain, she called the child, in her eye a tear

By the decree of the All-Singer
Cavain descended from the sky
To the ring of wild worlds below
Laden with naught but his long wings and his spear

[Chorus]

For his divine blood, Cavain was blessed
For his mortal blood, cursed to die
In the turning of the ages
For his numbered year, Cavain dared not to rest

Wings, feet and Gates carried him between
The worlds that danced around bright Aes
Found other winged sky-dancers
Sea-eyed nyads, dryads in the forests clean

[Chorus]

Cavain's wandering found worlds too wild
Overgrown and torn by the tides
All lives lived in fear of the flame
Only ashes left behind the fae of fire

To his side, Cavain called the wild herd
To learn the order of the gods
To raise great cities of crystal
But the pyran would not heed his kindest word

[Chorus]

Followers of the flame called for war
Every city reduced to ash
Cavain raised his banner to them
To fight back the flame for all of time, he swore

Before his spear, the fiery fae fell
Destructive blazes laid to rest
Never again to raise a flame
Cavain's kingdom ever under peaceful spell

[Chorus]

In honor of Cavain's divine call
Of Aes the cloud-veiled Sky-Dancer
White Kingdom was named the new land
To Cavain was given lordship over all

Seasons turn, as seasons often do
The Night has passed beyond our sight
But to his royal lineage
The races of fae still pay their given due

For without the gifts of Cavain's line
To stream and spire and hill and sky
Devouring fire would consume all
So sing to the raven-manes and I sing mine

[Chorus]

[Chorus]

For more books by
Erica Lindquist & Aron Christensen,
visit us at **LLStories.com**